The HONORABLES

DUTY BEFORE Desire

Elizabeth Boyce

Crimson Romance

New York   London   Toronto   Sydney   New Delhi

CRIMSON

Crimson Romance
An Imprint of Simon & Schuster, Inc.
1230 Avenue of the Americas
New York, NY 10020

ISBN 978-1-4405-8502-9
ISBN 978-1-4405-8503-6(ebook)

For Tara Gelsomino. Thank you for seeing me through.

Chapter One

Lord Sheridan Zouche was having trouble with his linen. A thin, damp fog wreaked havoc with his cravat, to say nothing of the sorry state of his collar. Grimacing, he plucked at the wilting material.

"Devil take it," he muttered. "Anyone know if Dewhurst carries a looking glass in his bag?" he called out. "On second thought, no. Perhaps it's better if I don't know how shabby I appear."

"Where the hell do you think you are?" snapped the giant at his side. Norman Wynford-Scott jostled Sheri's shoulder with an oversized paw. "For once in your life, would you be serious?"

Witnessing the normally unflappable man in a veritable lather did wonders for Sheri's spirits. "Right you are," he said, leaving his neckcloth to its fate. He spun sharply on boots freshly blackened and polished with champagne to an immaculate shine and addressed the remaining occupants of his coach. "Step lively, lads. This way. Hop to."

Henry De Vere clambered out, rubbing sleep from his deep-green eyes. "Shouldn't be chipper at this ungodly hour. It's deuced rude." To their immediate north, the Thames was a hard, steel gray in the pre-dawn gloaming. Henry's jaw cracked on a yawn.

"The secret is not to go to bed. At least," Sheri said with a smile, "not to sleep."

Glowering darkly, Henry muttered invective against the menace of confirmed bachelors. Married just two weeks ago, he'd spent most of the ride through Mayfair and Chelsea grousing at Sheridan for robbing him of his domestic comforts.

The last occupant of the coach, Harrison Dyer, descended from the carriage with a long, flat box tucked under one arm and a grim set to his stubbled jaw. "Tyrrel is here ahead of us." He indicated with his chin the black carriage at the far end of Battersea Fields.

Two men stood near the vehicle while a third, solitary figure, dim in the gray mist, paced a short distance away. A distinctive limp identified the man as Lord Tyrrel. The orange ember of a cigarillo intensified, then faded, as Tyrrel drew on it.

"I'll speak to his men." Harrison clapped Sheri's back and strode to meet the seconds of the offended party.

It had been deuced bad luck that Tyrrel walked into his wife's bedchamber two nights ago. The man hadn't been expected back from his hunting trip for another week, and he'd not made so much as a peep as he entered the house. It was well known that her ladyship had a string of paramours over the last five years, of whom Sheri was just the most recent.

Having already spent several nights together, Sheri and Sybil had moved beyond the fundamentals of coitus and were becoming a little more creative in their bed play. That particular evening had involved various foodstuffs. Sybil had been lying on her stomach, and Sheri had scooped dollops of blancmange in a line down the column of her spine. Naked and aroused, he'd been poised above her on hands and knees, licking and nibbling his way up her back, at the moment her husband entered the room.

Sybil had gasped and started to move, setting all the bits of dessert to quivering like frightened baby bunnies. Perhaps he lacked some vital instinct for survival, Sheri reflected, or maybe he was just too accustomed to his dissipated pastimes. In any event, when Lord Tyrrel happened upon them, Sheri didn't make a run for his breeches; rather, he'd laid a calming hand on Sybil's haunch and met the furious, shocked glare of his host with a steady, amused gaze. Then he'd offered the man a spoon.

He was more than a bit nonplussed over being the instrument by which Tyrrel chose to restore his manly honor.

A dull rumble announced the approach of another carriage. Within seconds, a hackney coach pulled in behind Sheri's equipage, and Brandon Dewhurst hopped out, surgery bag in hand.

"Sorry I'm late," he said. He spoke to the driver, then joined Sheri, Norman, and Henry. After another moment, Harrison returned from his *tête-à-tête* with Tyrrel's representatives. In the center of their protective ring, Sheri slowly turned to meet the eyes of each man. He couldn't help but feel a lump of gratitude in his chest.

Tasked with naming his seconds for the duel, Sheri had quickly dispatched notes to his tight-knit group of friends, the Honorables. They'd been drinking companions at Oxford, meeting frequently at The Hog's Teeth tavern, facing the crucible of those final steps into adulthood around a rough-hewn table. "The Honorables" derived from the fact that though each man was the scion of an aristocratic family, none of them would inherit a title. They were each The Honorable Mr. So-and-so.

Technically, he, *Lord* Sheridan, second son of the Marquess of Lothgard, was not honorable—literally and figuratively—but courtesy title notwithstanding, he was legally a Mister, just like his friends.

Now, on the dueling ground of Battersea Fields, Sheri had never felt the appropriateness of the name more. Pressing a hand to his chest, Sheri bowed. "Thank you all for coming, gentlemen."

Henry lifted his hat and swiped a hand through his hair. "Was that a note of sincerity I detected? Don't tell us you're actually worried."

"He should be," Norman snapped. "Tyrrel is reputed to be a crack shot." Standing well over six and a half feet tall, the large man's disapproval seemed to fall quite a distance before it reached Sheri.

With a dismissive flick of his hand, Sheri scoffed. "How good could he be? He returned home early from his trip. I'd wager he challenged me after already having been bested by every beast in Scotland, who laughed him over the border with his tail 'twixt his legs."

Crossing his arms, Norman muttered, "Unless he came home early because he shot them all and had nothing left to do."

Squinting at the lightening sky, Harrison said, "Nothing to fear, Norm. Tyrrel intends to shoot wide. It's satisfaction he wants, not blood. Our Lothario will be seducing the ladies tonight." His brandy eyes flicked to Sheri. "It's time."

Brandon held up a hand. "Just a moment." He produced a flask from the inside pocket of his great coat and unscrewed the cap. "A dollop of Dutch courage."

Sheri took a swig of the gin. Nerves he would never admit to had kept him awake for nearly twenty-four hours, so he appreciated the stringent vapor of juniper that curled up the back of his nose and sharpened his focus.

After passing the drink around, the circle broke up. Harrison met Tyrrel's second at the weapons table to inspect and load the pistols, while Brandon took a position off to the side, surgery bag at the ready. Norman loped to the center of the field and fished out a handkerchief, as Henry and Tyrrel's other man paced off the distance.

With all the fellows busy at their appointed tasks, Sheri was left alone. A pang of loneliness, or maybe nostalgia, ached in his chest. Turning so the others couldn't see him, he fumbled at his waist to detach the fob that secured his omnipresent quizzing glass to his person by means of a silver chain. The silver fob was round, a little larger than a guinea, and puffed like a delicate sea biscuit. Embellished with the Zouche family crest, the fob reflected the weak morning light in undulating gray lines.

Pressing his thumbnail into a recess on the edge, Sheri popped the fob open, revealing a miniature portrait of a young girl, which he cradled in his palm. She smiled at him shyly, her lively brown eyes hinting at impishness. Not for the first time, Sheri felt a rush of gratitude to the portraitist who had managed so perfectly to capture the way Grace's lower lip curled over her teeth when she smiled and the stubborn lick of brown hair that liked to escape her ribbons.

"Miss you, Grace," he said as he always did, as he always had done. *Miss you, Sheri!* she used to call back when he took his leave of her cottage. She hadn't mastered many words in her twelve years, but those three had always rung out clear and true.

"I won't ask if you've got any sway up there," he murmured. "I don't suppose I've a single favor to call in, even if you had. But if you could spare a few moments to be with me now, I'd be much obliged. You'd laugh yourself silly at the scrape I've gotten myself into this time, Grace, you really would. So maybe linger a bit for the entertainment, if nothing else." He smiled sadly, a poor imitation of the expression captured in the tiny portrait. "And if things go badly here, then we'll see each other soon. We'll play snakes and ladders, all right?"

"Sheridan!" called Henry.

Sheri snapped the fob shut and returned it to its place on his waistcoat, then went to his mark.

Twelve paces away, Tyrrel joined Sheri on the field of honor. The challenger gave Sheri a long, hard stare.

Beneath the other man's scrutiny, a vague feeling of embarrassment stole through Sheridan at being caught up in something as sordid as a duel. In his long, storied career of fornicating, this was the first time he'd been called out. On the surface, it seemed remarkable that after sleeping with dozens of married women he'd not once been called to task for it, but Sheri was meticulous about discretion. He was interested only in seeking pleasure with enthusiastic partners, not in causing trouble for the women he bedded, their lawful husbands, or—most importantly—himself.

Inside his kid gloves, which he'd purchased for the occasion of his first duel, Sheri's palms began to perspire.

The seconds broke away from the weapons table, each making for their respective principal. Harrison held the gun—one of the two he always carried about his own person—across his flat palms and presented it to Sheri.

It didn't look like much. The stock was fashioned of dark wood, with a brass cap on the end of the handle he supposed would be good for coshing one's opponent over the head, should one's shot go astray. The barrel, he believed it was called, was simple and unadorned.

"You get the lucky one," Harrison said. "This is the same pistol Brandon used to put an end to the scoundrel who abducted Mrs. Dewhurst."

That had been last fall, back when Mrs. Dewhurst was still Miss Robbins. Sheri had a particular fondness for Mrs. Dewhurst. Maybe the gun that had defended her life would, indeed, serve him well. He would take all the help he could get right now.

Gingerly, he took the thing in his hand. It was heavier than he'd expected. "I just depress this lever here, do I?"

Harrison snorted. When Sheri didn't respond in kind, the man's eyes widened. "Tell me you know how to shoot a gun, Zouche."

"Never touched one before in my life."

"What?" Harrison blurted. "How … ?" He cut himself off with a sharp gesture. "Never mind. Doesn't matter." Turning in a tight circle, he blew his lips out in exasperation before leaning in to hiss, "Why the devil did you choose pistols if you've never fired one? Are you trying to get yourself killed?"

Raising a russet brow, Sheri ticked off items on his fingers. "My other option was fencing, which: One, takes too damned long. Two, I do not engage in exercise resulting in effusive perspiration before three o'clock. Three, I've a distaste for practicing fancy footwork with another man—I prefer my dancing partners to be female. Four, it's piratical and uncivilized in these modern times. And five, I plan to delope, in any event. I tupped the man's wife, which he and I and everyone else knows. Drawing his blood would only further humiliate the poor bastard. Let Tyrrel have his tantrum, and then we can all tell him what a fine, brave boy he is and return to our own beds."

Harrison tipped his head into his hand. A heavy sigh poured from him. "Yes, Sheridan, you just depress the little lever. Be sure to point the gun well away from your own foot."

The seconds cleared the field. Norman stood between the combatants and to the side. He rattled off the rules of the duel. Then he raised his arm, holding aloft a white handkerchief.

Tyrrel turned to the side, his right foot leading. Sheri imitated the stance.

Norman released the scrap of material. It seemed to be a long time in falling.

Lord Tyrrel lifted his arm, gun pointed skyward.

Sheri's abdomen released a knot of anxiety he hadn't known he'd been holding. He pointed his own weapon to the ground, at a forty-five-degree angle away from Tyrrel.

The handkerchief alighted on the dew-silvered grass.

With the lightest squeeze of Sheri's finger, his pistol erupted. The noise slammed into his ear with the force of a pugilist's fist. A gout of turf spurted into the air much closer to Sheri's feet than he'd intended, startling the hell out of him. Bluish-white smoke snaked from the gun to mingle with the thinning morning fog.

"Oh, my god!" screeched a feminine voice. "I'm come too late!"

All heads swung to the woman bearing down upon them, one hand anchoring her fashionable hat in place, the other lifting the skirts of her perfectly *en mode* dress free of the damp grass.

"Tyrrel," Sybil cried, "did you kill him? I'll never forgive you if you did." This dramatic declaration despite Sheridan standing not ten feet away from her, whole and unharmed.

The pretty woman stopped at his side, chest heaving in a manner calculated to draw attention to her generous bosom. "My love, you're all right!" Looping her arm through Sheri's, she cast a scornful look on her husband. "I'm leaving you, Tyrrel. Lord Sheridan and I are eloping."

This was news to Sheridan.

"Is that so?" came the aggrieved reply from down the field.

"My lady," Sheri murmured, "might we discuss this at a more convenient time? Perhaps when your husband and I are not locked in a contest of honor?"

Her pale brows drew together; she tightened her grip on him. "But, Chère, I love you so. No man has ever made me feel like you do." She shouted down the field, "Do you hear that, Tyrrel? Lord Sheridan satisfies me in ways your dull, little brain could never imagine! And as for your—"

"Sybil," Sheri hissed. He shook her once, trying to silence her goading. "Stop it. Now."

"—no larger than my thumb and veers to the right, but Chère's endowed perfectly." She laughed, loud and jeering. "Why, our infant son has more in his clout than you've in your drawers."

A choked sound pulled Sheri's attention back down the field, to the man who had not yet taken his shot. Twelve paces away, Tyrrel's mouth twisted in a bitter sneer. He lowered his arm, training his pistol on the adulterous pair.

Instinctively moving to shield the woman, Lord Sheridan Zouche perceived the flash of Tyrrel's shot an instant before the bullet hit him.

• • •

That night, Sheri lay on his stomach, lengthwise, across an otto-man bench in the bedchamber of his rooms in Upper Brook Street. His arms dangled to either side. The fingers of his left hand

curled lightly around the club foot at the bottom of a walnut cab-
riole leg, while the fingers of the other grazed the page of the book
open on the floor beneath him. He read with his chin propped on
the generous cushioning, but the entertainment did little to dis-
tract him. His manservant, French, had set a snifter and bottle of
brandy on a silver tray on the floor, in easy reach of his wounded
employer. The air was lightly perfumed by the handful of bou-
quets he'd received—along with a veritable hillock of notes—from
various women of his acquaintance, expressing shock and dismay
at the news of his injury and wishes for a speedy recovery.

Beneath a bandage Brandon had wound about his hips, the
stitched gunshot wound throbbed—even the silk of his dressing
gown felt heavy on his sensitive skin. Thank God Sheri had only
been grazed, but the gash burned like the very devil. He reached
for his glass and propped up on an elbow, wincing at the sudden,
sharp pain that darted down his leg.

He returned his beverage to the tray and closed his eyes, his
cheek resting on the cushion. Sheri couldn't remember ever
hurting so much. Not that he'd imagined being shot would be
a lark, but neither had he anticipated the painful throbbing that
enveloped most of the right side of his body.

Brandon had left him some laudanum, but Sheri didn't want to
take it unless the pain became unbearable. So far, his discomfort
fell somewhere between terrible and beastly. Nothing he couldn't
live through.

He wished he had some company—female, preferably. Idly, he
wondered what his friend Elsa, Lady Fay, was doing this evening.
The beautiful young widow never failed to liven his spirits.

As if in answer to his wish, his door slammed against the
wall—but it wasn't Elsa come to minister to his wounds. Sheri's
eyes popped open in time to see his older brother striding into the
room, with French trotting just behind him.

"The Marquess of Lothgard," called the harried servant.

"Thank you, French," Sheri drawled. "If you'd be so good, perhaps a preparation of the medication Mr. Dewhurst recommended? I sense the imminent approach of a rather large pain."

French nodded and backed out of the room.

The marquess stopped several feet short of the ottoman. Sheri lazily pulled his gaze up his brother's form, noting, with a touch of envy, the fine breeches gracing his lordship's limbs. Sheri's new pantaloons had been a casualty of the morning's carnage—a senseless death.

He craned his neck to meet his sibling's thunderous expression. Eli's brown hair was a shade darker than Sheridan's, and his eyes almost black to Sheri's coffee-hued irises. The elder Zouche folded his arms across his broad chest, straining the shoulder seams of his evening coat. Every line of his noble form bristled with a sense of umbrage.

"Evening, Lothgard," Sheri said. "Kind of you to blow in for a visit."

His brother tapped a manicured finger against the opposite elbow. "It's all over Town that you were shot in the arse this morning."

"I did suffer an indignity to my fundament, it's true. However, the injury is not life-threatening, so you may put away your smelling salts."

Eli scoffed. "More's the pity. They say you deloped."

Sheri, silent, returned his gaze to his book.

"*And* that Lady Tyrrel made quite the memorable entrance."

When Sheri still made no response, his brother's toes appeared in his line of sight. Eli kicked Sheri's book, sending it skittering across the rug. "Blast it, Sheridan, look at me when I'm speaking to you."

Propping on his elbows, Sheri lifted a brow. "Shades of Pater," he remarked. "How many times did I hear just those words before the strap landed on my backside?"

Eli's face—much like Sheri's, but fuller, the skin slightly loose about the jaw, now that he was approaching forty—reddened. "Perhaps you should have better heeded our father's lessons. Not only did you bed a man's wife, you once more insulted his honor by refusing him a proper duel, and then making a scene with his wife! You may as well have spit in his face." The marquess's hands clenched and released at his sides. The heavy gold signet ring adorning the fourth finger of his right hand caught the light of a nearby candelabrum, flashing a rich yellow. "You're thirty years old, Sheridan. When will you behave like a grown man?"

Slowly, and with no small degree of discomfort, Sheri rolled onto his side and rose. He stood an inch shy of Eli's six feet, and he felt the disadvantage of being in a state of undress while the marquess was exquisitely garbed. Still, Sheridan was younger than his brother by nearly a decade, and for all his lackadaisical airs, he kept his body in prime condition with an hour of vigorous exercise each day—his preferred activities of dancing and bedding women depended upon physical stamina, after all. If Eli thought to intimidate him with paternalistic chiding, he would soon find Sheri was not so easily cowed.

"What masculine accomplishments do I lack, brother? Should I have cut Tyrrel down, as our sire would have done? Pray, enlighten me."

The hard lines around Eli's mouth softened a fraction. "Dammit, Sheridan," he muttered. With a heavy sigh, he retrieved the book he'd abused and idly flipped through the pages.

When Eli spoke again, his voice sounded altered, as though he parted with the words unwillingly. "When I heard about the duel," he said, "my first thought was how you'd always refused to touch a gun, and I wondered if you hadn't managed to shoot yourself in the rump."

"I had a quick course in handling the thing."

Eli snapped the book shut and met his younger brother's eyes. "You've become an embarrassment, Sheridan."

"The gossip will blow over in a few days, Lothgard."

"Not just the duel." Lothgard grimaced. "Deborah"—his wife—"tells me the ladies all call you Chère ..."

Sheri couldn't suppress a smile at the mention of his French nickname amongst many of the *ton*'s ladies. "It's just a silly little—"

"While I've heard the men," Lothgard continued, "call you *Share*. Share Zouche."

Sheri shifted his weight to his left foot. The right side of his body throbbed. "Honestly, that one is undeserved. There was only the one time." He frowned. "No, twice. But everyone involved had a fine time ... Oh, I suppose there was a third occasion, but there was a great deal of drinking involved that particular night ..."

His glib recitation tapered off as Lothgard's face grew more and more pained with every word. He didn't look angry anymore, just ... disappointed.

A ripple of defensiveness coursed through Sheri. How dare Lothgard come in here and moralize at him?

"Your reputation is abysmal," Lothgard said. "You are known only for your sexual exploits, rather than for anything of worth."

Sheri crossed his arms. "I contribute a great deal of worth, Lothgard. In fact, had Tyrrel walked into that room an hour earlier and witnessed the act his wife begged me to perform with a cucumber, he'd have thanked me for sparing him the task." He lifted his chin. "I should receive the Royal Guelphic Order for keeping Lady Tyrrel contained to her own boudoir while his lordship was away, rather than letting her menace an unsuspecting male populace."

Lothgard drew back. Squeezing his eyes shut, he pressed his third finger between his brows, as though suffering the headache.

Feeling the beginnings of victory, Sheri stooped over for his glass of brandy. Offering his brother a silent toast, Sheri brought the glass to his mouth.

"I didn't want to do this, but you leave me no choice."

Pausing with the snifter at his lips, Sheri raised a brow.

His brother opened the door. "French, please bring her ladyship here."

Sheri stiffened. "You didn't."

His brother smiled evilly. "I did."

"Elijah?" said a gentle, uncertain voice.

Sheri groaned. Just like that, he was defeated.

"Here, darling." Hopping into action like a footman, the marquess held the door wide to admit French escorting a petite woman. When she saw Sheri, her big brown eyes instantly filled.

"Oh, Sheridan!" She approached him in a rustle of evening silks, one gloved hand pressed to her cheek.

Delicate of health and guileless as a calf, his sister-in-law, Deborah, had always been a great favorite of his. Eleven years ago, when Sheri couldn't tell Eli's infant twins apart and suggested, in all seriousness, that they tattoo the boys' names onto the bottoms of their feet, Lothgard had erupted and called him a buffoon. Deborah had merely laughed her tinkling fairy laugh and tied different-colored ribbons about the babies' ankles until their uncle could distinguish them. Ever since, Sheri had doted on the woman.

"Pray, do not fret, Deborah," he said, gently squeezing her hand to reassure her of his vitality. "Tyrrel missed my heart by a mile. I may lose my leg yet," he joked, "but you can be sure I'll have the most fashionable peg leg in London. Something silver-plated and gold-tipped, I imagine, engraved with scrollwork, possibly set with rubies and sapphires. Or maybe I'll allow some promising artist to paint it with a masterpiece that follows me wherever I go. It would be the latest sensation—wearable art for amputees.

I predict wounded soldiers will soon be clamoring to have their wooden limbs frescoed with depictions of their battlefield heroics. What do you think?"

In a tense, silent moment, Deborah's lower lip quivered while the water level in her eyes rose to alarming heights before the flood finally spilled over the dam of her lids. She emitted only a small, plaintive whimper, worse by far than a loud show of distress. She did nothing to stem the flow of tears down her face, only stood there and quietly cried, her eyes still locked on Sheri's.

Lothgard wrapped his wife in his arms and drew her away from his brother, glaring accusingly at Sheri over her head while making soothing sounds.

A hot coil of guilt twisted in Sheri's gut. "Forgive me, Deborah. I was simply making light of the situation, which, obviously, was the incorrect course." He raised a hand, then let it fall uselessly to his side.

Deborah lifted her face and wiped her nose on a handkerchief Elijah had provided. "I can take no more, Sheridan," she said in a watery voice. "Anyone else, I'd know they were funning, but you very well might go out and have some gaudy false leg made and parade it all around Town, flaunting the fact that you'd lost your leg in a duel with your lover's husband.

"Do you never think of your nephews, Sheridan? What kind of example are you setting for them?"

His ass throbbed, and that hot coil twisted tighter, pinching his innards. He dropped onto the ottoman, sucking a breath through his teeth at the flare of pain. His discomfort was making him cross. "It was a jest," he ground out. "What would the twins know about it, anyway?" Sheri demanded. "I don't make a habit of discussing my private affairs with your offspring, my lady; do you?"

His eleven-year-old nephews were called Crispin and Webb. Sheri had thus far refrained from telling Eli and Deborah that he'd always thought the boys' monikers sounded like the name of a legal partnership. He could very nearly see the engraved brass plate now: *Crispin & Webb, Solicitors at Law*. In his current state, he very nearly let loose out of spite.

The marchioness swayed on her feet. Eli helped her to a chair. Never possessed of a strong constitution to begin, the twins' birth had very nearly killed Deborah, and she'd never quite recovered from the ordeal. She passed her days navigating from one resting spot to another. Pain was her constant companion; any activity more strenuous than a sedate stroll was beyond her, but she put on her sweet smile and did her best to move about in Society. Sheri was glad he'd kept his spiteful remark between his teeth and was sorry he'd ever thought to lash out at her.

Husband and wife exchanged a look. "Things have not gone well, I take it?" Deborah asked.

Hands clasped behind his back, Lothgard once more looked the formidable nobleman. His nose sliced a negative through the air. "Sheridan won't hear a word I say."

"He's always gone his own way."

Lothgard blew out a snort. "Down the devil's highway, more like."

"I worry about your mother, too—what must she make of all this?"

There they went again, treating Sheridan like a recalcitrant child, speaking as though he were not in the same room.

"Our mother," he interjected, "is too busy kicking up her heels in Bath to pay any heed to London gossip. If I have in any way discombobulated her, you can be sure she'll let me know."

"Yes, you can be sure she will." Eli stood behind Deborah's chair and rested his hand on her shoulder. "Both of us wrote to her today."

"What, both of you? One missive wasn't enough?"

Deborah parted her hands in her lap. "We wished to assure your lady mother that we were aware of the situation."

"And that we would handle it," Eli pronounced down the length of his aristocratic nose.

"Handle?" Sheri echoed. "How must I be handled?"

In her soft, soft voice, Deborah said, "You must marry, Sheridan."

For a while, no one spoke. In the silence, the aroma of flowers became oppressive. Sheri's head began aching in earnest, his skull beating in sympathy with the angry pulse of his wound. He wanted that laudanum, after all.

He opened his mouth to formulate an argument, but the marquess cut him dead with a look. "Your days of indulging your every base desire are at an end, Sheridan. If it were just myself, I'd cut you loose and let you fornicate your way through all of England." At his wife's gasp, he winced. "Sorry, my dear," he hastily apologized. "But it's not just me," he went on, addressing his brother once more. "It's Mother, and Deborah, and the boys. You're ruining our family's name and causing them embarrassment. Deborah has persuaded me to grant you one last chance: if you wish to remain an acknowledged member of this family, you will do your duty and wed."

Damn Elijah!

Knowing there would be no winning with his brother, Sheridan turned to his sister-in-law. "Sister," he began, his tone conciliatory, "please forgive me for causing you any shred of humiliation. You know I'd never willingly do you harm."

The woman's lower lip trembled. She made a little, muffled sound.

Sheri went to where she sat and, repressing his own whimper, knelt before her like a penitent seeking absolution. He took her hand and pressed a kiss to the back of it. Her nose reddened. "I see now that things have gotten out of hand. I'd no idea Lady Tyrrel would make such a to-do this morning, and I recognized at once that there would be scandal. I see now, though, that this is not the first time my behavior has brought you grief, is it?"

Sniffling, Deborah shook her head. "Oh, Sheridan, if you'd heard what the ladies all say. Half of them think you're the Lord's gift to womankind, while the other half think you're the devil incarnate. No matter which side they fall on, every one of them loves nothing better than swapping tales about you: *Where will Chère Zouche be tonight? Who is he wooing now? Have you seen his new coat? Can you credit the way he looked at Lady Whistleton at the ball? Do you suppose he's taken her to bed?* It never ends!" She cast a hurt look at the flowers arrayed around the room, stand-ins for the women who'd subjected her to their tattle.

"Well, it ends now," he vowed, squeezing her hand and gazing earnestly into her eyes. "There's no need to bring marriage into things; I will be a reformed man without all that, I swear."

Deborah shook her head. "I pity you, Sheridan—truly, I do. You're missing out on the good things in life, and you don't even realize it. Goodness knows you love women and they love you right back, but we're nothing more to you than …" A fierce blush flooded her face. "Bed partners," she finished in a whisper.

"That isn't so," he protested. The pain in his flank drove him to hands and knees, his face almost to the rug, so that now he was practically groveling at Deborah's feet. "I live to make women happy—not just *that* way, either. Don't look at me like that," he yelled. "Your pity is insufferable."

His affairs had been for the pleasure of the women he bedded— his own, too, naturally—but he'd never once touched a woman selfishly. A woman's pleasure was Sheridan's greatest joy. To think that all the time he'd been pleasuring women in his bed, he'd been hurting Deborah every bit as much.

A guttural moan vibrated in his throat. Perspiration damped his hairline.

"Perhaps we should take our leave, my dear," said Eli.

Yes, Sheridan cried to himself. *Begone, and take your witch of guilt with you.* It was just the pain that had his mind in such a muddle, he assumed. Once he felt better, his mind would set itself to rights.

"Sheridan?" Deborah's hand touched his chest. Sheri's eyes opened; he found he was laying on the floor, his sister-in-law crouched beside him.

"Deborah," he rasped. "I'm so sorry. Every bit of unhappiness I caused you, I wish I could take it for myself."

She smiled sadly. "I think you shall." She took his hand. "Don't you love me, Sheridan?"

"You're the sister I always wanted," he replied in a rough voice. Grace was never far from his thoughts. "I couldn't have picked a better sister for myself. I'm grateful every day that Elijah chose you."

Her angelic smile was a blessing. His eyes started to drift closed. *I really must summon French with that medicine.*

"Do you acknowledge that you have caused me a great deal of social embarrassment with your indiscreet behavior?"

"Of course, darling, I already did."

"And would you like to make it up to me?"

"If I can, certainly." There were several jewelers Sheri patronized when he needed to make amends with a woman. Through the haze of pain, he wondered whether Deborah would prefer a new fan or a pearl bracelet.

Her face filled his vision as she leaned over him. Sheridan sensed the bulk of Elijah behind her, physically supporting his wife. "Then get married, Sheridan. You've made every woman in the *ton* happy, and now it's my turn. Find a wife. Tell me you will, Sheridan. You've never once broken your word to me. Tell me you'll marry and be a good husband and stop your wicked sinning."

"Yes, Deborah, I shall marry."

A moment later they were gone, and Sheri was on the floor, gutted and raw by the promise he'd made. He wouldn't go back on his word to Deborah—not ever. It would be the end of any relationship Sheri hoped to have with his brother and nephews in the future—not to mention with Deborah herself.

Even now, the flowers and letters filling his chamber, which had marked the happiest part of his life, were the funereal arrangements for that same time of life. It was over. Gone. Dead.

Sheri would marry.

Somewhere in the back of his mind, a rallying thought: hadn't he always been prepared for this eventuality? *In Case of Crisis, Wed* ...

Sheridan stiffened. Yes, he would have a happy bride in no time.

Quickly, he rose to his feet. And just as quickly collapsed on the ottoman. His leg felt like hot, liquid lead. "French," he bellowed. "The laudanum. Now."

He might not have a happy bride in *no time*. But soon, he thought, rubbing his hand over the battered rump. Soon.

Chapter Two

Three weeks later

If this was Home, Arcadia wanted nothing to do with it.

This place, this England her mother had rhapsodized about, was all wrong.

To begin, it was cold. Arcadia had arrived yesterday morning and had been shivering ever since. She'd stepped off the boat on legs as wobbly as a newborn foal's—still weak from the fever and stomach illness that had plagued her since somewhere off the coast of Spain—and into a drizzly atmosphere possessed of the kind of cool dampness that seeped all the way down to her bones. Not even the carriage rug draped across her lap warded off her tremors.

From her seat in the landau, she gazed listlessly across Hyde Park, her hands pressing the comforting weight of her reticule to her tender stomach in an attempt to still its roiling. *This* was the park that had captured her mother's imagination, this alien place with its gloomy sky and acres of faded grass and balding trees? For this, the landscape equivalent of dirty dishwater, Arcadia had left India?

"Put your arms down, child," fussed her aunt, Lady Delafield. "Clutching yourself so will make everyone think you're ill." Her ladyship's pinch-mouthed disapproval was echoed by the black, beady-eyed stare of the stuffed partridge perched in her turban.

"I *am* ill," Arcadia protested, "and cold."

She didn't add it to her litany of complaints, but she was also dreadfully uncomfortable in her new, ill-fitting clothes. Papa never would have forced her into this suffocating costume. Back on the station in the *mofussil*, she'd worn saris suited to the Indian climate—unless they were visited by other members of the Raj, of course, in which case Arcadia had donned something approximating English dress. Now, however, she was encased in numerous layers of undergarments and even a corset. Before this morning, she had never even seen a corset. She'd thought Poorvaja, her *ayah*, was playing a trick on her when she showed Arcadia the contraption and said Lady Delafield expected her to wear it beneath her clothes. Arcadia had peered incredulously at the woman, but Poorvaja had simply shrugged.

Her aunt sniffed. "Nonsense. You're simply suffering seasickness-in-reverse from being on land for the first time in months. It will pass in a day or two. September is our warmest time of year! You couldn't possibly be cold."

Behind her, Arcadia heard an indelicate snort. She didn't turn around, but could very well picture the look on the face of Poorvaja, who was riding beside a groom on the hard bench behind them. Arcadia might well attribute her chill to her persistent ailment, except Poorvaja had likewise relentlessly cursed the temperature— and she was as healthy as an ox.

Their open carriage stopped while Lady Delafield exchanged greetings with a gentleman on horseback.

"Niece, you are in luck!" Lady Delafield exclaimed. "Here is Sir Godwin Prickering, one of our foremost literary talents. Sir Godwin, allow me to present my niece, Miss Parks, lately of Hyderabad, India."

The thin man wore a scarlet neckcloth. Against his snowy shirt, it looked like a gash across his throat. Arcadia fought to repress a shudder. From his saddle, the man made a slight bow. "Your servant, Miss Parks," he said in a lazy drawl.

"Pleased to make your acquaintance, sir," she replied.

"How cheering it is to have an English rose returned to her native soil—although you have certainly flourished in the ..." His compliment trailed away as he finally took a good look at her, undoubtedly seeing her pale, sickly cast, perhaps even wondering at how she looked like an uncooked goat sausage.

When the landau lurched into motion again, Arcadia's stomach clenched alarmingly. She closed her eyes; watching the scenery just exacerbated her nausea.

As they rolled on, Lady Delafield leaned over. "On no account should you have anything to do with that scribbler. Pity you did not come six months ago," her ladyship tutted. "Had you been here during the Season, we might have—no, we mightn't have," she interrupted herself, pulling upright and sighing. "No good ever came of false regrets." Arcadia cracked an eye to see her aunt glowering into the middle distance, her scythe of a nose looming over hollow cheeks. "Your father should have sent you to us when you were much younger, as dear Lucretia wished to do. You'd have been properly educated and groomed to catch a fine husband. With your dowry and connections, you could have had a lord. Now, we must set our sights much lower. Although not as low as a poet, I daresay."

Lady Delafield had taken it into her head that her niece had come to London for the purpose of finding an English husband. Arcadia needn't have left India to accomplish that feat. The Raj teemed with eligible men in want of wives. Despite the remoteness of her father's post, Englishmen started visiting the station on specious claims of East India Company business soon after Arcadia's sixteenth birthday. By then, her mother was long dead, and her father, Sir Thaddeus Parks, had no mind to see his only child—his only remaining blood relative—removed to Delhi or Bombay by a husband. When other Company factors came to stay, Sir Thaddeus sent Arcadia to Poorvaja's family in a nearby village, summoning his daughter again only after the threat of courtship had gone.

The sky steadily dimmed as the team of four horses paraded them around Hyde Park in lonely splendor. The side-to-side rocking of the landau made Arcadia's insides slosh. Her head pounded; perspiration beaded on her temples.

"You can't imagine the great sea of people one meets in the park during the fashionable hour in the Season." Lady Delafield sat a little straighter, warming to her subject. "Anyone worth knowing is here. One still meets friends this time of year, to be sure, but nothing like the crowds to be found in the spring. The air is positively thick with consequence!"

For a few fleeting seconds, Lady Delafield's stern features became animated, peeling years off her age. Her enthusiasm in describing the social hour reminded Arcadia so much of her mother, she felt a pang of grief she'd not experienced in many years. Her chest constricted painfully. Combined with the unease in her middle and the rhythmic aching of her head, she feared she really might be sick right here in Lady Delafield's fine landau.

"Aunt," she said, wrapping the cord of her reticule around her gloved hand, "my stomach … I think I'm going to vomit."

Her aunt's mouth popped open on a gasp. "Don't *say* such an indelicate thing," she hissed. "And in public, too! Your father truly did let you go native, didn't he? Have you no refinement?" She leaned back in her seat, moisture welling in her eyes. The partridge on her turban eyed Arcadia dolefully. "I can't credit such a thing— my own niece! Oh, my poor sister must be turning in her grave." Waving a hand, she called, "Coachman, stop!"

While Lady Delafield indulged in the third fit of the vapors she'd had since clapping eyes on her niece's "sun-spoiled" complexion yesterday, Arcadia half-fell from the carriage and staggered to a convenient knot of shrubbery a short distance away, where she fell to her knees and emptied the contents of her stomach.

In the aftermath, she felt lightheaded with exhaustion. A hand settled on her back. Blinking her bleary eyes, Arcadia saw the silhouette of a woman in a bonnet and startled.

"Hush, Jalanili," said the familiar voice calling her by the familiar nickname. "It's only me." Crouching beside her, Poorvaja produced a handkerchief from her apron pocket and patted

Arcadia's mouth. Her berry-brown lips quirked. "I look as foolish in these ridiculous clothes as you do, eh?" She swept a hand down the front of her new English dress.

Her mind still muddled, Arcadia peered at the woman who had been her wet nurse as an infant, then the nurse and governess of her childhood, and now her lady's maid and companion. Poorvaja's dear face featured in her earliest memories, and although the Indian woman was only fourteen years her senior, the ayah had, in many ways, been more of a mother to Arcadia than Lucretia Parks. Suddenly swamped with emotion, Arcadia threw her arms around Poorvaja and burst into tears. "I want to go home," she cried.

Poorvaja let out a little *oof* when Arcadia hit her, thumping down on her backside. Then her strong arms wrapped about Arcadia's shoulders. "There, there, Jalanili. We've only just arrived! This is your country, your people."

Arcadia shook her head in the crook of her ayah's neck, feeling once more like a child in need of comforting. "Not my country. *India* is my country. That's where I belong. I don't know why I agreed to come here."

With a long sigh, Poorvaja helped Arcadia to her feet and led her away from the carriage at a stroll. "You had no choice," she reminded Arcadia as they rounded a little bend in the path. A thick grove of bushes and trees flanked them on either side, cutting Lady Delafield's carriage from their line of sight. Arcadia was grateful for the brief reprieve from her aunt.

Poorvaja's arm around the younger woman's waist gave a little squeeze. "The *sahib* left instructions for you to come here after his death."

Grimacing, Arcadia shrugged out of Poorvaja's grasp. "In six months, I'll reach my majority," she said, picking up her pace in spite of her aching body's protests.

The unfamiliar confines of the corset prevented her from drawing adequate breath. Even the fabrics of her clothes draped differently than the saris to which she was accustomed, making her walk differently.

Arcadia wanted to scream. The clothes, the weather, the country—none of it fit properly. None of it was home. Lifting her skirts a little, she tried to force her legs into their customary gait. "I could have devised a way to stay until my birthday, then no one could have told me what I had to do."

Behind her, Poorvaja snorted. "Child, you were just nineteen when the *sahib* passed. Where would you have hidden for two years?"

Not for the first time, Arcadia felt the injustice of time and distance. It had taken months to arrange her voyage from Bombay to London after Sir Thaddeus had succumbed to his final illness, and she'd had no say about the seven long months she'd spent at sea. While she might have been just nineteen when her life was thrown into turmoil, Arcadia was now almost her own woman, according to the law, and it seemed downright unfair that she be expected to follow plans made on her behalf when she was still but a child.

She glanced over her shoulder and saw she'd put a fair bit of distance between herself and Poorvaja. "I could have gone anywhere!" she called in Hindustani, defiantly raising the fist clutching her reticule and struggling to repress another wave of nausea rising from her gut. "That Mughal prince, Suri Shah, would have given me a place in his *zanana*."

Her friend tossed back her head and laughed before replying in the same language. "If you think to tell me you'd consent to being that pompous oaf's thirty-third wife—or his seventy-second concubine—then you're the fool here, Jalanili, not I."

A sharp retort formed on Arcadia's tongue. Then she walked into something solid and a hand clamped on her shoulder, causing her words to die in her throat. Startled, she glanced up at the stranger. A dusty scarf concealed the lower portion of his face, while a hat pulled low shadowed his eyes. In the failing light, it was nigh impossible to distinguish any features.

Powerful fingers dug into her upper arm. Arcadia gasped. He spoke, but she couldn't understand his unfamiliar accent. She shook her head. The bandit repeated himself impatiently, shaking her. Sluggishly, she made sense of the words.

"Don't want no trouble, I said." From somewhere, he produced a short knife. The dull blade was nicked and rusty, but Arcadia didn't doubt its ability to cause injury. "Give me the bag, nice and easy now, and we all go home to our suppers."

"Bag?" she echoed dumbly, not comprehending his meaning.

She heard a sound like a bellowing bull elephant from somewhere in the distance. Behind her, Poorvaja let out an angry stream of Hindustani curses.

The man glanced over Arcadia's shoulder at the irate Indian woman. He gave a warning jab to her stomach with his knife. Arcadia felt the threads of her too-tight dress part. A cold wash of fear doused her from tip to toe, paralyzing her. Had she sailed across oceans, traversed half the globe, simply to die at the hands of a common footpad?

"Gimme the bloody reticule."

The snarled command snapped her back to her senses. "No!" Arcadia shouted, attempting to move her reticule out of his reach. The silk satchel contained her dearest treasure from India. "Please, don't—"

Still weak with illness, she was no match for the larger, stronger man. He snatched her wrist and twisted. Arcadia yelped in pain and released the silk cords. The pouch tumbled from her grasp; the thief nabbed it before it touched the ground. Then the miscreant sprang towards the tree line.

Arcadia stumbled, catching herself on her hands. "Stop," she cried, pushing back upright and waving her arm. "Please, wait! That's mine!"

Poorvaja sprinted past her, arms pumping, shouting in Hindustani for the thieving son of a casteless whore to come back. Just as the ayah's extended fingertips brushed the thief's coat, the skirts of her new dress tangled around her ankles, and she went sprawling into a heap of leaves and shrubbery.

Arcadia screamed for her friend and lurched forward on legs that refused to cooperate. Moreover, her stomach contracted, hard. She bent double and retched again, this time right in the middle of the path. Shivers wracked her body.

"Good God!" called a masculine voice.

Then new hands were on her arms, gentler this time, pulling her upright and steadying her. An indistinct face swam in Arcadia's vision, with dark spots where eyes should be and a reddish smudge for the mouth.

"Are you all right, miss?" asked the man. This one held her non-threateningly, and even through the haze of her ailment, she found his warm, spicy scent appealing and the support of his arms comforting.

Blinking away tears, she pointed a shaky finger in the direction the thief had run. "He took my bag."

"Are you all right?" the man repeated. From the woods, she heard the villain stomping his getaway through crunchy leaves.

Arcadia beat her fist against a solid chest. "Thief! Go, please!"

"Now, now," the man said in patient, cultured tones. "There's nothing in your reticule you cannot replace. The important thing is that you are safe. Did the scoundrel harm you?"

Off to the side, Poorvaja shakily rose to her feet. "Help her," Arcadia murmured, worried her friend may have been injured in her fall.

"Hush, my dear." The man's voice was velvet against her ear. "Your maid is fine, I'm sure; it's you I'm worried about."

Poorvaja muttered a dark invective, which the man seemed not to notice.

"Please get my bag," Arcadia wailed, her voice tinny and distant in her own ears. The illness that had plagued her for months seemed to crash down upon her all at once.

The man muttered an oath Arcadia didn't understand. His outline started to fade. "I say, Norman," he called. "Do you see a blighter with a reticule over there in the woods?"

His words only made superficial sense. Arcadia recognized the sounds, but meaning did not follow. The sickness was overwhelming her now, and she was slipping into the darkness.

Another shadow appeared beside the first. This one was enormous—monstrous, even—a giant who could crush her under his fist as easily as swatting a fly.

A choked sound worked its way from Arcadia's throat. Her rescuer said something she couldn't distinguish, but she paid him no heed. Instead, she ran headlong into the sanctuary of her mind.

• • •

Sheri watched in disbelief as the sweaty woman slithered through his hands and landed at his feet in a heap, her limp hand flopping into the muck of her own vomit.

"What the devil?" Norman exclaimed when he skidded to a halt beside him an instant later. "Why didn't you catch her?"

"I didn't think she meant it! In my defense, ladies feign swoons all the time for attention, or to get out of trouble with their husbands. I'm not sure I've ever actually seen a real one before."

"Well, now you have."

Sheri sent his friend a withering look. "Go after the scoundrel, would you? He threatened her with a knife."

The two friends had been taking a ramble about the park while Sheri picked Norman's brain as to whether his brother could legally disown him over his marital status. Norman had been cheerfully explaining that Lothgard could bar Sheri from the family for any reason or none when the sounds of female distress had cut through the late afternoon. Without hesitation, Sheri had broken into a sprint. From a distance, he saw the masked fiend shake the woman and press a blade to her middle. Too far away to intervene, he'd bellowed in rage, hoping to scare the thief off. Woman and malefactor tussled briefly. For an instant, Sheri's blood ran cold, certain the lady would be stabbed to death before he could reach her.

When the other woman, dressed in maid's garb, chased after the thief, Sheri went for the lady, catching up to her just in time to witness her casting her accounts on the ground. Normally, he could scarcely stand being in the presence of his own sick when that unfortunate event happened, much less that of another person. But he hadn't even wavered before drawing her to her feet. She'd pleaded with him in a strange, lilting accent before collapsing.

While Norman went loping after the miscreant, Sheri crouched and took a good look at her. The woman wore a dowdy bonnet. Her dress was matronly and plain, but pulled sinfully tight across her breasts, as though they wanted to spring free of the confines of their muslin prison.

A few dark, damp curls clung to the woman's cheeks. Her complexion looked waxen, except for twin fever-blooms on high, prominent cheekbones. She had a strong, angular jaw, with the hint of a cleft bisecting her firm chin. It wasn't a beautiful face, and the aroma of regurgitated bile did nothing to improve his impression.

A pained gasp burst from her lips.

Unattractive and odoriferous she might be, but she was a woman in need of aid. "She can't breathe properly," he announced to no one, reaching behind her to release the fastenings of her dress and loosen the laces of her corset. His practiced adroitness with women's attire allowed him to accomplish the task in half a minute. At once, the unconscious woman's chest inflated as she dragged in a heavy breath.

He felt a touch lightheaded himself, with relief. "There's a good girl," he murmured, soothingly stroking her back through a sweat-damp chemise. Beneath his fingers, he detected welts where the corset laces had nipped far too hard into her tender flesh. The physical discomforts to which women subjected themselves for the sake of vanity never ceased to amaze him. He rubbed the marks, encouraging circulation in the abused rib cage.

There was a burst of indecipherable noise, and then the maid was trying to pull Sheri away from his foundling. The servant's pinched brown face and sharp gestures communicated all the ire he could not deduce from her words.

He batted away the angry woman's flailing hands. *Mine*, snapped his brain. *He'd* found her; *he'd* saved her from death-by-fashion; he'd deuced well be the one to continue tending her. Besides which, she'd come to harm on the maid's watch; Sheri had doubts as to her ability to properly see to her mistress.

The servant spat a few venomous words at him; Sheri was grateful he didn't understand them.

He scooped the unconscious woman into his arms and rose. He was too attuned to female bodies to help from noticing that he held a very nice one, even if her unflattering clothes disguised it. Her curves snugged right against him as he jostled her weight. Out of habit, he lowered his head to her cheek for a whiff of her feminine scent; he recoiled at the acrid fumes from the vomit he'd managed to forget.

In a strained voice, he asked the maid, "What is your mistress's name?"

"My word!" said an unfamiliar voice.

A group of onlookers formed a short distance away. Curious ladies and gentlemen had, evidently, been drawn away from the social hour by the same commotion that had alerted Sheri to trouble.

"What's going on?" called one of the men.

"Who is that?" asked another.

"Why, it's Lord Sheridan," said a lady. "Yoo-hoo, hello, Chère!" She tittered. The woman waved cheerfully. Sheri recognized her as someone he'd enjoyed a tumble with in the past. She gave him a saucy wink.

"Do you know this woman?" he asked, indicating the female in his arms. The lady kept preening, batting her eyelashes and smoothing a hand over her waist.

The crowd drew closer, forcing the maid to the edge of the path.

"Does anyone know her?" He looked from face to face, but his inquiry was met with blank stares, shrugs, and shaking heads.

Norman tromped back out of the woods, brushing leaves from his broad shoulders. He stood a full head taller than every other man present and addressed Sheri as though the crowd wasn't standing between them. "Sorry, Sheri, but the thief escaped. Has she still not come around?" he asked, pointing to Sheri's damsel.

"No," Sheri ground out, frustration and the beginnings of fear lapping at him. Now that he'd been holding her for a few moments, he felt how much heat she was generating. The sick woman was fevered, in need of proper care. "And as much help as any of them are," he said, jerking his chin at their audience, "you'd think she just fell from the sky. No one recognizes her."

"Neither do you, Zouche," said Marcus Tyson, whom Sheri recognized from his club. "But I see it hasn't stopped you taking her clothes off."

Laughter rippled through the group.

A flush of embarrassment heated his neck. Sheri's jaw ticked. His hands tightened on his burden. "There are ladies present, Tyson."

He made a decision. If these Society ninnies couldn't help him, he'd take care of the woman himself. "Come, Norman," he called. "Collect the maid. Is Dewhurst in Town? He'll know what to do."

Norman plowed through the crowd. "I don't see the maid. I think she's run off."

The whinny of a horse announced yet another newcomer. At the back of the crowd, Sir Godwin Prickering sat atop his mincing little gelding. Sheri would never have thought to apply the word "foppish" to an animal before he encountered the poet's mount.

"I say, Zouche," the man called, "whatever are you doing to Miss Parks? Your offensive touch has killed her!"

Sheri's brows shot up. "You know her?" he asked, incredulous.

A hush fell over the witnesses as they followed the exchange, eager to lap up new gossip.

The poet wiggled his shoulders as he straightened. "But of course," Sir Godwin said in a smug drawl, relishing his moment of superiority. "And I don't suppose Lady Delafield will care to hear you've molested her niece. Give her to me, and I'll deliver her back to her aunt."

"The hell I will," Sheri snapped. Homely and smelly she might be, but damn it all, he felt compelled to make sure his mystery woman was all right. He wouldn't trust Sir Godwin with the welfare of a slug, much less a young lady. He'd waltz in hell before he gave the obnoxious little oaf the satisfaction of claiming undeserved heroics.

Sir Godwin's lips thinned in a hard line. "See here, Zouche, I'm acquainted with the lady, while you have no such claim …" His voice trailed off as a distant rumbling quickly became louder.

The group parted to make way for a landau drawn by four horses. Lady Delafield craned her neck, the missing maid perched on the bench behind her. While Sheri had been locking horns with Sir Godwin, the servant had done something useful, namely, go for help.

"Lord Sheridan," cried Lady Delafield. "If you'd please be so good as to return my niece?" Her tone was brittle.

Sheri quickly made his way to the carriage. "My lady," he said, "your niece was accosted by a ruffian. I was only trying—"

A whimper drew his attention to the woman in his arms. Miss Parks was rousing from her swoon. Sharp pleats creased her brow as she regained consciousness. He watched, suddenly fascinated, as her eyes rolled behind lids before blinking open, her hazel gaze slowly focusing on his face.

Something in Sheri's chest lurched. "Hello again," he murmured. "Welcome back."

The footman and maid hopped down from the back of the carriage. In a few seconds, Sheri would have to hand over his charge. He held her a little tighter, reluctant to release the woman who, for a few moments, had been his to safeguard and protect.

A shadow crossed Miss Parks's eyes. She let out a fretful sound.

The footman opened the carriage door and let down the stairs. The maid tugged on Sheri's arm. He ignored them all.

"It's all right," he assured Miss Parks. "I've got you. You're safe now. If there's anything I can do to be of assistance—"

"Lord Sheridan!" snapped Lady Delafield.

Sheri looked up to see several women tittering into their hands, while the men shuffled and coughed uncomfortably. Norman met his eyes and jerked his head towards the landau.

Sheri deposited Miss Parks beside her aunt.

"She was sick," he informed her ladyship, "and I believe she has a fever. You must have her attended right away. Have you a carriage blanket? Oh, yes, here it is." He covered Miss Parks's lap and started tucking the rug snugly about her.

"What do you think you're doing?" hissed Lady Delafield. "Unhand my niece this instant, you rogue."

The insult stung Sheri like an angry wasp. He'd been called many a foul epithet in his time, and deserved most of them. But this time—this time he was trying to help the lady, not despoil her. That his reputation was so far gone that he couldn't rescue a maiden without drawing suspicion sat ill with him.

A rebuttal formed on his lips, but then he glanced at Miss Parks. Her cheeks blazed—far more color than could be accounted for by the fever. She was embarrassed to be seen with him, mortified by his touch.

Recalling Deborah's intelligence that half the *ton*'s ladies believed Sheri to be wickedness incarnate, he felt certain Lady Delafield and her niece were in that camp.

As he climbed out of the carriage, Sheri noted that the curious gazes of his peers were more mocking than admiring. Sir Godwin Prickering sat tall in his saddle as though he'd just won in the lists at an ancient joust.

"Damn it all," Sheri muttered, shouldering his way to Norman.

He really was a blackguard. A rogue. A rake.

Worst of all, he was a joke.

CHAPTER THREE

Sheridan stared out the window, watching gray clouds cross the sky like an armada of ships under full sail.

One of Henry De Vere's merchant ships was leaving soon. Perhaps, Sheri mused, he should be on it. Floating out there in the isolation of the deep blue sea held a great deal of appeal, as did the thought of a destination at journey's end where no one would have any reason to scorn him.

"Have you gone to sleep again?" Elsa asked.

Lifting his head from the back of the chair upon which he was reclining, he met Elsa's amused gaze in the mirror of her vanity. This little tradition of theirs, meeting in her dressing room once a week to exchange gossip, had begun while she was still married to the late, and little lamented, Lord Fay. It was one of the great attractions of married and widowed women, this being able to conduct a friendship with something of the same degree of intimacy he enjoyed with his male compatriots.

He sipped from a dainty Sèvres teacup and shook his head. "No," he drawled, "but I won't be long for the world with no more than a thimble-sized serving of tea." He directed his attention to Elsa's maid, who stood behind her mistress, styling her hair. "Foster, aren't there any cups in the house large enough for a man to properly fortify himself against the impending day?"

The maid shot him a disapproving look. "My lady doesn't cater to gentlemen, my lord."

Perhaps not in the tea service department, but Sheridan knew perfectly well that Elsa entertained lovers at her home with some degree of regularity, if not in the same numbers as Sheri's own bed-hopping. Elsa's honest sensuality was one of the things he admired most about her.

From the front pocket of his waistcoat, he plucked his quizzing glass. Squinting through it, he made a show of watching the maid work. "Is that hairstyle *meant* to resemble a basket weave, or is it just an unfortunate coincidence?"

Elsa sighed. "Please see if Cook can scrounge up a mug for Lord Sheridan." After the maid stalked from the room, her spine ramrod straight with wounded pride, Elsa chided, "Must you antagonize Foster so?"

Sheridan waved a dismissive hand and leaned back in his chair again. "*Pfft*. She enjoys our little sparring matches. You know, I think she nurtures a bit of a *tendre* for me."

"You *would* think so." Elsa opened a vanity drawer and withdrew a flask, silver inlaid with mother-of-pearl. She tipped a generous measure of clear liquid into her teacup. "You wanted some fortification, Chère. Here it is." She proffered the flask.

"Thank you, but I'd prefer to remain conscious, at least until afternoon tea. I've a fitting with my tailor at two."

Shrugging, she returned the bottle to its hiding place, took a sip of her drink, then adjusted the sash of her rose silk dressing gown. Elsa turned in her seat to face him and patted her knees. "So. What did you do yesterday?" She raised a brow, a teasing smile tugging at her full lips. There were dark circles beneath her glassy eyes, as if she hadn't gotten enough sleep, despite the advanced hour.

His right knee rocked side to side while he studied his friend's shrewd expression. *Hell.* She already knew about the incident in Hyde Park; he'd stake his best pair of gloves on it. Still, he saw no reason to hand over his balls on a silver salver.

"I had a consultation with my solicitor," he said. "Asked whether this proposal of Lothgard's is entirely legal. It turns out, the law holds no opinion whatsoever on disinheriting unmarried brothers."

"An unforgivable oversight," Elsa replied, reaching again for her cup.

This whole marriage business had Sheri's guts in knots. He wasn't cut out for it. He'd never be as religiously devoted to a woman as Lothgard was to Deborah, or as obscenely in love with his spouse as Brandon and Henry were with theirs. If he was to marry, he needed a wife who understood she was getting a bad deal, but would marry him, anyway.

There was only one such woman in existence. *In Case of Crisis, Wed...*

"Marry me," he said.

Elsa snorted.

"I'm in earnest." Sheri sat up. "Marry me, Elsa. My only option for keeping my place in my family is marriage, so why not you?"

At that, her eyes narrowed dangerously. "*Why not me?* What am I, Sheri, the old nag in the stable no one else wanted to ride to the hunt?"

"No!" He shot to his feet. "No, of course not, Elsa." He took her hands. "Marry me. We're friends. We love one another."

"As friends," she clarified, pulling her hands free. "You've cracked, dearest. We'd never suit, and you know it." Turning back to her vanity, she selected a perfume bottle and dabbed fragrance on her neck and wrists. "Now then, if we're done with that foolishness, finish telling me about your day."

Elsa's quick refusal shouldn't have surprised him, but it did. While they'd never been lovers, there was an undeniable affection between them, and he'd thought they had a sort of unspoken understanding. Neither of them was inclined to marry, but ... well ... *In Case of Crisis ...*

Sheridan scratched his ear. "I took my supper at home. Lady Tyrrel came 'round."

Elsa's eyes widened. "Her again? Then you enjoyed a better pudding last night than I did, you scoundrel, even though I dined at a duke's table."

Sheri had gone out to Sybil's carriage to prevent her from making another public spectacle. She'd thrown herself at him, declaring once more that she wanted to leave Tyrrel and elope with Sheri. He shuddered at the memory. "Hardly."

Elsa rose and crossed to the closet that housed her vast collection of gowns. "You've ruined the woman for her own husband," her voice floated out. "What else?"

"Wear something cheerful today, won't you?" Sheri returned. "The amber brocade, perhaps. Brighten up a gloomy day."

"Sheridan!" Elsa's head popped out the closet door. "Are you going to ignore the subject of the poor girl?"

"What poor girl?"

A slipper sailed out of the closet and struck him in the chest. "*Oof.* Good shot."

"You beast!" Elsa called. "No wonder Miss Parks fainted dead away at the sight of you."

Sheri lobbed the shoe back, smacking the door just over Elsa's head. She shrieked and ducked for cover.

He shifted lower into the chair and crossed his arms over his chest, trying to keep at bay the memory of Arcadia Parks's loss of consciousness and his reaction to it. Cradling her in the protection of his arms, he'd almost felt like the stupid gallant Deborah wanted to turn him into. For his pains, he'd been scorned and rebuffed.

"It wasn't quite like that," he returned, keeping to himself the part about Miss Parks emptying her stomach before falling into the mess.

"You didn't even catch the poor girl, I heard," Elsa continued, returning with the amber frock over her arm.

"How can you possibly know that?" he asked, bewildered. "Norman and her maid were the only ones there."

"I have my ways," she said in a mysterious tone.

"And stop calling her a *poor girl*," Sheridan snapped. "She's related to the Delafields; I doubt she's impoverished."

"Poor girl," Elsa quipped.

He hadn't caught the poor girl, though, had he? Nor had he cut a heroic figure when he'd fussed over her like an anxious nursemaid. The whole episode had been quite an embarrassment for him.

"Elsa," he groaned, "you're the only woman who knows me and loves me, anyway."

After hanging the selected dress on a hook in the wall beside the vanity, she joined him in his chair, nudging him over with her hip. Sheri obligingly wrapped his arm around her shoulders while she nestled against his chest.

"I do love you, you know," she said. "Behind the ridiculous quizzing glass, beyond the womanizing rake, I know there's a good man in there."

"You're the only person who thinks so. I could marry you for that. In fact, I think I shall."

She started to draw away, shaking her head. "Sheri ..."

"Think about it," he protested. "We're precisely the same. Our sense of humor, our zest for carnality, our—"

"We're *not* the same." Now there was real hurt in her eyes. "I've already done my duty at the altar, something you've blithely avoided all these years." Her brow furrowed, and the faint lines around her eyes deepened.

Sheri knew her marriage to Lord Fay hadn't been a love match, but she looked downright haunted. What hadn't she told him?

"I have no reason to marry ever again," she continued with heat, "and I won't—not unless I choose it. You think you know everything about me, Sheridan, but you don't. I would never break the vows of my marriage, and I wouldn't tolerate a husband who does, either. Not again. I'd rather die alone and have my corpse eaten by the dozen cats I'll surely own by that time than endure another miserable union. It's love or nothing for me."

He blinked in surprise. He'd never heard his friend speak like this. Cautiously, he reached a hand out and took her forearm in a gentle grip. "Was there someone, Elsa? Is there?"

She smiled sadly and shook her head. "But maybe there will be, someday. I deserve to be loved, don't I? And so do you, Sheri. I want that for you. Let's not waste ourselves on one another." Then she turned her back on him and drained her cup. He watched her twitch as though a shiver passed down her spine.

The dressing room door opened then, and Foster returned with a heavy mug, which she plonked down on a side table beside Sheridan without a word.

Elsa blinked and surreptitiously wiped her eyes with the back of her hand. "You should go call upon Miss Parks," she said as she lowered herself to her vanity stool so that her maid could resume her interrupted hair dressing. "Make sure she's recovered from the shock of meeting you."

Sheridan wanted to stay, to say something more, something comforting perhaps, but he knew when he was being dismissed. "Perhaps I shall. It would be just my luck, though, to take one look at the poor girl and cause her to expire for good."

CHAPTER FOUR

"Jalanili, open your lazy eyes. It's a sunny day, even if the air is as cold as a goat's devil heart. You should get out of bed today."

With a groan, Arcadia turned and covered her head with the pillow, stoutly refusing to acknowledge her ayah's wheedling.

"That Lord Sheridan sent flowers for you. They are cowslip, according to Lady Delafield. She says they convey wishes of good health. Don't you wish to see?"

It had been a week since the park, seven days since Arcadia had humiliated herself in front of Lord Sheridan, as she'd learned her rescuer was called—and all those important English people.

One hundred sixty-eight hours since she'd been threatened with a knife and robbed of the only possession she cared about. The attack hadn't lasted longer than a minute, but it had caused endless distress. When she closed her eyes, once more she felt the blade parting the threads of her clothes. Once more she knew fear.

No, she did not wish to see flowers from the Englishman at the center of that dreadful memory.

She curled in a ball on her side, her arms wrapped around her head. "Leave me alone," she moaned. "I think my fever has returned."

A hand snaked under the blanket and pinched her calf.

"Ow!" Arcadia's eyes flew open. Poorvaja stood at the bedside, hands planted on hips and a look on her face that declared she would not be played the fool. Her long braid swept forward over her shoulder, coming almost to her waist. One cocoa-brown finger tapped impatiently against the pleats of her aubergine sari.

"You've had no fever for two days," the Indian woman declared, "and your stomach has not troubled you since you awoke yesterday. It's time to be up and moving about again, unless you plan to make an invalid of yourself, like some soft English lady would do." She raised an imperious brow over a black-brown eye. "Is that your scheme? Now that we are in your England, do you intend to be waited on hand and foot, and carried about in a paladin chair?"

"No, it's just …" Arcadia started. "It's just not home."

"And perhaps it never will be," Poorvaja said bluntly. "But still you must get out of bed and stop feeling sorry for yourself."

There was a knock. The folds of Poorvaja's sari swished around her bare ankles as she crossed thick rugs to the door. Lady Delafield hovered beneath the doorjamb and peered at Arcadia.

"How are you this morning, niece? Better?"

"Burning with fever," Poorvaja supplied.

Lady Delafield turned her head sharply. "What? But yesterday you said she was improving!"

"Some Indian sicknesses are like this." Poorvaja gestured expansively at the bed. Arcadia went limp and did her best to look fevered. "They can go away and come back again for months—years, even. I think it must be dengue fever."

Lady Delafield paled and rapidly backed out of the door. "Perhaps I should send for the physician again," she called from a safe distance.

"No use," Poorvaja said, shooing the lady of the house away. "Your English doctors can do nothing for the dengue. She'll probably be dead tomorrow."

She slammed the door on her ladyship's stricken cry.

Arcadia clapped her hands over her mouth to smother a laugh. It was, she realized, the first time she'd so much as smiled since arriving on these wretched shores.

Her laughter died in her throat a moment later, when she recalled that her mother had, in fact, died of dengue fever when Arcadia was nine. Lady Lucretia Parks, like so many of the Raj before her, could not survive India.

Poorvaja seemed to realize her mistake in attributing Arcadia's phantom illness to dengue. "There now," she said, briskly pulling back the counterpane. "I have bought you some time free of your aunt, and in a few hours, you can impress her with your miraculous recovery."

"Thank you." Arcadia swung her legs over the side of the bed. "I wish she'd leave us alone forever, so we could go back to India."

Poorvaja sighed, her plum-colored lips parting to reveal white teeth. She looked out the window for a moment, then back to Arcadia. "Come, Jalanili, let us sit and breathe."

As she'd done for the entirety of her life, Arcadia took Poorvaja's hand, and the ayah led her to the rug. Neither heeded their exposed legs as they sat cross-legged on the floor facing one another.

"Close your eyes." Poorvaja slipped into Hindustani, a language comfortable to them both. "Turn your attention inward, Jalanili. Fill your belly, and feel your breath connect you to the earth."

They passed some time in this fashion, with Poorvaja leading Arcadia through some meditative breathing.

When the older woman seemed to be preparing to end the practice, Arcadia said, "Shall we practice some postures?"

"Do you feel well enough?"

Arcadia nodded.

"Very well. It will be good for us to train both our minds and bodies in this new place."

They moved through several yoga postures. After several days of inactivity, Arcadia's muscles protested the rigorous stretching, but she knew she'd feel much more herself soon. They concluded with *Śava-âsana*, the pose of the corpse. Lying on her back, Arcadia felt her limbs grow heavy against the soft rug, but it was a healthier languor than the fatigue imposed by illness.

"How do you feel?" Poorvaja asked.

"Better," Arcadia admitted.

A small smile played around her ayah's mouth. "You see?" Poorvaja touched two fingertips to Arcadia's sternum. "You have brought India with you. Peace is as close as your breath, Jalanili, not on another continent."

Sitting up on her heels, Arcadia tucked her night rail around her thighs. "But I was free there," she protested. "They've taken that away from me, Poorvaja. I lost Papa, and then India, and now they're going to make me marry."

Gracefully, the maid rose to her feet and crossed to the clothespress. "Who is this all-powerful *they*? Do not resent your aunt and uncle for carrying out your father's wishes. Instead, resent them for making you wear that awful corset."

Arcadia chuffed a laugh at Poorvaja's attempt to ease the stinging reminder that it had been Sir Thaddeus's will that laid out the plans for his daughter's return to England after his death. Warranted or not, his wishes still felt like a betrayal. After years of encouraging his daughter to adapt to India—allowing her to thrive like an orchid, rather than forcing her to be the sad, scraggly English rose the women of the Raj insisted on planting in their gardens—he had, at the last, uprooted her from the only home she'd known and cast her across an ocean to relatives she did not know, for the purpose of marrying her off to a stranger.

Arcadia raised her arms as Poorvaja approached with clean underthings. "I don't want to marry," she said, her voice muffled by the white chemise billowing around her head.

"A young woman should marry."

"*You're* not married," she pointed out.

Poorvaja shot her a dark look. "That is unkind, Arcadia." The maid's use of her given name, rather than the pet name by which she usually called her charge, conveyed the seriousness of her disapproval.

Arcadia's ayah had been married to a well-to-do farmer when she was thirteen years old, and became a mother shortly after turning fourteen. Sadly, the baby did not live long, and just days later, the farmer was crushed by an overturned oxcart. The family of Poorvaja's husband expected the young widow to perform *sati*, self-immolation, alongside the bodies of her husband and child. When she refused, her in-laws cast her off and shipped her back to her own family. In short order, she was hired by Sir Thaddeus Parks to serve as ayah to his soon-to-be-born infant daughter.

Poorvaja spoke little of this painful, turbulent time in her past, but Arcadia had pieced together the major details from bits she'd heard over the years.

"Marriage is expected of all women, in all places." Poorvaja cast a shrewd look at Arcadia from beneath her sooty lashes while she fitted Arcadia into one of her new dresses. The maid had let it out enough that blood could flow through Arcadia's torso, at least. "What do you do in a difficult yoga posture, Jalanili? Do you run from it?"

Arcadia suspected the woman had a lesson up her sleeve, but she couldn't see what her inability to clasp her hands behind her back had to do with marriage. "I breathe into it and try to relax until it comes easier."

"Ah." Poorvaja raised a finger. "You embrace the struggle. You dwell with it until it resolves, and then you are able to move on. You must embrace this struggle as well, my child, for the struggle is where life happens."

Her ayah had a dreadful habit of talking good sense, even when Arcadia didn't want to hear it. Restlessly, she surveyed the bedchamber. The furnishings were different than those to which she was accustomed. Most notably, her bed was draped with curtains for warmth, rather than netting to protect her from mosquitoes. It was all so alien and strange. Was this a struggle Arcadia even wished to embrace? How did one go about making a new life in a new land, anyway?

At last, her eyes came to rest on a small bouquet of flowers in a squat vase, cheerful yellow blooms on bright green stalks.

Poorvaja followed the line of Arcadia's gaze. "He must have paid dear for those. Nothing could bloom naturally in this frigid wasteland."

At this dark pronouncement, Arcadia chuckled. "You said yourself that we should go outside today. Lady Delafield says this is the warmest time of year. What shall become of us if it snows?"

The ayah's eyes rolled skyward. "Lord Vishnu preserve us."

A frantic rapping on the door brought Lady Delafield back into the chamber. "Lord Sheridan has come again."

Arcadia frowned. "Again? What do you mean?"

Her aunt clucked her tongue. "He has come every day to ask after you, and every day I've had to tell him you are still unwell." She started, seeming to notice for the first time that Arcadia was out of bed and dressed. "Why, you wicked beast! If you're well enough to be up, you're well enough to take tea with a suitor. Mind you, I don't approve of Lord Sheridan as a suitor, not in the least. I've only allowed him into the front parlor because I knew you were ill."

Her aunt's bewildering logic had Arcadia's head in a whirl. "If you do not wish me to see Lord Sheridan, why are you upset? I've no wish to see him, either. On this, we are in accord."

Lady Delafield cast her a withering look. "Because you are deceitful, niece. I cannot think my sister would like the lying, willful creature her only daughter has become. Lord Sheridan is no prize, but you could do worse—and you will, too, if you don't start behaving with some civility. If you think Lord Delafield and I mean to house a spinster for the rest of our lives, you're sorely mistaken, my girl."

It wasn't as if coming here had been Arcadia's idea. In less than a week, she had arrived in a new country, been attacked and robbed, and had suffered illness. As if all that wasn't enough, her aunt had first complained that Arcadia should have been sent to her years ago, and now she complained about the prospect of having her niece in the house for a length of time. There wasn't enough meditation in the world to make Arcadia comfortable with so much chaos.

"So I *should* see Lord Sheridan? Tell him I'll come down," she said, eager to placate her aunt. The thought of coming face to face with Lord Sheridan and the painful recollections he represented stirred her nerves, which she fought to quell.

"Too late," snapped Lady Delafield. "I've already sent him away."

Behind her ladyship's back, Poorvaja threw up her hands and rolled her eyes.

Ordinarily, Arcadia would have laughed at her maid's mischief, but now she experienced a cold knot of anxiety.

"You're here to marry," Lady Delafield pronounced with finality, "not to plague this house with your heathen antics."

CHAPTER FIVE

"Sheridan? What are you doing here?"

He looked up from the book of Epictetus he'd been browsing while waiting in a drawing room at Lothgard House. He'd asked to see his brother, but it was his sister-in-law who stood before him.

Setting the book aside, he rose and went to her. "Deborah, what a pleasant surprise. You look lovely this morning, my dear." He bent to buss her cheek, his customary greeting.

She drew back, out of reach. Her lips pulled thin, bracketed by lines.

He gave a tight smile, straightened. His fingertips skimmed over the heavy embroidery on his waistcoat on their way to pluck his quizzing glass from the pocket. He twirled it in his fingers, allowing the silver fob chain to wrap about his digits.

"Why have you come?"

"To kiss the Blarney Stone," he replied with simulated levity, not at all caring for the way his brother's sweet-tempered wife, who had once regarded him fondly, now seemed offended by the fact that he drew breath. "I'll settle for laying eyes upon my brother, however."

She raised her chin a notch, folded her hands at her waist. "Elijah isn't here."

"Is that Uncle Sheridan?"

One of the twins—he thought it was Crispin—popped his head through the open door.

The boy's face split into a wide grin when he spotted Sheri; he took a step into the parlor.

"Webb, get back." Deborah's voice cracked like a whip and her arm shot out, as though to bar her child from stepping on an adder.

Only, in this case, Sheri was the venomous serpent.

"Oh, come now, Deborah," he said, affronted. Extending his arm, he waved his nephew forward. "Let the lad come greet his uncle."

"No." Shooing the boy back into the corridor, she slid closed the pocket door and turned on her brother-in-law. Her brown eyes were large in her rounded face. "I don't feel comfortable having you around the boys, Sheridan. Just this morning, Crispin came home from the park with a bruised face. Do you know how he came to be injured?"

"Fell off his pony?" Sheri guessed.

Golden curls swayed as she slowly shook her head. "He fought with another boy. That child called you a …" She visibly wrestled with the epithet. "A name. And Crispin defended you."

Sheri winced. "Good of him, but he shouldn't have done that."

"No," Deborah agreed. "You're just what the other boy said."

Well.

"Boys scrap, Deborah."

"He didn't even know what the word meant, only that his uncle, his hero, had been insulted. Webb explained that a *monger* is someone who deals in particular goods, so Crispin said, in that case, he wants to be a whoremonger when he grows up, just like you."

Shame, cold and acidic, leaked from his gut and spread. "I hope you assured them I do not peddle flesh for a living."

Deborah took a few limping steps, her determined spirit more than making up for her physical frailty. "They go to school next year, and it will be worse. Not just a single boy taunting them in the park, but dozens." She shook her head and bit her lip, pausing before continuing on. "You may not come around the boys, Sheridan." Despite the fire in Deborah's eyes, her voice quavered. "Not until you've proven yourself reformed."

"By way of marriage?" he asked as kindly as he could, given that it was an agreement he'd made under duress. His hackles rose at the thought. Sheri had no wish to bring ill repute to his family, especially his young and impressionable nephews, but he had no need of a bride to keep him in line. "Things will be different, you have my word. I believe I'm well on my way, without the intercession of a wife. Just the other day, you may be interested to know, I rendered aid to a lady in need."

"Miss Parks," Deborah said. "Believe me, brother, I've heard all about *that*." Her shoulders heaved on a weary sigh. "You were found in a compromising position with the lady—"

"She was robbed," he clarified, "and sick. Mr. Wynford-Scott was there, as well as her servant."

Deborah pulled a kerchief from a pocket in her dress and dabbed the corners of her eyes. "It's been established that the maid was *not* there, that she arrived later in Lady Delafield's carriage. As far as I can gather, Miss Parks was alone with *two* men, and half-unclothed. Furthermore, you resisted returning Miss Parks to her aunt." She wrung the damp square of linen into a tight log. "Oh, Sheridan," she said, her voice thickening, "how *could* you? I hear nothing but 'What has that brother-in-law of yours done now, Lady Lothgard?' and 'Share Zouche has struck again!'"

She balled a fist and batted his arm. "That terrible Lady Tyrrel even had the audacity to ask if your depraved proclivities run in the family—and then she ... she ..." The woman's face crumpled. "She made a vulgar proposition towards Elijah and myself!"

His eyes widened at the thought of Sybil trying to lure Lothgard and Deborah into her bed. Deborah was so innocent, she'd probably never even heard of such an arrangement before Sheri's former lover put the suggestion to her. "My dear, I'm so sorry," he said, taking her by the hand and leading her to a chair. Crossing to the sideboard, he poured a cup of lemonade and presented it to her. "Please believe that nothing untoward happened with Miss Parks. I would never take advantage of a lady in such dire straits," he pointed out. "As a matter of fact, she has been abed with her illness ever since that unfortunate incident. This is all tawdry gossip and misunderstanding, don't you see?"

Deborah snuffled and swiped her nose with the wadded handkerchief. "But it's so easy to believe the worst, because it's happened before, over and over again. And that's why I can't have you in my home or around my children." She sipped the drink, coughed, and set it aside. "What sort of example are you setting for them, Sheridan? Is this the kind of behavior you wish them to emulate—this inveterate womanizing?"

One knee cocked out as he planted hands on hips. He'd had quite enough of these aspersions cast on him and his life. "And what's wrong with willing adults engaging in whatsoever activities they choose?" he demanded hotly. "If my nephews wish to sample the delights of the bedroom when they are older, then bravo to them, I say."

Deborah gasped in dismay. "Says the man who was shot by a jealous husband." Deborah rose to her feet. "You have to get out, Sheri. Right now. And don't come back until you've properly reformed."

Sheri made a curt bow and turned. His brother stood glowering in the parlor door. His face was red and still as stone. "I suggest you do as the marchioness bids, Sheridan. Do not darken our doorstep again."

• • •

After being evicted from his brother's house, Sheri found himself at something of a loss. He walked aimlessly through Mayfair, staring at the ground in front of his toes. The accusations of treating Miss Parks with impropriety stung, but he could shrug off the gossip as he had so often in the past. After all, the same tabbies who whispered behind his back welcomed his advances. Hypocrites, the lot of them, he fumed.

He did regret that Deborah had to face cruelty from the *ton*'s women. It wasn't fair that she was taunted with his indiscretions. The woman was innocent of everything except possessing a sweet, sensitive disposition. While Sheri's mother, the dowager marchioness, had a core of steel and could face down a hungry lion and have it purring at her feet inside three minutes, Deborah was not likewise hardened against the ravages of social scrutiny. She'd never understood that she couldn't be bosom bows with everyone, that some people were jealous of her lofty position and would pick and tear at her until there was nothing left.

His innards squirmed at the memory of the hurt in her eyes, at the courageous way she'd defended her children against Sheri's corrupting influence. Her idea of reforming him via marriage might be silly, but her heart was in the right place. She was a good woman, a good wife and mother. She didn't deserve the scorn of the *ton*.

Lifting his head, Sheri took stock of his surroundings. It was a nice day. The sun shone in a clear sky. The temperature was a little cooler than it had been the previous week, but a warm breeze— probably one of the last of the year—ruffled the hair peeking from beneath his hat at the nape of his neck. What to do on such a day, with the celestial orb spilling its glory on his quickly sinking spirits?

Where were the other Honorables on such a day, he wondered as he strolled past stately homes and gardens flaunting their Michaelmas blooms. Norman would have his nose in a tome, putting together a legal brief to assist some barrister's case. Brandon would be tending his patients, saving a life, delivering a baby, sawing off a gangrenous limb, something genuinely useful. Henry, meanwhile, was probably stuck behind his desk in the offices of De Vere and Sons, the shipping company he and his brother had founded. And Harrison, who'd recently taken a position with Henry's company, was probably in a stuffy warehouse or inspecting the dank cargo hold of a ship.

None of them would be out and about enjoying the fine weather. Instead, they were all busy being productive adults, a feat Sheri had never quite managed. It mattered little that, thanks to his inheritance and prudent investments, he didn't need to work to live a life of modest splendor; he was still bedeviled by the nagging suspicion that his life was utterly pointless.

Sometimes he thought he should do something better with his life, something more. An endeavor he could take pride in, such as the occupations of his friends. He'd spent a little time here and there dabbling with one idea and another. Last fall, Sheri had even taken it into his head that maybe he could be a surgeon, like Brandon Dewhurst. He'd gone so far as to attend a lecture and dissection demonstration. Even there, he'd only managed to squire Miss Robbins (now Mrs. Dewhurst) and her midwife friends past some disapproving men to their seats. Then he'd nearly shat through his teeth at the sights and smells that assailed him, putting a swift end to that professional calling.

Instead, he went on passing a meaningless existence, day after day allowing French to dress him in the latest fashions. He provided a male body to intersperse between females in some hostess's seating arrangement at supper and coaxed shy flowers away from the wall of the ballroom.

Perhaps that was why he kept calling on Miss Parks. She was a lady, and making ladies happy was what he did. It was, possibly, the only skill he could claim to have mastered.

At Delafield House, he was admitted and then shown into the now-familiar front parlor. After five minutes, Lady Delafield appeared. "Oh, Lord Sheridan," she said, coming forward with her thin hands extended. "You are everything kind and good to call upon us."

Her cheeks were bright with color, reminding him of the fever-blooms on Miss Parks's face when he'd happened upon her the other day.

"My lady," he murmured, taking her hands and bowing over them. "How fares your niece today? I hope her health is improving."

"Oh, my," said her ladyship, gesturing him to a seat. "Not at all better, I fear. In fact, I hear she is declining."

Sheri's brows drew together. "You hear? Have you not ascertained her condition for yourself?"

Lady Delafield shook her head, setting to shaking the curls interspersed with streaks of gray that circled her face. "Only from the door, my lord. Miss Parks may have some Indian disease. That maid of hers seems to think so. Although," she leaned toward him, her voice dropping to a conspiratorial whisper, "those people are known to lie. Not Christian, you know, so they don't scruple to tell the most outlandish falsehoods. My sister, Arcadia's mother, rest her soul, used to write of the trouble she had with her Indian servants."

A little knot of anxiety sat heavy behind Sheri's sternum. "Have you summoned anyone to attend her? My friend, Mr. Dewhurst, is a first-rate surgeon. If you'd allow me, I'll write him at once. He's just in Middlesex and could be here—"

Lady Delafield waved her hands. "No use, my lord, no use. That servant says it's likely dengue fever. If it is, there's nothing to be done. She'll either live or she won't."

Sheri gaped at the woman, incredulous. Just a few days ago, he'd held Miss Parks in his arms. Yes, she'd been sick, but to have arrived at the point of death so soon? She'd felt vital in his arms, so warm and soft and right.

After taking his leave of her ladyship, Sheri made his way to his club, where he took a seat in the bow window overlooking St. James's Street. He raised his finger, summoning a waiter for a glass of whiskey.

For more than an hour, he brooded as men passed before his window perch, unwilling to accept that Miss Parks was in mortal peril. Perhaps on another day, he might have taken this news better, but not today, not when he already detested everything about himself and the world around him.

There had been some little slice of his brain that thought the young lady was being coy by not seeing him this past week, that her supposed illness was overstated to string him along in some game of seduction. But of course she wasn't. She was an innocent. What would she know of such things? She was Miss Arcadia Parks, recently of India, and she was dying.

That vibrant girl, with those hazel eyes he'd only caught a glimpse of, and that haunting, melodious voice of which he hadn't heard nearly enough, would be snuffed out by some exotic disease. Perhaps Brandon *could* help, he reasoned. After all, his friend had been an Army surgeon overseas. In Spain, not India, but perhaps …

Not your place, he reminded himself. Lady Delafield had refused his offer of assistance. With no more than five minutes' acquaintance with Miss Parks, Sheri could claim no interest in her treatment, regardless of his preoccupation with the girl. He rolled his shoulders, cracked his neck, cursed. Helplessness did not sit well with him.

"Would you look at that!" The laughing exclamation from another patron shattered the sedate atmosphere of the club. Men leaped from their seats and crowded his way. For a terrifying instant, Sheri thought he was the object of attention.

Then a vision appeared on the street, framed by the window. Women. Two of them. Brazenly parading down the exclusively male provenance of St. James's Street. One woman was wrapped in a heavy pelisse and a brilliantly colored shawl that drew the eye like fireworks against the night sky. A sinking sensation in his chest, Sheri snapped his quizzing glass to his face, enlarging the woman in question. She walked with that stubborn chin leading the way. He'd know it anywhere, for he'd seen it from a distance of only inches when he'd cradled her to his chest. She walked in the company of her Indian maid, both females oblivious to the male audience lapping up the scene.

A brief instant of joy at seeing her in good health was followed by a wash of anger. She'd played him for a fool, after all. "Snatched from the jaws of death, are we?" he muttered darkly. What the devil was Arcadia Parks playing at?

As she came abreast of the window, Arcadia stopped. Her head turned, and she met his gaze through the glass. Her hazel eyes, which he'd just been recalling with the misty nostalgia one grants the nearly dead, squinted up at him, small and unremarkable. She studied him and frowned, as though he was the most depressing shop window display in London.

In a flash, he sized her up and found her just as wanting. Anger lapped at his mind, stoking the flames of his critique. How dare she and her aunt attempt to play his softer emotions? Who did she think she was? She was no one he would ever take notice of, unless he deigned to offer her a dance out of pity. She wasn't pretty. Her skin was overly browned by the sun, but still managed the feat of sallowness. Her attire was appalling. That shawl was a riot of jewel tones, while her pelisse was drab and too tight. Someone should tell her that constricting one's breasts in corsets and improperly fitted dresses did not make them appear bounteous—merely desperate for escape. Once already he'd had to rescue her from the folly of her attire, if she thought he'd do it again—

"Isn't that Miss Parks?" A man standing near Sheri nudged his shoulder. "The one you were with in Hyde Park? They just can't get enough of you, can they, Zouche? They go mad for wanting you. This one's thrown propriety to the wind. How do you do it?"

Laughter rippled through the gathering, while Arcadia's name was bandied about like a bottle of cheap wine.

A muscle in Sheri's jaw ticked, hearing them speak of her with such crassness. But really, a respectable woman did not walk down

St. James's Street, lined as it was with gentleman's clubs. It just was not done. Reputations had been ruined for less.

Still, she held his gaze. He could not look away. He was embarrassed for her, he told himself. She wasn't worth his anger. She was pitiful, really, in her desperation for attention.

"Now, now, gentlemen." His voice carried over the throng. "She is a recent émigré. Might we not give Miss Parks the benefit of the doubt?" Even as he spoke them, he sensed the fruitlessness of his words; her *faux pas* would be known far and wide before tea. But never let it be said that Sheridan Zouche participated in the social pillorying of a lady.

Suddenly, Arcadia's head snapped to the side, like a dog responding to a whistle. She launched farther down the street, deeper into ruin.

With a groan, Sheri pushed to his feet. He couldn't let her continue to make a spectacle of herself. Once again, it fell to him to rescue Miss Parks.

CHAPTER SIX

Fatigue lashed at her temples. Like a slave driver, Poorvaja pressed her onward. "Just a little farther, Jalanili," the woman said. "Soon, you may turn around and go home."

"It isn't home," she said by rote, her voice dull.

After Lady Delafield's rebuke, she felt even more strongly that England was not the place for her. Clearly, her aunt felt compelled to find her a husband solely out of familial obligation. She had no interest in Arcadia herself; she wished to marry her niece off as quickly as possible and get the imposition out from under her own roof.

Despite Arcadia's continuing weakness, taking a walk had seemed like a capital idea. She had to escape from that house, if only for an hour. Her aunt hadn't said a word when she and Poorvaja made to leave.

London was so large, so busy, so *loud*. So many people going and coming, such a variety of diversions and entertainments. Begrudgingly, she acknowledged a trickle of excitement coursing through her veins. Perhaps she could find something about this place to enjoy.

They'd wandered through Mayfair, then crossed the busy Piccadilly thoroughfare, before turning onto St. James's Street, which was blessedly quiet. They walked in the heavy shadows cast by distinguished, looming structures. The stuccoed exteriors radiated a chill of their own, one accentuated by the frosty stares cast in her direction by other pedestrians. Arcadia shivered, pulling her paisley Kashmir shawl closer about her shoulders. She wished her hair covered her nape, rather than being tucked uselessly beneath a straw bonnet. The collar of her pelisse did not come up as far as she'd have liked. The cool breeze dipped inside and raised gooseflesh on the back of her neck.

From the corner of her vision, Arcadia detected a hulking mass of humanity. She turned and found herself confronting a window full of men, all of them looking at her. What on earth were they doing? What was this place? Was this some strange English ritual she'd not yet learned about? Sitting front and center, enthroned like a king surrounded by his courtiers, was Lord Sheridan.

She hadn't wanted to see him again, had been sure that doing so would only remind her of that terrible day in Hyde Park. But now, impaled by his demanding gaze, she didn't think of being robbed. She thought of his arms beneath her, of gentle hands tucking a blanket around her thighs. They were scraps of memory, shredded by fever like the unraveling edge of a gossamer ribbon. But they were real memories, nonetheless. He had touched her, held her, even as his inscrutable brown eyes held her now.

It was an unnerving sensation. Arcadia did not care for it in the least.

"What are they doing, I wonder?"

Poorvaja's question broke the trance cast by Lord Sheridan's eyes. Arcadia turned to look where her ayah pointed at a row of carriages standing along the curb at a nearby corner.

"Is it some sort of procession?" Poorvaja glanced at Arcadia and raised her brows expectantly before continuing down the street.

"I don't know any more than you do," Arcadia replied. The sight of her ayah in English dress was still jarring, but the maid already seemed more comfortable in the clothes than Arcadia—of course, Poorvaja did not have to wear the same constricting undergarments.

The older woman's brown eyes twinkled. "I'm going to find out," she said, lifting her skirts and darting forward.

Arcadia chuckled. The excitement of being in a big city must be infectious, she supposed.

"Miss Parks?"

Startled by the sound of her name, Arcadia turned. Before her, as if she'd summoned him from the window, was Lord Sheridan.

Arcadia had not much experience with the English aristocracy. In India, the Raj developed its own pecking order based on position within the East India Company. Her father, a mere baronet, had been the highest-ranking factor in the region. Serving as *de facto* ambassador of the Company—and therefore of the British Empire itself—he was received by Mughal princes and powerful Indian merchants who wished to engage in trade with the Company.

To all of the Indian servants working in their house, Sir Thaddeus had been *sahib*, the master, while Lady Parks was *memsahib*, the master's woman. As such, they were afforded respect as though rulers of their own tiny kingdom.

Standing in the company of a genuine lord—and such a handsome one, too, dressed in a resplendent waistcoat embroidered with vines and leaves, topped by a striking coat of dark green and a hat with a brim that looked sharp enough to cut bread—Arcadia couldn't help but tremble a bit in her half boots.

"Lord Sheridan." Keeping her eyes downcast, she curtsied. As her knees bent, the strength sapped from her fatigued legs. Head suddenly swimming, she sank lower and lower, until her nose nearly touched the walk.

"Gracious me, I've never felt so distinguished in all my life." His cultured voice was rich with dry sarcasm.

Why must her body refuse to behave in front of this man? Humiliating herself in front of him once was enough for a lifetime, yet it was happening again. She'd known seeing him would be trouble. Cringing, Arcadia palmed the ground to push herself back up. Strong hands cupped her elbows as he assisted her. She swayed on her feet, her legs refusing to cooperate.

His brown eyes roved her face. Fine lines around them creased. "By Jove, you *are* ill. When I saw you out and about, I thought you'd been having a bit of fun at my expense."

Shaking her head, Arcadia pressed gloved fingertips to eyes that were burning, with fatigue or impending tears of embarrassment, she wasn't sure. "I don't understand. Whatever do you mean, my lord?"

Gently prising her hands free of her face, he tucked her arm into his and pulled her close to his side, subtly lending physical support as he strolled on toward the corner, where Poorvaja engaged in conversation with one of the carriage drivers. Arcadia kept her eyes downcast, allowing the brim of her bonnet to shield her.

"I've never had to put quite so much effort into seeing a woman," he said. "I'd begun to think I had imagined finding you in the park."

Startled, Arcadia glanced up at the nobleman. He had a proud bearing, fully at ease in his surroundings and the slightest bit haughty. And why not? He was a man of importance in this city. That he should expend any effort to see anyone was a surprise, much less go to trouble on her behalf.

"About that, my lord," she started, then pressed her lips together, uncertain what to say. The attack in the park was shocking, completely beyond anything she'd ever experienced. In the matter of seconds, she'd been robbed of her most valuable possession, become violently ill, and intimately handled by a strange man. Everything about it was twisted up inside her in a knot of fear and pain and the tiniest bit of pleasure. She had no idea how to begin to unravel that morass of emotion, or whether she should even attempt such a thing.

Instead of anything sensible, she blurted, "I do wish you had retrieved my property from that thief, as I asked you to do, instead of tending me, which my ayah could have done better."

He suddenly stopped, jerking her to a halt at his side. For a moment, he stared straight ahead. Then he looked down at her. "Did you just say all the words I think I heard? Surely, my ears must deceive me."

"I hesitate to complain, my lord," she rushed to assure him, "as I'm sure you did what you thought best. But Poorvaja could have taken care of me while you apprehended the criminal." She blinked against the sun, surprised to find that it—so much less intense than in India—pained her eyes.

"Miss Parks," the gentleman said, his polite tone a thin, icy crust over a lake of vexation, "I understand you are recently come to this quaint little island of ours. I don't know how you were raised in India, but here in jolly old England, a gentleman values the life of a lady above a reticule. Furthermore, most of us were taught from the cradle to thank those who have rendered us service, not to berate them for it."

Arcadia's mouth popped open in a surprised *O*. She'd meant to thank him; she had! She was building up to it, offering some constructive criticism, in the event he ever again found himself in a similar situation.

Before she could speak a word in her defense, he barreled on. His voice raised a notch in volume; the skin around his nose whitened. "*Further* furthermore, you have wandered onto St. James's Street, a bit of pavement entirely *verboten* to the gentler sex. Owing to your obvious physical impediments and general ignorance, I refrained from bringing this indiscretion to your notice. But as we are making free with one another's shortcomings, you should know this"—without taking his angry gaze from her, Lord Sheridan pointed behind himself to the bow window she'd seen him in, where she still detected the shadowy figures of a crowd watching them—"all those men in there believe you're offering yourself for sale. They think you're a whore."

"No." She shook her head in dismay. How could simply walking down one particular street mark her for a prostitute? How could she have known? There should be a sign, a warning.

When she offered no additional reply, Lord Sheridan tightened his hand around her upper arm and tugged her forward. She stumbled. Muttering to himself, the aristocrat gentled his grip. He put an arm around her waist and supported her elbow with his other hand. He was strong and deliciously warm, and smelled of leather and tea, good English aromas. In spite of herself, she leaned into his side and experienced a second of relaxation, of reprieve, as he bore her weight. Arcadia whimpered, wishing she could pull away, hating her weakness, detesting the way her body was so willing to accept comfort from this man who so clearly begrudged her the aid. She wished she could faint again, or better, die, and escape Lord Sheridan's wrath.

Down the street, oblivious to her mistress's plight, Poorvaja was speaking to one driver after another. *Whatever is going on?* Musing on the scene provided a useful distraction from the stern lord at her side and the blistering message he'd delivered.

The angry current of his silence made her innards squirm. She had no idea how to rectify the offense she'd given. From the mountain regions in northwestern India had come bloody tales of feuding tribes forever slaughtering one another over the smallest perceived insult. Had she unwittingly set off a fight between her family and his? The English didn't seem the type to engage in actual, physical combat over ownership of a goat, but there was undoubtedly some social equivalent. Arcadia's agitation rose in counterpoint to her quickly failing strength. Increasingly, she needed Lord Sheridan's support as her steps slowed.

"Shall I carry you again?" asked the infernal man-beast, his drawl rich with derision.

"Certainly not!"

Gritting her teeth, Arcadia dug deep into every reserve of fortitude she could muster. She would not wilt in his presence. She would carry herself all the way to … Where were they going, anyway? The distance between herself and Poorvaja seemed endless, and then what? She'd have to turn around and walk back to Delafield House. No matter. She'd haul herself to France on her own two feet before she let Lord Sheridan take her up in his arms. Her desperately needed nap would wait.

As she struggled onward, something in the nature of Lord Sheridan's demeanor shifted, became less hostile. His arm around her waist, while still as solid as a branch, softened.

"You know," he said, at last breaking the silence between them, "I have done a bit of thinking about your stolen reticule. The loss of it seems to mean a great deal to you."

"I care nothing for the bag," she said on a weary sigh. "It was an item inside the bag that I was heartbroken to lose."

"Heartbroken?" His hand patted her waist in a friendly fashion. "I do so regret hearing that the deprivation of this mystery trinket has caused you such anguish. As it seems to be my calling in life to render you aid, perhaps I might be of service in recovering your property."

Arcadia was the one to stop abruptly this time. It had not occurred to her that her lost treasure might be returned to her. She would have no idea where to begin looking, but a mighty lord would know just what to do.

A street vendor pushing a cart laden with fruits and vegetables swerved to avoid her. The merchant shouted a colorful remonstration, but he paled when Lord Sheridan produced a quizzing glass and stared icily at the man. The force of that glower had the man tugging his forelock, begging Lord Sheridan's pardon and offering Arcadia abject apologies.

Warmth pooled at the base of her spine as she watched Lord Sheridan silently cow the street vendor into submission with nothing more than the force of his glance. How noble he was, she thought, just like a Mughal prince. And she'd been foolish enough to offend him! His sharp response had hurt her feelings, but powerful men were entitled to demand respect from their inferiors, were they not? Some princes were known to have the tongues of overly chatty wives and concubines cut from their mouths.

In the future, she would be more cautious with her words, she decided. "Thank you, Lord Sheridan," she said when the grocer had rolled away with his wares.

"Not at all," he said lightly, as though he hadn't just demonstrated his superiority over another.

"If I may be so bold as to inquire," she said formally, "what is your title, Lord Sheridan? Are you a duke of the realm?"

The man threw back his head and laughed. At Arcadia's bewildered look, he explained, "I'm the son of the Marquess of Lothgard."

"So the title is your father's, not yours?"

His head bobbed side to side. "It belongs to my older brother now. My father is dead."

"As is mine," Arcadia supplied.

"You have my condolences."

She frowned. "Why are you called Lord Sheridan, if you are actually lord of nothing?" She was certain she'd learned this years ago when the tutor who served the station's children read her lessons, but it was all dusty and far away now.

"It's merely a courtesy title." The smile he bestowed upon her had a brittle edge to it.

She pondered this while they resumed their journey. "A courtesy to your father, you mean?"

"I wouldn't put it in such—"

"Because he," she said, gaining some clarity on the subject, "is the great man—not you. You merely shine in his reflected glory, without any of your own."

Lord Sheridan sucked a breath through his teeth. "You have an uncanny knack for striking a man where it hurts the most."

"I do not mean to insult you, my lord, merely to understand."

"For an Englishwoman," he said, "you know remarkably little about your own country, its customs, and its people."

As if that were Arcadia's fault! What say had she in her own raising or education? How dare this man with his undeserved arrogance find fault with her? To think she'd begun admiring him!

They were almost to Poorvaja now. Her ayah glanced over her shoulder, looked from Arcadia to Lord Sheridan and back again. "Jalanili!" she called, hailing them with a wave. "Shall I tell you what these carriages are for? They are all for hire. These drivers park here waiting for people to ask them to carry them places. Let us hire one and ride back to your aunt. It will be fun!"

"Oh, thank God." Arcadia could have wept for being delivered from having to trek back to Delafield House.

Arcadia started to step away from Lord Sheridan, but he pulled her back to his side. "Do you want my help recovering your stolen property or not?"

His pride was gravely wounded, she saw. Anger stiffened his spine so much she thought it might crack like dry tinder. But her own pride still smarted, too, from his remarks about her ignorance and insinuations against her morality. What sort of gentleman would go out of his way to make a woman feel so low?

"Thank you, Lord Nothing," she taunted, wanting to strike back at his cruelty, "but that won't be necessary."

"Very well." Lord Sheridan swept his hat from his head and bowed grandly, a gesture she felt sure must have been meant to insult her further. He straightened, turned, then paused. "I'll probably hate myself for asking," he said, pivoting back to regard her once more, "but would you please tell me what it is that was stolen from you? Just in case I happen upon it, you understand."

Reaching for Poorvaja's extended hands, Arcadia huffed. "A brooch," she said over her shoulder, "a jeweled peacock." The smirk slipped from his lips. "My father had it made for my mother when they first arrived in India, before I was born. If I still had it in my possession, I would take it and Poorvaja and sail back to India on the next ship." His eyes widened in something like wonder—or perhaps horror. "It's my father, my mother, and India, all wrapped into one, the only object I felt any attachment to, and now it's … Why do you look at me like that, Lord Sheridan?"

His eyes bored into hers, the intensity of his stare once again making her distinctly uncomfortable. His hand went to his waistcoat, his fingers toying with a silver fob.

Shaking his head slightly as though snapping himself out of some sort of daze, Lord Sheridan bowed. "As ever, Miss Parks," he said as he handed her the rest of the way into the carriage, "our time together has been uniquely experiential." He shut the door.

The words flummoxed Arcadia's vocabulary.

"What does that mean, 'uniquely experiential'?" Poorvaja asked as the carriage pulled forward.

"I think," Arcadia said, parsing out Latin roots, "it simply means 'an experience.' Something that happened."

"Hmm. That was certainly something that happened." A hint of mischievous smile twitched at her lips; Arcadia suspected her ayah had found the man rather dashing.

She just couldn't understand Lord Sheridan. Had his offer of help anything to do with what he'd told her, about a woman walking down that particular street? *They think you're offering yourself for sale.* Perhaps he was trying to protect her. Arcadia snorted at her own conjecture. The man was arrogant, selfish. He used a title that had nothing to do with him. There wasn't a benevolent bone in his body.

Well, it didn't matter. She wouldn't be seeing Lord Sheridan Zouche again.

But his statement that the peacock might be recovered had intrigued her. Resting her head against the carriage window frame, Arcadia tried to think how she might go about finding her stolen property, and tried to forget about arrogant, handsome men with strong arms and hollow offers of service.

CHAPTER SEVEN

Later that evening, Sheri met with some of his friends for supper. They congregated in the dining room of an inn called The Sea Maiden, which catered to the local shipping businesses.

The décor was of a nautical bent, which made no sense to Sheri. If he spent his life upon the waves, the last thing he'd want to see on the walls of an inn would be pictures of more infernal boats and battles at sea. He'd wish to lay eyes upon majestic mountains and verdant meadows, picturesque cottages and stately manor houses. And women, naturally; glorious, naked women. But then, there was no accounting for the tastes of those who deliberately flung themselves upon the deep, with only a thin shell of wood parting them from a cold, salty death.

At a round table, Sheri was joined by Henry De Vere and his bride, formerly Miss Claudia Baxter. Norman had managed to sneak off from the Inns of Court to dine with them, as well.

"Where's Harrison?" Sheri asked, lifting a glass of wine. "He's still in the city, is he not?"

Henry and his wife exchanged a concerned look. "You know how Harrison gets sometimes," Henry said. "I think he prefers to be left alone right now."

Sheri's heart sank. His glass hit the table with a *thunk*; some claret sloshed over the rim and puddled around the base. "Are you sure he's all right? Should he be left alone right now?" Harrison Dyer had always been the most reserved of their set and was sometimes given to bouts of melancholy. The others liked to tease Sheridan for his superficial airs and his little vanities, but he was just as capable as the next man of noticing the pain that sometimes lurked in the depths of their friend's eyes, and it worried him.

He looked from Henry to Norman. "What say you? Should we collect our wayward lamb and drag him out for a night of boon companionship?"

Norman raised a large hand to his face, pinching the bridge of his nose as though fatigued. "I think we should leave him be, Sheridan. He'll snap out of it soon enough; he always does."

"I'm sure he'll be fine," Claudia said while cutting a bite from her venison chop. "Henry says Mr. Dyer falls into these maudlin spells once or twice a year." She shot her husband a small, private smile. "When I met him before our wedding, he struck me as a very levelheaded sort of fellow. He'll come 'round in no time."

Sheri scoffed. "Will he? If I may be so bold, Mrs. De Vere, I think the other gentlemen and myself are in a better position to judge whether our friend of more than a decade will come 'round in no time or not."

Henry's fork clattered to his plate. "Now see here, Zouche—"

Claudia stayed her spouse with a hand on his arm. "This from a man who so recently required my husband to witness you being shot for debauching another man's wife. I'm not entirely convinced of the soundness of your judgment, my lord."

Norman, who'd been trying look preoccupied with a long swallow of his own wine, snorted. A gout of red liquid shot from his nose and splattered in the middle of the table.

Claudia screeched. Sheri and Henry jumped in their seats. All conversation in the dining room skittered to a halt while heads turned in their direction.

"Ow!" Norman bellowed, clapping a napkin to his face. "Laughing wine up the nose bleeding *hurts*." He wiped his face and raised his arm, signaling to all that he was fine.

A round of laughter and applause rippled through the room. Meanwhile, a waiter hurried over to daub up the mess and refill Norman's glass.

Glancing down, Sheri noticed a stain on his satin waistcoat. "Confound it, man, your nose-wine spoiled my ensemble." While he blotted at the mark with his napkin, he sent a rueful smile in Norman's direction, grateful for the distraction, which had lowered tempers around the table.

"Let's discuss something else, shall we?" Henry suggested. "Such as the trouble you and Norman got yourselves into last week."

The tall man frowned, his brows drawing together ponderously. "Do you mean the incident in the park? I wish I could have laid my hands on the blighter who attacked that girl."

"That's what I mean, yes." Ribbons of light skated across Henry's golden hair when he tilted his head. "All the talk says the two of you were found alone with the lady, whose dress was open."

Sheri winced. He'd not yet had an opportunity to speak to Norman about the wild gossip flying around.

"What the deuce?" Where Sheri would have begun shouting at such an allegation, Norman's voice dropped in volume, so that everyone had to lean closer to hear. "Forgive me, Mrs. De Vere." He nodded his apology to Claudia. "My tongue is running away from me." Snapping his eyes back to Henry, he continued, "That's an infamous lie, and you know it. The woman was attacked and robbed. Sheri tended her while I attempted to apprehend the villain."

Henry's hands flew up in a placating gesture. "Calm down, big man. While I'm sure Sheri has perpetrated all manner of depravity in Hyde Park, I never believed a word of that codswallop for a second, since it involved you."

Claudia waved. "Never mind all your ridiculous male posturing. Is the lady all right? Was she harmed?"

The corner of Sheri's mouth twitched as he remembered his earlier encounter today. Though no longer suffering fever, Arcadia was still weak as a kitten and had no business tromping about London—right down St. James's Street, of all places. His scandalous kitten had claws, too, and wasn't afraid to turn them against him. He couldn't help but admire her pluck in refusing his offer to carry her. Willful chit. And damn, but she'd felt too good as he'd assisted her with an arm curved about her waist, good enough to make him forget that in word and deed, Arcadia Parks had brought him nothing but trouble. Altogether, he'd walked away from his second experience with Miss Parks feeling like he did after a bout at the boxing club—invigorated, if a little bloody.

He cleared his throat, trying to rasp the memory of her plumeria-and-sandalwood scent from his nose—a vast improvement over the bile he'd sniffed on her their first meeting. "Miss Parks came through the ordeal a little rattled, and deprived of a valuable trinket, but otherwise not much the worse."

Claudia's soft gray-blue eyes narrowed thoughtfully. "What happened? You are more put off by this woman than you're saying."

Incredulous, Sheri looked at Henry.

That man shrugged. "I don't know how she does it. I barely need speak a word to her. She reads faces like most of us read books. It's remarkable."

Claudia preened at the compliment. "So, Sheri," she pressed, "what did this Miss Parks do to put you in such a fine fettle?"

Drawing a breath, Sheri considered. A gentleman shouldn't speak ill of a lady, but this one got under his skin like no other. She'd mocked him, called him *Lord Nothing*. She couldn't know it, of course, but she had, with those two words, succinctly encapsulated all of Sheridan's doubts and insecurities.

Fingers of heat stretched up the back of his neck as he felt the hated sobriquet burrow under his skin, spreading shame and resurrecting his ire against Miss Arcadia Parks. Who was she, anyway? Some plain-faced chit with a sing-song accent and no idea how the British aristocracy—to which she, herself, was related—worked. It wasn't exactly advanced trigonometry. Even some Indian-bred colonial should have a grasp on the ins and outs of courtesy titles and shouldn't go about insulting people who happen to have them.

"She's a terrific scold," he said at last. "Had the audacity to complain that my rescue did not meet her exacting standards."

A wide grin split Claudia's face. "Did she, indeed? Oh, I like her immensely already. She's my hero, in fact, for giving the lofty Lord Sheridan a taste of comeuppance. You must introduce me to her, so that I might shake her hand."

Gesturing at the impish female, Sheri looked at Henry. "Control your woman, would you?"

"I couldn't if I wanted to, but I don't. I like her this way." Henry and his wife exchanged another soppy smile, and if the movement of their arms was any indication, Sheri believed they were exchanging gropes beneath the tablecloth, as well.

"*Ugh*. Newlywed couples," he muttered. Seeing two of his friends, first Brandon, then Henry, fall so blissfully into the parson's trap had been a trial for Sheri. So much sugary, marital happiness impeded his digestion.

Turning to Norman, he tried to block out the minor obscenities he had no doubt were happening across the table. Not that he objected to discreet public lewdness in principle—he just didn't care to witness his friends engaged in it.

"Zouche," Norman hissed, "how serious is this gossip about the two of us and Miss Parks? How widespread?" He went a little white around the lips. "God's teeth, is it in the scandal sheets?"

Sheri batted away his friend's questions with a dismissive flick of his wrist. "It's just petty, idle gossip. You know how it is, always some outlandish tale going around. Sort of a fictional story written by communal effort. Entertainment for the easily bored, you see? It will all be over in a few days when some other poor sod's mishap is seized upon and blown out of proportion."

He didn't tell Norman about Miss Parks's most recent misadventure on St. James's Street. That additional grist would keep the gossip mill churning for some time.

Norman frowned. "I don't like it, Sheri. I've been making a good name for myself at the Inn. My last supervising barrister credited my work for him winning the case. The paper I presented on civil suits brought *in forma pauperis* was well received. I could be called to the bar any day now, but I'll never make barrister with you dragging my name through the muck."

Sheri snorted. "Resist, if you can, the temptation to fall into a fit of hysterics. As someone who has been attached to unsavory gossip a time or two, heed my words: it will all be over soon."

He hoped. Learning that his nephew wanted to grow up to be a whoremonger *just like Uncle Sheri* had struck him unexpectedly hard. He *was* a corrupting influence, on his nephews and Norman and God only knew what other innocents.

And now, when he should be orchestrating his *tour du réforme*, Arcadia Parks and her missing peacock occupied too much room in his head. He touched the fob at his waist, tracing the family crest with a fingertip.

She wants to go back to India.

Maybe that information, like the vexing woman attached to it, should mean nothing to him. But maybe, maybe, it would be useful.

Chapter Eight

By the following morning, word of Arcadia's stroll down St. James's Street had reached Delafield House by way of Lady Delafield's tattle sheet. The lady had screamed and then fainted. Arcadia had dispatched a footman for her ladyship's smelling salts. When she recovered from her swoon, her aunt had ordered Arcadia confined to her room. For three days, ominous silence had filled the house. Lady Delafield refused to see Arcadia, other than to inform her that she would not leave her room, upon pain of thrashing. Whether or not the threat of violence was sincere, Arcadia did not care to learn.

So she bided her time, continuing her recuperation with regular meals, rest, and daily yoga practice. Despite the renewal of her physical strength, peace of mind continued to evade her. She could not forget the shame she had inadvertently brought upon herself with her reckless constitutional, or the dreadful man at the center of it. Lord Sheridan had dunked her into the scandal broth.

Outside, London enjoyed a clear morning sky dotted with fluffy clouds, betraying no hint of the firestorm she'd ignited. Her room overlooked the small garden behind the house, but she could hear the omnipresent rumble of life passing through the streets. How she hated it here. How she longed to throw her window open and escape, to return to India. How long could her aunt and uncle keep her a prisoner in their house?

As if in answer to her unspoken question, her door opened. "Arcadia," said Lady Delafield.

Turning from the window, Arcadia nodded. "Good morning, Aunt."

The older woman studied Arcadia. "I suppose this is the best that maid of yours could do," she said on a resigned sigh. "Well, make yourself ready. I'm taking you for an outing."

Stunned by her sudden liberation, Arcadia did not pause to wonder what, exactly, Lady Delafield found lacking in her appearance. She wore one of the few English-style dresses she'd brought with her from India, ivory poplin with flowers embroidered on the skirt and bodice. Since her long bout with illness, the dress was a bit loose in the waist, but Arcadia found that preferable to being squeezed within an inch of her life in the dresses Lady Delafield had provided.

Calling for Poorvaja, Arcadia quickly pulled on her gloves, took up her favorite Kashmir shawl, and donned a simple, light green bonnet before hurrying after her aunt.

When she reached the carriage, a footman handed her up. Poorvaja made to follow her into the landau, but Lady Delafield hissed and made a cutting motion with her hand. "To the back with you."

As they rolled away from the curb, Lady Delafield sniffed. "Must you bring her everywhere, niece?"

Arcadia pretended not to have heard. "Where are we going?"

"The British Museum. You were permitted to go native in that heathen country. You need to experience your own culture."

Despite her aunt's frosty hauteur, Arcadia couldn't repress a spurt of pleasurable anticipation. The British Museum! Here, at last, was something worthwhile. Even as a child, she'd been captivated by her father's descriptions of the great halls filled with art and antiquities from all around the world. It had sounded much more intriguing than her mother's memories of glittering Society functions.

By the time they arrived at the entrance on Great Russell Street, Arcadia was fairly bouncing in her seat. Lady Delafield presented tickets to the porter at the door, and they were shown into a grand entrance hall. The expansive marble-tiled floor was caged in by walls decorated with Grecian half columns. A large sculpture of a seated man resided between two arched iron gateways that led into the museum proper, while another statue of some bewigged fellow loomed over a few chairs situated against another wall.

Eager to discover the riches within, Arcadia took Poorvaja's hand and hurried toward the gate. Marveling in the accomplishments of Man and Nature, Arcadia and Poorvaja stared wide-eyed at the great treasures on display. Eventually, they reached a gallery empty of other visitors. A brass plate informed them this was the Towneley Marbles, a collection of Greek and Roman statuary.

"Oh, there's my friend Mrs. Durrant." Lady Delafield turned to wave to a woman in the gallery they'd just passed through. "Stay here, niece; I shall return shortly."

After her aunt scurried off, Arcadia turned to examine the *Discobolus*, which was situated in the center of the gallery floor. The statue was a visually arresting depiction of a perfect (and perfectly naked!) male specimen, his legs bent and torso twisted, right arm extended behind him, preparing to hurl the discus in his hand. From toes gripping the ground to shoulders bulging with exertion, every inch of the young athlete's body spoke to his powerful virility.

As she slowly circled the marble base, her eager gaze took in every slope of muscle and line of sinew. She'd never seen a naked man before, only glimpsed the occasional shirtless Indian laborer or fisherman from a distance. How astonishing that here, in the middle of the British Museum, was a naked man to satisfy the curiosity of any inquisitive young lady. Arcadia paused, tilting her head to better consider the rippled muscles of *Discobolus*'s arms and chest. She couldn't help but draw comparisons between the ancient Roman and Lord Sheridan. Though she'd not seen that gentleman in such a state of undress—where had that thought come from!—he must be similarly muscled. He'd carried her with ease the first time they met, and the arm he'd clamped about her on St. James's Street had never once faltered in its support, even while he'd berated her.

An unwelcome sensation tugged at her belly as she continued looking at the naked man and thinking of Lord Sheridan. She tightened her shawl against hardening nipples. *Just the cold,* she assured herself.

She heard her aunt's voice drifting closer from behind her.

"... Must marry her off as soon as possible," Lady Delafield was saying. "Then she'll be someone else's problem."

The other woman tittered.

Arcadia clenched her teeth.

"Further," her aunt went on, "I must get rid of that ayah. My niece has been too long under the influence of a heathen servant."

Arcadia's ears rang as though they'd been boxed. *Get rid* of Poorvaja? Might Lady Delafield also so blithely suggest Arcadia *get rid* of an arm, or perhaps an eyeball? Even now, her beloved companion was at the far end of the gallery, studying at an elaborately decorated Grecian urn. As if sensing Arcadia's attention, she turned and pointed at the vase, her broad smile saying *Can you believe we're really here?* Poorvaja, too, had been entranced by Sir Thaddeus's tales of London's cultural wonders. Many was the time Arcadia had found her ayah looking at the plates in a book about the British capital, her slim, brown finger tracing the edifice of this palace or the lines of that monument.

Her hands tightly fisted in her shawl, Arcadia rounded on her aunt. "Why not just return Poorvaja and me to India and be done with it? Neither of us wants to be here. Mightn't we just agree this arrangement has been a terrible mistake and wash our hands of each other?"

Lady Delafield grabbed Arcadia's arm and pinched, hard. Shocked, Arcadia jerked out of her aunt's grasp. The loose skin about her ladyship's jaw quivered in undisguised fury. "No, gel, we most certainly shall *not* wash our hands of each other. You are Lucretia's daughter, the only living thing left of my sister. You might have no regard for your dear mother's memory, but I *will* do right by my sister. I will see you properly settled, you may be sure of it. Send you back to India, indeed. *Harrumph!*"

Poorvaja scurried over to investigate the commotion. Arcadia shook her head, warning her away from Lady Delafield's line of fire. The ayah hesitated, then pointedly turned her back on the squabble.

A man strolled in from the far end of the gallery, near the Grecian urn. For a few seconds, Arcadia did not recognize him, but the man's languid air and red cravat tickled her memory. The poet, Sir Something-or-other. His eyes swept the room, caught on Poorvaja, then darted to Arcadia. They shared an instant of contact before Mrs. Durrant had her say.

"Why, Lady Delafield," the woman said, "I hardly know what to make of this shocking display. Children are the greatest blessing and lowest curse of a woman's life."

As if overcome, Lady Delafield nodded, her expression one of unmitigated suffering. Sniffing, she fished a handkerchief from her reticule and dabbed at her cheeks. She drew a deep breath and exhaled slowly. "Lord Delafield and I were never blessed with children of our own, you know. I'd hopes that my niece might provide us, at last, with an outlet for our paternal feelings. Alas, I think it's not to be …"

While Lady Delafield gave vent to her familial frustrations, Arcadia watched the poet approach Poorvaja, beakish nose leading the way, and engage her in what appeared to be stilted conversation. Poorvaja, eyes wide, took a half step back from the gentleman.

Arcadia sidled away from her aunt to rescue her friend from the intrusive scribbler. As she approached, Poorvaja glanced anxiously at her. *All well?* Arcadia nodded, trying to convey confidence she did not feel. What a mess she'd made of everything, from losing her precious heirloom her first day in England, to offending her relatives, Lord Sheridan, and all their fine, London Society with her ignorance.

"Miss Parks." The poet bowed, his gaze slipping over her figure as he straightened. "What an unexpected pleasure, finding you here in these dusty halls. And Lady Delafield!" He interrupted the other women's *tête-à-tête* to make a florid bow to Arcadia's aunt and receive an introduction to Mrs. Durrant. With a girlish giggle, the baroness waved the poet back over to Arcadia and resumed her discussion.

"I trust you ladies are enjoying the exhibits?" Sir Godwin inquired upon returning to Arcadia's side.

"Yes, well ..." Arcadia's eyes cut to where her aunt and Mrs. Durrant stood with their heads together, discussing Arcadia as if she was a clogged irrigation ditch or a cobra in the laundry, a problem to be solved. "It's been very illuminating, Sir ..." she faltered.

"Godwin," he supplied with an affable smile. "Sir Godwin Prickering, at your service, Miss Parks. What a challenge it must be to find yourself cast upon foreign shores, thrust into the company of so many strangers, and expected to learn their names and adapt to their ways at once."

Arcadia blinked. "Yes," she said. "Precisely." At last, she thought, a sympathetic soul.

"And you, Miss Poorvaja? How do you find London?"

The Indian woman's nose wrinkled; she looked at the man askance. In a sensible wool dress and plain gray bonnet, with her sleek black braid hanging down her back, Poorvaja's entire countenance brooked no nonsense.

Arcadia, too, was a bit taken aback by Sir Godwin's question. Not once had any person ever called her ayah "Miss" Poorvaja. Her surprise was followed by a rush of gratitude for the gentleman's consideration.

"White," Poorvaja answered, her voice tinged with suspicion. "I find London very, very white."

The poet chuckled, his laugh sounding like *hip-hip-hip*. "You have us there, Miss Poorvaja. We are a sunless, pallid breed." Turning to Arcadia, he once again examined her. While she was sensible of his appraisal, his gaze did not cause her that uncomfortable rush of awareness that Lord Sheridan's did. "You look much improved since last we met, if I may say so, Miss Parks. I trust you are recovered from your unfortunate encounter with that cad in the park."

How did he know about the footpad? Unless he meant the *other* cad. "Do you refer to Lord Sheridan?"

"Well … I don't like to name names." Sir Godwin flicked dust from his sleeve. "*Some* names, in particular, should not be uttered in polite company."

Lady Delafield had alluded to Lord Sheridan being unsuitable, and here was another who seemed to find him lacking. Arcadia looked over her shoulder to confirm her aunt was still occupied with Mrs. Durrant.

Leaning closer to Sir Godwin, she whispered loudly, "You do not care for that gentleman?"

"Zouche"—the poet's lip curled as he uttered the hated name, in contradiction with his previous edict—"does not merit the designation of 'gentleman.' To say I do not care for him would be to say the ocean is damp. It would be to say the pyramids of Giza are getting on in years. It would be to say this institution"—he turned on the toe of a tasseled boot as if to encompass the whole of the museum—"has a few trinkets of passing interest. In short, Miss Parks, to say I do not care for that gentleman would be an understatement of criminal proportions."

A man and a woman entered the gallery. While the man kept his eyes carefully averted from Sir Godwin's theatrical performance, the woman on his arm peered with interest. Even when the man turned, hauling her about to face a relief depicting a Bacchanal, Arcadia could practically see the woman's ears straining to overhear their conversation.

Arcadia made a patting motion. "He *is* a bit arrogant," she said in a low voice, hoping to placate Sir Godwin's temper. "And a touch high-handed," she added, recalling how he always insisted on doing things his own way, never taking her wishes into consideration.

"Oh, my dear Miss Parks, you are too generous. Is she not, Miss Poorvaja?"

The ayah had begun to edge away, but his question stopped her from making good her escape. She shot a glance at Arcadia and remained silent.

"You have not long been in our little society here, Miss Parks," Sir Godwin continued. To the side of the gallery, the eavesdropping woman leaned farther away from her companion and tilted her head, the better, Arcadia assumed, to discern the subject of Sir Godwin's ire. "He is the worst sort of scoundrel."

"Oh, come now," Arcadia gently chided. "Surely, you exaggerate. Twice he has come to my aid." She didn't care to be in the position of defending Lord Sheridan, but he had, in his own, infuriating way, rendered her assistance when she'd needed it. And he'd offered a gleam of hope with his suggestion of recovering her brooch. "Lord Sh—" She stopped herself at Sir Godwin's glower. "*That gentleman* has a certain charm, I'll grant." Arcadia's gaze slid to the nude *Discobolus*. Heat swept her cheekbones. She cleared her throat. "Some women might find such a person … compelling."

The poet scoffed and scuffed the floor with a toe, like a sulking boy. Arcadia and Poorvaja exchanged an amused smile.

"Let's not speak of that unpleasant subject any longer," Arcadia said. Thoughts of Lord Sheridan always created a muddle of feelings she did not care for. "What brought you to the museum today, sir?"

With the subject turned to himself, Sir Godwin brightened and waved an arm. "Nourishment, Miss Parks. I come seeking nourishment for my poor, starving soul. Whenever I feel my powers of creativity on the wane, I strike out on a pilgrimage of poverty, my heart open to receive whatever alms of ingenuity the Muses see fit to grant."

Gracious. What a mouthful. Lord Sheridan, too, had a fondness for using many words to express brief thoughts, Arcadia recalled. *No!* she scolded herself. *No more thinking about Lord Sheridan.*

The writer guided her and Poorvaja to a nearby statue. Arcadia's brows rose at the sight of a naked female torso. At least the woman's lower half was covered, unlike the male athlete, although the marble fabric clinging to her left leg from thigh to foot revealed as much as it concealed. The end of the fabric draped over her right arm, while her left was poised in the air, her hand curled in an attitude of grasping … something. But her hand was empty.

"Behold the Towneley Venus," said Sir Godwin. His long, curved nose rose in the air as he gazed up into the goddess's face. "Such sublimity. Such beauty. Note, if you will, the graceful curve of her cheek, the tender fullness of her lip. One wonders whether she is about to smile, or rebuke a hopeful lover. I find in her the essence of feminine mystique. I come here often to sit at her feet and seek divine guidance for my work." His eyes gleamed with admiration.

"I think you just like to see the undressed lady," Poorvaja stated, unimpressed.

Arcadia turned her head, hiding an indelicate snort.

The poet turned his eyes on Poorvaja, his lids half-lowered. "I *always* find much here to inspire me."

Poorvaja's cheeks went ruddy, and she ducked her head, then scurried over to Lady Delafield and Mrs. Durrant.

"Sir, that was not well done of you," Arcadia scolded. "Poorvaja is not used to such talk." Not that she was, either. The tips of her ears were fairly scalding from the flirtation laced in the poet's words—and he'd accused Lord Sheridan of improper behavior with ladies!

Sir Godwin's fingers dallied in the folds of his red cravat. His eyes once more roved the voluptuous goddess while he addressed her. "Forgive me, Miss Parks. I was overcome by … poetry. It happens, you understand, in the presence of such beauty. Words tend to erupt forth when I am so … inspired."

His gaze turned on her, then, but Arcadia steadfastly kept her own fixed on the statue. This level of verbal play was far beyond her.

"She looks sad," Arcadia blurted. "Did you ever notice?"

"No."

"She's meant to be holding something." She pointed at the vacant palm. "Venus is missing a belonging. Perhaps an object of great value."

"That doesn't make her sad," Sir Godwin drawled, "merely incomplete."

Arcadia wanted to point out that the loss of something dear, that feeling of incompleteness, could make one sad and unmoored. But she did not feel inclined to open herself up to criticism for such an opinion. Being deviled by Lord Sheridan for her foolishness in losing the brooch had been enough of that kind of scrutiny.

Lady Delafield joined them, her nose more pinched than ever. "Niece, time we were off."

Sir Godwin bowed and took his leave of the ladies.

As they departed the gallery, Arcadia cast a final, lingering look on *Discobolus*. With her own feelings of incompleteness and loss, strange that she would be so drawn to the ancient athlete rather than to the goddess, with whom she was in perfect sympathy.

• • •

At seven o'clock, her aunt's maid arrived to help Arcadia dress for supper.

"Where is Poorvaja?" Arcadia asked. The ayah had been absent from her room since they'd returned from the museum. Recalling the words of her aunt earlier, she was anxious to lay eyes upon her friend.

The maid cast a furtive look at the closed door. "Not supposed to talk to you about that, miss," she whispered out the side of her mouth. "Just put your dress on, please."

Another layer of apprehension wrapped around the cold stone in Arcadia's torso. She prepared for supper mechanically, allowing the maid to dress and style her as she would.

In the parlor, Arcadia found her uncle and aunt calmly sipping tea.

"Good evening, Uncle. Aunt."

Lord Delafield stood and made her a slight bow, light from the candelabra slipping over his bald, waxed scalp. "Arcadia, have a seat." He gestured to a chair adjacent to the settee he shared with his wife. His other hand stroked his white beard as he regarded her.

Arcadia sat on the edge of the chair, eyes lowered, hands folded demurely in her lap, doing her best to look meek and contrite. She still wasn't entirely sure what she'd done wrong, other than walk down St. James's Street. More than *doing* wrong, Arcadia sensed that she *was* wrong, that she wasn't English enough to suit her aunt, not enough like her mother.

When her uncle resumed his cup of tea and talking over the newspapers with Lady Delafield, Arcadia risked a glance. Her aunt wore a beaded evening gown, a turban topped with two fluffy white plumes, and three looping strands of pearls. Uncle Delafield, too, looked dressed for an evening out in his knee breeches, white stockings, and velvet slippers. Whatever their plans, they did not include Arcadia.

A few minutes later, the butler announced supper. Lord Delafield offered one arm to his wife, the other to his niece, and squired them to the table, a pretty little family tableau.

By the time a course of roasted partridge and creamed parsnips arrived, Arcadia's nerves were frayed to the breaking point. She'd not been able to eat a bite with this terrible suspense looming over her like the blade of a guillotine.

"May I ask you a question, Uncle?" she said, interrupting Lady Delafield's recitation of the works of art they had encountered at the British Museum.

Lord Delafield paused with his fork poised at his lips. He lowered his hand. "Yes, Arcadia?"

"What's to be done with me, my lord? My lady aunt has been angry with me since I arrived." She cut a glance across the table; Lady Delafield shook her head, in warning or disagreement or dismay, she had no idea. "I didn't know not to walk down that particular street, my lord. You must believe me."

Her uncle blinked in surprise. "The St. James's business? Yes, yes, I believe you, girl. Just one of those quirks about London."

The knot in her middle relaxed a fraction, and Arcadia exhaled properly for what felt like the first time in days.

"Although," Lord Delafield continued, "it *is* a rule, unwritten as it may be, and you broke it."

Arcadia's mouth went dry. "I'm sorry," she managed. "But now I know, and nothing like it will happen—"

Lady Delafield's fork clattered to her plate. "And you lost my sister's brooch. And you argued with me in public today. And you force that terrible servant upon us incessantly. And you lie, and you bring scandal to our door, *and and and*!" Pressing the backs of her fingers to her mouth, her ladyship turned her head, as though she couldn't bear the sight of her niece another minute.

Calmly patting his mouth with his napkin, Lord Delafield leaned back in his chair. "Your aunt has a cousin, Fisk, with the living in a village near Derby."

"So, he is my cousin, as well?"

"He's a vicar," her aunt supplied. "A man of impeccable moral fiber."

"I've written," Lord Delafield said, reaching for his wine, "invited him to come up to Town soon as he can to see if you're suitable."

"Suitable?" Arcadia echoed dumbly, for the ground had suddenly shifted beneath her chair.

"To be his bride!" Lord Delafield chuckled before tucking back into his supper. "You'll be mistress of your own establishment before Christmas. Won't that be nice?"

No! Marriage would ruin everything. She'd never make it back to India if she was married off to an Englishman. She'd be trapped on this frigid canker of an island for the rest of her life.

Arcadia clenched her dinner knife in a death grip. "What … surprising news," she managed, forcing her fingers to release the cutlery. She took up her glass of wine; the rosé sloshed in her trembling hand. "What of Poorvaja?" she asked after a fortifying gulp. "She will come with me, will she not?"

Her aunt's lips parted, but Lord Delafield raised a hand. "Your former nursemaid's services are no longer required," he said simply. "She's been dismissed."

Arcadia shot to her feet. "What?" she screeched. "How could you?"

"I gave her a reference," her uncle protested. "She can find employment."

"Where is she?"

"Not my concern," said Lord Delafield. "Nor yours, for that matter." He waggled his fork at her. "Sit down, gel. Eat your supper."

Sit down? Eat? How could Arcadia sit down when Poorvaja had been turned out on the streets? How could she eat, knowing that her ayah had no food to fill her own belly?

Poorvaja could be anywhere in this dreadful city. Lost, with nowhere to turn. Anything could happen to her. The footpad who'd accosted Arcadia in Hyde Park wasn't the worst London had to offer. Poorvaja might be snatched off the street. Raped. Killed. Who would notice the loss of one Indian woman?

Even if her aunt and uncle couldn't recognize it, Poorvaja was far more than a servant; she was Arcadia's family. She couldn't abandon her now. But what could Arcadia do? She knew as little of the city and its ways as Poorvaja. If she went barreling out into the streets, she'd soon be as lost as her beloved ayah.

With a heavy *thud*, Arcadia fell back into her chair. A gnawing sense of loss opened in her heart. *Oh, Poorvaja.* What could she do? *What could she do?*

"There now," Lady Delafield said with a sniff, "you're behaving more the thing already. I was perfectly correct about that maid's influence over you. Reverend Fisk will be just the husband to set you to rights."

Husband. The word caused a sick roiling in her gut.

What could she do? She had no one to appeal to for help—

Well. There might be one person. One man who had offered her help.

Arcadia still believed his offer had not been sincere, but with nowhere else to turn, she had to try.

CHAPTER NINE

My lord,

> *I must speak with you on a matter of great urgency.*
> *- AP*

"And?" Sheri turned the note over and frowned at his own name scrawled on the other side. He flapped the nearly empty page at French. "Is this all?"

"Yes, my lord," his manservant answered.

"Is the messenger awaiting a reply?"

French shook his head. "She gave no instructions beyond delivering the letter into your hands."

"She?"

"A maid, I believe, sir, judging by her dress."

Sheri snorted. Leave it to Miss Parks (whom he presumed to be the cryptic AP) to botch something as simple as a clandestine communication. "Useful information, a time and place, would be too much to hope for," he groused.

And, naturally, being Miss Parks, her missive carried the tone of a summons. Nary a *please* or *upon your leisure* to be seen.

What could she have to say that was so important? Sheri thought she had made her dislike of him perfectly clear. He might have been a bit … stringent … in listing her faults, but she didn't have to be quite so emphatic in her refusal of his offer of help in finding her stolen property.

The tale of Miss Parks's promenade down St. James's had London's gossips abuzz. His involvement in the fiasco was also known, but, unjust it might be, it was not he whose reputation suffered as a result of the misadventure.

In the depths of his soul, Sheri's bruised pride took a bit of pleasure in Miss Parks's scandal. Really, just the very tiniest amount of pleasure. A crumb, which he was properly ashamed of himself for feeling and which he tried to ignore.

Still, the mystery presented by her note was not one Sheri could ignore, and so, lacking any other direction, he sent a note 'round to Lord Delafield, openly, by way of French, requesting the honor of Miss Parks's company for an afternoon ride in Hyde Park. So quickly came his lordship's affirmative reply, Sheri wondered whether the lady had actually been given any notice or say in the matter.

The following afternoon, he presented his card to Delafield's footman and was escorted into the front parlor, where he was left resting on his nankeen-clad laurels with nary a cup of tea for distraction. His eyes skated over the furnishings he'd seen the several times he'd attempted to call upon Miss Parks. In particular, his eye was drawn by a decorative screen in the corner comprised of a gilt-framed triptych of floral banalities. The garish thing was an affront to good taste.

At last, Delafield came into the parlor. Gray of beard and bald of head, the baron's clothes looked a little tired, a touch loose in the knees and elbows, where they had stretched from much use.

"Zouche," he said, waving Sheri into a chair while he took his own seat. Incongruously, the older man looked like a schoolboy in the headmaster's desk, sitting with back straight, leaned slightly forward, legs together, hands fisted on his knees. "M' wife has bid me to inform you that her niece is all but engaged to another, and she wishes to know—"

"*Ahem!*"

Lord Delafield's gaze flicked to the screen in the corner.

Had an audience, did they? Through his quizzing glass, Sheri regarded the older man. "You were saying, sirrah?"

Delafield tucked his chin. "Miss Parks is a gentlewoman of good breeding, noble connection, and some fortune." He spoke slowly and nodded as he went, as though reciting from a script.

The baron cleared his throat. "She—Lady Delafield, that is— wishes you to know—"

"*Ahem!*"

"—wishes *to* know," Delafield corrected, voice raised and obviously ruffled by the off-stage prompts of this scene's director, "whether you plan to present a rival claim for the gel's hand, and if not, to tell you to sod off."

"*Oh!*"

His lordship gave a mutinous smile at the affronted gasp, triumphant in his moment of improvisational rebellion.

"So," the reluctant actor concluded, "what are your intentions towards Miss Parks?"

Before Sheri could stop it, a laugh blurted from his lips; he attempted to cover it with a cough but might have just made himself sound like a vital organ was about to erupt from his mouth. His *intentions*? Good Lord, he couldn't remember the last time anyone had asked Sheridan to declare his intentions towards a woman. In the past, his designs had always been straightforward: either he meant to dance with a woman, bed her, or charm her with witty conversation at social gatherings. Sometimes a combination of more than one of those options, but those were the only intentions he ever had.

To his mind, this was simple, too. He was only responding to her request for a meeting. But the Delafields didn't know that, he realized. While he might ask Elsa to go for a drive without anyone batting an eye, one did not engage the company of a young, unmarried miss unless one had *intentions*, honorable or otherwise. He knew this; he did. But he had no prior experience in calling upon a respectable young lady for a solo outing. Shouldn't this conversation with a male relative occur somewhere down the line, not before the horses had left the starting gate? Ye gods, for the sin of granting Miss Parks's wish for a surreptitious conversation, he'd inadvertently blundered into a courtship.

"It's a little soon to say," he prevaricated.

The older man's lips retreated into the white bristles of his mustache and beard, his brow creased in a deep, severe eleven.

Their unseen audience tutted.

"That is," Sheridan hastened to add, "I've only just met Miss Parks. She's an interesting young lady, isn't she? One doesn't encounter a girl like her often." *Ever.* He'd never met anyone who was so well traveled, yet disastrously innocent; or one with a sing-song voice that said the most outrageous things. "Which is why I thought it would be nice to get to know her a bit by going for a drive."

He tapped his quizzing glass against his palm. Realizing he probably appeared an anxious suitor, he stuffed it back into his pocket. Sheridan was thirty years old and had more experience with females than any other ten men put together. He did not get *nervous* over some Indian-bred chit.

"She's to be married," Delafield stated, "and soon. Won't have you wrecking everything."

Odd. Miss Parks had mentioned nothing about an engagement, pending or otherwise. She'd given every indication of wanting to return to India, but how could she do so if she was wed?

"If I may be so bold as to inquire, my lord, who is the lucky bridegroom?"

"The Reverend Mr. Fisk, cousin of my wife. D'you know him?"

"I'm afraid I haven't had the pleasure."

Perhaps this was the answer to the mysterious summons: Miss Parks must want rescuing from her drab country vicar. "Well," Sheri said, rising smoothly, "I can assure you, my lord *and lady*," he loudly added for the screen's benefit, "that I most certainly harbor no improper intentions towards Miss Parks. We're just off for a little drive."

"Glad to know it," his lordship drawled.

A moment later, Miss Parks appeared. She wore a blush muslin dress that was too pale a color for her. A woman possessed of her strong features should complement them with bolder fashions.

As if she secretly agreed with him, her shoulders were once more draped with the silk shawl he'd seen her wear before. It was a stunning cerulean blue, edged in a paisley motif, each crooked, jewel-tone teardrop embroidered with intricate floral designs.

Atop all perched a straw bonnet trimmed with enough lace to clearly point to Lady Delafield's influence.

Ordinarily, such a mismatched ensemble would have given him dyspepsia. But on Miss Parks, the look was charming. It was so very *her*, he supposed.

He sketched a bow. "Miss Parks."

She curtsied in return. "Lord *Sheridan*." She emphasized his name when she said it, turning it into a playful reminder of the outrageous *Lord Nothing* nickname she'd given him.

She was teasing him. He liked that, he realized. He liked it a great deal. And he liked the way his name sounded in her unusual voice, like the opening peal of an aria.

"Shall we?"

As they exited the house, Sheri expected the ever-present Poorvaja to fall into step behind them, but the Indian woman was nowhere to be seen.

"Could I truly be so fortunate as to have you all to myself?" Sheri couldn't resist whispering. He was rewarded with a delightful pinkening of Miss Parks's cheeks. "Where is your Miss Poorvaja?"

Something flashed through her eyes, and then was gone. She cast a furtive glance over her shoulder. "My aunt says it is permissible for a lady and a gentleman to ride alone in an open carriage." She nodded to the smart curricle standing at the curb.

"And thank God for that," he said, jauntily leaping into the seat after handing her into the curricle he'd bought for a song from a viscount with pockets to let a few months back. "Lest I'd have had to rack my brain to concoct a plan equal to your cunning missive."

He flashed her a grin as he snapped the ribbons, setting the matched pair of bays to a lively step. The day was overcast, but the clouds were high and nonthreatening. Though the air was still warm, one could feel summer leaching away; the atmosphere had the faintest undercurrent of the coming autumn chill. It was a perfect day for a drive. Sheri, at heart a city creature, wished, for once, to be out in the countryside. Miss Parks might enjoy seeing something of her new homeland that wasn't paved or soot-covered.

Several moments passed in silence while Sheri contended with traffic. "Where are we going?" she inquired. "Isn't Hyde Park in the other direction?"

"We can go there, if you wish." Sheri nimbly directed the horses around a porter unloading a wagon parked before a draper's shop. "I thought revisiting the scene of the unpleasantness you experienced there might distress you."

Miss Parks's wide eyes flew to his. "That is most considerate, my lord. Thank you."

He barked a laugh at her surprise. "I really am a civilized sort, Miss Parks. You and I seem to have a knack for aggravating one another." He nudged her arm with a playful elbow. "Admit it: deep down, you know I'm not too terrible. Elsewise, why call upon me to rescue you?"

"What makes you think I need rescuing?"

A teasing reply at the ready, Sheri glanced down in time to see her lift her chin, a shadow catching in the dimple there, highlighting her stubbornness. She raised one golden-brown brow, silently pressing her challenge.

With that small gesture, Sheri felt as if he'd been walloped over the head. In the days since he'd last seen her, the lady beside him had vastly improved in looks with the return of her health. Gone was the greenish, smelly urchin he'd plucked out of a puddle of her own sick in Hyde Park. Gone, too, was the pinched and exhausted female he'd nearly had to carry down St. James's Street. Quite suddenly, Sheri realized that Miss Parks was not at all plain, but arresting, with beguiling hazel eyes set above strong cheekbones, and a complexion appealingly, if unfashionably, bronzed from a lifetime in the Indian sun.

How could he, Lord Sheridan Zouche, dedicated appreciator of womankind, have failed to notice Miss Parks's potential? She'd never be a classic beauty, but God knew the *ton* had enough of those to sink a ship. Miss Parks was blessed with the kind of bones that would ensure she aged gracefully. Twenty years from now, she'd still turn heads. Hell, fifty years from now, she'd still be lovely.

Her fingers snapped in front of his face. "Lord Sheridan?"

He blinked. "Terrible traffic today. *Hyup!*" he called to the horses, urging them across Pall Mall, and then into St. James's Park. After handing the reins over to his tiger, Sheri assisted Miss Parks out of the carriage.

"You haven't answered my questions," she complained.

"And you haven't answered mine," he rejoined, eager to move past the way he'd been staring at her like an imbecile.

A scowl was her only response.

Tucking her hand into his arm, Sheri led her to The Mall. At this time of day, the *beau monde* would all have flocked to Hyde Park for the fashionable hour, making the promenade here a place of relative privacy.

Sheri was pleased by the strength he detected in Miss Parks through their point of contact. Her delicate hand rested lightly on his arm. She did not rely on him overmuch for support; her steps were even and sure. A little knot of worry he hadn't even been aware of lugging about in his chest eased.

For some minutes, they strolled in silence through the stately old trees lining the pebbled walk. Sheri enjoyed stretching his legs with a woman on his arm. It had been a long time since he'd had the simple pleasure of a woman's company. Not that Miss Parks's company was exactly simple, he reminded himself.

"What was it you wished to discuss?" he asked. "A matter of utmost importance, I believe you said."

She angled towards him. The fringe of her shawl swung against his thigh. His breath hitched. Ye gods, he'd been far too long without a woman if some strings swatting his leg could affect him so.

"My response will answer one of your questions. And you're right, I do need help. I didn't know who else to turn to." Her earlier bravado slipped away like a discarded mask; now weighty concern seemed to pull down her shoulders.

Whatever differences he and Miss Parks had had in the past, he hated to see a woman in distress. As a gentleman, it had been bred into his very marrow to come to the aid of a lady in need. Furthermore, there had been Grace, for whom he'd have turned the world upside down, only for the reward of her open smiles.

"Miss you, Sheri ..."

Stepping off the walk, he pulled her around the large trunk of a tree to shield her from public view.

"Miss Parks, what's happened?" He took her hand in both of his and rubbed circles with his thumbs. Her slender fingers curled delicately around his. Even through the gloves they both wore, her gentle touch heated his palms.

When she met his gaze, her eyes were full of sorrow. "It's Poorvaja. My uncle has cast her out."

"Cast her out?" Sheri echoed. "To where?"

"That's just it, I don't know!" Miss Parks threw up her hands in a helpless gesture. "She's a stranger here, like me. She has nowhere to go. Who would take her in? She'll be lost. Something terrible will happen if I don't find her, I just know it." Slowly, sadly, she shook her head from side to side. "I cannot abandon her. Poorvaja is my ayah. She is family to me."

Sheri had only a rough idea what the office of ayah entailed, but he well understood the ties that bind family together. Hadn't he agreed to find a wife he didn't want just to please his own family? And then there was the family of his own making, the Honorables, his brothers-by-choice. The men who had stood at his side during that early morning duel would do anything for him, as he would for them.

No, one did not abandon family, and one certainly did not cast family aside, he thought, sparing a sour thought for his own brother, who had threatened just that if Sheri did not fall in line with his dictates.

"Will you help me find her? Please?"

Without answering, Sheri turned on his heel. He plucked his quizzing glass from his pocket and jounced it against his palm. Miss Parks tugged his elbow. "My lord, please. Will you answer me?"

"I'm thinking," Sheri answered over his shoulder, his tone clipped. "It's not a particular talent, so you'll have to give me a moment."

What a conundrum. Shame on Delafield for tossing out Miss Parks's beloved ayah. Difficult enough for the average household servant to find employment, but at least there were employment offices and an informal network among the working class to help one another find placements. What were the chances that Poorvaja knew where to locate an employment office in London, or even that such a thing existed? The woman hadn't been in England long enough to make friends with the maids at neighboring houses to hear of openings that way, either.

"How long has she been gone?" he asked, spinning about.

"Two days." Miss Parks wrung the cords of her curricle in tight fists at her waist.

Oof. With nowhere to go, Poorvaja was at risk of being waylaid by a cutthroat or footpad, or "rescued" by one of the many unscrupulous pimps and procuresses who snatched lost lambs off the streets and forced them into the flesh trade. From what he'd seen of the Indian woman, she was made of stern stuff, but as time passed, she would become desperate. After two days, she could be anywhere in the city—or even beyond. The hair on Sheri's nape stood on end. Good God, the woman really would be lost.

"And what will you do if you find her?" he demanded. "Will your uncle take her back in?"

"I … I'm not sure," Miss Parks admitted. "I'll figure something out. It won't be for long, only until we can return to India—"

The quizzing glass smacked into his hand; he stuffed it back into his waistcoat. "And will your intended," he demanded, snatching her wrist and pulling her close, "the Reverend Mr. Cousin Whatsit, join your little exodus to the promised land?"

Her eyes went wide and round. She batted his shoulder with the side of a fist. Sheri held firm and pulled her closer. Frustration of all sorts licked his veins. Most immediately, he was angry about the loyal and lively ayah having been discarded into the gutter. His family's edict that he marry still bristled. And, as his aching flesh reminded him, he'd been celibate for months now, ever since that disastrous night with Sybil.

Yes, well, he thought, admiring the fiery way Miss Parks yanked herself free of his grasp and stomped his toe for good measure, perhaps something could be done about each and every one of his frustrations. The idea had been circling the perimeter of his brain ever since his encounter with Miss Parks on St. James's Street. Now he felt sure of its soundness.

"He isn't my intended," Miss Parks snapped, indignantly drawing her shawl tight across her bosom. The pale pink of her dress was far and away outdone by the livid flush across her prominent cheekbones. Her eyes nearly crackled with anger, and that stubborn chin jutted defiantly. She was glorious. "I told you

I'm going back to India, and I am—alone. I have no intention of marrying Mr. Fisk, nor any other Englishman."

"An admirable sentiment, I'm sure," he said, planting his hands on his hips. "But you're wrong about one thing, Miss Parks. You will marry."

Her mouth opened; he raised a hand to forestall her protest. "Oh, don't squawk at me. I'm not proposing you should marry your country parson." At the perturbed tilt of her head, he felt a smile slide into place. "Rather, I propose that you should marry me."

CHAPTER TEN

Before Arcadia could absorb Lord Sheridan's statement, her body reacted. For the first time since arriving on this frigid island, Arcadia felt heat. Her ears burned as if boxed. The rest of her, however, went numb. She ducked around the tree and immediately stumbled on a root. He was behind her at once with warm, steadying hands bracketing her waist.

Pulling free, Arcadia wheeled about to face him. "What madness is this?"

As he stepped closer once more, the vines on his waistcoat seemed to snake and writhe across his chest. She was giddy, Arcadia realized, retreating until her back touched rough bark.

A determined gleam shone in his eyes. He shook his head once. "Not madness. It's perfect. Marry me."

Pressing a hand to her temple, Arcadia tried to clear her head. How had her plea for assistance in finding Poorvaja turned into … whatever this was. "Why are you saying this?"

"Because I wish to engage you in a contract of matrimony. *Marry me* are words we English typically associate with the concept."

"I know that!" she snapped, annoyance blowing the cobwebs out of her skull better than a brisk cup of tea. "What I don't understand is why you would ask me. Is this a poor demonstration of British humor?"

He pressed a hand to his chest, affecting a wounded expression. "On the contrary, I am entirely sincere. My family requires that I marry, as yours does you. Our union is the solution to both of our problems. Straightforward enough."

Somewhere in the last two minutes, the man had taken leave of his senses. It was the only explanation.

"There's nothing straightforward about it. We're strangers! What a rash idea."

Witnesses. She needed witnesses. The last time she'd been caught alone with a man in a London park, she had been accosted and robbed of her most valued belonging, and here she was, once more at the mercy of a lunatic. Fresh air seemed to have a deleterious effect on the British male sensibility. Arcadia eased to the side, planning to make a break for the promenade.

She managed half a step towards freedom before Lord Sheridan's arms shot out, caging her in. Her palms braced against his chest, and she shoved. She might as well have been trying to push the tree out of her path, for all he gave way.

"Let me by," she demanded tartly. "I'm not marrying you, nor anyone else. I don't want to marry at all."

Grinning wide, he clapped her on the shoulder. "Neither do I!" his mouth said, but his expression and tone suggested, *Yes! Now you have it,* as if Arcadia had finally grasped some arcane mathematical concept.

Pressing the heels of her hands into her eyes, Arcadia moaned. Then she lifted her head and met his infuriatingly amused expression. "My lord, please return me to my uncle's house. Clearly, asking you for help was a mistake. You've proved your point. I'm sorry for wasting your time."

Lord Sheridan took her elbow and guided her back to the path, but instead of heading back towards the carriage, he continued down The Mall. She dug her heels into the gravel, resisting. There were other people here, the witnesses she'd wanted. Two gentlemen rode horses at a sedate walk a short distance away. There was a harried maid herding four children, and even an officer in his scarlet coat strolling with a lady. Arcadia drew a breath, preparing to scream.

"Hear me out, Miss Parks," Lord Sheridan said rapidly in a low tone. "Carlton House is just over there," he said, pointing to a high wall edging the parkland. "If you scream, you'll have the Royal Guard on us." He flashed her that charming smile. "Wales would find it endlessly amusing that my proposal of marriage brought a woman to hysterics, but let's not give him more ammunition to use against me, hmm?"

She blinked, for a moment taken aback by what he'd said. "*Wales?* Are you on such familiar terms with the Regent?"

The man shrugged. "My brother is a marquess, as was my father before him. I've spent more time at court than I care to remember. Our beloved quasi monarch sometimes finds me diverting of a dull evening. But returning to the topic at hand, will you please grant me the opportunity to tell you my idea? This was your secret meeting, do recall, and you're the one who asked my help. I'm trying to give it to you, if you'd leave off waving down those fellows over there long enough to listen."

Arcadia lowered the hand she had been waving to catch the attention of the passing horseback riders. "Very well," she said, huffing a sigh. "If I hear your plan, will you accept my rejection and return me to my uncle's house?" She had to think up a new way to hunt for Poorvaja, since Lord Sheridan had turned out a disappointment. There was no time to lose.

"Agreed." Lord Sheridan nodded. "If you do not agree my suggestion is a staggering work of genius, then you shall be free to engage yourself to the Right Reverend Mr. Dullston."

"Fisk." Arcadia suppressed a laugh. She wouldn't be charmed by this lunatic. She wouldn't. "His name is Mr. Fisk."

Waving away the correction as no consequence, Sheridan proclaimed, "The germ of my brilliant plan came to me the moment you revealed to me that you had lost a peacock."

This time, she couldn't help but chuckle. "Oh? And why is that?"

He cut her a withering look and stopped. "Doubt me, do you, my little peahen? I see I shall have to prove myself at every step."

Fiddling at his waist, he soon produced the fob leashed to his ever-present quizzing glass, unhooked it from the chain, and held it out on his palm.

Arcadia took the silver object. It was round and light, hollow. On the face, worked in beautiful relief, was a crest featuring a peacock, tail fanned, surrounded by several words in Latin.

"Good gracious! That is quite a coincidence," she allowed. "What does this say?" She pointed to the script.

"*Dum vivo ego serviturus,*" he answered. "*While I live, I serve.* The Zouche family motto." His brown eyes danced with humor. "Perhaps I'm fated to be forever serving you, one peafowl to another."

She scowled. "An avian device is hardly a sound basis for matrimony, my lord."

"Indeed not," he agreed in a tone that said he didn't *really* agree and was about to tell her why. He clasped his hands behind his back as he continued their walk. Arcadia's fingers closed around the fob and held it to her chest as they strolled. It felt good in her hand, warm from riding close to his body.

"And yet," Lord Sheridan continued, "when our paths kept crossing, I could not help but think perhaps there was something … fated, if you will, about our meeting. The coincidence of the peacock bore out my supposition, and hearing your wish to return to India quite decided me on the matter.

"If I may be frank, Miss Parks, I've no more desire for a wife than you have for a husband. If you do me the great favor of marrying me, I will do you the favor of absenting myself from your life at the earliest opportunity. You may return to India, alone and unfettered. I'll stand on the quay and wave you off with a hurrah and a basket full of sweets for the voyage."

"Why would you do such a thing?"

"Because you'll be my wife," he said as if that made things any more clear. When she shook her head, he huffed. "Don't you see, Arcadia?" She glanced up at the sound of her given name. It rumbled against her ear in his deep, cultured voice. So pleasant. "If we marry, then we're married. Legally bound, forever and ever, 'til death do us part." He bobbed his head from side to side. "Or much sooner than that, if you go back to your side of the globe and leave me to mine. But it'll be done. Duty discharged, no one can make us marry anyone else, because we'll already be married to each other."

She hated to admit it, but his idea did make a certain, deranged, kind of sense.

Leaning down, he peeked under the brim of her bonnet. "You agree with me." He touched her jaw with a finger. "I see it on your face."

He sounded far too sure of himself for her liking. "What about Poorvaja? You've said nothing of her. Since we're being frank, Lord Sheridan, your marriage problem is none of my concern."

He scoffed. "And yet you'd like me to make your lost ayah *my* concern." Beneath her right hand, his forearm tightened. He cut a tight arc, turning them around to face the other direction. His strides were longer than before as he led her back towards his carriage.

Suddenly, their time together was running out too quickly. After he deposited her back at Delafield House, then what? Arcadia had no other plan in place to rescue Poorvaja and escape England before her guardians forced her into marriage.

"Wait," she begged, once more dragging her heels, this time to delay their return to the curricle. "Please. There's a stone in my shoe." When his steps slowed, she darted to a nearby bench and sat, her right hand latched onto the seat beside her thigh to lock herself in place; her other hand still gripped his fob. Lord Sheridan stalked to where she huddled on the cold stone seat, lean and sleek, like a tiger on the prowl, his eyes locked on her as if she was the sambar he would fall upon and devour. Her shawl slid down her right arm, the rich colors giving way to the soft pink of her English dress, making her feel even more exposed and vulnerable.

Swallowing hard, she forced herself to hold his gaze. To crumble now would be to consign both herself and Poorvaja to bleak fates. "This is the price of your help in finding Poorvaja? Marriage?"

"Everything has a price, Arcadia. This is mine." Slowly, he lowered himself to sit beside her, still holding her eyes captive in the snare of his own warm, brown gaze. It wasn't fair. He was too handsome, too enticing. With the back of his finger, he brushed a loose strand of hair from her cheek.

"It might sound too high a cost, but I think you'll find my terms more than reasonable." His fingers dropped to her shoulder and skimmed down her arm, lightly caressing, until he plucked her shawl from where it had fallen and tucked it back in place. "In exchange for your promise to marry me, you may keep whatever dowry you bring to our union. I assume you've some fortune you plan to live on back in India?"

"Six thousand pounds. It's to be mine on my next birthday, or given to my husband when I wed."

His eyes bugged. "Six?" Groaning as if pained, he tipped his head back, giving her a clear view of the intricate knot of his pristine white cravat and the crisp points of his collar. He cleared his throat. "Yes, well, I don't need it. Keep it. I will begin at once to assist you in finding Miss Poorvaja. I will tell your uncle that, as part of our betrothal agreement, he must also help in recovering her, then continue to employ her until we are wed, at which time I will employ Miss Poorvaja myself. You shall not be parted from your ayah, my dear."

"Can you really do that? Force my aunt and uncle to take Poorvaja back in?"

He raised a brow. "Ever the skeptic. Yes, my darling little Doubting Thomas, I can make them take her back in. For the chance to connect the lowly Delafield barony to the Lothgard marquisate, I believe your relations—her ladyship, in particular—would do a great deal more than employ a certain servant."

"But ... but what if they are cruel to her? My aunt ..." Remembering how Lady Delafield had often wiped her hand after touching something Poorvaja had handled, how she called the Hindu woman a "brown heathen," the casual cruelty with which the ayah had been discarded after years of faithful service, Arcadia hung her head. She felt small and ashamed of her family. Her friend should not be subjected to such acts of bigotry and meanness.

Lord Sheridan took her hand and simply held it for a moment. "If they are unkind to her, even once, you've only to tell me, and I will right the matter. Needs be, I'll bring her into my household at once. I'll need help preparing our new house ahead of your arrival, in any event."

Arcadia drew a raspy breath, her throat suddenly thick with emotion. Her fist pulsed around the silver fob like the beating of her own heart. She choked on a laugh-cry. "Our new house?"

He gave her a lopsided grin, the one she'd already picked out as his real smile, distinct from the flawlessly charming one he presented most of the time. "I can't set up housekeeping in my bachelor rooms on Upper Brook. Not that I'd mind sharing cozy quarters, but poor French would expire of shame if I brought a new wife home to such mean circumstances, so I'll find a place to let."

"French?"

"My manservant. Being elevated to the position of valet, with a footman or two to lord over, will swell his head beyond bearing, but I suppose there's no help for it. Poorvaja will be your lady's maid, of course—unless you'd rather she be housekeeper, in which case she can lord over French, as well."

Arcadia laughed softly at his description of the servant, then caught herself being swept up by his pretty words of a new house with a toplofty valet and Poorvaja leading a household staff. Her gaze swung across the promenade to the grass on the far side, where a boy in short pants kicked a ball back and forth with an older girl. Could Arcadia really trust Lord Sheridan to keep his word? A plethora of *what-ifs* rattled through her mind.

"If I'm to leave, why go to all that trouble? A house, footmen … none of that is necessary."

He shifted, stretching his legs out and crossing his booted ankles. Reclined so, he reminded her once more of a tiger, specifically the one Poorvaja's uncle kept, a large male called Zizu who had been taken in as an orphaned cub, his mother felled by English hunters. When Arcadia accompanied her ayah on trips to her family home, she'd loved to visit Zizu. Hour after hour, she watched the animal through the iron bars of his enclosure. Zizu's striped hide rippled sleekly over powerful muscles as he slunk through the trees. Even lounging in the shade, his ear occasionally twitching at an annoying fly, the great cat was fearsome, silently communicating feline disdain for the small human on the other side of the fence. When he yawned and stretched, claws like knives extended from his large paws.

Where, Arcadia wondered, did Lord Sheridan hide his claws?

Leaning back, the man beside her winked. "We've some work to do, peahen, to make them believe." He spread his hands. "As well, there will likely be some bit of time before your departure. I don't expect we'll ride to the docks straight from the altar, so we might as well have the proper trappings. We must establish, beyond a doubt, that we intend a true union before you abandon your poor husband."

She chortled at the idea of Lord Sheridan, the very pinnacle of masculine beauty and arrogance, ever being a poor *anything*.

Dipping his head, he *smoldered* at her. His lips pursed slightly, in a way that suggested kissing, she imagined. Not that she imagined kissing Lord Sheridan. Just generally, she meant. A general kissing fashion.

"Yes, well, we won't really be married. Not … not *really*."

What a thing to say! She didn't know why she'd done it, except his nearness, his warm scent, and the curve of that lip had scrambled her brains and had her wishing he'd hold her hand again, or even—heavens—kiss her.

At once, his expression sobered. "On the contrary, love, our marriage will be consummated. I'll not have you crying foul and asking for an annulment later, nor will anyone else be able to take this away from us. This will be a true marriage in every sense, even if only for one night."

Her stomach rolled. So. This was the true cost. Not just her name on a marriage certificate to rattle in their families' faces, but her body, as well. She had to become his wife in deed, not just in name.

Dropping her head, she opened her hand and once more examined the fob in her palm. A pretty little bauble. Why couldn't it have portrayed a typical device, like a lion, or a griffin, or a … goodness, even a puffin. He wouldn't have thought twice about Arcadia and her peacock, would never have concocted this plan.

But then, he might not have been willing to help her find Poorvaja, either.

She hated England. It had taken everything from her—her home in India, her brooch, her ayah. Regaining what she'd lost could cost her the independence she required to live on her terms, to return to India and the life she'd loved.

With a weary sigh, she twiddled the fob, turning it over and around in her fingers. Along the edge, she spotted a hinge. Without thought, she located the latch opposite the hinge and pressed her thumb into it.

With a crisp *snick*, the fob popped open. She blinked, surprised by the smiling face of a girl set into one half of the silver shell. Beside her, Arcadia felt Lord Sheridan tense, but he made no move to take the miniature portrait away from her.

The child, who looked eight or nine, had rosy cheeks and a wide, happy smile, her bottom lip concealing her teeth. Her brown eyes were set unusually wide and tilted down at the corners.

"Grace. My little sister."

Arcadia glanced up at the guarded tone in his voice, the caution something she'd not heard from him before.

Looking from the wary man to the child in the picture, Arcadia offered, "I see the resemblance. You've the same color eyes, and there's … *oooh*," she cooed, "the sweet little lick of hair on her forehead." She chuckled softly. "My hair never liked to cooperate at that age, either. Truth be told, it still doesn't, most of the time." She passed the fob back to Lord Sheridan. "Grace looks like a happy child."

His tight smile didn't touch his eyes. "She was."

"I'm so sorry."

He didn't acknowledge her condolences, just gazed at the little picture cradled in his hand. "She loved doing that," he said, nodding to indicate the children playing with their ball across the way. "Whenever I visited her, she'd cozen me into taking her outside to kick the ball, whatever the weather. Didn't matter if it was raining buckets, or if there was a foot of snow on the ground. The only ball she had was a castoff from Eli and me. Old leather cracked, falling apart at the seams. Eventually, I bought her a new one. When I gave it to her, she cried and wouldn't have anything to do with it, so we played with the ratty old one until …" His voice faltered. "Until the last time we played."

"How long ago?"

"Ten years this past summer, a few months after this portrait was done. She was twelve."

So long, yet his grief was still fresh. That Lord Sheridan was capable of such deep feeling wasn't precisely a shocking revelation, but it did unsettle her somewhat. He did a fine job of presenting himself as elevated beyond common mortals, with his perfectly tailored clothing, his withering insults, his debonair manners.

Clearing his throat, he closed the fob, then busied himself reattaching it to the quizzing glass chain.

Arcadia wanted to hear more about Grace. Had his sister not lived with Lord Sheridan's family? Why had he had to visit her? She didn't dare ask, though; clearly, it was a tender subject.

Tilting her face to the sky, she saw that the clouds that had blanketed the sky all day had taken on a lavender cast. "It's getting late."

Lord Sheridan drew his feet in, propped his elbows on his knees. He plucked his hat off and raked his hair with his other hand. It was the first time Arcadia had seen his head bare. Thick, russet waves fell forward, concealing his eyes. His head hung low, shoulder blades jutting like wings trying to burst past the fabric of his coat. Between them, his back sloped into the vulnerable hollow of his spine. Arcadia longed to run her fingers down it, to soothe the long-ago hurts that pained him still.

Abruptly, he straightened and extended his arm along the back of the bench, his hand just behind her shoulder. Not quite touching, but she felt it there. "It's your choice, Arcadia. I've never taken a woman to bed with anything less than her avid consent. I'm not about to force my own wife, but neither will I take you to wife without your agreement to the consummation."

"Must I choose now? May I have a little time?"

A thick brow arched, sardonic, above a dark eye. "While you dither, where is your ayah? Is Poorvaja safe in a warm bed, or has she been forced to labor in a Spitalfields factory, perhaps against her will? Maybe a pimp has offered her shelter and food, for which she will have to repay him by selling her body. Or—"

"Stop!" Arcadia cried. "Don't you think I've already imagined every dreadful thing that could happen to her?"

He chuffed a breath. "No, peahen, I don't believe you have. London is home to vices not yet dreamed of in your little Indian idyll and knows ways to hurt and demean that I pray you never see in your nightmares."

He sounded older just then, and tired.

Tired, Arcadia understood. She was weary, too. Worn nearly to the bone by this bleak city and its strange ways. And yet, she knew her life was better than most. She'd been part of the Raj in India, *de facto* ambassador of the British Empire by virtue of her father's place with the East India Company. But she'd witnessed suffering there, deprivation and hardship that flashed through the chinks in the wall. Lepers begging outside temples, weaving women who earned extra coin by offering themselves to British soldiers, children who ate no more in a day but a single bowl of rice and a cup of goat's milk. Compared to them, Arcadia had been blessed with abundance. She'd never known a day of hunger or a night without a blanket. Who was she to now balk at giving herself to a man—an attractive one, at that—just once, in exchange for Poorvaja's safe return?

Even Poorvaja herself held a dim view of Arcadia's protests against marriage. It was what everyone around Arcadia expected of her. If she could not avoid the inevitable, might she not take some portion of that fate for herself and do something good with it?

Still ... still. It was hard to reconcile the image of a younger Lord Sheridan happily playing in the rain with the man issuing this hard demand. Shouldn't he help her, for no reason other than she'd asked it of him? Wasn't that the English way?

Mayhap it was the English way, but it wasn't *his* way, not this creature with his eyes rendered fathomless by the gloaming, his exquisite male beauty shrouded in linen and wool. Had he been the spice merchant in the village marketplace, she might have known how to haggle with him; had he been a Company factor, she might have known how best to appeal to his sensibilities; but this aristocrat was something entirely beyond her ken. What could she do but accede to his bargain?

Back on the station in the *mofussil*, when the *memsahibs* gathered and complaints started flowing along with the tea, this oft-repeated advice would flow from one of the senior women: *Think of England*. Whatever hardship India threw their way, women of the Raj could master. In India, they were ambassadors of the Empire and were expected to behave as such. Thoughts of Home inspired them to buck up and do whatever needful to see things through.

Well, Arcadia's thoughts of home flowed across the sea in the opposite direction, but the advice held. If she wanted to help Poorvaja, if she wanted to return to her version of Home, she must do whatever it took.

Firming her spine, she told him, "I will marry you, but I want my brooch, too. You offered to help me find it, as well, remember."

His eyes crinkled at the corners. "Naturally. While we're turning London inside out to find your wayward servant, we might as well dig up your lost treasure, too. Anything else you'd like to add to the list? The Holy Grail, perhaps?"

Arcadia scowled at the grinning Lord Sheridan. "Don't you dare laugh at me! This is serious."

Chuckling softly, his arm insinuated itself around her shoulders and slid down her back. His hand wrapped around her waist, and he tugged her close to his side. "I'm not laughing at you, I swear."

"You're laughing right now!"

His other hand cupped her cheek while the hand around her waist slid down to her hip and hitched her even closer. Arcadia suddenly found herself pressed against a warm, solid wall of male chest, her face just inches from his.

"You shall have your brooch and your ayah and anything else you want, my dear little peahen." His eyes darted to her lips; his head angled closer to hers. "Now kiss me, Arcadia. Kiss me and be mine."

Chapter Eleven

Arcadia took a deep breath.

Closing her eyes, she lifted her chin to seal her bargain with this laughing devil. More gently than she could have thought possible, he covered her mouth with his. A deep shock thudded through her body. Her chin trembled beneath the tender onslaught of his kiss, her teeth lightly chattering, as if she'd taken chill. Yet it wasn't the cold that possessed her, but the overwhelming sensations he'd aroused in her.

She brought a hand between them, thinking to push him away. Instead, her disloyal fingers gripped his lapel, clinging for all she was worth.

Back and forth his lips moved over hers, devastatingly tender. His hand moved to her nape; his fingers slid beneath the back of her bonnet and tangled in her hair. For long minutes, he sipped from her bottom lip and teased the corners of her mouth. Soft exhalations of contentment vibrated through his throat, as if he'd slipped into a hot bath and planned to stay for a while. Not once did he press for more.

More.

The idea possessed her like an imperative. She wanted more of his kiss, of his hands on her body. And heaven help her, she wanted to touch him, to see the marble statue wrought in living flesh.

With a groan, she tipped her head back, wantonly offering herself.

Abruptly, he drew back, ending the kiss just as she was desperate for more of it. She blinked her eyes open. The corner of his mouth, that weapon of sensual destruction, quirked. Was he laughing at her again?

Drawing a shaky breath, Arcadia fought to steady her wrecked nerves. "I suppose you could tell that was my first kiss. I'm sorry if it wasn't to your liking."

"*Shh, shh, shh ...*" Pressing a finger to her lips, he bent his head to her ear. "It was entirely to my liking, Arcadia," he whispered. The sound, *the feel*, of her own name carried on his breath, hot against her earlobe, sent shivers dancing across her skin. "Consummating our union won't be a hardship to either of us. Already, I'm anticipating the next time I can taste your sweet lips. But today ..." He retreated a bit, cut his eyes to the promenade. "Today I'd rather not embroil my fiancée in a public indecency scandal."

Following his gaze, Arcadia gasped. A knot of five or six men stood not ten feet away, leering at them. Merciful Krishna, she'd forgotten they weren't alone; it had only felt that way when Lord Sheridan's kiss obliterated her wits.

"Don't stop now," called one of the men in a rough accent.

"Aye," added a second, "this is better'n the show at Fanny Mae's. She was jus' startin' to get hot, man. Keep at it—this way!" He pumped his arms and hips in a lewd gyration, accompanied by grunts of *ungh-ungh-ungh.* The entire group burst into raucous guffaws.

Arcadia wondered that her face didn't incinerate from the humiliation. Laughing, Lord Sheridan wrapped his arms about her, shielding her face against his shoulder.

"Sorry, lads," he called in return, "show's over. But you're the first to know that this lovely girl just agreed to marry me."

A rousing cheer rose from their small audience. Pulling Arcadia to her feet, Lord Sheridan led her to the group and handed out coins. "A drink on me," he told the men.

His gift was met with more cheers and congratulations. The men all pumped Lord Sheridan's hand and kissed Arcadia's cheek.

"A bonny bride," announced one of the men in a Scots burr. "She'll give you a fine passel o' bairns."

Arcadia's cheeks flamed once more. Lord Sheridan caught her eye and winked.

The man who'd first called to them slapped the back of his hand against Lord Sheridan's waistcoat. "'Oo shall we drink to?"

Clapping the fellow's shoulder, her affianced husband turned a beaming smile on Arcadia. "Raise your glass to the health of my bride, Miss Parks, and to me, Sheridan Zouche, the luckiest man in England."

His tone was so affectionate, she almost believed he meant it. *We have to make them believe.*

"Never say you're Share Zouche!" cried another of the men, his hands clapped to his head, his expression one of disbelief.

"The very same," Lord Sheridan affirmed with a nod.

"Oh, ain't we seen somethin' tonight, boys! Share Zouche slain by a bit o' muslin."

After another round of good wishes, more kisses on her cheek (and one adventuresome pinch on her bottom), Arcadia and Lord Sheridan took their leave of the group and returned to the carriage.

Lord Sheridan whistled while he drove, a jaunty melody Arcadia did not recognize.

"Why did you do that, my lord?"

Stopping abruptly, his lips still pursed, he tossed a questioning look at her. "Do what, peahen?"

Why did you kiss me like I was precious to you? she wanted to ask. *Why did you introduce me with such pride?* But she was intensely aware of the groom seated on the perch behind them. She shifted her weight from one hip to the other. "Those men back there. They were familiar and rude, yet you did not correct them. In India, no one would dare speak that way to a Company official. And should a peasant offend the person of a Mughal prince or any of his wives or concubines, the penalty would be severe and immediate."

He looked at her askance. "Did your father ever have anyone chucked in gaol for impugning his dignity?"

Arcadia shook her head. "No. But I remember a neighboring factor who boasted that he'd had seven Indian men lashed the month before, one of them for staring too long at his wife."

"Good God! What did the other six do?"

"Nothing. He said it was good policy to remind the natives who's in charge. There are always rumblings of uprisings against the Raj. He was doing his part to suppress it."

"And you wish to go back there? Doesn't sound a very appealing place."

How could Arcadia explain? Sitting high in Lord Sheridan's curricle afforded her a good view of the street. The buildings here were too tall, caging her in. Her ears were fatigued from hearing nothing but English all day long. Every breath filled her nose with unfamiliar smells. When it wasn't actively stinking, London's aromas were heavy and dull. Arcadia missed the lively scent of curries cutting through the hot morning as she and Poorvaja did shopping in the market, the heady aroma of incense wafting from the Hindu temple, the sultry fragrance of flowers scenting the nighttime air.

"Yes, I'm sure," she said. "Besides, can you honestly tell me England is any better?"

After a moment of charged silence he cleared his throat, then returned to the earlier topic. "Well, this is London. Here, the unwashed masses hold no one in reverence, excepting perhaps our ailing king and the Duke of Wellington. Note, if you will, that I am neither of those august persons. Given half a chance, any butcher or laundress would think nothing of marching right up to Prinny and giving him a scold over how much he spent renovating Carlton House yet again, or the abysmal state of the roads. An exceedingly minor aristocrat such as myself, living a worthless life of pleasure and indulgence, is just the sort to attract the well-deserved anger of honest laborers. I'm better served currying the mob's favor, rather than feeding their antagonism. Heroically strong I may be," he said, waggling his brow as he rounded the corner to her street, "but not even I can fight off an entire pack of the irate downtrodden."

Behind the light self-mockery of his speech, Arcadia sensed something deeper. Lord Sheridan hadn't said that the mob might *perceive* his life as worthless, he'd said that it *was* worthless. Coming on the heels of the discovery of his lost, beloved sister, Grace, Arcadia couldn't so quickly dismiss the statement as just a poor choice of words. Perhaps he meant nothing by it, but maybe—

"Here we are." They'd arrived at Delafield House. He rounded the carriage, then handed her down. "Best I speak to your uncle now. We've been racing news of our engagement all the way to your door."

A prickling sensation crawled over her neck, as though she was being observed. Pausing with one foot poised on the bottom step of the front stoop, Arcadia glanced over her shoulder, as if she might espy the gossip winging its way through Town. Instead, she saw a figure emerge from behind a gardenia bush across the lane. The gathering twilight obliterated the person's features, but tatty skirts and diminutive stature revealed her sex. The woman stumbled over the curb, righted herself, and continued towards Delafield House.

Recognition jolted through Arcadia. She cried wordlessly, fingers digging into Lord Sheridan's arm, just as the woman extended a beseeching hand.

Alerted by Arcadia's sound of distress, the groom tending Lord Sheridan's horses shouted, "Off with you! Take your begging elsewhere." Dropping the horses' lead, he stomped into the street and raised a hand to strike the shabby woman.

Falling to her knees in the middle of the road, the woman raised an arm to shield herself. "Jalanili!" she cried.

"*Rukiye!* Stop!" Arcadia darted in front of the horses, startling the beasts. Heads tossing and harness jangling, the whinnying cattle took the groom's attention away from Poorvaja, allowing Arcadia to reach her ayah before the fellow harmed her.

"Miss Parks!"

Arcadia dropped at Poorvaja's side, heedless of the muck-strewn cobbles digging into her knees, and threw her arms around the other woman's shoulders. "I'm here," she said in Hindustani. "You're all right now. You're home."

Her ayah's body shook. Silently cursing the damp English air, Arcadia embraced her all the more fiercely. "Come inside now," she continued in a hushed voice. "Let's get you warm."

A whimper escaped Poorvaja's throat. She shook her head against the crook of Arcadia's neck.

Perplexed, Arcadia put her hands on Poorvaja's shoulders and pulled back. "Don't worry about my uncle," she said. "Everything will be …" Her voice died in her throat when she got a good look at Poorvaja. A dark bruise marred her jaw on one side. Dirt smudged her face. The skirt of her formerly plain but clean dress was half-soaked and caked with all manner of unknown filth.

"What …?" Arcadia breathed. "What happened?"

Lord Sheridan crouched to place a carriage blanket around Poorvaja's shoulders.

"Help me get her inside." Arcadia held one of Poorvaja's arms and nodded him to the other.

"No," he answered firmly. "She can't go in there."

Betrayal stabbed her gut; she sucked a deep breath. "You promised!" she protested. "You said—"

"I know what I said," he hissed. "But safe to say we both assumed everything would be settled with your relations before we found Miss Poorvaja. I haven't spoken to your uncle yet."

"Do it now!" she snapped, flinging her arm. "Speak away!"

Straightening, he planted hands on his hips and glowered down at her before turning on a heel. He didn't walk away, just stood there a few seconds. Thinking, Arcadia presumed, as he'd done earlier in the park.

While he busied himself with useless cogitation, Arcadia helped Poorvaja to her feet and wrapped a supporting arm around her waist. Only two days gone, but the Indian woman felt thinner already. What on earth had befallen her during her ordeal?

Murmuring encouragement, Arcadia tried to help Poorvaja to the door but was met with resistance. "No, no," Poorvaja moaned.

"It's all right," Arcadia assured her. "Just come inside. I'll sort it out."

Turning around again, Lord Sheridan took one look at Arcadia's meager progress and sighed. "Let me take her." Without awaiting her reply, he scooped Poorvaja up and carried her to his curricle.

"What are you doing?" Arcadia hurried after him.

He stopped and looked at Arcadia, his expression registering exasperation. "I said I'd take her. The words *just* left my mouth. Literally seconds ago." He turned sharply and resumed his course.

Arcadia lifted the hem of her skirt and hurried after him. "You needn't be snide. I thought you meant you'd take her into the house. Look at her, she's shivering and hurt. She needs help."

"I shall see she has it." Lord Sheridan lifted Poorvaja and deposited her into the seat Arcadia had occupied just a few minutes ago. The horses had calmed from their fright, and the groom scrambled back to his place at the rear of the vehicle.

Poorvaja seemed half-senseless. Her head lolled, and her eyes were glassy when they settled on Arcadia. "Jalanili?" she said faintly.

"Yes, it's me. I'm here." A sob caught in Arcadia's chest. She tore at Lord Sheridan's sleeve as he made to go past her. "Where are you going? I have to help her. She needs me!"

He grabbed her by the waist, his large hands nipping into her soft flesh. "What will you do for her, huh?" He shook her once for emphasis; she held his shoulders to steady herself. Closing his eyes, he took a deep breath. When he opened his eyes once more, he was calmer. His thumbs rubbed her sides. "Arcadia, Poorvaja needs tending now, not in an hour or two, after I've asked your uncle for your hand and convinced him to allow her back in the house and said, 'By the way, my lord, that same servant of whom we were just speaking is on the front step in dire need of medical attention.'" He paused, fingers raising to rub the back of his neck. "Allow me to take her to my brother's home, Lothgard House. I swear, she will have the very best care. In the morning, I will return to speak to your uncle and arrange to reunite you with Poorvaja as soon as possible."

He pulled her close and dropped his head. For a second, she thought he meant to kiss her. But he stopped short, simply holding her gaze from a distance of several inches.

"But ... she's all I have."

"Trust me Arcadia. Please."

He wasn't merely trying to reason with her. Beneath that brilliant confidence, Lord Sheridan longed for her trust, her approval. What choice did she have but to give it to him? "All right," she said, nodding. Then again, more confidently, "All right. Yes."

After all, she had reached out to Lord Sheridan to enlist his aid in finding Poorvaja, and he'd agreed to help. He deserved at least this much trust.

He gave her a small smile. "Good," he said, stepping back.

"Poorvaja." Arcadia moved to pat the woman's knee. "You must go with Lord Sheridan now. He's going to—"

"Arcadia!" came her aunt's voice. "Is that you?"

Whirling about, Arcadia saw the older woman standing in the open door, hand curved above her eyes, peering into the dusk.

"Indeed, we have returned." Lord Sheridan snapped Arcadia's arm into his own and hustled her right up the steps, stopping just before Lady Delafield, blocking her view of the curricle. "Apologies for the commotion out here. The horses were startled by a cat. Miss Parks kindly kept me company while my groom set them to rights."

He threw a dazzling smile at her aunt. "Thank you for permitting me the honor of your niece's company, Lady Delafield. Perhaps next time, you'd be so good as to join us? I've noticed your astonishing turbans, and I wonder if you might give me some secrets to pass along to my mother. She despairs of finding a milliner who can properly complement her tastes"—here he leaned in, his voice dropping to a conspiratorial whisper—"but I suspect you know just the person, hmm?"

"Oh! Thank you, Lord Sheridan." Touching a hand just behind her ear, her ladyship preened, turning her head to showcase the rabbit foot and clover adorning today's headpiece. "I should be most honored to share my milliner with the dowager marchioness. Tell her she must see—"

"*Ah-ah!*" Lord Sheridan raised a hand. "Next time, dear lady, next time. There's something so life-affirming about anticipation, isn't there? And what could give a man more reason to arise in the morning than the promise of time spent with a paragon of fashion?"

One more flash of his charming smile dazzled Lady Delafield into speechlessness. He touched a finger to his hat brim and bowed. "Fair ladies, I bid you a good evening. Until we meet again." As he turned, he caught Arcadia's eye and winked, then skipped down the steps whistling a jaunty tune, seemingly without a care in the world.

Taking her cue, Arcadia hustled her aunt into the house and closed the door before she noticed the passenger in the curricle. In the entry hall, Arcadia bent her head while removing her bonnet and gloves, silently beseeching whomever might be listening to watch over Poorvaja. The larger part of her wanted to race after Lord Sheridan, so that she might tend her friend herself. But that would be foolishness, she knew. Lord Sheridan and his noble brother were plenty capable of providing care.

"Well, gel, tell me what happened," Lady Delafield insisted.

Caught out in her reverie, Arcadia opened her lips, then closed them again. She couldn't very well tell her aunt about her secret bargain with Lord Sheridan, or the moments-ago discovery of Poorvaja.

"We took a walk," she finally managed.

"Whom did you see?" Lady Delafield prompted.

Arcadia licked her lips. "See?"

"Which people of note did you greet? It was the fashionable hour; someone of consequence must have been present. And Lord Sheridan being such a favorite of all the ladies, he must have introduced you to several."

"Oh." Crossing to the staircase, Arcadia shook her head. "We didn't go to Hyde Park. Lord Sheridan took me to The Mall."

Her ladyship sputtered. "Wha—The Mall? But no one's gone there during the fashionable hour for years and years!"

"There were people," Arcadia assured her. "Some children playing, gentlemen riding, others …" Recalling the ribald jests and congratulations from the working-class men, her ears heated.

"Who cares about gutter waifs mucking in the dirt! Honestly, Arcadia, if you hadn't Lucretia's eyes, I'd wonder if you were her daughter at all. You've not got a tenth of my sister's good sense." Wagging a finger, Lady Delafield continued, "Why, I didn't permit an outing with a known rake so you could swan about Town as you please. The point of the exercise was to be seen with the brother of the Marquess of Lothgard by those worth being seen by. Not go to Hyde Park, indeed," she added in a dark mutter. Chuffing a breath, she planted a fist on her waist. "If there is any saving grace to this debacle, it is that you almost assuredly were not seen by anyone of good society at The Mall, unlike that fiasco on St. James's Street."

For once, Arcadia didn't mind her aunt's scold. While she was harangued for her many flaws, Lord Sheridan was carrying Poorvaja to safety. Aiding a loved one shouldn't have felt like rebellion, but it did. Knowing she'd succeeded in thwarting the Delafields' exile of Poorvaja sent a heady sense of triumph trilling through Arcadia's bones.

"I apologize, my lady," she said, dipping her knees for good measure. She could afford to be graciously humble now, to her aunt's face, with her plans for escape set in motion. "I did not know that particular park was off limits. During our promenade, Lord Sheridan pointed out the residence of the Prince Regent. How funny, that his royal highness's own neighborhood is not considered a good address."

When her aunt made no reply, she made for the staircase, but paused with her hand on the bannister. Perhaps it was anxiety for Poorvaja, or her exposure to Lord Sheridan's grief for his sister, but Arcadia felt a welling of sadness and anger in equal parts rising in her chest. Turning, she added, "I wish I had the good fortune of my mother's guidance now. She was everything good and gracious when I was a child. After she died, both my father and Poorvaja made sure I never wanted for love or care." The scuffed toe of her half boot nudged her a single step closer to her aunt. "But since coming here, I have felt motherless in a way I never have before. I never knew the sensible adult you describe, only the lady who smelled of her favorite peppermint candies and told me stories about a faraway wonderland called London. I'd give anything to have her here to help me find my way through Society and offer her wisdom in matters of courtship and matrimony."

Lady Delafield's throat bobbed on a hard swallow. "Why, niece, I've done everything for you just the way my sister would have wanted. Your uncle and I have afforded you every—"

"She was *my mother*," Arcadia snapped, pressing a hand to her chest and gliding closer to her aunt. As she advanced, Lady Delafield retreated by slow degrees. "Always with you it is *my poor sister* this or *dear Lucretia* that. You never acknowledge that Lady Lucretia Parks was my mother—*my mother*—or that I lost her when I was but a child. After she died, not once did you correspond with me. I only knew you existed because Mama told me she had a silly, shallow little sister who'd more than once made a spectacle of herself trying to snare a rich husband."

Arcadia snapped her teeth together, but it was too late. The words were out.

Lady Delafield's face paled; her lips whitened around the edges.

The women shared a long, pain-filled gaze. Apologizing would be the right thing to do, but Arcadia wouldn't. Not again. Since docking in London, all Arcadia had done was apologize, and she was done with it.

"I shall take supper in my room," she said at last.

Her aunt gave no reply. She didn't seem to be breathing.

Turning sharply, Arcadia darted up the stairs to her room and closed the door behind her. Throwing herself into a chair, she buried her face in her arms and finally permitted the overwhelming emotions of the day to pour forth in hot tears. Even as sobs shook her shoulders, she forced herself to remain quiet, lest her relatives overhear and take exception at her outburst.

After a time, she straightened and scrubbed her knuckles across her eyes. At the wash stand, she poured water into the basin and splashed some onto her face, then pressed a square of flannel to her heated cheeks.

Arcadia scarcely knew what to make of herself anymore. Lady Delafield had needled her from the beginning, but it wasn't like Arcadia to be deliberately cruel. Her aunt obviously worshiped the memory of her older sister; divulging the unkind things Lucretia had once said about her had been needlessly vicious.

It had been the same with Lord Sheridan in the beginning, too, she reflected. His arrogance and sharp wit had goaded her into saying and doing all sorts of regrettable things. Now she knew he wasn't quite as callous as he'd first appeared, but his charm had an almost worse effect on her than his cool disdain. Just this evening, she'd gone and agreed to marry the man, despite promising herself she wouldn't marry any Englishman. His scheme to release her so she could return to India had appealed to her sense of reason, but she couldn't deny that she responded to him as a man, too. The feeling of his strong arms around her waist and his hard chest pressed to her own had been just as compelling in swaying her decision as his promise of freedom.

She was surprised when a housemaid delivered a supper tray; she'd half-expected Lady Delafield to withhold food from her in punishment for their exchange downstairs. Worry for Poorvaja had regained supremacy in the noxious, emotional stew simmering in her gut, and she had little appetite for the portion of lamb and new potatoes on her plate. After forcing down a few bites, Arcadia set the tray in the corridor, then prepared herself for bed.

Desperate to find some sense of peace, she sank to her knees in the center of her rug. *Please let Lord Sheridan take good care of Poorvaja.* She trusted him to keep his word; she did. And yet, she couldn't help but think she herself could do the job better. It was natural, she supposed. She loved Poorvaja, while Lord Sheridan did not. To Arcadia, the Indian woman was her entire family. To Lord Sheridan, she was a chip in their matrimonial bargain.

"All will be well," she murmured, rearranging herself into a cross-legged sitting position. "All manner of things will be well."

Closing her eyes, Arcadia drew and released a deep breath, training her attention on the sensation of respiration. Behind her lids, nebulous blues and purples and greens floated across a sea of black. A faintly luminous corona formed in the center, concentric rings of color and darkness.

This. Yes. For a few blissful moments, Arcadia was free. Her worries and fears were still there, and the side of her nose itched. But for the briefest time, none of those sensations mastered her. She dwelt alongside them in peace, observing them from a distance as one might a stranger passing on the road. There was only Arcadia, her breath, and the wide universe inside herself.

CHAPTER TWELVE

The woman's head lolled as the curricle rolled swiftly through the darkening streets of Mayfair. "Jalanili," she murmured. Fishing under the bench, Sheri pulled out a flask and offered it, unsure whether she was actually conscious. "Try a nip? It's Madeira. My friend imports it from America."

One black eye cracked open and rolled in his direction. He jiggled the silver container, sloshing the liquid. "The legality of obtaining the stuff is a little dubious, so I must swear you to secrecy, all right?" Poorvaja made no reply, nor any move towards the drink. Stopped at an intersection, he popped the lid and took a swig. "*Mmm,*" he hummed in exaggerated appreciation as he held it to her lips, as if trying to cajole an infant into eating mashed peas. "Comes from Charleston. Ever heard of the place?"

She turned her head, giving him another view of her bruised jaw. Someone had struck her. A flame of anger stoked in his belly.

"Who did that, Miss Poorvaja?" he asked, determined to hunt down the offending coward and give him a taste of his own sauce. "Who hurt you?"

She shrank into the blanket, her silence tinged with an undercurrent of fear.

Right. Not the time for questions. He wedged the flask beneath his thigh before guiding the horses through a break in the traffic. A moment later, Poorvaja's eyes were once more closed. She slumped heavily against his shoulder and pitched forward when he struck a rut in the road, forcing him to grab the neck of her dress to steady her.

"No, you don't," he said, pulling the senseless woman back. "Your Miss Parks will have my head on a platter if anything happens to you." He drove the rest of the way to Lothgard House one-handed, his other arm anchoring Poorvaja to his side.

At his brother's house, the butler, Giles, raised an imperious brow when he opened the door. "I'm sorry, Lord Sheridan, but you are not allowed entrance." He sounded not the least sorry, the ornery old goat. The servant shut the door.

Jamming his foot in the doorway before it closed, Sheri shouldered his way past the sputtering servant. "Sorry myself, Giles, but I'll give you the satisfaction of slamming the door in my face another day."

"My lord, I must insist that you leave," the butler said dryly, unperturbed by Sheri's behavior. Giles had been in Eli's service since the time of the marquess's marriage and was well accustomed to the Zouche family scapegrace.

"Can't do that, Giles," Sheri said, striding across the shining marble floor. "As you can see, I've a woman here who needs—"

Clang! Clang! Clang!

Poorvaja startled and thrashed in his arms. Instinctively, Sheri tightened his grip and hunched protectively over her, wheeling to locate the source of the clamor.

Giles was ringing the bronze alarum bell hanging from a heavy iron sconce near the door, alerting the house to an emergency—in this case, Sheri.

"Oh, for God's sake!" Sheri bellowed as footmen swarmed from every corner and crevice to answer the call.

"Intruder!" Giles pointed at Sheri. Quickly, he snapped off orders, instructing two footmen to hold Sheri and dispatching another to locate his lordship. There was a decided note of glee in the butler's tone. This was probably the most fun he'd had in years.

"Giles," Sheri heard his older brother call from the top of the stairs. "Is it a fire? Do we need to evacuate?" The marquess trotted into view, half-dressed for the evening, an intricately embroidered waistcoat fitted atop a shirt still open at the collar and cuffs. "Is it—Christ Almighty!" he exclaimed, pulling to a halt.

Sheri raised his brows. "An honest mistake, but nay, brother, it's only me."

"You aren't permitted here," the marquess snapped. "Giles," he rounded on the butler, jabbing his thick index finger into the opposite palm, "I gave you explicit instructions—"

"Oh, save it for a rainy day, Eli," Sheri groaned. "Giles did nothing wrong. And call off the hounds, would you?" He shot a withering glare at the footman on his left side, whose hand hovered as if to snatch Sheri's arm. "I come on an errand of mercy." He hoisted Poorvaja in explanation. The carriage blanket bundled around her torso effectively bound her arms, but her feet kicked wildly, solidly connecting with the rib cage of the hovering footman. "Good shot, Miss Poorvaja," Sheri commended in a low voice, "but please still yourself." The effort of holding onto her was beginning to make Sheri's back complain. "If you'd just direct me to an unoccupied room," he said to the marquess, "I'd be much obliged."

Lothgard's lip curled in a sneer of distaste. "Have you taken all leave of your senses? How dare you bring one of your doxies into my wife's home!"

"She isn't a—"

"Elijah?" Deborah slowly descended the stairs, her hand tightly gripping the mahogany bannister. She, too, was partly dressed for the evening. Her golden hair had been prettily arranged in a cascade of shining curls sprinkled with diamond hairpins that winked in the light, but she wore only a silk wrapper. "Sheridan? Who is that?" A shadow of concern crossed her face as she nodded toward Poorvaja.

"My fiancée's ayah," Sheri blurted before his brother could supply his own, mistaken interpretation.

"Your what?" Eli said, at the same instant Deborah asked, "What happened to her?"

The lines around Deborah's mouth deepened as she crossed the foyer. At her beckoning gesture, Sheri leaned over, as if presenting a swaddled babe in arms, instead of a grown woman. Poorvaja shrank against Sheri, her dark eyes wide and fearful.

"Her face!" Deborah cried. "She's injured."

"That's why I'm here," Sheri said. "Long story, but Miss Poorvaja can't stay with Miss Parks at the moment. Please, may she stay here tonight? I want to call a surgeon for her."

"Of course," Deborah said immediately. "This way."

The marchioness led Sheri upstairs to a guest chamber. Lothgard followed on Sheri's heels. "Miss Parks? Not the chit who paraded in front of White's in broad daylight?"

"That's the one," Sheri answered.

The marquess made a choking sound. "You can't be serious! Her name's been splashed in the scandal sheets at least twice. Naturally, you've been tangled up in it all. But scandal is all anyone knows of her—she hasn't been presented; she's barely connected." Lothgard hissed into Sheri's ear, "Have you compromised the girl? Is that what this is about?"

Pausing at the bedchamber door while Deborah, a footman, and a maid raced ahead to prepare the room, Sheri gave his brother a quelling look. "I would thank you not to speak so freely of my intended," he said in a frosty tone. Although referring to any woman as his *intended* raised the hairs on the back of Sheri's neck, the chagrined expression on his brother's face almost made that unpleasantness worthwhile. Almost.

"Come in," Deborah called.

Sheri carried Poorvaja into the chamber and gratefully deposited her onto the bed. He made a sound of warning when the woman flung off the carriage blanket and lurched upright. "I think not, madam," he said, gently but firmly pushing her shoulders back to the mattress.

Poorvaja shook her head. "No, no. Jalanili. Please."

"Miss Parks knows you're here," Sheri assured her. "She asked me to have your injuries tended. You're safe now, upon my honor. And if you aren't well enough to go home tomorrow, then I shall bring Miss Parks to you."

"Shall we send for my physician," Deborah inquired, "or do you prefer someone else?"

Sheri'd never before been responsible for the well-being of anyone besides himself. The sense of responsibility he'd felt when he first took custody of Poorvaja grew heavier with every decision thrust upon him. Arcadia was depending on him to take the best possible care of her ayah, and Sheri didn't dare fail this first test of trust.

Raking his hands through his hair, he gripped the back of his head and blew out a breath. "I want Dewhurst."

"That surgeon friend of yours?" Lothgard asked from where he hovered in the doorway. "I thought he'd married and relocated?"

"Just to Middlesex." Elmwood, the small estate where Brandon now resided with his wife and her young brother, lay in the countryside not far outside of London.

"Still, it would be two hours before he could be here, at the earliest," the marquess pointed out. "That's too long."

Indeed, Poorvaja's eyes rolled, half-closed, while she whimpered.

Growling, Sheri took several restless strides and kicked the brick hearth. "Shit! Sorry, Deborah."

Lothgard was right. Sheri trusted no one more than Brandon, but calling his friend wasn't a viable option.

"McGully, then," he said, naming the master surgeon-anatomist with whom Brandon had lived and worked for years.

His brother nodded. "I'll see to it."

Heaving a sigh, Sheri pulled a handkerchief from his pocket and mopped his brow and upper lip. This was but a small taste of what it must be like to have an entire family and household in one's care. If making decisions for one ayah was so agonizing,

Sheri and Arcadia were doing the right thing in planning to go their separate ways. Both of them would live much nicer, simpler lives without the burden of the other.

A maid entered with a pitcher of water. Deborah poured some into a glass and sat on the edge of the bed. "Miss Poor ... I'm sorry," she glanced at Sheri.

"Poorvaja," he supplied.

"Miss Poorvaja," Deborah began again, "my name is Lady Lothgard. Would you care for some water?" She offered the glass. "Perhaps tea?"

The Indian woman gave no sign of comprehension. Her eyelids fluttered weakly, and she mumbled beneath her breath. Deborah touched her shoulder. Poorvaja flinched.

"Ye gods, how badly is she injured?" Sheri nibbled anxiously on his thumbnail, spoiling his manicure. Where the devil was that surgeon?

"Why don't you go wait for Mr. McGully to arrive?"

He shrugged off Deborah's suggestion. "Lothgard can meet him."

"Sheridan." The little marchioness gave him a long look, her brow furrowed and lips pursed. "You're in the way," she finally said.

It was the closest thing to a harsh remark the woman had ever uttered at him.

Jamming his hands into his pockets, he strode out of the room and made his way to his brother's study. The marquess was seated behind his large desk, nursing a tumbler of whiskey. When Sheri entered, Lothgard gestured to another drink, already poured.

Sheri took both the glass and the decanter and headed right back out the door.

"*Sheridaaan.*" The marquess's voice held a note of warning.

"Later, Eli. Please."

Without a backwards glance, Sheri made for the billiards room. After lighting a candelabrum, he spotted a bottle of spirits resting beside a box of cigarillos on a side table. He'd forgotten his brother kept the male sanctuary well stocked with the essentials. He considered returning Lothgard's purloined whiskey, but thought better of it after he downed his first drink and poured another. His lordship could spare the liquor, and Sheri needed ample fortification.

With the whiskey's pleasant burn spreading through his belly, Sheri racked the balls and selected a cue from the rack. Carefully lining up his first shot, he drove the cue ball into the triangular formation with a sharp *crack*.

Sheri had never been much of an academic, but there was an elegance to the clean geometry of billiards that he found appealing. Examining the arrangement of little spheres and picking out shots; exerting just the right degree of force to bounce the cue ball off a cushion so it angled just so and sank a ball into his chosen pocket; the satisfaction of a clear bed … it was all restful in its own way.

Deep into his second game and his third drink, he heard the front bell ring. *McGully. Thank God.* Rounding the corner of the table, he blew out a breath, feeling the smallest part of his nerves ease.

Soon, Poorvaja would be better. When he'd suggested his bargain to Arcadia Parks—his help in locating her ayah in exchange for her hand in matrimony—he never dreamed his half of the deal would be fulfilled so quickly, and without the least effort on his part. While he'd not had a firm plan in place for hunting down a lone nursemaid in a city of half a million inhabitants, he'd thought there would be some process involved. He would have hired a Bow Street Runner, maybe posted a reward notice in the *Times*, that sort of thing. He'd imagined passing along progress reports to his overwrought intended. *Not much to tell, I'm afraid*, he'd say, or, *Happy news, there's been a sighting.* There would have been a certain romance to it: Arcadia beside herself with worry, Sheri the steady pillar she depended upon to lead the rescue effort. She would have been grateful to him for everything he'd done to reunite her with Poorvaja. She'd have felt indebted.

He leaned over the rail, training his eye beyond the cue ball to the cushion behind it, picturing the sharp angle it would take to strike his chosen ball.

But with the search over before it had begun, what hold did he have on Arcadia Parks? What did she need him for? What if … what if she reneged on their agreement and refused to marry him? The cue ball spun wildly, missing his target. Sheri cursed, stalked around the table, and chalked his cue.

Without permission from her guardian, Lord Delafield, Sheri and Arcadia could not be officially betrothed. Her promise alone wasn't enough to bind her to him. In the park earlier, he'd done all he could to ensure the match. He'd publicly kissed her, then announced their names. What he'd not anticipated was the fire that had instantly stoked his groin the instant his lips collided with Arcadia's. The first time he'd encountered her in Hyde Park and he'd lifted her into his arms, he had appreciated the way her soft curves snugged against his body, but nothing had prepared him for the wave of lust that had nearly knocked him senseless when they'd kissed.

She'd felt it, too, he'd bet his life. He'd sensed her blood leaping in the veins beneath his fingers. She had tipped her head back, wordlessly inviting him to ravish her throat. He'd been nearly undone by the urge to mount her then and there, to claim her for his own. It had taken every scrap of self-control to break that kiss. It was unnerving, the force of it, as disturbing as the weight of his sudden responsibility for Poorvaja. He wasn't used to it.

It was his prolonged celibacy, he decided, lining up another shot. That was all. There wasn't anything special about Arcadia

Parks in particular; she was just the first woman he'd kissed in months.

But I did it, didn't I? he thought with a sense of vindication as a ball tipped over the lip of felt into the wicker pocket. He'd kissed her in front of those men. Spread coin around to ingratiate him in their minds. Behind the laborers, he'd spotted a couple more men he knew in passing, one a solicitor, the other a gentleman of leisure, like himself. Sheri had announced his name and Arcadia's for their benefit, knowing those two would spread the tale right where he wanted it—into the ears of Society. By the time he knocked at the door of Delafield House tomorrow, half of Mayfair would know Sheridan Zouche was engaged to Arcadia Parks. The indiscretion of their public kiss would be excused as the exuberance of the moment, evidence of their impending joy. Sheri was a known voluptuary; no one would look askance at him kissing his bride in public.

But even if Sheri was given a collective wink, Arcadia would not be so fortunate. She was compromised, even if just. Crying off would guarantee her ruin.

But, Sheri, said a little voice in the back of his mind that sounded suspiciously like Grace, *haven't you already guaranteed her ruin?*

He scowled at the tip of his cue. *Awfully insightful for a twelve-year-old, little sister,* he silently retorted, kicking back another measure of the peaty whiskey.

Miss you, Sheri.

Miss you, too, Gracie.

He sucked his teeth. Grace had never possessed the mental capacity to string together such an eloquent remark in her all-too-brief life, but the point was annoyingly sound. The very crux of his arrangement with Arcadia—their promised separation—would assure she'd never be welcome in London Society again. Sheri could play the heartbroken, abandoned husband and worm his way back into the good graces (and beds) of Society's matrons, but Arcadia would never be given such a chance. Already viewed as an outsider, she would be further scorned as a faithless wife.

Even if, at the moment, she thought she'd shake England's dust from her heels and never return, shouldn't she be fully informed before making a decision as life-altering as marriage? Sheri had the impression that Arcadia's life in India had been unconventional, to say the least. Though an English gentlewoman by birth, she was remarkably ignorant of Society's ways. When he'd attended Eton, Sheri had met a couple of lads born in India and returned to England for schooling. At twelve, they'd known as little about England as Arcadia did at—Lord, how old was she, anyway? Twenty, he presumed. Hadn't she mentioned something about inheriting on her next birthday?

In such a circumstance, the right thing to do would be to present her with all the facts and allow her to make her choice from there, even if it meant releasing her from her promise. Maybe she would like to leave open the possibility of returning to England sometime in the future. Maybe she'd like to leave open the possibility of marrying someone else.

He shuddered, physically repulsed by the thought, but why? Sheri had never harbored possessive feelings towards prior lovers. The women who took Sheri to bed were all goddesses in his mind, granting him the boon of pleasure while he returned it in kind. They parted friends, Sheri grateful for the time they'd enjoyed while recognizing that those women would go on to share their beds with others, just as he would.

Perhaps it was as simple as the fact that he'd never framed another woman in his mind as his potential spouse. Well, except for Elsa the time he'd regrettably proposed to her. Even then, it had been more a matter of casual convenience. He hadn't felt the primal sense of urgency to wed her and bed her he felt with Arcadia. If she slipped away, then ... then ...

He blinked, rubbed his bleary eyes. He'd have to start over, was all. Arcadia Parks presented Sheri the opportunity to fulfill his familial duty of marriage without the risk of actually having to alter the life he'd rather enjoyed living these past thirty years. It would be easy enough to find some insipid little miss to take to wife, some milquetoast creature with the proper accomplishments and a socially ambitious mama.

Of course, he reflected, Arcadia's aunt, Lady Delafield, was just as covetous of the connection to the Zouche family as any matron at Almack's. The crucial difference was that Arcadia did not share that ambition. She cared nothing about Sheri's family. She scorned his aristocratic ways.

Lord Nothing. He laughed at the memory of her haughty set-down. Saucy minx.

"What's so funny?" asked a little voice.

Turning to the door, Sheri saw two pairs of brown eyes peering owlishly at him.

"What're you rogues doing?" he asked, propping himself on the upright cue. "Sneaking out past bedtime? Hoping to get into your father's brandy? You'll have to fight me for it."

Giggling and grinning, his eleven-year-old twin nephews tumbled into the room on a cloud of billowing white nightshirts.

Identical at a glance, the boys had the brown eyes and straight, full brows of their Zouche forebears, but Deborah's blood had granted them lighter hair and complexions less prone to bronzing in the sun. Good-looking little rascals. In about ten years, Sheri predicted, they'd be cutting quite a swath, leaving heaps of discarded petticoats and broken hearts in their wake. He was able to discern Crispin by the impish gleam in his eye, and Webb by the wary way he glanced over his shoulder at the door.

"We never go to sleep when Nurse says," announced Crispin, who still sported the bruise on his cheekbone from his fight defending Sheri's worthless honor. "We were reading when Giles rang the bell. We heard Papa holler, so we knew it was you."

"No, *I* was reading," Webb corrected his brother. "*You* were trying to determine whether you could bite your own toenails."

"*Blech!*" Sheri stuck out his tongue and shuddered for comedic effect. "What a revolting endeavor. That's the most disgusting thing I've heard all day." Rather than chagrined, the irrepressible Crispin looked rather pleased with himself. "So ..." Craning his neck, Sheri glanced at the boy's bare toes. "Did you succeed?"

The boy dutifully extended his foot for inspection. "I managed my large toe, but couldn't turn my ankle far enough to reach the others," he reported.

"I'm not sure whether to wish you better luck next time or suggest you find a new field of study."

After a moment of consideration, Crispin said, "Our tutor says scientific experiments have to be repeated, so I should try again." Drifting to his uncle's side, he tugged the quizzing glass from Sheri's waistcoat and used it to examine a scab on his arm.

Behold, the future Marquess of Lothgard, Sheri thought. Not for the first time, he wished his own brother long life and abundant health. It was difficult to picture Crispin taking the reins of the marquisate, running the estates, sitting in the Lords, and heading the family.

"Gnawing your own toes is *not* a scientific experiment," Webb said. The more serious-minded twin, twenty-two minutes younger than his brother, had taken an interest in the billiards table. While he scanned the balls scattered across the felt, he continued, "To be considered valid, an experiment must take place in a controlled environment and be repeatable."

"I can do it again tomorrow night," Crispin declared. "And I'll wear the same nightshirt to bed, so everything's the same."

With a world-weary sigh, Webb palmed the cue ball and rolled it hard towards the rail. It bounced off the cushion to the other side, then careened back again, striking a ball and shooting it into a corner pocket.

Sheri let out a low whistle. "Did you mean to do that?"

Webb wrinkled his nose. "It's just lines, Uncle Sheri."

True enough, but Webb took Sheri's own visualization of the table to a higher level. He swept the tip of his cue towards the rack of sticks. "Have you actually played before? Care to try your hand at a game?"

The lad eyed the implements with a longing gleam in his eye while worrying his bottom lip between his teeth. "Best not. We'd get in trouble."

Sheri scoffed. "For being out of bed? There was an uproar. Nurse will understand."

Webb shook his head. "No, I mean … it's that …"

"We aren't supposed to talk to you," Crispin provided. "Mama gets sad when she hears your name, and Papa is terrifically angry." He lifted the quizzing glass to his face, blinked his magnified eye, and said in a credible imitation of his sire, "T'would be best if you mites forgot you had an uncle."

Sheri's cheeks went oddly numb, and not just from the quantity of alcohol he'd imbibed. "He said that?" It came out a raspy whisper.

It was one thing for Lothgard to order Sheri away from the twins for the time being, but it was quite another for the marquess to tell the boys to forget their uncle existed. Sheri might not be the most shining example of a son or a brother, but he was a demmed good uncle. Not being permitted to see the boys again would be … Well, it would be like losing Grace all over again. His heart squeezed at the mental image of the simple cross marking her small grave.

Death took loved ones, and there was nothing to be done about it, but he could prevent being barred from his nephews' lives. Lothgard's demand that he marry still rankled, but Sheri wouldn't permit his own pride to come between him and his family. Any thought of releasing Arcadia Parks from their agreement was swept from his mind. They'd both given their promise. They *would* marry. He'd make sure of it.

"And Grandmama is coming from Bath," Webb said. "I heard Papa tell Giles that the dowager marchioness was to be admitted, but not you." He tugged his brother's arm. "We'd better go, Crisp."

The elder boy *harrumphed*. "Don't want to. We never get to see you anymore, Uncle Sheri." His face brightened. "You could come sleep in our room! We'll nick biscuits from the kitchen and eat them in bed."

Sheri managed a half-hearted smile. "Not tonight. Another time, promise. Run along now."

"Yes, sir," Crispin said glumly, returning the quizzing glass.

"Good lad," Sheri said, ruffling the boy's hair.

"Good night, Uncle Sheri," Webb said, unexpectedly throwing his arms around his uncle's waist.

Sheri returned the embrace and kissed the top of his nephew's head. "Good night, Webb," he rasped, his throat constricting. "Thank you for coming to see me. Do try to keep your brother out of trouble." Webb nodded against Sheri's chest.

As Crispin opened the door, the sound of voices grew closer.

Webb stiffened. Sheri patted his back. "Go, go," he urged in a whisper. On silent feet, the twins darted down the corridor away from the approaching adults.

Quickly, Sheri leaned over the table and frowned as if considering his next shot. Seconds later, Lothgard entered with another man. Sheri recognized the short, gray fellow as McGully, the surgeon.

Sometime since Sheri'd purloined his whiskey, his brother had finished dressing for whatever evening plans had been spoiled by Sheri's arrival. The simple elegance of the marquess's navy coat balanced the richly embellished waistcoat to perfection. Sheri felt a frisson of envy at the artistry of the ensemble. French was an excellent valet, but Lothgard's man, Powell, was a visionary.

Once, Sheri had cornered the servant and told him to name his price. The price Powell named sent Sheri right back to French's ministrations.

"Mr. McGully has treated your ... friend," Lothgard said.

"How did you find her, sir?" Sheri inquired, shaking the surgeon's hand.

"*Och*, a wee bit battered, my lord," McGully replied. The Scotsman removed his spectacles and held them to the light, squinting through the lenses. "Besides what you've seen on her face, there are extensive contusions around her trunk. Ribs bruised, but no' broken. A strained shoulder from, I think, her arm being twisted behind her back." He huffed onto the lenses, polished them with a kerchief, and replaced them on his face.

Sheri winced. "Good God. What happened?"

"I'd hoped you might answer me that, lad. The woman said not a word. She tolerated my examination and let me bandage her up, but she wouldn't answer my questions and refused the medicine I offered to help with the pain and allow her to sleep. Lady Lothgard is with her now, trying to coax her into taking it."

"Will she be all right?"

"Oh, yes, a few days of rest will see her well again. Mind that rib, though. Light duty for a month."

Sheri thanked the surgeon, then headed up to see Poorvaja for himself. He wished he could get word to Arcadia and relieve the worry he knew must be bedeviling her, but he had no way to contact her tonight. Tomorrow morning would have to be soon enough.

Deborah answered his light rap on the door. She looked over her shoulder at the patient, then gestured Sheri back into the corridor and closed the door behind them.

"I spoke to McGully," he said. "How is she?"

Deborah shook her golden head, one hand clutching her wrapper closed at her neck. "It's hard to say. She doesn't speak English."

"She does," Sheri assured her. "I've heard her myself."

"Well, she wouldn't speak to me. She kept saying one word over and over: *Jalanili*."

"That's what she calls Miss Parks."

The little marchioness tilted her head and regarded him. "Are you really engaged to Miss Parks?"

"As good as. I've already spoken to the lady, and plan to speak to her uncle in the morning."

A sweet smile spread over his sister-in-law's face. "Oh, Sheridan, I'm so glad."

"Are you?" he asked, cautious. "Lothgard isn't, even though he's the one who insisted I find a bride."

"Elijah worries," she said. "Nothing is ever right until he sees that it is. You'll just have to show him that Miss Parks is the lady for you. I'm ready to love her, though, if she has captured your heart."

Guilt trickled down his spine at Deborah's sweet, unaffected generosity. "Yes, well …"

Her smile broadened, crinkling the corners of her eyes. "We'll try not to crowd you too much," Deborah said, misreading his reticence. "But I am eager to welcome her to the family, and the timing couldn't be better. You can announce your betrothal at our ball in two weeks' time."

"But that's your birthday ball," Sheri protested, politely refraining from mentioning that he'd not received an invitation for the annual festivity. Black sheep flirting with disownment had no room to complain when they were cut from family parties. "You must be the center of adoration the entire evening."

"I'm happy to share the glory. Besides …" A pained expression crossed her face; she lowered her eyes.

Owing to the constant pain in her bones, Deborah hadn't been capable of dancing in years. Lothgard's dedication to the annual celebration of his wife's natal day was commendable, but the ball should have given way to some other festivity long ago.

"I should check on Miss Poorvaja," he said.

"Yes, do." Deborah gripped his wrist. "Mr. McGully left some medicine, but she wouldn't take it for me, I'm sorry to say."

"Don't fret, my dear. I'll see to it. Thank you for everything you've done this evening." He squeezed her hand, then headed into the sickroom.

Most of the candles had been extinguished, but one remained burning on the bedside table, and the coals glowing in the grate provided more illumination. Poorvaja was sitting up in the bed, back erect, not reclined against the pillow. Her dirty, torn dress had been replaced with a white, long-sleeved nightdress buttoned up to her chin. The pear-green coverlet draped across her lap revealed the outline of crossed legs. Despite her upright posture, her eyes were closed and remained so when Sheri entered; was she asleep, after all?

He crept forward on the balls of his feet. Spotting the bottle of medicine and a spoon, he debated with himself over what to do. If she was resting, disturbing her to take laudanum was silly. But then, she might awake in pain during the night—pain that could be preemptively avoided by a dose now.

"Miss Poorvaja?" he whispered.

The sitting woman remained still as a statue. Her black hair fell loose about her shoulders; rumpled and tangled, it cloaked her back and brushed the covers. He allowed his hand to drift close to her shoulder. If she did not respond to a light touch, he would leave her be. Her complete stillness, contrasted with the slightly wild look created by her hair and the discolored injuries beneath her skin, unnerved him somewhat. A tremor passed down his arm.

"What do you want?" she said before his fingertips made contact, her eyes still closed.

He jerked his hand back and yelped, then covered the unmanly reaction by clearing his throat and clasping his hands behind his back. "I came to see how you are faring and ask if you are in need of anything."

Poorvaja's shoulders crested through the curtain of her hair as she inhaled, then vanished again on her sigh. Her eyelids parted. "No."

Taking up the medicine bottle, Sheri fiddled with the stopper. "McGully has left some medicine for you." She shook her head. "It'll help with any pain."

Her eyes were hard when they found his. "Take your opium away," she said, regal as a queen. "I'll have none of it."

He cracked a smile at her tone, so similar was it to Arcadia's. Sheri pulled over a chair and took a seat. Poorvaja averted her eyes from his appraising gaze, but rather than maidenly shyness or servile submission, her lowered face felt more like a dismissal. She did not look at him because he did not interest her.

Her indifference presented a challenge. Sheri might have to get approval from Lord Delafield before he could marry Arcadia, but winning Poorvaja was just as important—perhaps more so, in the grand scheme of things. Sheri very much doubted Arcadia Parks, headstrong as she was, ever did anything without her ayah's approval. Even if he could prevent Arcadia from crying off their match, he would have to win Poorvaja over, too.

Judging by the sparse gray strands in her black hair and fine lines around her eyes and mouth, Poorvaja couldn't have more than a few years' seniority over him. Looking past the swelling and bruising marring her jawline, he saw a pretty face with round cheeks and full, plum-colored lips. And though she might have spent the last twenty years in the service of one headstrong English girl, she was still a woman—and women could be charmed.

For the first time since the poor, battered creature had been put in his care hours ago, Sheri felt more in his element. He was just having a chat with a pretty girl, something he did all the time. Changing his tack, he said, "Even if your pain is not too much, consider that you now share a roof with eleven-year-old twin boys. Rendering yourself insensible might be the only way to get any uninterrupted sleep."

At this, her eyes cut in his direction, her lips quirking to the side.

"Aaah, I see you're familiar with the feral creature that is the adolescent male. Did you have brothers?"

She shook her head. In her lap, her slender brown fingers laced together first one way, then another. "Only two older sisters, much to my parents' sorrow."

"Speaking from experience, allow me to assure you you've missed out on nothing by not having an older brother. They're dreadful brutes and only gain a superficial polish of civility over the years when it comes to their younger siblings. Mine still likes to order me about just as he did in the nursery. I was never so happy in my life as I was the day Elijah left for Eton. I crowned myself with a wreath crafted of twigs from my mother's trained wisteria, then ransacked my brother's room for any treasures he may have left behind. Found a veritable sweet shop squirreled away in a trunk. I sat in the middle of his bed and gorged myself on the spoils of my conquest."

"Oppressed, were you?" Poorvaja asked, that wry smile still in place.

"Quite brutally," he assured her. "Elijah used to sit on my chest, pin my arms, and allow his phlegm to dangle above my face, then suck it back up just before it reached me. There should be a special military division devoted to systematizing big brother torture techniques for use in interrogation settings."

Left unsaid was the stomachache that had hounded him the remainder of that day and kept him awake that night frequenting the chamber pot. Left even more unsaid was the accompanying ache in his chest that had settled in not long after the last bite of toffee, a dull, hollow place created by his brother's absence. But perhaps Poorvaja knew that sad destiny of younger siblings, being resigned to forever say goodbye to those idol-tormentors.

"But you have encountered boys somewhere," he deduced, drawing away from his own ruminations. Reclining, he crossed his arms over his middle. "Do they roam the Indian countryside in packs as they do here in England?"

Poorvaja, too, relaxed her posture, leaning back against the headboard. "I have many male cousins. Thirty-something, at last count."

"*What?*"

"My father's brother, Gyan, is head of our family. In his *zenana*, he keeps six wives and five concubines. After our lessons, the first wife turned the boys out of doors and told them she would snip a toe off any who dared return before dark." Sheri must have still looked shocked by her revelation about thirty male cousins (*How many girls were there?*), for she added, "My other uncles and aunts have children, too, but none so many as Gyan."

"I should hope not." To his own ears, Sheri sounded like a stuffy old coot, scandalized by wicked, heathen ways. He'd heard of harems, of course, and like any man with hot blood and a functioning brain, had sometimes fantasized about having so many women attending his needs and desires. Meeting someone who'd spent time in one sapped a bit of the eroticism out of his lewd daydreams. Nowhere in his imagination had scores of children been running about, with lessons and harried mothers.

"Crispin and Webb won't be worse than anything you're used to, then."

Sighing, Poorvaja turned her eyes to the canopy draped over the bed. "That was a long time ago. Most of those boys are men now. There are still a few youngsters. Gyan's youngest wife is no older than Jalanili."

"Why do you call Arcadia that—Jalanili?"

"It means a *water* ..." Her dark brows drew together on a frown of concentration. "Spirit? Or fairy? I don't know the English word."

Sheri tapped his lip. "A water nymph?"

Poorvaja shrugged. "Perhaps." She hooked her hair behind her ears. "Arcadia was born blue, not breathing. The English doctor who'd come to the *mofussil* said the baby was dead and told me to take her away to spare Lady Parks the sight. She looked like a water ... what you said."

"Nymph."

"Yes. Perfect and blue. When I held her, that tiny purple mouth opened, and she drew breath and cried and took right to my breast. My beautiful little *Jalanili*."

She almost whispered this last in a tone of reverence, of love. She sounded like ... Well, she sounded like a mother. And she must have been, to have been the newborn Arcadia's wet nurse. As he'd heard nothing of Poorvaja's own child, Sheri presumed there was tragedy in the woman's past. How much had she lost? A child, at least, but perhaps a husband or lover, too. She'd left India and her extended family behind to accompany the daughter of her heart to a new, foreign land, only to have Arcadia, too, prised from her.

Despite all, she exuded a calm, determined air. She'd been knocked down by life, and quite literally by the brute who had beaten her, but Poorvaja wouldn't stay down for long. He admired her strength.

It occurred to Sheri that this Indian ayah was the closest he'd ever have to a mother-in-law. The realization made him smile. He'd proudly claim her as such, too. Wouldn't that just stick in his mother's craw? The thought of the dowager marchioness having to share the "parents of the couple" role with a wet nurse-governess-companion was absolutely delightful. He chuckled to himself, picturing the head table at the wedding breakfast and the splash such a scene would cause.

Poorvaja slanted a questioning look at him.

He waved his hand. "Don't mind me. A little too much whiskey, is all. Gives me the giggles. If you won't take your medicine, would you at least tell me, please, who caused your injuries?"

The sudden shift in conversation caught Poorvaja off guard. Her hand went to her face. "I don't want Jalanili to know."

"I'm afraid she already knows. She saw you, remember?"

"No, I mean ..." She ducked her head, her hands twisting in the bed linen. "I don't want her to know what happened."

Sheri went still inside. "I vow, Miss Poorvaja, that whatever you confide here will not find its way to Arcadia by my lips. If you choose to tell her at a later time, that's your decision to make." But if he heard a name, or any useful information, Sheri would hunt down the swine who caused Poorvaja harm and visit the same hurts upon that bastard tenfold.

"Well," she began, gingerly at first. "Jalanili's uncle, Lord Delafield, told me I had to leave, that his wife takes care of staff decisions, but she couldn't stand to look at me." Poorvaja's eyes flashed at the memory; her voice grew stronger. "The first night I tried to spend near the house, but a man with a stick said I was disturbing the respectable people." A watchman, Sheri surmised. "When I would not go, he chased after me, so ..." She pressed her fingers above her brow. Sheri passed a glass of water to her. "Thank you," she said, after a long sip. "That first night, I walked, not knowing where to go. By the time the sun came up, I thought to myself to work as an ayah again until I found a way to get to Jalanili. But what to do?" she asked, shrugging. "Go door to door, hoping someone would take me in? By nighttime again, I was hungry, but more thirsty. I had only two small coins in my pocket, so I went to a place with drink. I asked for water, but the man there laughed and gave me beer. I was so thirsty, I drank it very fast. It went right to my head," she added with a rueful smile.

"Happens to us all," Sheri assured her.

"Not to Jalanili," Poorvaja stoutly declared.

"Excepting that paragon, naturally," he teased in return.

"After that, I walked some more, until I saw a large building, all lit up, with many fine carriages coming and going. Lots of *sahibs* and *memsahibs* in one place! A good place to find work, with so many people to approach in a short time, yes?"

Sheri frowned. "What was the building?" he asked, trying to place Poorvaja's location during this portion of her narration.

"A theater, I believe," she answered. "Someone said the play would be ending soon."

Drury Lane, then.

"There were other women standing near the building, too. I went to one and asked what she was doing, and she said she was working."

Sheri felt himself blanch, knowing all too well what sorts of women worked Drury Lane after dark. "Oh no."

"So I said, 'Me, as well,' and waited beside her. The woman said I couldn't stand in her spot. I explained that it was important for me to find work, but she only grew angrier. Not a good temper, I thought, to display before young children."

Sheri snorted. "She wasn't looking for work around children. I'm afraid you encountered some Drury Lane vestals—ladies of the night," he clarified at her baffled expression.

"Whores, you mean?"

He nodded.

She laughed once, dry and humorless. "There were no prostitutes on Jalanili's little station, and the only two in the nearby village were sisters who kept their own house, so it took me a little time to realize the sort of work that woman and the others were looking for, but I did figure it out. Unfortunately, it was after she hit me."

His eyes widened. "A *woman* did this to you?"

"Three of them," she said, ticking her chin up. "Two of her friends came to help when they heard her screaming."

A chill passed down Sheri's spine at her cold, satisfied smile. If he'd previously found Poorvaja a bit intimidating, his opinion had just shifted to *mildly terrifying*. He'd do well never to land on her bad side.

Surreptitiously wiping sweaty palms against his trousers, he asked, "How did you make it back to Delafield House today?"

She blinked. "I walked," she said, as if it should have been obvious.

Badly injured and half-starving as she'd been, though, Sheri wouldn't have thought any less of Poorvaja if she'd just curled up in a gutter somewhere and quietly expired. That she'd had the fortitude to find her way back to Arcadia after her harrowing few days was further testament to her indomitable nature.

Sheri could think of no person more deserving of his help. What better way to reward her loyalty and perseverance in the face of such adversity than to make possible the voyage home she and Arcadia both desired?

Should everything go as he planned, he would soon marry Poorvaja's charge and then have the authority and ability to make good on his intentions.

"Well, I see why you wouldn't want Arcadia knowing you'd scrapped with a bunch of street cats, so your secret is safe with me, but it's a demmed good tale. You made a fine showing," he said, chucking her on the shoulder in a friendly manner.

Poorvaja grinned, seeming inordinately pleased with herself. Bloodthirsty wench.

"We both need to rest up," Sheri said, rising to leave. "You, to regain your health, and me, to regain my sobriety. Tomorrow morning, I've a bride to claim."

CHAPTER THIRTEEN

In Lady Delafield's parlor, four days after accepting Lord Sheridan's proposal, Arcadia sat upon a tufted ottoman across the room from her aunt, her stomach all in knots as they awaited the arrival of their much-anticipated guest. A neatly displayed selection of savory tartlets and flaky scones on the sideboard attested to the expectation of many visitors, although only the Marchioness of Lothgard was scheduled to call. A pot of pekoe steamed merrily beside the sugar bowl and cream pitcher. For the past several days, Arcadia had been nibbling on everything in sight in a futile attempt to settle her nerves and alleviate the boredom of confinement in her room. An appealing aroma wafted over from the tray of tartlets, onions, and—Arcadia sniffed—was that thyme? Her stomach gave an audible grumble.

"Do not forget what I told you," Lady Delafield instructed loudly over the impolite sounds of Arcadia's anxious appetite. "Curtsy, and keep your eyes down, sensible of the great honor it is to meet Lady Lothgard. But do not appear cowed. You must give the impression that you will do credit to the marquess's family."

Lady Delafield glanced up from her embroidery hoop and regarded her niece over the rims of her pince-nez. Today, Arcadia's aunt wore a dress featuring long sleeves and a high collar trimmed with lace, as well as a white cap festooned with more frothy lace. The ensemble looked enviously warm compared to Arcadia's cap-sleeved dress of sprig muslin, which Lady Delafield said emphasized her youthfulness. At least her ladyship had not objected to Arcadia's shawl.

"If I ought not be cowed," Arcadia mused, "is there a farm beast I should emulate? A goose, perhaps?" Goodness, but those scones looked good. The golden tops, brushed with butter, gleamed dully. And a dish of clotted cream beside them, too. Her mouth watered.

Her ladyship *harrumphed*. "Impudent girl! Lady Lothgard will expect better manners than that in Lord Sheridan's wife. Already, your name is connected to some rather unfortunate business. If your besmirched reputation convinces the marchioness you are not a suitable *parti*, you might find yourself married to a baker, missy. You cannot rely upon poor Reverend Fisk to renew his interest now that your uncle has had to tell him you are not eligible for his consideration, after all."

Oh, bother Reverend Fisk. To the best of Arcadia's knowledge, there had been no interest expressed by her unknown cousin, anyway, only her Delafield relations trying to foist her off on the vicar. And Lady Delafield likely would have cheerfully pushed the fellow off a cliff to clear the way for the more advantageous match.

Three mornings ago, Lord Sheridan had made good on his promises. The day after whisking Poorvaja away, he'd arrived at Delafield House just as the clock chimed eleven. Anxious to know how her ayah fared, Arcadia had run to the window each time she heard a carriage or horse in the street, and so she'd caught a glimpse of him from the landing above the entrance hall just as the butler admitted him.

Stepping into a shaft of sunlight cast through the transom, he'd paused to remove his hat and gloves. Even she, who knew nothing of English men's fashion, could see he'd taken greater care with his appearance than his usual, impeccable toilette. His gray-blue frock coat fit him like a second skin, accentuating the breadth of his shoulders and skimming his sides as they tapered to lean hips, while cutting away in the front to reveal a gray silk waistcoat, free of any adornment save his silver fob. In the sunshine, his cravat was almost blindingly white; an iridescent black pearl nestled in the center of the crisp, precise knot. Charcoal trousers clung to his muscled thighs before disappearing into black top boots that gleamed like the pearl at his throat.

The sight of his splendid male beauty hit Arcadia in the solar plexus. The air rushed from her lungs in a soft *whoosh*. His eyes cut to where she stood, and her heart seized. It wasn't just his ensemble that was perfection. Lord Sheridan's sensual lips held a firm line; his eyes glinted with supreme confidence. The very air around him crackled. Arcadia felt drawn to him like air helpless to resist the pull of a raging inferno. He gave her a nod, the gesture filled with determination. *All will be well*, he seemed to say.

A short time later, Lord Delafield had called both Arcadia and her aunt to his study. Arcadia tried to look surprised when Lord Delafield announced that Lord Sheridan Zouche had done her the very great compliment of requesting her hand in marriage.

Lady Delafield shrieked, then burst into tears. "He's a rogue!" she wailed. "But such a connection. Oh, husband, what's to be done?" Lord Delafield opened his mouth, but his wife seemed to have finished wrestling with the matter. "You're right; of course she must accept." Her ladyship issued thanks to heaven, immediately after which she commenced hyperventilating, necessitating the summoning of her maid with her vinaigrette. There didn't seem to be much reaction left for Arcadia herself to express, and so she remained quiet.

Lord Delafield tried to stem his wife's mounting enthusiasm, warning that there were "one or two peculiarities" attached to Lord Sheridan's proposal, but her ladyship would hear nothing to diminish her jubilation.

When Lord Sheridan returned to the study to formally propose, Lady Delafield refused to quit the room, taking it as her due that she witness Arcadia's moment of triumph, which was, she proclaimed, every bit hers, as well. Arcadia felt her aunt's eyes, feverish with ecstasy, on her as Lord Sheridan took her hand and dropped to bended knee. She'd scarcely heard his pretty little speech, so embarrassing did she find the entire scene.

There was one small moment that felt entirely her own, when she must have missed her cue to reply. Lord Sheridan gave her hand a private squeeze. Arcadia met his gaze, warm with knowing humor, and felt herself overcome with wonder. How could this be real? How could this gorgeous man be meant for her? He wasn't, not really, but—oh, just for this instant, she could pretend it was all real, that he truly did want to marry her, and she actually was the happiest woman on earth. And so she'd answered yes, her voice thick, and his grin split her heart right in two. He stood then, his eyes never leaving hers, the awareness between them quickening. She craved a kiss, like the one they'd shared in the park to seal their bargain. His eyes dropped to her lips, and her eyes went to his. Her toes curled.

Then Aunt Delafield broke into applause, shattering the spell. Lord Sheridan pecked Arcadia's cheek then turned so they could accept congratulations from her aunt and uncle.

The only intelligence she had of Poorvaja came just after Lord Sheridan's proposal, when Lady Delafield had been occupied recovering from her nerves, and her uncle had gone to fetch a bottle of champagne. In those stolen seconds, Arcadia whispered an inquiry after her friend. Lord Sheridan had assured her that Poorvaja was in good hands at Lothgard House.

That afternoon, upon learning that Poorvaja's return was a condition of the betrothal, Lady Delafield had turned on her niece with an accusing finger. "Conspirator!" She threatened to call the betrothal off, but neighbors, having caught wind of the gossip ignited by their kiss in the park, began arriving to offer felicitations. It was too late to end the engagement without losing face. Instead, Lady Delafield once more confined the bride-to-be to her room. Poorvaja had not yet returned, and Arcadia had heard nothing more about her friend's recovery.

Now freed from her room for the first time since that day, Arcadia would not risk her precarious liberty by asking Lady Lothgard about Poorvaja's health. "Forgive me, Aunt, I don't mean to be disrespectful. Things are so very different here, even some of the words you use are unfamiliar."

Quiet blanketed the room, interrupted only by the gentle sound of the embroidery floss as it was drawn through the fabric. Arcadia had nothing to keep her own hands occupied, and the refreshments only tortured her empty stomach, so she stared wistfully instead at the *trompe l'oeil* chimney board painted with—of all things—a fire. It was cruel, she thought, to tease a cold person with a fire that offered no heat.

"Why must I sit all the way over here, my lady?" she asked a few minutes later, shifting on her stool. A plush chair neighbored her perch, but Aunt Delafield had insisted the low ottoman made Arcadia seem daintier than she was, a neat little feat of visual trickery akin to the chimneypiece's empty promise of warmth.

"Evenly distributing ourselves will soothe her ladyship's nerves. We would not wish to crowd her and seem grasping or vulgar."

Arcadia glanced around the empty sitting area. "Yes, I see what you mean. This is certainly preferable to being all in a heap."

Her aunt's eyes narrowed on her.

Arcadia smiled innocently.

Just then, the butler entered and presented a salver bearing the coveted calling card. Lady Delafield jumped to her feet. "Up, girl, up!" she yelped. She took her niece's hand and towed her into the center of the room. Then she dithered with the embroidery hoop in her other hand, dancing in a little circle before stuffing it behind a decorative pillow on the sofa.

The butler appeared in the doorway again and cleared his throat. "The Marchioness and Marquess of Lothgard," he pronounced grandly, stepping aside to bow in a couple, rather than the expected lone lady.

Arcadia only caught a glimpse of the august personages before she followed her aunt's lead and sank into a deep curtsy. When she rose, she saw a tall man with dark hair and eyes. He was good-looking, she supposed, in a regular sort of way. Similar to Lord Sheridan in coloring, the marquess was not as aggressively handsome as his younger brother. The lines about his eyes and silver wings in his hair helped her estimate his age at about forty. At his side, the marchioness was golden and small. Her figure was soft and maternal, an impression carried out by the kind smile she trained on Arcadia.

"My lord, my lady," Lady Delafield gasped, her eyes wide with awe, "how good of you to come. What an honor it is to have *both* of you in our home."

"Madam," the marquess said with a nod, drawing his wife further into the room. "Thank you for receiving me. You were expecting only my wife, and I pray you'll forgive my impertinence in coming unannounced."

As they cleared the door, another couple was revealed behind Lord and Lady Lothgard. The surprising sight of Lord Sheridan's teasing smile struck a blow to Arcadia's heart, but the woman beside him sent it spinning crazily in her chest.

"Poorvaja!" she cried, rushing forward to embrace her friend, forgetting her duty to greet the, ostensibly, more important guests.

At her rain of kisses and murmured concern, Poorvaja laughed and waved her back. "I'm well, Jalanili, I'm well." The ayah squeezed Arcadia's upper arms. "How are *you*?" She studied the younger woman's face just as Arcadia was drinking in the details of Poorvaja's fading bruises. "Getting fat, I see," she stated bluntly. "Has she locked you up again?" Poorvaja's chin ticked towards the center of the room.

Lord Sheridan, who had been smiling fondly at the reunion between the two friends, now turned his attention to his hostess.

Lady Delafield gaped at Poorvaja. "What do you think you're—" Her eyes cut to the noble persons watching the scene and modulated her tone. "The servant's entrance is around the side of the house, you know," she said to Poorvaja, as though scolding a naughty puppy. "Next time, be sure to use the correct door, please."

"Miss Poorvaja has been an honored guest in our home these past days." Lord Lothgard's mild tone was belied by the steely set of his posture.

"Though the circumstance of our meeting was most unfortunate," chimed in the little marchioness, "I am delighted to have made Miss Poorvaja's acquaintance, and am proud to call her a friend." Her cheeks were pale, like a china doll that had yet to have the blush painted on, and the round eyes she turned to Arcadia furthered the impression of a delicate nature.

"Deborah," Lord Sheridan said, taking Arcadia's hand and guiding her to his family, "Lothgard, please allow me the great pleasure of introducing you to Miss Parks, lately of ... Where was it, my dear?"

"Hyderabad," Arcadia supplied.

"Hyderabad, India," Lord Sheridan concluded. "Arcadia, this stuffy bloke is my brother, the Marquess of Something-or-other, and his wife, the marchioness, who is entirely too good for him."

Casting a rueful smile at his brother, Lothgard bowed. "Enchanted, Miss Parks. By what miracle my scoundrel of a brother has convinced you to marry him I shall never know."

"Oh, Elijah, stop your teasing," the marchioness gently chided. "You mustn't mind their squabbling, Miss Parks. Our family isn't as uncouth as these two would make us out to be."

"Worse, I fear," Lord Lothgard drawled. "She hasn't met the twins."

Arcadia took the marchioness's proffered hands. "Not at all, my lady." Drawing a breath, she uttered the few words she'd prepared for this meeting. "I'm delighted to meet you, Lady Lothgard. I have not made many friends here yet, and I hope that I shall prove myself worthy to be yours." Glancing at Poorvaja, who gave her a nod, she added, "From the bottom of my heart, I thank you for taking such good care of Poorvaja. I'd hoped to hear from you word of her progress, but you have exceeded my dreams by actually bringing her here today, healthy and strong once more. How can I repay your kindness?"

"Oh, isn't she the dearest thing in the world?" Lady Lothgard beamed like Arcadia was the Second Coming. "It was our pleasure, my dear, I assure you. Of course you and I shall be good friends. You must think nothing of any sort of debt—we are to be family now, after all. But Sheridan"—she turned to the younger man—"why have you left Miss Parks in such suspense all this time?"

"It was not my intention to do so, Deborah. Each day, I attempted to call upon Miss Parks to tell her how her friend fared. Each day, my call was rebuffed." He allowed a pregnant pause to fill the room. "The footman said you weren't at home, Arcadia. But Miss Poorvaja has implied that might not have been the case."

All eyes turned to Lady Delafield. The woman's trembling set her many lace ruffles to quivering like autumn leaves in the breeze. Her face blanched, then flushed. She swayed on her feet. Arcadia feared the woman would shortly faint in self-defense.

"The footman was not mistaken," Arcadia blurted. "I wasn't home. My lady aunt has taken me shopping every day this week in preparation for our wedding."

Lord Lothgard's shoulders eased, and Lady Lothgard's sweet smile returned. But Lord Sheridan was not fooled, Arcadia saw. His brow arched as he leveled a speaking glance on her, but he said no more. Poorvaja snorted, muttering a Hindustani oath beneath her breath before strolling to the sideboard and helping herself to tea.

As though freed from a daze, Lady Delafield blinked. "Tea!" she chirped. "Fine idea. Please, everyone be seated. Poorvaja, help me serve our guests."

While her aunt fluttered about, Lord Sheridan took Arcadia's elbow. After several days apart, seeing him again was a shock to her system. Tingles danced over her scalp as he bent his head to her ear. "Did she lock you up? Is it true?"

Arcadia licked her lips. "It's good to see you again, my lord. Thank you for everything you've done."

Lord Sheridan's jaw tightened. "Tell me, woman."

She nodded.

He cursed and pulled a hand down the lower half of his face. "Where is your uncle? Did he know? He will answer for this—"

"Please don't," Arcadia whispered, acutely aware that the company was watching them. "It's over now. I just sat in my room and ate and read and meditated. It wasn't so bad, really. The worst part was not knowing about Poorvaja, but she's here now and …" His eyes searched her face. Arcadia swallowed. "Please."

Mouth drawn, he looked away. A muscle in his jaw flexed. Unconsciously, it seemed, his hand went to his waist. Briefly, he touched the fob, which she now knew contained the portrait of his deceased sister, Grace. Then he pulled out his quizzing glass and held it to his eye.

"Madam," he called to Arcadia's aunt, "I must put you in touch with my manservant, French. He's set about finding Miss Parks and I a new abode to call our own. No doubt your recent shopping excursions have formed the seed of my bride's *trousseau*, but French will let you know what linens and furnishings my wife will require for her marital home. I know you will want to give your niece the best." His chilly voice brooked no argument. "The very finest money can buy."

Lady Delafield's mouth popped open. "Well … naturally, my lord," she said, passing a cup of tea to the marchioness. "Her dowry will amply afford all the necessary accouterments for your new establishment."

He clucked his tongue. "*Not* her dowry." His smile could have turned hot tea to ice. "After all, my lady, it wouldn't be a wedding gift if she pays for it from her own dowry, now would it?"

"Bu … bu …" Lady Delafield stammered.

Oh, she could kiss him. Arcadia might not have wanted her aunt's petty cruelties revealed before Lord and Lady Lothgard, but in her deepest heart, she took satisfaction in Lord Sheridan's neat *riposte*.

The marchioness staged an intervention for the sputtering hostess. "On the topic of the wedding, might we discuss the ball? Lady Delafield, my husband and I would like to use our upcoming annual ball as the occasion for an official betrothal announcement. Of course, I'd welcome any additions you might wish to make to the guest list …"

While Lady Delafield recovered herself, Lord Sheridan and Poorvaja exchanged a silent communication. The ayah took a seat, perching herself beside Lady Lothgard.

"Miss Poorvaja," Lord Sheridan said, speaking over his sister-in-law, "I see you've some tea, but no refreshments as yet. What do you have on offer there, Lady Delafield?"

The older woman straightened and glanced over her shoulder at the buffet. "Cook has provided scones, biscuits, tartlets—"

"A little of everything for Miss Poorvaja, if you'd be so good, my lady." He guided Arcadia to a chair, settled her into it, and kissed her hand. "And for Miss Parks, too."

For a moment, Arcadia was sure her aunt would refuse. Her nose pinched and eyes flashed defiance. But then, astonishingly, Lady Delafield bent her stiff neck and set to filling two plates with delicacies.

Arcadia quailed, wondering what her aunt would do in retribution for Lord Sheridan humiliating her before Lord and Lady Lothgard. But he put his hand on her shoulder, and she knew he was still there, standing behind her. And he'd served a warning to her aunt.

For now, Arcadia was safe. The heat of his hand cupped around her arm spread, infiltrating her heart, and she wondered whether that vulnerable organ could possibly remain unharmed.

CHAPTER FOURTEEN

When Sheri arrived at Delafield House the following day, it was with a much different mindset than he'd had just the day prior, a call he'd approached with the grim determination of a general rallying the troops to battle. Having to beg Lothgard to attend what was supposed to be a ladies' tea had been an excruciating exercise in the art of groveling, but his inability to see Arcadia for three days had been alarming, given the circumstances. Already, he knew the Delafields capable of turning a woman out into the streets; what might they do to their niece?

Learning that Arcadia had been punished, sent to her room like a recalcitrant child, made Sheri want to punch a wall. Witnessing Arcadia, whom he well knew to be impertinent and a bit saucy, shrink into herself and even lie to protect her detestable aunt was an outrage. His engagement to Arcadia Parks might be a farce, but that didn't mean he would allow her to be mistreated, either.

His impulse had been to throw Lady Delafield into a closet, lock the door, and throw away the key. See how the harridan liked a bit of her own treatment. Then he'd run Delafield to ground and make him answer for the sins that had been committed against the women in his household. Mostly, he wanted to spirit Arcadia away to safety as he had Poorvaja.

Over the course of their visit, Sheri had beheld aspects of Arcadia he'd not yet seen. There'd been a vulnerable sweetness there; her voice had trembled when she thanked Deborah for the care Poorvaja had received. And her eyes had been filled with hope when she'd asked Deborah to be her friend, as though she desperately wanted it to be true, and he'd silently seconded his sister-in-law's claim that Miss Parks was the dearest thing in the world—at least in that moment. He had no doubt she could turn biting on him again in an instant.

But wasn't that kind of unpredictability exactly what he enjoyed in a woman?

Lord and Lady Delafield were nowhere to be seen when Sheri was shown into the now-familiar parlor. In short order, Arcadia and Poorvaja made their appearance. He helped them into his coach.

"Where are you taking us?" Poorvaja demanded hotly as the coach started forward.

He regarded her with amusement. Sheri might have come to her rescue in her hour of need and persuaded her to share confidences with him, but Poorvaja's instinct to protect Arcadia rested for no man, not even erstwhile heroes. "I'm abducting you to my lair of villainy," he drawled in reply.

The ayah leveled a gaze on him. He met it. Held it. At last the woman lowered her eyes and muttered something in an unfamiliar language.

Arcadia made a sound in her throat and replied in the same Indian dialect. If Arcadia Parks's English sounded like she was about to sing, this was her voice in full melody. He had no idea what the woman said as she directed what sounded like a heated few sentences at her ayah; he just let the music of her voice wash over him like the loveliest aria ever composed. Sheridan could very happily wallow in her voice for hours.

This was her greatest beauty, he decided. Arcadia might not be the most conventionally pretty woman he'd ever beheld, but her voice was astonishing.

He didn't realize his eyes had closed until they drifted open at the sound of his name tucked inside a nest of that melodious language. He felt like he was coming out of some sort of trance. When they regained focus, both women were watching him from the opposite seat.

"So, Lord Sheridan," said Miss Parks, "where *are* we going?"

"A jeweler I frequent. Not too far from here. And call me Sheri, won't you, Arcadia? All my friends do."

Her hazel eyes clouded. "Are we friends?"

"Well, we …" His neck felt hot under the collar. His breezy request wasn't quite so simple anymore, not with her staring at him like that. They were compatriots of a sort, he and Arcadia. And when she'd told Deborah how she wished to be her friend, Sheri had found himself suddenly longing she'd ask for his friendship, too. Although, God knew, he was not in the habit of kissing his friends the way he'd kissed Arcadia at The Mall, nor did he typically fantasize about undressing his friends the way he imagined doing to his bride.

"Speechless, Lord Nothing?" A teasing smile played around Arcadia's lips. "I think I shall call you that," she proclaimed. "It suits you better than Sheri."

Saucy minx. "As you wish, my dear, but be advised: all of Society may take to calling you Lady Nothing once we're wed."

Her smile faltered. He winked.

When they arrived at the shop tucked away in a quiet side street off the bustling Strand, Poorvaja lingered on the sidewalk. "Go ahead, Jalanili. I wish to stretch my legs."

He wanted to ask Poorvaja if she desired them to stroll with her, but his other companion was already opening the door. He hurried to hold it for her.

The little shop was like a jewel itself, all glittering glass cases and polished brass fittings. When the proprietor stepped out from the back room, his eyes lit. "Good afternoon, Lord Sheridan. What a pleasant surprise."

"Afternoon, Tulliver." Sheridan had been a customer here for years. Mr. Tulliver was a skilled gold- and silversmith. Both Sheridan's quizzing glass and his fob had been the craftsman's work. There had also been the occasional gift to soothe the sting of parting when he ended his dalliance with this or that lady.

Speaking of ladies, Tulliver regarded Miss Parks, eyes all agleam. Undoubtedly, he assumed Sheri was here to purchase a bauble for the woman.

"Mr. Tulliver, this is Miss Parks, niece of Lord and Lady Delafield. And my affianced bride, I'm delighted to say," he added, lest the fellow get the impression she was another of Sheri's soon-to-be castoff mistresses.

Arcadia politely accepted Tulliver's compliments, but she clearly had no patience for chatting with the proprietor. She stalked the length of the counter, examining the case's contents.

"Is there something in particular you are looking for, Miss Parks?" Tulliver asked. "Lord Sheridan has impeccable taste, so if you have difficulty making a choice, I know he'd—"

"I'm looking for a peacock," Arcadia interjected. "A jeweled brooch. It was stolen from me."

The man's face paled. "Can you describe it for me, please?"

"It's about this size and shape." She formed a circle with her index fingers and thumbs, with the tips only overlapping to the first joint. "It's large," she said a little apologetically. "The body is an elongated sapphire teardrop, with a smaller sapphire and black and white enameling for the head, and a small garnet for the eye. The tail feathers are worked in gold, set all along with emeralds, golden topaz, and sapphires for the spots."

It sounded gaudy, Sheridan thought, but the thing must've been worth a fortune. No matter Arcadia claimed keeping it with her allowed her to feel connected to her deceased parents and India and whatnot, something that valuable should have been locked up in a strongbox, not riding in a reticule in Hyde Park.

The jeweler let out a low moan. "I saw it, Miss Parks. I did. About a week ago, a man brought it in, wanting to sell it. It's absolutely exquisite; the craftsmanship is divine; the filigree work on the tail feathers is some of the finest goldsmithing I've ever had the honor of laying my eyes upon. And that sapphire!"

"Tulliver," Sheridan said, bringing the man back to earth. He propped his gloved hand on the counter, rapping with a knuckle. "Who brought it here? Where is the peacock now?"

The man shook his head sadly. "That's just it, Lord Sheridan, I don't know where it is now. I figured the peacock was stolen. I'd never seen the man before in my life, and he wouldn't give me his name, either. I don't deal in stolen goods; the guild would have my skin, and word would get out; my reputation would be in tatters, and I'd be sunk. I didn't want anything to do with it, so I sent him on his way."

At Arcadia's choked sound of dismay, Tulliver wrung his hands. "If I'd known the rightful owner would come looking for it, I'd have bought it from him and held onto it for you, never mind the cost or the consequences."

"Nonsense," Sheri dismissed. "We wouldn't have you risking your livelihood." Disappointing to learn they'd missed the peacock by days, but Sheridan hadn't really expected they'd be fortunate enough to find it sitting in the case of the first shop they entered, either. It was remarkable that Tulliver had seen it at all.

"How about the man?" Sheri pressed. They didn't have the brooch this time, but finding out who was trying to sell it would be useful to their investigation.

"He was a short fellow," Tulliver said, "heavy in the middle. Round, pink face. His eyes were blue, I think—no, brown. No, on second thought, they *were* blue."

"That's not the man who attacked me," Arcadia said, her tone despondent. "I didn't get a good look at his face, but he was taller than I am, and I didn't notice a heavy belly." Her eyes were swimming with sadness when they moved to Sheridan. "Now what?"

They were a very pretty hazel, Sheri thought. Shades of brown and green and blue all mixed up like tiny mosaics. And they were so expressive, holding nothing back. All of her pain was right there for him to see.

Snapping himself out of cataloging Miss Parks's attractions, he said, "If you hear anything, Tulliver, do send word to me, won't you?"

"Of course, my lord. And again, Miss Parks, I'm sorry I could not be more helpful."

"You were most helpful," Arcadia assured him. "Lord Sheridan, compensate Mr. Tulliver for his service."

Why, the managing little baggage! What did she think she was doing, ordering him and his money about? And to think he'd been silently complimenting her eyes. His own narrowed on that stubborn chin of hers with its not-quite cleft. She raised a brow, impatient.

Biting his tongue for the moment, Sheri fished a coin from his pocket and passed it across the counter. "Thank you again, Tulliver. Do be in touch."

He took Arcadia's arm and removed her from the store before she decided to make him give the jeweler his hat.

He hissed into her ear, "In the future, I would thank you to allow me to handle any financial considerations that arise."

Her eyes widened. "I did allow you to handle it. In fact, I asked you to. You did an excellent job, by the by."

As they stepped towards the coach, Poorvaja hailed them from a short distance away. When Sheri saw the companion the ayah had picked up, he groaned.

"I'm haunted," he said.

Poorvaja walked alongside Sir Godwin. Stopping in front of Sheri and Arcadia, the poet greeted them, sweeping his hat from his head and executing a florid bow. Righting himself, he said, "I was in my favorite coffee shop, working on a new composition—inspired by our little meeting at the museum, I might add—when I sighted Miss Poorvaja on the street. I rushed to hail her, hoping you, Miss Parks, might be nearby." He pressed a hand to his chest. "Fortune smiles upon her unworthy son this day, and grants me a glimpse of your glowing countenance."

A blush swept over Arcadia's cheekbones. "Sir Godwin, you are much too bold in your praise." She didn't sound entirely displeased, however.

"What meeting at the museum?" Sheri demanded.

"I hesitate to contradict a lady," said Sir Godwin, ignoring Sheridan entirely, "but I fear my poor words do not do justice to the arresting beauty that surrounds you." He glanced at the ayah, as if weighing whether Poorvaja would castigate him for heaping such treacle on her mistress. Reaching into his pocket, Sir Godwin withdrew a handkerchief. Sheridan sighted the initials GP embroidered on the corner. "Might I beg a favor of you, Miss Parks?"

"What is it, sir?"

The poet extended his hand; the little scrap of linen caught in his fingertips fluttered in the breeze.

"Would you be so good as to touch my handkerchief?"

Sheri scoffed. God, how he despised Godwin Prickering, his flattering words sashaying around with all the sincerity of a whore's arousal. His betrothed should not be subjected to the ignominy of insincere gallantry. "Of all the idiotic—"

"I'd be happy to oblige, sir," Arcadia startled him by interjecting. Far from looking put off by the ludicrous request, she smiled shyly as she plucked one cream kid glove from a hand.

Prickering handed the handkerchief to Poorvaja, who scowled at the object before passing it on.

The use of an intermediary further annoyed Sheri. Really, the oaf was standing two feet from Arcadia, not twenty; this show of humble admiration was … Well, it was stupid, is what it was. And what the devil was Arcadia doing meeting this buffoon at the museum? She was engaged to *him*, by Jove. Their arrangement was not one that demanded fidelity, but Sheri couldn't bear the thought of his bride trysting with an imbecile.

Arcadia rolled the material between her bare fingertips. "How long must I hold it?"

"Just another moment," the poet replied. He gestured to the shop they'd exited. "Out hunting your peacock?" He cast a cool look in Sheridan's direction. "Good of you to assist the lady, Zouche, but do you think it seemly, parading her about to institutions of commerce without a chaperon?"

"But Poorvaja was with us," Arcadia protested.

Godwin raised a thready brow. "Miss Poorvaja was on the Strand, in fact, not chaperoning you. Fortunate it was me who found her and returned her to you, Miss Parks, and that you were not discovered by those who do not sympathize with your struggle to acclimate to our ways. You must take better care." Glancing at the Indian woman, he added, "Both of you."

Poorvaja lowered her head, eyes downcast. Her mouth, Sheridan noted, firmed mulishly. No doubt she wished to give the pompous man a piece of her mind.

"That's quite enough of that." Sheridan snatched the handkerchief from Arcadia and slapped it against Sir Godwin's stomach. "Take your snot rag and be off with you, Prickering. My fiancée and I don't require a chaperon to do a bit of shopping."

Clenching the material to his chest, the poet affected a stricken mien. "*Fiancée?* Say it is not so, Miss Parks!"

"I'm afraid it is so," his Indian-bred chit replied in good cheer.

"Well … well." Sir Godwin blinked, then cleared his throat. "My thanks for the token, Miss Parks. I shall treasure it. And now I bid you good day, in the hopes that I'll soon have the pleasure of your company once more. Miss Parks. Miss Poorvaja." His gaze slid to Sheridan. "Zouche." He smirked, then turned to head back towards the Strand.

There had been a challenge for Sheridan in that exchange with Miss Parks, a gauntlet thrown. Sheri was not in the habit of competing for the attention of a woman, much less his own bride. It was insulting that Sir Godwin might consider himself a worthy opponent to Sheridan in any sense; even more infuriating was that Miss Parks seemed taken in by the man's blatant groveling.

"Where shall we go now?" Arcadia asked, pulling her glove back on.

"It's time to return you to Lord Delafield's house," Sheri snapped, his eyes returning to the dwindling figure of Sir Godwin.

As they settled back into his coach, Arcadia laced her fingers in her lap. Beside her, her companion stared out the window.

"Why did you tell Sir Godwin about the peacock?" Sheri inquired.

Her eyes widened a fraction. "I was not aware my stolen property is a secret."

Sheri pulled out his quizzing glass and tapped it against his thigh. "And what is this about the museum? Which museum? When?"

Ye gods, just listen to him. He sounded like a jealous wife. Of Godwin Prickering, no less. This was turning into a very bad business. Sheri had been too long without a woman. For a multitude of reasons, he needed to get Arcadia Parks wedded and bedded. That would allow him to think straight once more.

"By happenstance, we encountered Sir Godwin at the British Museum about a week ago," Arcadia said. "I told him about the brooch then. He is very kind. A little silly, yes, but harmless."

Sheri grunted. He was gratified to hear her call the other man silly, although she had no idea of the history of Sheridan's rivalry with the fellow, how far each had gone over the years to devil the other.

It wasn't his place to involve Arcadia in his years-long spat, though. It was her damned brooch; she was welcome to enlist all of London in searching for it, if she wished—although some immature, begrudging part of him felt he did have a claim on the hunt. It was *their* quest, his and hers.

"Back in India," Arcadia said after a moment, "merchants would come to our house to show us their wares. The *durzi*—the tailor—brought trunks filled with silks and muslins in every color of the rainbow. And other merchants, too—we never left the station to buy such goods; they came to us." She paused; Sheri watched a flicker of sadness cross her features, briefly rendering them softer. She must have been remembering, once again comparing her ancestral home to the one of her birth, and once more finding England lacking.

But then she smiled suddenly, dazzling him. "This way is preferable," she stated, "even though we only made it to a single shop. It's wonderful to go out and meet people, to see something of the city. And we gathered useful information on our very first day!" The animation of her delighted voice once again swept him up in a spell. "Thank you for taking me, Sheri."

"It's been my very great pleasure," he assured her, shaken by how good her pleasure made him feel.

"May we go again tomorrow?" Her eyes sparkling with hope, she grasped her hands at her chest.

Lord, but her voice was an unexpected aphrodisiac. Pitched against him in such a way, he didn't know that he—that any man—could deny her. Suddenly, he thought about hearing his name on her lips again, this time in a voice thick with passion. A familiar rush to his groin had him shifting in his seat, tightening his thighs to try to staunch the erection.

Too long in an empty bed, old man.

"I don't know that I can contrive to take you out shopping two days in a row," he said. "Though we're engaged there are still proprieties to observe. It pains me to admit as much, but Sir

Godwin was right about that. It might be best if I ask around at a few places on my own."

The young woman fell into a thoughtful silence until they arrived at her uncle's house. When he helped her alight from the carriage, she took his hand tightly and continued to hold as she reached the pavement. Energy quickened the scant inches separating them, enticing Sheri to risk drawing a little closer yet.

Arcadia's mouth firm, her expression mirrored the one he'd seen on Poorvaja earlier. He had the darting thought that it was a familial resemblance. "We *shall* go tomorrow," Arcadia declared, her voice low. "I know you won't let me down."

Something inside his chest gave way, done in by her naïve determination expressed in that seductress's voice. "I wouldn't dream of disappointing a lady. I shall look forward to it," he capitulated with a nod, returning the squeeze of her hand before releasing it.

And damnation, but he was. He couldn't wait to see Arcadia Parks again tomorrow.

CHAPTER FIFTEEN

The morning post brought a note from Sheri, inviting Arcadia to once more go shopping. If it pleased Miss Parks, Sheridan would like to introduce her to a friend of his, a respectable matron named Mrs. De Vere who would chaperon their excursion.

Arcadia quickly accepted the invitation, curious about this Mrs. De Vere. Had Arcadia planned to stay in England, she would've liked to cultivate a circle of friends. Alas, it was not to be. With Poorvaja safely returned and the hunt for her brooch underway, Arcadia would not reside in England much longer.

At the appointed time, Sheri arrived with the "respectable matron," a lively young woman of an age with Arcadia. Sheri had a harried look about him as he made the introduction.

"Miss Parks, permit me to make you known to Mrs. Claudia De Vere."

"I'm in alt to finally meet you," declared Mrs. De Vere, pressing her cheek to Arcadia's as if they were old bows. "Lord Sheridan has told us so much about you."

"Lord Sheridan doesn't know much about me," Arcadia said. "I fear what he has told you must not have been very pleasant." She cast a wary look at the man in question. The air around him bristled. Had she been too pushy in requesting another day of searching? She'd enjoyed yesterday so much, she'd selfishly sought the pleasure of his company again.

How greedy I've become here, she thought. In India, she never used to want more of anything. Arcadia had been perfectly content with her life and everything in it. But in England, nothing was good enough. She wanted less of her aunt, more of Sheri—but less of Sheri, too, she reminded herself, for the man turned her emotions inside out. Just one more reason to return to her sensible life in the *mofussil*, where everything was right and good and enough.

Mrs. De Vere laughed, silvery and bright. "On the contrary, what he's said has convinced me that you and I are destined to be great friends. Why else should I have badgered him so for an introduction?"

The thought of anyone wanting to meet her, of going to the trouble of seeking her out, was novel and a little flattering. She felt her spine straighten a fraction.

Soon they were on their way. In the coach, Mrs. De Vere leaned over, nudging Arcadia's shoulder with her own. "Ready to find The Item?"

"Did Lord Sheridan tell you about my peacock?"

"A little." Mrs. De Vere patted Arcadia's knee and cooed. "I'm terribly sorry you were accosted in Hyde Park. What bad luck! Nothing of the sort has ever happened to me."

"You're more likely to be the one doing the accosting, my dear Mrs. De Vere," Sheri drawled from the opposite seat.

That lady opened her mouth, shut it again, then sighed.

"I know a brooch must seem a silly thing to care so much about," Arcadia said, "but, to me, it represents my entire life before I came to England."

"Not in the least," Mrs. De Vere assured her. "A lost family heirloom is no small thing. What a Grand Quest this is!"

Arcadia wasn't sure how Mrs. De Vere managed to verbally capitalize her words, but it was an interesting trick. She thought she might practice her own enunciation later, in the privacy of her room, and see if she could manage it herself.

"Thank you, Mrs. De Vere, you're very kind to assist us."

"Claudia, if you will." The young matron smoothed a hand over her skirts. "You must forgive my eagerness. It's just that when Lord Sheridan came to see my husband and me last evening, and he lamented your need for a chaperon, I volunteered my services. For once, Sheri didn't seem to mind my scheming."

At Claudia's use of the familiar name for Lord Sheridan, a little worm of jealousy slithered through Arcadia's heart.

When they arrived at the jeweler's shop, Sheri opened the carriage door and handed the ladies down. Arcadia closely observed his interaction with his friend's wife. Was it her imagination that the smile he bestowed upon Arcadia was a little wider than the one he'd given Claudia? Was there a special warmth in his brown eyes? Did he grasp her hand a little longer?

Was it all just wishful thinking on her part?

Inside the shop, Sheri conferred with the shopkeeper while Claudia looped her arm through Arcadia's and drew her along the cases of goods, pointing out sparkling baubles that caught her eye.

"Tell me something of yourself, Arcadia," Claudia said, pausing to admire a hairpin adorned with opals and aquamarines, "for you were right earlier: Sheri hasn't told me very much, just enough to make me eager to learn more."

"You must be quite friendly with Lord Sheridan," she said, a touch stiffly, "to call him Sheri. He invited me to do so, as well."

At once, Claudia seemed to understand the other woman's feelings. "I'm allowed the intimacy because I'm married to Mr. De Vere, and for no other reason. My Henry and Sheri are longtime friends from back in their Oxford days. Only Lord Sheridan's closest companions call him Sheri—most Society ladies call him Chère."

"Chère is a French endearment, is it not? Why is he called this by so many?"

Claudia suddenly interested herself in a gold lily strung on a velvet ribbon. "Oh, it's a trifle," she said with forced breeziness. "Just a small thing. Nothing, really. He's ... popular with the ladies."

He must be very popular, indeed—more even than Sir Godwin's dire warnings suggested—for ladies to call him Chère, as if he was the collective beau of all the *ton*'s women.

"But you must not think badly of him," Claudia hastened to add, her hand darting over the countertop to cover Arcadia's. "Sheri is … Sheri. He has a good heart and is as loyal a friend as ever you could hope to meet. And most of his reputation is undeserved, I'm sure. He just likes to make women happy, to dance attendance on the wallflowers at balls, flatter the older ladies with flirtation, that kind of thing."

Claudia couldn't know it, but her explanations weren't helping Arcadia's feminine pride. Was their engagement just another of Sheri's charity cases? She was grateful for his help, but apparently he'd do the same for any other woman; there wasn't anything special about her that drew his interest, besides her willingness to marry him and then go away. Once more, she felt mortified by insisting he bring her out again today. Small wonder he'd brought another woman along to divert Arcadia. He couldn't wait to be rid of her, just like her aunt and uncle.

"I long to hear about your life in India," Claudia intruded on her gloomy thoughts. "I read a history of the subcontinent ages ago, and one of my brothers was stationed there for a few years, but he spent most of his time in Calcutta amongst the army officers and wives. I yearn to hear from someone who *really* lived there, as you did."

Grateful for the opportunity to think of something besides Sheri, Arcadia told Claudia a little about her day-to-day life on the station, about their *khansama*—or head servant—Harit, whose rigid correctness would rival the starched manners of any English butler. She mentioned her summer trips with Poorvaja to visit the ayah's family in the mountains. There, in the *zenana* with all the women and children, her days had been spent playing, gorging herself on mangoes picked right off the trees until her stomach hurt, and learning the practice of yoga from the first wife.

"Yoga?" Claudia perked, the dreamy expression on her face giving way to excitement. "In the history I read, there were illustrations of a yogi with his arms and legs all twisted about. Can you do that?"

"Some days I do better than others," Arcadia demurred, "but I try. Yoga is much more than the *asanas*, though; it's a disciplined way of life. I must confess, I'm not as dedicated to the whole system as many Indians. I never felt quite right about claiming another culture for my own, but the women in the *zenana* were always good enough to let me join in *asana* practice."

"Oh, you must show me! Would you, please?" Claudia clasped her hands at her chest. "It would be thrilling to see a person do the things I've only read about."

Laughing, Arcadia waved her hands. "All right, all right! Poorvaja is who you really want to watch, as she is much better at the postures than I. But I'll speak with her. I'm certain we can give you a demonstration sometime."

She failed to divulge that she might not—probably wouldn't—be here to demonstrate yoga postures. Not if she succeeded in quickly finding the peacock and escaping this country.

She perceived a presence behind her. Turning about, Arcadia found Sheri looming over her, his jaw hanging slightly ajar, a strange expression on his face.

"Lord Sheridan," she ventured. "Sheri, are you quite well?"

All at once he blinked, and his jaw snapped shut. "Fine, thank you. Shopkeep's neither seen nor heard anything about your peacock, though he was able to offer the names of a few businesses less particular in sourcing their wares. We should look elsewhere."

He turned sharply and strode out the door.

With a smart flick of her wrist, Claudia opened her fan to cover a laugh; her eyes danced above the ivory-and-silk accessory. "Gracious, but you're leading him a merry chase," she said.

"Mrs. De Vere," Sheri said once they were all outside, "would you mind giving Miss Parks and I a moment to decide our next course of action?"

Claudia cast a sidelong glance at Sheri, then a knowing smile at Arcadia. "I'll be at Gunter's, having an ice. Order for you two, as well, shall I? Don't be long."

As the young matron strolled off in the direction of Berkeley Square, Sheri drew Arcadia into an alleyway between buildings.

"My lord?" Arcadia asked in confusion.

He pushed her back to the wall and cupped her cheek in his hand, tipping her face. The shadows of the buildings on either side gave his face a cool, bluish cast, but his eyes flashed hot beneath the brim of his tall beaver hat.

He lowered his mouth to hers, kissing her once, twice. Pulling back slightly, he hovered but an inch away, a hum filling the tiny space between their faces. The sound came from her, she realized, as if she'd just enjoyed a delicious morning stretch.

"There," he said, lifting his head further. "It's deuced difficult to contrive to kiss my own fiancée. I've been telling myself for days that your lips couldn't possibly be as soft as I remember, but they are." He slanted a smile. "Astonishing."

"Is that ..." Arcadia's heart pounded in her throat. She wanted him to kiss her again, but she didn't know how to ask, or whether he'd like her to. Even though he claimed to like kissing her, Sheri wasn't left breathless by the experience as Arcadia was. Maybe this was just part of his *Make them believe* campaign, to play the part of a doting suitor.

"Is that what, peahen?"

Arcadia swallowed her nerves. "Is that all?"

His eyes flicked down, perhaps in thought, perhaps to where her breasts were slowly smooshing against his chest. Arcadia couldn't help herself. He was so solid, like a heavenly body with his own gravitational pull. And as he did not rebuff her entrance into his orbit, she carried on slowly crashing into him until her cheek rested against his chest. His chin tucked alongside her temple. Eyes drifting closed, her body attuned itself to the steady beat of his heart. That regular *thump-thump* was a point of meditative focus stronger than her own breath, so vital and alive.

"No," he breathed against her temple, his hands slipping over the globes of her bottom and tugging her snug against him, "no, by God, that's not all."

His words thrilled her; the feeling of his possessive touch ignited a fire of need in her belly. On a soft cry, she lifted her face and brought her mouth full against his. One hand still on her bottom, the other came to her back, and he pulled her even closer. Sheri's kiss became openmouthed, the tip of his tongue gently tracing her bottom lip. Tentative, Arcadia parted her own lips and was rewarded with his moan of approval as his tongue swept into her mouth.

She brought her hands to his shoulders and rose to her toes, reveling in the sweet invasion of his body into hers. His fingers clutched tight at her back, while the hand at her bottom kneaded and squeezed. His hand moved between her legs from behind, probing through her clothes at her sex.

"Oh!" Arcadia gasped at the rush of sensation. His mouth found her throat, trailing fire along her neck while his heavy thigh parted her knees and found the juncture between her thighs. Arcadia clutched his shoulders, his neck, anywhere she could find purchase. His hands came to her waist, and he guided her hips back and forth, building the most exquisite pressure in her intimate flesh.

His own hips canted in rhythm with hers, the hard ridge of his flesh trapped between their bellies, undeniable and rude, while he ground against her through her skirts. One hand came to her breast, the pad of his thumb teasing her nipple to aching.

Not ten feet away, the alley opened onto the street, from which any passerby might get an eyeful of what they were doing. Sheri was angled to shield her from view, but that wouldn't be enough to stop a determined voyeur. Swamped by the overwhelming rush of pleasure and conflicting sense of shame, a sob rose in Arcadia's throat. She gripped his neck and brought his mouth back to hers, trying in her inexpert way to return to their tamer kisses of earlier.

His grip on her hips loosened. One hand rubbed soothingly along her flank. "Peahen?"

"Please," she whispered, her hands trembling and eyes closed against humiliation. "Please don't."

Sheri's forehead dropped to the crook of her neck. She was surprised to discover his breathing was as ragged as hers.

"Of course," he said. "Of course." Kissing her temple, he withdrew his leg from between hers. "Don't cry, Arcadia," he murmured. "It's my fault. I'm a rank bastard." His eyes scanned her face, his heavy brows creased in concern. "You just wanted a kiss, didn't you, peahen? I should have realized. Forgot you were a virgin, forgot myself—" Abruptly, he turned his back. His shoulders expanded, rose and fell as he took several breaths.

Arcadia used the moment to set herself to rights, fluffing out her skirts and smoothing a hand over her waist.

"I'm sorry, Arcadia," he said over his shoulder, his voice barren of its usual warmth. "I shouldn't have taken such liberties." Avoiding her gaze, he took her arm and guided her out of the alleyway, back onto the street.

She wanted to reach out to him, to tell him she wasn't upset by what he'd done—by what *they'd* done. Until she thought of the possibility of being discovered, she'd very much enjoyed what he'd made her body feel. She still felt restless and unsatisfied and wished there were some private place where he could give her more of those wonderful feelings.

"Sheri?" she ventured, pulling him to a stop.

But when he looked down at her, his eyes bleak, her courage withered and died.

"We should find Mrs. De Vere with all due haste," he said. "There's nothing so desperately sad as a half-melted ice."

Chapter Sixteen

There was a great deal involved, Arcadia soon learned, in preparing for a sham marriage. With a little less than a fortnight before the Lothgards' ball, at which she would be presented to Society and her betrothal to Sheri officially announced, attention quickly turned to making Arcadia a bride worthy of the Zouche family—or at least one who would not humiliate them.

That was how Lady Delafield framed the situation, in any event.

Lady Lothgard merely swooped in to take Arcadia shopping. "You can't know how delightful it is to have another lady in the family at last," she said as her carriage bore them towards Bond Street. "I've only my husband and sons to outfit. What fun it shall be to consider the cut of a bodice rather than a frock coat."

Today, her ladyship wore a gray and pink pinstriped muslin frock and a handsome bonnet with a low crown, the brim tilted back to frame her doll-like face. The marchioness's hand gripped the ivory handle of a cane.

"Does Lady Lothgard—that is, the Dowager Lady Lothgard—not accompany you on outings?" Arcadia asked.

She'd heard rumblings that Sheri's mother had recently alighted on Lothgard House, but Arcadia had yet to be introduced to her future mother-in-law. The meeting caused her no small degree of anxiety.

The carriage jostled on a rut. Lady Lothgard's eyes flinched shut; she sucked a quick breath.

"My lady?" Arcadia touched the other woman's knee.

Her entire body tense, the marchioness shook her head. She exhaled slowly, her shoulders relaxing by small increments. "There," she said with a weary smile, the lines in her forehead deepening. "Forgive me, Miss Parks. I'm well. As well as I ever am.

What did you ask? Oh, yes," she said to herself, pressing a finger to her brow, "Lady Lothgard. My mother-in-law resides in Bath, so I do not often have the pleasure of her company."

"She is in Town now, though?"

"Mmm."

Shouldn't the dowager have called upon Arcadia? Or should Arcadia call upon her? She'd no idea how these things were handled. Her aunt was still barely speaking to Arcadia, and Poorvaja knew less than she.

She wished Sheri were here to ask, but she hadn't seen him since the day before yesterday, when he'd introduced her to Claudia De Vere. When he'd pulled her into a dark alley and darker pleasures.

Arcadia's eyes traced a paisley swirl on her shawl, and she felt lost. If only Lucretia Parks had thought to leave her daughter some instructions. Arcadia frowned. While she was making useless wishes, she might as well wish her mother hadn't died at all and was here to guide her through London Society, rather than buried in the churchyard of a tiny Anglican church in Hyderabad. A pang of missing her mother shot up Arcadia's throat, catching her breath.

"She always takes several days recuperating from the journey to Town," the marchioness said. "I've scarcely seen her myself, and she's living in my house. On a related topic"—her smile warmed—"it occurs to me that you and I shall very soon have the same mother-in-law. That makes us sisters."

"Sisters?" Arcadia echoed.

Lady Lothgard reached for her hand. "Please call me Deborah. And will you permit me the use of your Christian name?"

"I … I suppose, yes."

"Excellent."

Deborah inhaled, her quiet smile illuminating her from the inside out. Her happiness caused Arcadia no small agitation. When she and Sheri had agreed on their plan, she'd not thought of his family. Having no siblings of her own, it hadn't occurred to Arcadia that she was obtaining a brother and sister through her marriage. And nephews, too, although she'd yet to meet the infamous Crispin and Webb.

Now Arcadia had more family than she'd ever had—or shortly would, in any event—and while they rolled out the rug of welcome, she was planning to leave them all. It didn't seem right to allow the sweet noblewoman to call her a sister.

"Deborah …" Arcadia's voice faltered.

"Arcadia," Deborah returned, giggling like a young girl. Cutting her eyes out the window, she gasped. "We're here!"

The carriage door flew open. "Surprise!" shouted Claudia De Vere, laughing at Arcadia's stunned expression.

"Missus … Claudia," Arcadia stammered, clambering out, "what are you doing here?"

"Her ladyship invited me," Claudia said, bending her swan-like neck to the marchioness. "As if the pleasure of seeing you again wasn't enticement enough, when Lady Lothgard said she was bringing you to Madame Doucet—"

"Who?"

"—I couldn't possibly say no." Claudia looped her arm through Arcadia's and pointed out a black painted door. No signage suggested this was any sort of shop, and curtains drawn across the interior of the windows prevented her from glancing inside the brick-fronted building. "There's a waiting list for her services two years long. Why, just last month, I heard the Countess of Wagener burst into tears in the middle of the street because Madame refused to outfit Lady Wagener's daughter for the girl's debut ball—*next year*. No one gets in to see her on such short notice, unless, of course, one is at least a marchioness. *And* a Zouche."

Leaning heavily on her cane, Deborah led the way to the mysterious black door. "You make Madame sound like a dragon, Mrs. De Vere!" she protested. "Madame Doucet is my modiste,

Arcadia. She isn't a snob, merely overworked. I'm most fortunate to have found her when she was new to London. She outfitted me for my wedding, and I've been with her ever since."

Despite Deborah's reassurances, Arcadia's knees knocked beneath her terrifically unfashionable skirts. The only dresses she owned were those she'd brought with her from India and the handful Lady Delafield had made ahead of her arrival—and those far too small.

Another facet of the scheme Arcadia had not considered was the impact marrying into a fashion-forward set would have on her wardrobe. When she returned to India, she would have no use for gowns commissioned for London ballrooms. And while her dowry could more than bear the expense of new garments, that money was meant to provide her primary support for the rest of her life. Unwise expenditures today could translate into lean times twenty years from now.

Still … it wouldn't hurt to look. One gown would not send her to the workhouse.

A shop girl opened the door and escorted the trio to a sumptuously appointed seating area where three glasses of champagne awaited them on a tray atop a gilt table. Deborah looked perfectly serene in the opulent surroundings, while Claudia craned her neck this way and that, drinking in every detail while she sipped her beverage.

Arcadia tried to relax. She took a mouthful of the wine and attempted to focus on the sensation of bubbles popping against her tongue and the insides of her cheeks. If she closed her eyes and really concentrated, she could even hear them fizzing against her teeth.

A velvet curtain swooshed aside. "*Bonjour!*"

Arcadia startled, sending champagne shooting up the back of her nose. Through watering eyes, she saw a dark-haired wisp of a woman swathed in black approach Deborah with outstretched hands. "*Ça-va, beauté?*" the woman asked, leaning down to place two Gallic kisses on either of Deborah's cheeks.

Averting her face, Arcadia coughed into her hand to clear her throat. She sniffed and dabbed her eyes with the back of a finger. Feeling more composed, she turned back, only to find herself the focus of Madame Doucet's gimlet eye. Then the modiste trained her attention on Claudia, who shrank back in her seat.

Madame Doucet laughed once, then cocked her head at Deborah. "You say you bring me Chère's bride, *mais ...*" Shoulders hunched to her ears, Madame spread her hands towards Arcadia and Claudia. Her eyes cut from one to the other. With a snort, she shook her head. "*Non. Pas possible.*" Then back to Deborah. "*Vraiment?*"

With a gesture, Deborah bid Arcadia rise. "Madame Doucet, this is Miss Parks, Lord Sheridan's bride. She is in need of a gown for her betrothal ball next week."

The Frenchwoman bristled. "*Mais, marquise,* that is your birthday *fête!*"

Was it? Arcadia's stomach sank. "My lady, I didn't know," she said in a rush. "I wouldn't dream of intruding—"

"And now it is to be a betrothal ball, as well," Deborah said. "Even more reason to celebrate. What a happy occasion it shall be." The golden-haired woman smiled serenely, but Arcadia noted a tightness around her eyes. Recalling the jolt in the carriage, she wondered how much pain the marchioness lived with every day.

Madame Doucet held her hands out to Deborah in supplication. "Already, I have created for you a gown of such *magnificence,* it will be impossible to outdo myself. No one will give her even a look, not with you already the queen of the night." Crossing her arms, the modiste sniffed, as if to put a period on the matter.

Deborah's soft bosom rose and fell on a sigh. "I understand, madame. I suppose we've no choice but to go elsewhere. Perhaps Mrs. Fowler would be willing to take our custom."

"Penny Fowler ... pah," the Frenchwoman grumbled. Her mouth twisted to the side. Dark eyes moved from Arcadia to Deborah and back again. Madame Doucet stepped closer to Arcadia, then closer yet, until the toes of her black shoes tapped against Arcadia's scuffed half boots. The modiste lifted her patrician nose and leaned forward, one thin brow raised. Palms damp, Arcadia gripped her skirts but stood firm.

After a moment, Madame Doucet's intense expression softened. "Ah." She smiled coyly. Stepping back, hands folded at her waist, she tilted her head, this time her gaze studying Arcadia from head to toes. *"Oui. C'est bon.* This, I can work with. For Chère." She clapped twice, and the velvet curtain parted again. The girl who'd admitted them to the shop appeared, and Madame rattled off instructions. The girl nodded and scurried away.

"Come, *mademoiselle.*" She shooed Arcadia towards the back room. *"Rapidement.* There's no time to lose."

Arcadia cast a silent, desperate plea for help over her shoulder. Claudia's wide, blue-gray eyes met Arcadia's over the mouth of her champagne glass.

"We'll be along in a moment, my dear," Deborah assured, lifting her own glass in toast.

In no time, the Frenchwoman had Arcadia standing on a pedestal in the back room in naught but her shift. Dress forms stood sentry around the room, the headless torsos arrayed in gowns of various stages of completion. Attended by a flock of seamstress-acolytes, the modiste scrutinized Arcadia with the careful diligence of a nit-picker, poking her waist and hips, lifting her arms, peering at her ankles, even demanding to see her teeth.

"Quel âge avez-vous?" Madame inquired, flattening her fingers against Arcadia's cheeks and tugging them back towards her ears. "How old?" she repeated at Arcadia's confused expression.

"Twenty."

"Your skin is five years older than the rest of you. Too much sun."

"I've lived in India all my life," Arcadia defended. "It can't be helped."

Madame Doucet muttered to herself in French, then resumed her appraisal of Arcadia's form.

Arcadia had assumed there would be measuring involved in the process, but Madame Doucet used no tape measure, only her hands and expert eye. Occasionally, she barked over her shoulder to an underling who jotted notes in a little notebook with a pencil.

In the midst of this chaos, Deborah and Claudia appeared, the front-room girl following, carrying a chair for Deborah. Claudia had managed to procure a refill of her champagne glass. Finding a spot to stand between a half-finished riding habit and a stunning ball gown, Claudia gave a jaunty wave and applied herself to her wine. Arcadia, who had never cared for the head-muddling effects of alcohol, now wondered if it would be gauche to take a slurp from her friend's glass in the spirit of making it through this ordeal with her sanity intact.

At the conclusion of Madame Doucet's inspection, Arcadia expected she'd be presented with a selection of colors and fabrics from which she might choose, and that there would be some discussion over what style of gown she might like to have. But in this, too, she was mistaken. Madame spoke to one of her girls, who scurried into another room and returned with a sketchbook and two bolts of cloth.

The Frenchwoman flipped through the journal to a page and, with a flourish, turned it for Arcadia and the other ladies to see. "*Et voilà*," Madame declared. "This is the gown for you."

Upon sighting the fashion plate, Lady Lothgard and Claudia gasped in awe.

Arcadia gasped in horror. She cast a stricken look at Madame Doucet. "I couldn't possibly!"

The modiste blinked. "May I ask mademoiselle why not?"

Her finger circled round and round the drawing's upper portions. "There's just so much … there. How about this one?" She pointed to the perfectly lovely—and far more modest—dress depicted on the facing page.

The sketchbook slammed shut on her finger. Arcadia yelped. "*Non!* That is a morning dress, foolish child. This gown has been waiting for your collarbones to come through my doors. They *demand* this gown."

"It's lovely," Arcadia prevaricated. "Perhaps just not for me." Never in her life had she worn anything half so daring. Never in her life had she *seen* anything half so daring. Surely, no woman would actually step into public with so much flesh on display?

"You must!" Claudia interjected. "It's the absolute crack."

"It's exquisite," Deborah added. "Oh, Arcadia you'll look a dream. Sheridan will be beside himself with admiration."

Arcadia balked. Claudia cajoled. Arcadia cringed. The modiste stomped and threw her arms about and declared that she would make mademoiselle this gown, or nothing. Deborah begged Arcadia to reconsider.

Outnumbered, outflanked, and entirely out of her depth, Arcadia capitulated.

"*Bon,*" Madame said with a sharp nod. Taking up a scrap of creamy silk, through which her hand was perfectly visible, the modiste's lips carved a wicked smile. Arcadia cringed.

"Mademoiselle, your underthings."

Arcadia whimpered.

• • •

The afternoon continued in a similar vein as the morning, only Arcadia wished even more to run screaming.

"Dancing master?" she yelped at Deborah. "I don't need … That is to say … I can't dance."

On the voyage west, a couple of the ship's officers had offered to teach her a few dances, but Arcadia had gratefully fallen ill before she was subjected to their tutelage. The notion of an English ball was anathema to every notion of propriety Poorvaja had taught her.

Claudia, who had joined them in the carriage, playfully slapped Arcadia's arm. "Oh, it'll be fun. Henry—Mr. De Vere, that is—has agreed to come. He and I will dance with you, so you won't be alone."

And therein lies the problem. Arcadia was fond of dancing. In the *zenana*, she and the other girls had kicked up their heels to the infectious twang of sitars and swayed their hips to the beat of drums. It wasn't dancing itself to which Arcadia objected, but the idea of doing it in the company of men. In India, only dancing girls and prostitutes did such a thing. Already, by walking down St. James's Street, Arcadia had inadvertently advertised herself as a lady of questionable character. English society held differing views on the matter, but Arcadia could not so easily excise and discard a piece of her upbringing.

In her marrow, she knew that dancing in front of men—with men!—wearing the scandalous dress Madame Doucet was creating for her, would seal her fate as a notorious woman.

"And perhaps her ladyship will join us," Deborah said, her eyes brightening. "How much easier it would be to meet in an informal setting, rather than at something stuffier, hmm?"

Oh, this just took the cake. Lewd public behavior and a mother-in-law to witness. Fantastic. Marvelous.

"I shouldn't mind making her ladyship's acquaintance at a tea. Or a supper. Or during my next lifetime, perhaps."

Claudia laughed. "Courage, Arcadia. Take heart: at least you aren't burdened with a mother-in-law who watched you grow up from infancy and continues to hold against you the time you had an accident on her century-old chair the first time you sat at her formal dining table at the age of six."

Despite Claudia's valiant effort at distracting her with amusing anecdotes, Arcadia's apprehension grew. By the time they entered Deborah's music room and Arcadia saw the lithe man posed beside a grandiose pianoforte, her stomach was all queasy acid. At the ladies' entrance, a second man seated at the instrument played a few lively bars of music while the first man sprang into motion, skipping and twirling. Breeches so obscenely tight they might have actually been hose revealed every bulge—muscly and otherwise—of the dancer's lower body. Her cheeks heated, and she tamped down on the urge to bolt. He pranced to a stop just in front of her and made a pretty leg, his bow perfectly timed to the pianist's concluding flourish.

"*Buongiorno, bella.* Let's dance."

Lady Lothgard and Claudia clapped appreciatively.

Arcadia died inside.

There was some small consolation in the fact that the dancing master, Signore Bonelli, did not strip her down and take inventory of her every defect as the modiste had done. (He did insist upon seeing her feet and substituting her own footwear for a pair of simple dancing slippers.) Yet it became readily apparent that he was dealing with an unwilling pupil, and the Italian struggled to maintain his equanimity.

"One, two, three, *hop*! In time with the music. If *signorina* would please hop. A small jump, that means. Your feet must leave the ground, signorina. *Si,* Signorina Parks, I am addressing you. Look at Signora De Vere, how she bounds like a majestic gazelle. Do as she does. Bend your knees, extend, and hop, signorina, hop! *Dio mio,* woman, do your knees not bend?"

"Signore Bonelli," Deborah said from her seat off to the side, "perhaps a pause for refreshment?" She rang a small silver bell on the table beside her.

Though she did not understand the dark invective the dancing master muttered in Italian as he stalked past on his way to the terrace, Arcadia was coming to recognize that she was hopeless in any language.

The musician bent his head to the keyboard and continued playing quietly for his own entertainment while a footman pushed in a laden tea cart and poured the ladies glasses of lemonade. Claudia took her drink and strolled to the other side of the room to gaze at an impressively large landscape.

"I'm sorry," Arcadia said as she sank into a chair beside Deborah. "You must think me quite inept." She took a sip of her beverage. It was tart and wonderfully cool. In spite of making a hash of the several country dances Signore Bonelli had attempted to teach her over the last hour, she was damp from exertion and felt the beginnings of a blister on her foot.

"Not at all," Deborah assured, her eyes crinkling with a smile. "These things take time. You're doing wonderfully."

Arcadia knew perfectly well that she was not *doing wonderfully*. Though it was kindly meant, Deborah's undeserved praise left Arcadia feeling hollow. Incredibly, she found herself wishing Sheri were here to issue one of his biting witticisms. When he'd scolded her for setting foot on the wrong London street, at least she'd had something to fight back against. Countermanding the petite marchioness, on the other hand, was nearly impossible. How could one refuse a woman so unflinchingly good?

And yet, the ball was a sword over her neck. She had to try for a stay of execution. "Deborah," she ventured, "is the ball really necessary—for a betrothal announcement, I mean? It is your birthday celebration, after all. May Lord Sheridan and I make our announcement at another event, such as …" Blast. Arcadia didn't know any other Society events. "A supper!" she blurted, suddenly inspired. "You mentioned earlier that you might have a supper. We could use that."

The older woman tilted her head quizzically. "A supper for our two families only. You must be introduced to Society, Arcadia dear. A ball is customary." She frowned. "Is it …" She sounded as uncertain as Arcadia felt. "Is it not what you wish? The ball?" Moisture rimmed her brown eyes; she pressed her hands to her cheeks. "I've overstepped, haven't I? It's your wedding, Arcadia, of course you must have whatever you'd like."

"Oh no," Arcadia breathed, taking Deborah's hand, feeling the very worst villain for upsetting the delicate woman. "No no no. The ball is … it's fine. Wonderful. I just hate to put you to so much trouble. The dress, the dancing lessons."

On a sigh, Deborah's fretful frown vanished. "It's no trouble, my dear. You cannot know how happy you've made our family. We would give you a hundred dresses. A dozen balls."

Arcadia shook her head. "How can that be? I've done nothing to earn your regard."

On the contrary, she'd done everything to earn the sweet lady's scorn. If Deborah knew what Arcadia and Sheri had planned, she would not be so free with sharing her modiste.

The door opened, admitting a gentleman Arcadia did not recognize. But Claudia's adoring smile revealed the identity of the handsome, golden-haired man.

"I heard there was to be dancing," Mr. De Vere announced to the room at large, "but I see only three splendid beauties at their ease. If this is what passes for a dancing lesson these days, then I'm happy to learn the steps of the latest craze."

Laughing, Claudia looped her arm through her husband's and drew him to Deborah and Arcadia. "We were only recovering our breath for a moment, Henry. Beware, Signore Bonelli is quite demanding. Before the day is out, Miss Parks and I shall be ready to make our debut at the ballet, will we not?"

Before Arcadia could protest the assessment, Claudia said, "Miss Parks, this is my Mr. De Vere." Awareness pulsed between the married couple. Arcadia didn't think she imagined how Henry's shoulders squared a bit more, that his chin notched upward with pride at being named *her* Mr. De Vere.

"A pleasure, Miss Parks." Mr. De Vere's hooded green eyes studied her with friendly assessment. "Claudia has been in alt since making your acquaintance the other day. I've heard little but rhapsodies over the delightful Miss Parks."

"Your wife is all kindness, sir, but I fear she has poised you for disappointment."

"Ladies are always too modest," Henry declared. "My darling bride is many things, Miss Parks, but *all kindness* is not one of them. Believe you me, if she has something other than a stellar opinion about you or any other person, I should hear about it. For my money, you're as good as beatified." He winked at his wife, then cast his gaze about. "Where is that wastrel, Zouche?"

Yes, where was her betrothed, Arcadia wondered.

Signore Bonelli, looking much more composed than when she'd seen him last, re-entered from the terrace. Waving his hands, he stopped the pianist's melodic trifling. "Are we ready to try again, ladies?"

"Perhaps skip ahead to the waltz, signore," Deborah suggested. "We'll leave the country dances to another day."

"Si, si!" he enthused, clasping his hands at his chest. "Every lady can waltz and, what's more" —he punctuated with a finger thrust skyward—"every lady *loves* to waltz. *Grazie,* my lady, for the excellent suggestion."

"Would you mind continuing without me?" Deborah asked. Her face looked a bit drawn, the luster of her eyes dimmed. The day's activities must have fatigued the poor lady. After assuring her they would soldier on in her absence, the dancing master escorted Deborah to the door, bowing and scraping every step of the way.

"Partner with Henry," Claudia whispered. "He's excellent at leading. You won't have any trouble."

But when Mr. De Vere gallantly offered Arcadia his hand, Bonelli would have none of it. "Signorina requires the very best instruction. She must have my guidance."

The Italian's palm rested on Arcadia's waist, and he caught her hand up in his other. She felt caged. Besides Arcadia's father, Sheri was the only man who had ever touched her like this. Her heart had beat faster when he'd held her, but with pleasure, not the unease currently squeezing through her limbs.

"Place your free hand on my shoulder, please." Bonelli's voice was low, his head canted close to her face.

Arcadia drew back. "No." He glowered and tugged her back into his grasp. "I don't want to dance," she insisted.

Claudia slanted a look at her. "Everything all right over there?" She and Henry were in position. Mr. De Vere's fingertips, Arcadia noted, drew circles on his wife's back. Arcadia didn't want Signore Bonelli touching her like that.

The dancing master grasped her arm and turned her aside. "The Marchioness of Lothgard wants you to waltz," he hissed so that the others could not hear. "Lord Lothgard is paying my exorbitant fee to teach you to waltz. Lord Sheridan expects his bride to waltz. Who are you to refuse?"

Who was she, indeed. Arcadia's objections to public dancing were subjective, she reminded herself, the product of being raised by her Indian ayah. Had she received more of her mother's guiding influence, or had she been sent to England at a younger age, Arcadia would have dreamed of her first London ball with starry eyes. Her apprehension shamed her, but she could not will it away.

Turning her attention to her breath for a few seconds, she attempted to distance herself from the discomfort. She raised her quaking hand to the Italian man's shoulder. He smirked. "*Bene.*" At his signal, the pianist struck the opening chord. Bonelli swept her in an arc. "*One*-two-three, *one*-two-three."

Arcadia tried to follow the pattern of his feet with her own, but the unwelcome weight of his hand on her waist made it difficult to concentrate.

"Left-right-left, left-right-left." The grip of his fingers tightened around her hand as he pulled her into a dizzying circle. The room was a blur of color and music and the sound of Claudia's laughter. Henry dipped his head and kissed his wife's jaw. The lady's hand slid from his shoulder to curve around the nape of his neck.

Arcadia averted her eyes from the intimate display and stumbled on yet another turn. Her heel came down, hard, on Signore Bonelli's instep. The Italian released her and threw his arms up. "It cannot be done!" he cried. "I cannot teach her to dance."

"You know this from one lesson?" Arcadia demanded, hands moving to her hips.

"Most of my students understand to pick their feet up off the floor, instead of shuffling about like an arthritic mole as you do."

"Please," Henry said, raising a placating hand, "allow me to dance with Miss Parks. She's overwhelmed by your expertise, signore."

Arcadia wasn't sure whether or not that was an insult, and the Italian couldn't seem to puzzle it out, either. After a moment, he relented on a huff. He and Claudia moved to the side to observe while Henry and Arcadia waltzed.

This was worse. Infinitely. Henry smiled and tried to tease her, but her skin crawled with the same sense of dread when he touched her. Moreover, Arcadia was standing in the arms of her friend's husband—while that same friend looked on, no less—and no one gave it a second thought!

Arcadia felt wretched. Her feet behaved a little better this time, but every step, every turn, she was acutely aware that others were watching her dance indecently with a man. A man she'd just met.

A man who was not Sheri, to whom she had been promised in marriage.

"You see," Henry said, dipping his head to meet her eyes. "You only wanted for an Englishman to show you the way of it. You're getting it now."

Arcadia's answering smile wavered.

Henry's brows drew together. "Miss Parks? Don't give Bonelli another thought. Those Continentals can be so high-handed. I hear you met with the French dressmaker who has the ladies all in a thrall, too."

Blinking back hot prickles, Arcadia nodded. She stomped Henry's foot.

He winced, but covered it with a grin and manfully carried on.

"Oh, I'm sorry," she cried.

"Think nothing of it, Miss Parks. Rarely have my toes been trod by so fetching a partner." He gave her waist a squeeze. It was probably supposed to be friendly, to reassure her. But Arcadia's heart beat double time against her ribs as another wave of distress rolled through her.

Missing the beat, she stepped on poor Henry's toes again.

And again.

And.

Again.

At last, even that stalwart gentleman had to bring the lesson to a halt. "Good progress, Miss Parks," he managed through clenched teeth as he hobbled off, his wife rushing to attend him.

The lump that had been riding around in Arcadia's chest since the moment Madame Doucet stripped her to her chemise rose to her throat and up her nose, burning all the way, finally exiting through her eyes in the form of scalding tears that splashed onto her cheeks.

Face lowered, Arcadia ran for the door, and plowed directly into a body.

A soft, small body that let out a startled yelp as it collided with Arcadia and was knocked onto the floor in a cloud of rice powder and jewels and umbrage. The older woman hit her bottom and rocked onto her back, splayed legs shooting straight into the air, satin skirts flying over her head.

"No!" Arcadia gasped. *Do not let it be her!*

Three steps away, Sheri watched the woman go down. A brow lifted over a coffee-hued eye. "Mother," he said to the heap of indignation on the floor, "allow me to introduce you to Miss Parks."

Chapter Seventeen

"Get me up this instant!" the dowager marchioness squawked.

Reaching into the tangle of aubergine satin, Sheri plucked his mother off the floor and set her back on tottering feet. He kept a steadying hand on her arm while she settled. "All right, madam?"

"An inkling of things to come, no doubt," the dowager muttered blackly. Of Arcadia, she demanded, "Well, gel, what have you to say for yourself?"

"Oh, my lady," Arcadia moaned. She looked utterly stricken, her lightly tanned face devoid of color except for two red splotches high on her cheekbones. Her mosaic eyes were wide and bright with tears, some of which had already been shed. The evidence was on her cheeks, where silvery tracks ran to her chin, and the tip of her nose was rather pink and soggy, now that he had a good look.

Behind her, the music room was like a reenactment of the aftermath of a battle in miniature. Henry De Vere was the walking wounded, turning in small, limping circles, while Claudia was trying to order him into a chair so she could nurse him in the field surgery. A spindly man of Mediterranean coloring, who must have been the dancing instructor, was the defeated general tearing his hair and weeping to the heavens. And through it all, the piper—or the pianist, in this case—went on playing the battle standard. A Viennese waltz was the score of this skirmish.

"My lady," Arcadia repeated, reaching a hand toward the dowager, then drawing it back. "I beg your pardon."

"Sheridan," his mother said, turning her head to address him, "you will complete the introduction now, so we can cease this infernal dancing about in the doorway."

"It would be my eternal delight. Mother, I am honored to present Miss Arcadia Parks. My dear, this ambrosial creature before you is the Dowager Marchioness of Lothgard, who is widely rumored to be my mother."

"Wicked child!"

He ought not goad his mother. Since luncheon, she had rung a peal over his head for dueling with Tyrrel and making the Zouche name a byword. If he did not reform, the dowager warned, not only would she endorse Eli's plan to cut him for the good of the family, she would also remove him from her will.

It was difficult to mind the thin ice beneath his feet when he saw his quip had the desired effect. Arcadia did not smile, but a little of the strain eased from her features. She regained her composure well enough to execute a pretty curtsy. "My lady."

"So you've said," the dowager drawled. "As far as I know, I've still got my wits, if you haven't just dashed them right out of my skull. Should I come to the point of forgetting my own identity, it's a comfort to know I can rely upon you to remind me of it, Miss Parks."

Arcadia ducked her face. "My … yes, ma'am."

In her highest heeled slippers, Sheri's mother stood just shy of five feet tall, but she managed to fill whatever room she occupied with the force of her consequence. Brushing past Arcadia, she strode into the music room, instantly drawing all eyes. "Sir," she said to Henry, "from your clumping gait, I deduce you, too, have had an adventurous encounter with Miss Parks. What has my son unleashed upon us?"

Sheri cupped his hand beneath Arcadia's elbow and drew her back into the room. He was surprised she permitted him the contact, but glad of it. "What the devil happened here?" he asked.

"I was learning the waltz," she answered grimly.

"And the result was this carnage?"

Color flooded her neck and jaw, and Sheri wanted to brush his fingertips over her, to feel the warmth of her blood rushing to the surface at the bidding of her emotions. He wanted to uncover more of that skin and learn in how many places he could elicit just such a rosy response.

"I didn't mean to," she said. "I just didn't care for, for all the …" Her voice faded. He followed the line of her gaze to where Henry was seated with Claudia perched on the arm of his chair, holding a glass of lemonade to his lips as if he was a damned invalid. And Henry, the besotted fool, lapped up the coddling without a scrap of shame.

"What didn't you care for, Arcadia?"

She cast a guilty look at him, then studied her toes. "The touching," she whispered.

Smoke clouded his brain. *The touching?* "Who?" His right hand flexed, then curled into a fist. "Who touched you? That Italian weasel?"

"And Mr. De Vere."

"I suppose Henry called him out on it; that explains his limp. But he'll never harm another innocent again, upon my honor. I'll snip his offensive fingers off with—wait." His brows snapped together. "*And* Mr. De Vere? Both of them?"

She nodded miserably. "I can't dance. I'm sorry, Sheri."

Pressing his palms together, Sheri brought his fingers to his lips and tried to puzzle his way through that one, to no avail. "I feel one statement does not naturally follow the other. What does your inability to dance have to do with the dancing master and Mr. De Vere molesting you?"

Her eyes widened. "Oh, no, nothing like that, my lord." She cast a furtive look at his mother, who was, in return, eyeing them with undisguised curiosity.

"Enough," Sheri said. "Everyone out, please. No, you stay," he said, pointing to the pianist. "Miss Parks wishes to demonstrate her newfound aptitude. After we dance, we shall join you all in the drawing room for tea."

"Signore!" cried the dancing master. "You must not attempt the minuet. And she's hopeless at the waltz. *I tried*, you must believe me."

The worm had done something to upset his fiancée. The extent of the offense remained to be seen, so Sheri withheld declaring punishment, but something primal and bloodthirsty stirred in his bones. He wouldn't mind poking his fives at the Italian's chin.

"Demmit, man, if I wanted a minuet at my betrothal ball, I'd marry Great-aunt Minerva."

Shooing the lot of them from the room, Sheri closed the door and went to Arcadia. She stood in the center of the room, slender and tall and graceful even in stillness. *Cannot dance, my eye.* If she couldn't dance, he was the king of Scotland.

At the pianoforte, the hired musician began a waltz, his fingers running embellishments up and down the ivories.

"I owe you an apology," Sheri said.

Her lashes fluttered once, twice. "For the other day?"

"I shouldn't have done what I did. You wanted a kiss, not …" Not to be shoved against a dirty brick wall and treated like one of his experienced lovers who could find their pleasure in a hurried coupling. Not to be subjected to his ravenous lust. Her hand drifted up from her side. Sheri took it, cradled it in both of his. Her fingers were slim and delicate, not meant to be bruised in some back alley assignation. "We struck a bargain. One night."

"We did."

The knot of hair at her nape was loose. Silken chestnut drapes curved gently about her temples and ears, framing the windows of her dazzling eyes. He longed to sink his hands into those strands, to prove he could behave better than a rutting beast.

Good God, if it were known how he'd made such a muck of kissing a virgin, he'd be more of a laughingstock than he'd already become. He wouldn't have even his reputation as a skillful lover left to hang his hat upon.

The musician reached the end of the piece, the final chord hanging in the abrupt silence.

"Another," Sheri requested. When the music began, he extended his hand, palm up. "Miss Parks, would you do me the honor?"

She eyed his hand warily. *She didn't like the touch.* Perhaps he shouldn't have asked her to dance. Perhaps he should have just gotten on with pounding the daylights out of Bonelli and De Vere and her uncle and anyone else who had caused her harm. The list was gaining length. It might be time to ask Harry to teach him to shoot. Pistols would be more efficient couriers of justice than fisticuffs.

During his brief sojourn in violent fantasy land, Arcadia slipped her hand into his. "I'm a menace," she warned as his hand nestled neatly into the small of her back like it belonged there. "Thus far, I have crunched underfoot the toes of every gentleman who has attempted to waltz with me." Her other hand came to his shoulder. He didn't tell her she was standing closer than strictly proper.

"You haven't danced with the right man." Sheri's foot swept to the side as he leaned into the music, pulling Arcadia with him.

"That's what Mr. De Vere said." Her face remained solemn. "Claudia may not forgive me for crippling her husband."

He snorted. "It would take stouter feet than yours to do him lasting harm, peahen. Besides," he added, closing his eyes to appreciate the sensation of her hip swaying gently as they danced, "Henry may have correctly stated the problem, but he was *not* the right man."

"And I suppose you are?" she asked tartly.

Sheri's eyes opened.

Her lips quirked to the side, one brow arched in challenge.

Unable to resist, Sheri drew her closer and executed a wide turn, causing his thigh to brush against hers. "You're waltzing with me perfectly well. My toes are wonderfully intact."

Her mouth screwed up and her back tensed. Sheri noticed how firm the muscles there felt below his hand. And the arm that she held aloft carried its own weight; her hand rested only lightly upon his. Arcadia Parks was strong.

The revelation further stirred his blood. At every turn, she had proved his presuppositions wrong. How would she surprise him next?

"I wish to say something," her melodious voice pronounced.

Yes, please. Anything. He'd happily listen to her read French's household ledger for the joy of holding that voice in his ears.

At his nod, her chin firmed. "At the risk of sounding ungrateful, my lord, the events of today do not rest easy with me."

She related her trip to Madame Doucet and the disaster of her dancing lesson, as well as the reasons why she found both objectionable.

"It must sound like foolishness to you." She worried her bottom lip between her teeth, her eyes anxious.

It did, in truth. It had never crossed Sheri's mind that an Englishwoman would find a ball distasteful for cultural reasons, much less that a chit half raised in a harem would harbor more stringent notions of modesty than any other maiden in London. The more Sheri learned of this *zenana* of hers, the more it sounded like a convent rather than a harem.

His face must have betrayed some of his thoughts, for her step suddenly faltered. He secured her with his arm and kept right on waltzing.

"I will try," she said, her tone imploring. "I don't wish to embarrass your family."

"Oh, the family can go hang." To her startled expression, he gave a rueful smile. "If anyone should be embarrassed, it is I. Mother was in a rare lather because of my manifold sins. I should have put her off when she insisted on meeting you, but I didn't suspect she'd be so uncivil."

"To be fair, she likely did not suspect she would be knocked to the ground by her prospective daughter-in-law."

"Deborah has never done anything half so brutal."

"Of course not," Arcadia muttered. "She'd never have to."

Sheri chuckled. It felt wonderful to laugh with a pretty woman in his arms and music—damn, were they already on to a new tune?—buoying them on a cloud. "Indeed, if my dear sister-in-law wished Mother cast to the depths, she'd need only ask, and who could resist her?"

"Not I," Arcadia answered. "I agreed to wear an obscene gown because I couldn't bear to hurt her feelings."

The mental image that jolted to mind thudded right to his groin. He did his level best to ignore it. "I'm convinced her unassailable kindness is really a Machiavellian device to enact the most angelic tyranny in history."

"A reasonable conclusion."

They shared a look of warm humor, which did little to blunt the edge of desire now slicing him from within, little by little. Nor did it lighten the burden of knowing he must raise a subject that had the potential to undo them both.

"Miss Parks," he said haltingly. "Arcadia."

"Yes?" She offered a teasing smile. Her hip deliberately nudged his hand. Saucy wench. Maddening, delectable, impossible wench. Below her breath, she hummed along with the melody. Through her breasts pressed lightly to his chest, Sheri felt the vibration. On the next turn, he lifted her off her feet. She laughed as her skirts swung wide, the hand on his shoulder clasping him tight, like she'd never let go.

"I'm afraid, peahen, that you might not fully grasp what our arrangement means."

The laughter in her eyes remained. "It means you will marry me and find my peacock and send me back to India. Quite a bargain in exchange for my participation."

Damn him. He should remain silent. He should marry her as planned and take her to bed, slake his lust upon her lean, strong body and learn what his name sounded like when cried in ecstasy in that rich voice. Then, and only then, could he let her go.

"It means you can never return to England. Not to good society, at least. And it means you can never lawfully marry another man. You'll never have children that are recognized as legitimate. Are you prepared to give that up?"

Well. That wiped the smile right off her face, as he knew it would.

For himself, Sheri had no concern on the subject of issue. Unless some freak accident wiped his brother and both nephews from the face of the earth, the Lothgard marquisate demanded no sons of Sheri's blood. He could safely plan on leading a quasi bachelorhood for the remainder of his life.

He was a cad for thinking so, but the perplexed frown that drew her lips downward was adorable. The shallow dip in her chin deepened to a dimple he was sorely tempted to taste.

"What are you saying?" she asked. "What if I'm not prepared to relinquish those things?"

"Then I won't hold you to our agreement. You'll be free to go."

Arcadia broke from his grasp. Quick breaths caused the bodice of her dress to draw tight across her breasts. Despite the matronly neckline, the tight fit of the top left little to the imagination.

"That's just it; I won't be free to go." Panting, she turned her face toward the French windows. The pink tip of her tongue swiped across her lip at a bead of perspiration. "If I don't marry you, they'll force me to marry elsewhere. Poorvaja and I will be stuck here. If I marry you," she gestured with an arm, "at least I'll be able to return to India. Those things, a husband and children, those were the price of my coming to England in the first place."

But even that had not really been her choice, he knew. She sounded so resigned to her fate, he almost offered to rescue her from it. He could pay for her passage to India, kidnap her from her aunt and uncle, and smuggle her onto the next ship sailing for Bombay. That would be the noble thing to do. Possibly the right thing to do.

But then he would be in the same grim predicament he'd been in before striking a deal with an Indian colonial. He would still be on the hook to find a bride, and had little hope of encountering another so willing and eager to leave him to live his life in peace.

And so he did not offer to be the gallant knight she so desperately needed.

"So you willingly hold to our arrangement?"

She nodded without hesitation. "Absolutely."

He bent his neck. "Very well." Taking her once more into his arms, he resumed their interrupted waltz. He rested his chin alongside her temple. "And I vow not to press untoward advances on you again. I hope you'll permit me some minor displays of affection for the sake of convincing the world of our match, but otherwise, I shall be the picture of propriety. I shan't trouble you for more than our agreed-upon wedding night. You still haven't said whether you accept my apology, by the by."

"Haven't I? Of course I do," she answered. She was warm and pliant in his arms and smelled like verbena and the dream of distant shores.

"Arcadia?" he said after a moment.

"Hm?"

"Don't change. Not for Deborah, not for my mother, and damned well not for me. I like you just the way you are, you know. Be as modest or as scandalous as you like. Don't dance at our ball, or dance every set—with me, or whomever you wish. I shall be content, so long as you are."

She slanted a look at him brimming with confusion. "Truly?"

He grunted his assent.

The clouds of confusion dissipated on a beaming smile. Her eyes were stained glass, illuminated from within. "You're my best friend, Sheri. The very best thing about England."

The unexpected remark hit him with the force of a cannonball packed with guilt in lieu of gunpowder. She knew the cost and she was willing to pay. He would have everything he wanted, a night with Arcadia, and then a lifetime of liberation. Why, then, did their bargain feel like impending disaster?

CHAPTER EIGHTEEN

"Have I told you yet how enchanting you look this evening?"

"Not in those precise words, my lord," Arcadia whispered back, meeting Sheri's warm gaze. "Thus far, you have called me *beautiful, resplendent,* and *breathtaking. Enchanting* is a new entry to the list."

"I hope you've plenty of ink and parchment, for it shall not be the final word you hear on the subject, I vow." His eyes made another slow perusal of her person from tip to toe, lingering on her bosom, causing no end of embarrassment.

After another visit to Madame Doucet for a final fitting, Arcadia now suffered the indignity of this obscene dress. A sheer overlayer of pistachio silk floated above a cloth-of-gold underdress. The skirts were cut on the bias below the high waist, accentuating the nip of her waist and the flare of her hips. The bodice was nothing more than two swags of the green silk draped perilously low, meeting in a deep vee between her breasts. Tiny gold beads were sewn into the folds, adding gleam rather than sparkle. An edge of the gold underdress peeked above the green, but all of her tugging and cursing had afforded her only another scant inch of decency.

As it was, the tops of Arcadia's breasts erupted over the low neckline, presented with great fanfare like two pale sweet dumplings on a gold offering platter in a Hindu temple.

In the back, her shoulder blades were also exposed, leaving her feeling half-naked. Perversely, her hands, one part she cared nothing about covering, were encased in white satin gloves that reached all the way to her elbows.

Despite stringently protesting the event, Poorvaja had spent two hours dressing Arcadia's hair. Each strand had been carefully wrapped around a curling rod, then finger-combed to achieve loose waves. The ayah then lightly oiled her fingers and deftly twisted sections from the left side up to the crown of Arcadia's head, creating a shining, fanciful swirl. The remainder had been left to cascade loose over Arcadia's right shoulder.

The glint of appreciation in Sheri's eyes as he once more followed the trail of her hair to the gulley between her breasts might not have been too bad, were they in private. But there had been no private moments of late. In the nearly two weeks since renewing their agreement at her dancing lesson, Sheri had been the very picture of a dutiful fiancé, calling often and taking Arcadia for drives or out looking for her peacock (no luck on that front). They'd been to see the menagerie at the Tower and to the theater. On days he didn't come to call, he sent little gifts of flowers, candies, and ribbons.

He'd courted her for all to see, a man besotted by his bride. Lies. All lies. The moment she called him her best friend, a barrier had dropped between them like a portcullis slamming home. His courtship had been empty of the frank exchanges she had most appreciated about him.

As the door opened to admit the first guests, he gave her a secret smile, and Arcadia's heart performed a somersault. Why must he be such a very convincing liar? Then she was smiling at faces she'd soon forget, repeating names she'd never remember. Sheri introduced her as *my darling Miss Parks* and called her *the woman who has made me the happiest of men*. And all these people—the same ones who had tittered about her fainting spell in Hyde Park and repeated unkind things about her after she'd walked down St. James's Street—swallowed Sheri's sugary, whopping falsehoods and wished them happy.

Could she and Sheri really get away with this? What if someone discovered their plan to marry and separate, and put a stop to it? What if she was, after all, forced to marry Cousin ... Oh, gracious, what was his name?

"Cousin Cyril!" Lady Delafield enthused as she accepted a buss on the cheek from a gentleman, "what a marvelous surprise! Allow me to make you known to our dear Lucretia's daughter, Miss Arcadia Parks."

The man Arcadia had narrowly evaded was nothing like the old, doddering country parson she'd envisaged when her uncle first mentioned sending for her mother's cousin to come marry the family *enfant terrible*. To be sure, a little age showed at the corners of the vicar's eyes and in his thinning hair. But he retained youthful good looks, aided, perhaps, by strong bones—including the family chin, which showed much more favorably on a male than on a female like herself, Arcadia noted. His somber black-and-white attire only set him apart from the glittering gathering.

Reverend Mr. Cousin Cyril Fisk bowed over her hand, then kissed her cheek. At her side, she felt Sheri stiffen.

"You've the look of your mother," her cousin said, a wistful gleam in his eye. "A rare flower she was, Lucretia. You can't imagine the torment I suffered in having you offered before me, then snatched away at once."

His eyes flitted to Arcadia's décolletage.

"Darling, who is this?" Sheri interjected, his tone polite, but the flash of his teeth promising new kinds of suffering.

She felt a feminine thrill, while holding back a giggle. Almost, she regretted not having had the opportunity to get to know Fisk as a suitor, if he could inspire jealousy in the great Chère Zouche. If she must tolerate the adoring looks three-quarters of the females present cast in the direction of her intended, then certainly he could survive her being admired by one country parson.

Sir Godwin came, too, and Arcadia was glad to see him, despite—or perhaps, a little because of—a repetition of Sheri's possessive display. Soon after him came the De Veres. Claudia kissed Arcadia's cheek and made her turn a circle so she could see the finished gown. With a promise to talk later, Claudia took her husband's arm and disappeared into the ballroom. Arcadia was grateful for the vivacious young matron's friendship. Her social circle in London was embarrassingly small. She missed the closeness of the little English community of the station, and the rowdy fun of the *zenana* at Poorvaja's family home.

Mr. and Mrs. Dewhurst, who were also particular friends of Sheri's, greeted her very kindly. Mrs. Dewhurst clung tightly to her husband's sleeve as they moved down the line, and Arcadia wondered if that elfin lady might not also be daunted by the grand gathering.

A giant appeared, wearing dark blue breeches and a matching coat, with a slapdash knot tied in his cravat. "A pleasure to see you again, Miss Parks." He sketched a bow.

He certainly looked familiar, and she wouldn't think she'd forget meeting a man of such memorable stature, but she couldn't place a name to his face. "Have we met, sir?"

"Not formally," Sheri said. "Mr. Wynford-Scott was with me that day in Hyde Park."

"Oh, yes," she said, as her memory supplied the vague outline of a hulking shadow, the fear of which had caused her to cringe against Sheri for protection. "Thank you for your assistance, Mr. Wynford-Scott. It means a great deal that you came to the aid of a stranger."

The tips of his ears pinkened. "My pleasure, ma'am."

Too soon, the receiving line broke up. Sheri escorted Arcadia into the ballroom and, for the first time, she began to understand the full scope of a London ball. Around her were women draped in expensive silks and satins and glittering jewels, but all Arcadia could see were breasts, everywhere creamy, fluffy mounds of flesh popping out of bodices like cotton bolls. Men wore breeches every bit as tight as Signore Bonelli's. Their fine frock coats were cut away, drawing attention to their uniquely masculine attributes. Cloaked as it might be with refined manners and luxurious trappings, there was no concealing the true purpose of the ball: it was a mating ritual, plain and simple. Why else would all in attendance so shamelessly advertise their private areas? The air was rife with sexual potential.

And Arcadia was on the arm of the most flagrantly virile male of the lot. Lord Nothing, she had once called him, but now she saw his domain for what it truly was. Female eyes followed their slow progress. Lips pouted and parted. Fans tapped bared collarbones. A collective sigh of *Chère* rose from the female portion of the throng like a hot wind sighing through the *mofussil* hills in the dry season. There was no lady Sheri did not know. He seemed to have a word to drop in every pearl-adorned ear. In a realm of fleshly desires, Lord Sheridan Zouche was king.

From these women, Arcadia expected to meet with unkindness spurred by jealousy. After all, she had claim to the man they all wanted. Instead, she was most frequently greeted and dismissed while the ladies went right on throwing themselves at Sheri. There were a few smirks, and one or two sympathetic smiles from the older women, but that was all. No claws. No hair-pulling. Some innate feminine knowledge inside Arcadia recognized that she was not perceived as a threat. Even at her betrothal ball, no one believed Arcadia had won Sheri's heart.

She very much feared that his attentive courtship had managed to bamboozle only one person: her.

As previously decided, he brought her to the ornate sofa that had been placed on a raised dais centered against the far wall. Since the marchioness would not dance, either, Arcadia and Deborah were given a joint throne from which to oversee the ball.

"Here we are, my love," Sheri said grandly, kissing her hand before relinquishing it. He pivoted and bowed. "Miss Poorvaja, would you favor me with the opening set?"

Arcadia's mouth popped open in surprise. Taking to heart Sheri's claim that she might do anything she wished, she had asked Poorvaja to attend the ball. Her aunt would have a fit of the vapors over a servant attending the ball as a guest, but Arcadia didn't care. Poorvaja was more family than anyone else. In answer to her young mistress's grand gesture of sentiment and flouting of convention, Poorvaja had flatly refused. Jalanili was free to make a public disgrace if she wished, but she would not take part in the orgy.

Swiveling about, Arcadia witnessed the astonishing sight of her ayah in a ballroom. True, she sat in a chair pressed to the wall with her knitting in her lap, but there she was. As she'd arranged Arcadia's hair and prognosticated her charge's moral bankruptcy earlier in the evening, Poorvaja had given no hint that she had changed her mind about attending herself. She'd even added a lace collar to her plain, gray woolen dress.

At first, Poorvaja did not respond directly to Sheri's invitation. But her needles flew faster, and her face turned a dusky rose. "You're a bad man," she finally pronounced without raising her eyes. "I should skewer your heart and feed it to a dog."

Several guests gasped, but Sheri only grinned. "As you say, madam." He winked at Arcadia before dashing off to secure another partner. In moments, he was leading a beanpole of a miss with an overbite and spots away from the wall to join other couples in one of several square formations.

The opening notes of the dance rang through the ballroom. Partners bowed and curtsied. Arcadia's pulse leaped in her throat. The women truly *were* going to dance in public, Arcadia realized in a daze, and she had agreed to do the same for the supper waltz.

In horrified fascination, Arcadia watched the dancers extend their arms into the centers of the squares and begin rotating the shapes with intricate little skips and hops. Her eyes tracked the movements of one group, then the next. She spotted Claudia and Mr. De Vere, but Arcadia's friends danced with other people, not each other. Mr. De Vere being in the company of another woman did not faze her, but the sight of Claudia in the arms of the towering Mr. Wynford-Scott made Arcadia flinch.

This is how things are done in England, she reminded herself. *Claudia is not doing anything immoral.* As she spun, Claudia kicked back her head and laughed, carefree and having a wonderful time. Despite her own misgivings, Arcadia smiled at her friend's enjoyment.

Inevitably, her wandering gaze arrested on Sheri. He carried himself with a noble bearing she had only seen in one other man: Suri Shah, the Mughal prince. Not even Lord Lothgard matched his younger brother's air of self-assurance.

He danced with the fluid grace of a man perfectly at ease in his own skin. His emerald coat defined the slope of his broad, muscled shoulders and accentuated the lines of his torso all the way to his slender waist. White breeches clung audaciously to his thighs, allowing Arcadia to watch his muscles play with every perfectly executed maneuver of the dance, a marble statue in motion.

His attention was fixed on his dancing partner, as though the wallflower were the only woman in existence. His sinful lips, turned up just slightly at the corner, bestowed the woman with a private smile Arcadia knew all too well.

Unwelcome jealousy crept through her bones. But then she saw the wallflower's brilliant smile, how utterly delighted she was to dance with handsome Lord Sheridan. After her, he chose a heavy-set matron of middling years for his next partner, and then he sat out a set to pay court to a white-haired crone who had been nodding off in the corner. He flirted outrageously with the old woman and her friends. The sound of their scandalized laughter carried over the room.

"Lest you think he's doing this for your benefit"—Deborah leaned over to touch Arcadia's arm—"you should know he's always like this. The beauties who flock around him, they haven't a chance. Not in a ballroom. Sheri always chooses the girls who are overlooked, the matrons who've been left behind."

Chère, they called him. Their dear. *He likes to make women happy,* Claudia had told Arcadia once. She saw the truth of those words in action. While gentleman after gentleman slipped away to the card room, Sheri spent each set with a woman who would otherwise have remained unnoticed. For most of those ladies, their set with Sheri was the only one they danced all night.

Rather than a burden, it became a pleasure to watch Sheri pay attendance to these other women. And yet she couldn't help but feel a bit of moroseness on her own behalf. While Sheri brought genuine pleasure to these other ladies, the compliments he paid Arcadia were meant to impress others, not her. How lovely it must be to have Sheridan Zouche want nothing more than to make one smile for one's benefit alone, instead of for the benefit of an audience.

She remembered the way he'd kissed her that day in the alley, so wild and deep and free, how every stroke of his tongue and rub of his thigh against her secret flesh had seemed focused on giving her the greatest possible pleasure in the least time possible. It had been reckless and overwhelming. Even now, her breasts tingled at the memory. She shifted her legs against a faint aching between her thighs. Yet even then, there had been potential onlookers on the nearby sidewalk. Their first kiss, too, had had an audience. What would Sheri do when it was just the two of them on their wedding night? Would he lose ardor with a lack of witnesses, or would the privacy free him to truly unleash his passions?

There were but two weeks remaining before that fateful night, when Arcadia's questions would be answered.

"Do you not dance at your own celebration, Miss Parks?" Sir Godwin stood at the edge of the dais, dressed all in black but for his usual red cravat. In deference to the formality of the occasion, perhaps, his neckcloth was scarlet satin, the fabric shining slick against his throat, like a ghastly wound.

"No, sir, I do not," she replied. "It is Lady Lothgard's special night, as well, and as you see, she and I have committed ourselves to an evening of sedentary leisure."

"Might you make an exception for one who can claim your friendship earlier than any other knave present?"

Giggling, Arcadia shook her head. "I'm afraid not, Sir Godwin."

"Alas," he sighed, "you wound me. Fair goddesses, remain upon your plinth, and I shall worship and venerate from afar." Bowing, he took a seat beside Poorvaja. The two did not converse. He simply watched her knitting needles as if he were in a stupor.

Finally, the moment Arcadia had been dreading arrived. Walking shoulder to shoulder, Sheri and Lord Lothgard approached the dais. The marquess was a little taller than Sheri and a bit thicker through the middle, and his years wore well on his face. But Sheri was in no way the lesser man. Sheri ... Well, Sheri swaggered. Leaving stately consequence to the marquess, the younger Zouche trained slumberous eyes on Arcadia, his mouth kicking up on one side in an insolent smile.

Arcadia's heart stuttered in her chest. Her underarms went clammy, and the inside of her mouth became a desert.

The men stopped and bowed to Arcadia and Deborah like courtiers before their queens. In unison, they stepped onto the dais and helped the ladies to their feet.

The marquess raised his hand for silence, but an expectant hush already blanketed the room.

"Friends," his voice easily carried over the assembly, "I thank you for honoring us with your presence tonight for this, the annual commemoration of my lovely wife's birthday." Cheers and applause swept the room. He raised Deborah's hand to his lips. The marchioness shyly ducked her head against Lothgard's shoulder.

Turning once more to the crowd, Lothgard said, "We've another cause for celebration tonight. It is my great honor to announce the betrothal of my brother, Lord Sheridan Zouche, to Miss Arcadia Parks. On behalf of our family, I extend my welcome and familial affection to Miss Parks."

The marquess shook Sheri's hand, then bussed Arcadia on the cheek, while Deborah hugged and kissed both of them. Arcadia's aunt and uncle stood beside the dais. And so did Poorvaja. The dowager held herself apart from Arcadia's family, but it didn't matter. The sight of Poorvaja bravely facing down a ballroom full of half-naked Englishpersons had Arcadia's heart near to bursting.

Sheri came to her side and offered his arm. "Shall we, my dear?" His eyes conveyed another layer of question. *Are you sure?*

Not at all. But she nodded anyway and stepped off the dais. She'd agreed to do this. She *could* do this.

In the center of the brightly illuminated ballroom, with hundreds of eyes looking on, Arcadia stepped into Sheri's arms, not just to participate in an activity anathema to her upbringing, but to lead the way.

"Breathe, peahen," Sheri reminded her. "And smile. You're happy, remember?"

Beating back the herd of elephants stampeding through her stomach, Arcadia jerked her lips up. "*You're* happy," she corrected, tilting her head and batting her eyelashes as other women had. "I, on the other hand, would rather be on fire."

A crease appeared in his cheek just as his hand slipped around her waist and the music began. He twirled her into the opening steps of the waltz.

Almost immediately, she faltered; Sheri's arm held firm, and he performed a graceful turn. Arcadia's eyes darted to the onlookers, but no one else seemed to have detected the misstep. Claudia caught her notice and waved.

"Don't look at them, Arcadia, look at me."

He wasn't nervous in the least, drat the man. Years of dancing with hopeless partners had trained him for this very moment. Sheri hummed along with the tune, genuine enjoyment shining in his eyes.

"*One* two three, *one* two three," he encouraged beneath his breath. "That's it; you're doing marvelously. No one will suspect you didn't know how to dance before last week, and they'll never guess how many toes were sacrificed to the cause."

Arcadia's lips tugged in amusement. "Don't make me laugh," she warned. "I'll lose track of my feet and land us both in a heap."

One finger curled lightly against her back, a teasing touch no one else would notice. "I might not mind landing in a heap with you, peahen. Shall we give it a try and see what happens?"

Her cheeks heated, and his insolent grin deepened. "That's a remarkably fetching shade of pink. I should like to see you wearing nothing but that. Do you know I think you're the most intrepid lady of my acquaintance?"

Arcadia gave him an arch look. "Don't suppose I didn't hear that naughty remark."

"The what?"

"The naughty remark."

"The what?"

"The … Oh! Don't laugh at me."

"I like the way you say 'naughty.' It makes me want to misbehave for the pleasure of hearing that word upon your lips." His gaze traveled to her mouth, and lingered there. "In fact, I like the way you say everything. Your voice is sinfully delicious. If it were a pastry, I'd gorge myself on it and gain five stone. I'm a glutton for your voice, Miss Parks."

His own voice, pitched low and rumbling in his chest as he complimented her so outrageously, made her joints feel loose. Arcadia's breath caught, lifting her breasts further from their precarious confinement. She felt womanly and good and didn't much care who saw.

But then, suddenly, the music ended. Arcadia blinked. "Over already?"

Sheri tucked her to his side to lead her to the dining room. "Nothing simpler. Painless. In time, you may even find the activity pleasurable."

He was being wicked again. *Naughty.* And she liked it. It was the first glimmer she'd seen, since her dancing lesson, of the man who teased and argued. She'd seen Lord Sheridan nearly every day, but she'd missed Sheri. She'd missed her friend.

"It was a triumph," she said, slanting a look up at him. "Silly to you, I know, but a triumph for me."

He leaned over and said in her ear, "Victory becomes you, peahen. Well done." And the warmth was in his smile again, as well as the little bit of longing in his eyes that she sometimes glimpsed, a yearning boy who wanted so much to please and to be pleasing.

"Thank you, Sheri. I couldn't have done it without you."

He waggled his brows. "Naturally not."

After a pleasant supper topped by a splendid birthday cake and several toasts raised in honor of the marchioness and the betrothed couple, the dancing resumed. Once more, Sheri led spinsters and antidotes out onto the floor. Deborah had retired after supper, so Arcadia had the raised sofa all to herself. Poorvaja had abandoned her post and slipped away at some point. Arcadia was grateful her dear ayah had made the effort to come, even if she hadn't been able to see the ball through to the end. In fact, she reflected, feeling pleasantly full from her meal and a little bit tired, the ball wasn't nearly so tawdry as it had first seemed. The clothes were indecent, of course, but everyone had been so lovely, it was hard to keep thinking of the ball as a cesspool of orgiastic excess.

Soon, she spotted Claudia making her way over, towing Mrs. Dewhurst behind her. The two women climbed onto the dais. Claudia plopped onto the sofa beside Arcadia in a billow of rose muslin. "What a crush!" the woman exclaimed.

"Is that good?" Arcadia asked.

"Not always, but in this case, yes," Claudia said. "Everything has been perfect, wouldn't you say, Lorna?"

Mrs. Dewhurst's turquoise eyes swept the room. "Most agreeable," she agreed. "You and Sheri make a handsome couple, Miss Parks. It was a pleasure to watch you dance."

"Please," Arcadia said, "if you're on *Sheri* basis with my intended, then you must call me Arcadia, as well."

"And I'm Lorna." She tucked a wayward corkscrew curl behind her ear, then nudged Claudia to make room for her on the seat.

Claudia clapped. "Now that we're all cozy, I must tell you the brilliant idea I've had, Arcadia."

"Another scheme? You warned me yourself—"

"There is no potential for this one to end in catastrophe. I swear it to you upon my brother's life."

Arcadia leaned forward to look over at Lorna. "Does she have a brother?"

Above cheeks generously sprinkled with freckles, Lorna's eyes danced. "Many, in fact. She may value them very cheap."

"I never would!" Claudia protested. "Oh, you're both abominable. I adore you immensely. This is exactly like being with my sisters. Anyway, if you're quite finished heaping scorn upon my head, then I shall tell you The Plan." Her eyes went wide with import.

"How do you do that?" Arcadia marveled.

"I told Lorna about the yoga demonstration you promised me, and she is also rabidly interested."

"Not my precise words …"

"I suggested," Claudia continued, "and Lorna agreed, that Elmwood would be the perfect venue. It's not too far from Town, but out in the country just a bit, so it will be nice and private."

"The gentlemen could come, too," Lorna suggested, "and we'll make a small party of it. Nothing much, just a day or two, as I know you're beset with wedding plans. You might like a little break from it, though."

"Indeed I would, though it might be best to wait until after the wedding." The idea of escaping the city was vastly appealing, so Arcadia readily agreed to the idea—The Plan, in Claudia parlance.

"Good heavens, what is she doing?"

Arcadia tracked the direction of Claudia's attention. Across the room, a raven-haired beauty in amethyst silk was weaving through the glittering mass on unsteady legs. Heads turned as she passed.

"Sheri," the woman called. "Sheri, Chère, Share! Where are you?"

At that moment, Arcadia's bridegroom was squiring an elderly lady about the perimeter of the chamber. Glancing over his shoulder, he frowned at the newcomer, then returned his charming smile to the old woman. He settled her into a chair and accepted her pinch on his cheek, then hurried to intercept the lady in purple.

The beauty ran the last several steps and threw her arms around his neck. He swung her in a circle.

Arcadia's throat constricted. "Who is that?" she rasped.

"Lady Fay. Elsa," Claudia said. "Oh, but you mustn't, you mustn't think …"

Elsa the Beautiful lifted onto her toes and pushed her mouth full against Sheri's.

The ballroom was rapidly falling silent. And the night was rapidly losing the rosy glow Arcadia had imagined after the victory of her waltz. All night, she'd watched her fiancé pay court to other women and she'd found it endearing, but this … This was not attention offered to a lonely old widow or a hopelessly shy spinster. Sheri had his hands on another woman. Had kissed another woman right in front of her.

This fascinating tidbit was not lost on the crowd. Heads swiveled from Arcadia to Sheri and Elsa and back again. "Chère," the people said again, but this time it wasn't an admiring sigh. This time it was an ominous rumble.

Sheri lifted his face from Elsa's and brought his eyes to Arcadia's. One instant. Two women. Pain sliced Arcadia's heart to ribbons, but she denied herself the right to it even as her soul cried out. Their understanding comprised of a cold marriage contract and a premeditated separation. Fidelity was not in the offering. In fact, Sheri had made it abundantly clear that he neither promised nor demanded fidelity. He'd spoken of illegitimate children, as if her eventual partnering with another man was a foregone conclusion. Why on earth, then, would she think he would be faithful to her, even for the duration of their brief, false betrothal?

But she had thought it, foolishly. Assumed. And it had been proven wrong, like every assumption she'd had about this man.

Then he grabbed Elsa's wrist and dragged her across the ballroom to the dais.

No. Arcadia did not want this. She did not want to meet his mistress. Had he been born in another place, Sheri might have assembled the largest *zenana* in India. Women would line up for miles to be a wife or concubine of the great Chère Zouche, happy for whatever scrap of his attention they might grab for themselves.

But not Arcadia. Her heart was not unselfish enough to share a man. Not this man, anyway.

Raw panic drove Arcadia to her feet, preparing her to fly, but the determined set of Sheri's jaw held her in place. His mouth was a hard slash as he tugged the stumbling, giggling Lady Fay to his side.

"Elsa," he said tightly, "you have the honor of meeting my betrothed, Miss Parks. Arcadia, my love, this is—"

"*My love?*" Elsa slapped Sheri's shoulder and threw her head back, howling laughter spilling from her beautiful throat and soft breasts bouncing on their purple bed. Her laughter put lie to Sheri's pretty words, exposed them for the hollow noise they were.

For the first time tonight, Arcadia was ashamed. Presenting herself in a shocking state of undress had not done it. Publicly dancing in mixed company had not done it. But Elsa, with her endless, knowing laughter, shamed her to the core.

CHAPTER NINETEEN

Sheri saw her eyes shutter, and he felt like he'd just been robbed of the sun. God knew he deserved to wallow in darkness, and he'd begun to suspect that he would do just that on the day Arcadia sailed for India. But that day was not yet come, and he would not allow Elsa's embarrassing display to take the light from him prematurely.

Standing on the dais before him, Arcadia was a goddess, gorgeous and unfathomable. Madame Doucet's ingenious gown of green and gold clung to her bronzed skin like the patina of long ages. The light slipped over the twists and curls of her sun-kissed hair, turning it into a river of liquid gold that flowed over her exposed, kissable shoulders to the promised land of her breasts. All night, he'd wanted to worship at her feet. To tell her how damned proud he was of her for finding the courage to wear that dress and dance in his arms. And after he offered his veneration, he wanted to worship her with his body.

That bit wouldn't happen, of course, but a man could dream.

Damn Elsa and her bloody, gin-soaked laughter. He was so angry he could shake her.

Keenly aware of the onlookers pressing in around them, ravenous for a spectacle, he quickly acted to allay the damage. He sent Arcadia a pleading look. *Stay there,* he mouthed. Forcing a laugh, he turned with Elsa and scanned the room. His brother had a hand on their mother's shoulder, seemingly restraining her from flaying Sheri then and there. And Lady Delafield was as puce as her turban.

"My dear, it wasn't *that* funny," he drawled, pinching the inside of Elsa's arm.

"Owww," she complained, but at least she'd ceased that infernal laughing.

From his prodigious elevation, Norman's gaze found Sheri's. An unspoken request was met with a nod, and the other man came to them, gently nudging his way through the crowd, mumbling "Excuse me. I beg your pardon. I'm so sorry," to everyone he passed.

Sheri whispered his instructions to the big man. Norman's paw wrapped around Elsa's elbow. "Well, if it's cake you want, Lady Fay, then it's cake you shall have." Norman, bless him, employed a tone he must have been cultivating for courtroom use as part of his barrister training. Sonorous and authoritative with just the right amount of dull, he conveyed respectability in a way Sheri never could.

Elsa sputtered. "I don't want—"

"To inconvenience the cook," Norman interjected, inexorably drawing Elsa from the room at a sedate, respectable pace. "You are all consideration, my lady. But it's already been cut. We'll just slip into the kitchen and nick a slice."

Huffing through his nose, Sheri hustled back to Arcadia. Claudia and Lorna flanked her now, handmaidens of the golden goddess.

"Will you dance with me?" He'd no right to make the request. She had granted his one waltz. "Let them see all is well between us."

The corners of her eyes tightened as something crackled to life inside the mosaics. Then it was gone, replaced by a false smile. "I should love to dance, but—" Her eyes slid over his shoulder. Sheri pivoted. Brandon and Henry were nearing the stage.

"Mr. De Vere," Arcadia said, "would you grant me the opportunity to redeem myself, if I promise to spare your toes?"

Henry shot a wary look at Sheri, but gave a slight bow. "It should be my honor, madam." He took Arcadia's hand and whisked her to the floor for the final waltz of the night.

Brandon led his wife out, leaving Sheri to partner with Claudia. The music began, and Sheri maneuvered to keep an eye on Arcadia.

If Sheri thought he possessed some special power that granted Arcadia the talent of dancing, he was instantly disabused of that notion. Not only did she not stumble once, but she floated in Henry's hands as if on a cloud. She bent her head, which shone like polished heartwood, close to hear something Henry said. She laughed gaily and swayed her hips. Sheri knew exactly what Henry's hands were experiencing, and he was livid.

The touching. She hadn't liked the touching of dancing. Yes, well, Sheri understood now and didn't much care for it any longer, either.

"Good thing I'm not looking to you for a boost to my self-esteem."

Sheri startled. His eyes snapped to Claudia.

"Merciful heavens, you forgot you were dancing with me, didn't you?"

"Of course not!" *Yes.*

She lifted a skeptical brow. "You should be smoothing things over with your fiancée, in any event."

"I will," he insisted, "just as soon as this dance is over. I had to give Norm some time to remove Elsa. Arcadia and I will make a sanguine departure, not run screaming from the room in the wake of impropriety."

Claudia's light brown brows drew together on a frown. "That was very badly done of Lady Fay."

Sheri was a gentleman, and Elsa had been his friend for many years. So he would refrain from agreeing with Claudia and further wishing the woman in question to perdition. "She was simply caught up in a moment of high spirits."

When the dance ended, Sheri deposited Claudia with her husband and collected his wife-to-be. Arcadia said nothing to him, but offered words of thanks and farewell to everyone they encountered. He ground his teeth in frustration at the glacial pace. He spotted Poorvaja near the door and, when they finally reached it, he asked her to accompany them.

He opened the door to a drawing room and gestured the women inside. Arcadia, seeing that Norman and Elsa were within, balked. "Please, peahen." He touched her lower back, and she bolted into the room as if prodded by a hot poker.

Sheri turned to close the door and was astonished to see Sir Godwin Prickering hurrying up the corridor in hot pursuit, his face nearly as red as his stupid cravat.

"Unbelievable!" The anger Sheri had been holding at bay licked up his spine. "It is bad enough that you constantly moon after Miss Parks and plague her with your prosy verse, but to give chase at our betrothal ball! I should call you out."

The poet's eyes flashed. Tucking his nose into the air, he shot back, "The same betrothal ball at which you quite publicly pursued another woman, need I remind you. Perhaps it is I who should call *you* out, sirrah, since you've no care for the lady's honor."

Sheri's pulse pounded in his temples. "Stay out of it, you contemptible widgeon," he ground out, then slammed the door in Sir Godwin's supercilious face.

Pivoting on the heel of his dancing shoe, Sheri wasted no time with preliminaries. "Norman, you're here to make sure she"—he pointed at Elsa—"doesn't try to escape. But you're also a solicitor, so I expect you to honor the cone of silence," he said, describing a circle with his hands.

"You aren't my client, Zouche," the tall man said. "And besides—"

"Damnation!" Sheri dug through his pockets until he turned up a half shilling, which he slapped into Norm's palm. "Now I'm your client. Be quiet, try not to hear anything, and make sure Elsa stays put. And Miss Poorvaja"—he rounded to face the ayah—"is chaperoning, since *some* of us," he said with a speaking look at Elsa, who slouched in a wingback chair, "have demonstrated a marked inability to behave in accordance with the strictures of good society."

"Don' you dare rip up at me," Elsa slurred. "I din' do nothin' I haven't done a thousan' times before."

The sudden spike of pressure behind his eyeballs might have popped them right from of his head. "One does not kiss the bridegroom on the mouth in the middle of his betrothal ball, Elsa, especially when one is not the bridegroom's bride. Were you absent the day that concept was introduced at finishing school?"

She scowled darkly. "You're become a sanc …" Her head nodded; she jerked it up, blinked. "Sanctimonious ol' prig."

"Miss Parks." Sheri swiveled, giving his sotted friend his back. His fiancée stood before the hearth, her shoulders and arms limned by the firelight behind her, so lovely, his breath caught. He cleared his throat. "Arcadia, I apologize for what you saw in the ballroom. Elsa—Lady Fay, that is—is a friend of mine, nothing more. But our greeting was … over-exuberant. And for that I most sincerely beg your pardon."

He did not add that Elsa had tripped and hurtled headlong into him, that he'd grabbed her up and spun to expend the momentum and prevent them from bowling over ancient Lady Dane, whom he'd just seen to her seat. Nor did he add that Elsa was inebriated to the point of impaired judgment, although that last was abundantly obvious to all and sundry. Why she'd chosen to put in her appearance after supper and three sheets to the wind, he had no idea. Likely Elsa didn't, either.

"My lord," Arcadia said, lifting a hand, "you needn't explain yourself to me. You must do as you wish, of course."

Elsa snorted. She dug a flask out of her reticule, different from the one Sheri had seen in her boudoir. "No wonder you picked her over me, Sheri." She twisted off the top and sniffed the contents.

"She's got much lower expectations inna husband than I've." She tipped the flask to her lips. Norman plucked it from her hand. "Hey!" she squawked.

The drunkard spoke truth, and it stoked hot flames in Sheri's belly. Arcadia *should* have higher expectations. She deserved the same loyalty and respect she gave her friends, not to be humiliated by her groom at her own betrothal ball.

Kicking her legs up over the arm of her chair and swinging her feet, Elsa addressed Arcadia directly. "Iss true, you know." Her glassy eyes crossed, then regained focus. "Sheri's been my frien' for years and years. We've never been lovers; we just compare notes." At a prompting nudge from Norman, she added, "An' I'm sorry for kissing Sheri at your ball. Beg pardon. It was very bad, and I shan't do it again. You may cane my palms if you'd like." She extended her hands; her head fell back to the arm of the chair, and she burst into laughter.

On a weary sigh, Norman lifted her into his arms. "I'll see she gets home."

Sheri nodded his thanks. While his friends cleared the room, he pulled out his quizzing glass and spun it on its chain at his side.

There was a fraught silence emanating from the woman behind him. *Women*, he corrected himself. Poorvaja was still present. But the Indian woman was tranquil in her silence. The tension all radiated from his bride.

He turned to meet her gaze. Their eyes held for a long moment. He wanted to take her in his arms and remind her what a real kiss felt like. He'd put her in front of a mirror and let her see what his passion looked like, so she'd never again mistake his intentions.

Never again. That sounded like a very long time. But he and Arcadia didn't have a very long time, only the duration of her sojourn in England. He was being hospitable. Ensuring her stay was comfortable. After she left, Sheri would kiss any number of women with whatsoever intention he damned well pleased. Eventually. That was the bargain.

"Please leave us, Poorvaja," Arcadia said, her eyes still holding Sheri's.

"Jalanili—"

"Please." She turned her face, giving him her profile—that straight nose and stubborn chin that teetered close to unfeminine but drove him wilder than any dumpling-cheeked maid had ever done. "I should like a moment alone with Lord Sheridan." She added something else in Hindustani. He couldn't help wondering what it was, but he'd been in the suds with enough women over the years to have a fair idea. *I'll dispatch him with the candlestick; you make sure the coast is clear* wouldn't have been entirely unreasonable.

The door closed behind Poorvaja. Arcadia stepped closer to Sheri. She tilted her head and peered into his eyes. His palms itched to pull her close and touch her everywhere, to feel her body against his once again.

"The gallery is empty, Sheri," she whispered. "You're all alone on stage, with no one to applaud your performance."

Gallery? Stage? What the devil was the woman going on about? But did it matter when she was so near that he could lose himself in trying to find the exact place where the tan on her face and upper chest gave way to the creamy swells of her breasts? There was no precise line of demarcation, but a gradual shift from one to the next, as the pale rays of dawn slowly gained intensity, until suddenly they were the brilliant gold of midday. He rubbed the back of his neck to keep his fingers away from her.

His tongue was thick in his mouth. Clumsy. "What—" he rasped. Cleared his throat. "What happened earlier, Arcadia. I'm sorry. I had to clear it up right away. I couldn't have you thinking anything untoward was happening between Elsa and me."

Her lashes lowered, casting crescent shadows on her high cheekbones. "She said you chose me over her. Did she wish to marry you? Does she still?"

Memories of that foolish morning flipped through his mind. "I asked her," he admitted. "Proposed."

"Do you love her?" The question was quiet and shaded with compassion.

"No."

Slowly, so she saw what he was about, Sheri took one strand of her brown hair, felt the warm silk slide between his fingers. When he reached the end of the strand, he lightly strafed his fingertips along the edge of her bodice and watched, mesmerized, as the faintest blush appeared in the wake of his touch, coloring the beautiful contours of her flesh. She was soft and silken, and he hungered to lay his mouth where his fingers had been and drink the taste of her into his mouth.

Mirroring the languor of his movements, Arcadia slowly brought her hand to his face. Somehow, she'd removed a glove without him noticing. Interesting, as he hadn't been able to tear his eyes away from her all night. Her palm hovered a hairbreadth away from him. He felt its heat. A whimper-groan arose in his chest, so much did he want her to touch him.

Fingers, one, then two, came to rest on his jaw, no heavier than a moth. So lightly he might have dreamed it, her nails traced his face, picking out the texture of his evening whiskers.

"Would you prefer to marry Lady Fay?" The warmth of her voice undulated across his throat.

What was a Lady Fay? Language lost meaning. All the blood had been diverted to the front of his body, his eyes and nose and fingers and ears, the better to sense every aspect of her. But mostly the blood was pooling in his cock. His golden goddess was to hand, and he was not kissing her or driving himself between her legs and that was wrong.

"Unf," he said.

She swayed closer yet, and his primitive brain registered a woman falling and so he caught her by the breast.

"You promised not to touch me."

"Did I?" He knew he had, more fool he. Why would he ever promise such a thing? Instead, he should have promised to fuck her until she forgot her own name. He loosened his grip, his fingers closing together and swirling across her nipple.

Her hazel eyes were bright. A line of white teeth flashed between her parted lips. Her bared throat revealed a thrumming pulse that beckoned to his tongue. He lowered his head.

She suddenly stepped back, out of reach, and he was left wanting and cold. "Keep your promises, my lord. And keep your hands to yourself."

CHAPTER TWENTY

Married.

Arcadia didn't feel married. But having only been in that state since morning, and with no point of reference for evaluating her experience against, perhaps this fatigued annoyance was what matrimony felt like.

"It's an awful lot of bother, isn't it?"

Poorvaja's eyes flicked to hers in the mirror, then returned to her work as she carefully brushed Arcadia's hair, pausing periodically to anoint it with oil. "You are a bride only once, Jalanili."

True, but it was the second time today she'd been put through an extensive toilette regimen. Before dawn, Arcadia awoke at Delafield House for the last time. She and Poorvaja had shared a few minutes of meditation, followed by yoga postures. Then it was right into a tub redolent of sandalwood. She could have happily lingered in the bath for hours, but her ayah attacked with a special scrubbing powder to make her skin glow, pink and new.

The Arcadia Parks who met Lord Sheridan at church was the image of proper English maidenhood, laced and buttoned, gloved and bonneted, only her freshly scrubbed face bared to the chill October air. Sheri, too, had taken pains with his preparations. His hair was still damp at the ends, his cheeks freshly shaved, his skin carrying the brisk note of cologne recently applied. In a tailed frock coat, ivory brocade waistcoat, and buff trousers, he'd been splendidly handsome. Sober before the vicar, yet Sheri's lips had twitched with a spark of deviltry as he vowed … *with my body, I thee worship.*

Her thumb worried the gold band on the fourth finger of her left hand like a tongue prodding at an aching tooth. Two weeks since the betrothal ball, and the memory of Sheri kissing Lady Fay still stung. Playing along with his pretend courtship created too many confusing emotions. One of the few things Arcadia knew of a certain was that she did not fit into his world. During that first waltz that robbed her of her senses, Sheri told her he liked her just as she was and exhorted her not change for anyone. *He certainly hasn't changed for you.*

After the ceremony, they had come to Lothgard House for breakfast, then Poorvaja whisked Arcadia upstairs to begin preparations for supper. This evening, Arcadia would be neither the immodest dancer, nor the blushing bride. She would be something else, something closer to who she was at heart. She was done apologizing for who she was and who she wasn't. She lifted her chin and watched in the mirror as Poorvaja parted her hair down the center and gathered it at the nape. She was Arcadia Zouche now, and soon she would be going home.

"You make the mistake of supposing your wedding day is for you."

Arcadia lifted a brow. "Is it not?"

"Not only you." Poorvaja bent at the waist to examine her handiwork, making minute adjustments to the tucked ends of Arcadia's hair. "There are two families also, yes? People who have cared for you both and dreamed of this day and who want to see—" Her voice suddenly hitched. "Who want to see you happy." She swiped an eye with the back of her wrist.

The ayah's other hand rested on Arcadia's shoulder. Arcadia pressed her cheek to it. "You are everything to me, Poorvaja. Mother and sister and friend."

"And you are the daughter of my heart, Jalanili." She cracked a wry smile. "Which is why you must now let me have my fun. Turn around," she directed, reaching for a little pot of *kajal* on the dressing table.

She bent close, her familiar scent a soothing accompaniment to the gentle strokes of the thin brush she swept below Arcadia's eyes.

"He's going to stick it in you."

Arcadia blinked. "I ... ah ..." she stammered.

"Since the *memsahib* is not here, it is my duty to tell you."

Her cheeks flamed. Arcadia didn't think her mother would have approached the topic with quite that degree of candor. "All ... all right."

"His man part."

"Yes, I understand. Thank you." Arcadia had not spent eleven summers of her life in a *zenana* and not picked up a fact or two.

Poorvaja gripped Arcadia's chin and turned her head. "That's how you get a baby." The memory of something lost and sad echoed faintly through her words. Finished with the *kajal*, she turned to Arcadia's attire laid out on the bed.

Twisting in the chair, Arcadia's hands gripped the posts. Peeking from beneath the edge of a white sari banded with blue and orange, Poorvaja's bare brown feet were small and worn. Strands of silver that had not been there when they left India now threaded through the dark braid hanging heavy down her spine.

"There will be no baby," she directed to her ayah's back. "We're going home."

Poorvaja's hands stilled. "The nonsense you talk. Lord Sheridan lives here."

"He will continue to do so. I told you I wouldn't stay here."

"That was before. Stand up."

Poorvaja helped Arcadia into a white petticoat, then an underskirt and blouse of crimson silk, the skirt, neckline, and short sleeves heavily adorned with gold beading and embroidery in intricate paisley and scrolls.

Practiced fingers tightened the skirt's laces at her waist. "You might ask your husband to send me back to India."

"I would never send you away, Poorvaja. You know that."

"I wasn't giving voice to fear, Jalanili; I was suggesting. You don't need me anymore."

A bead of anxiety trickled down Arcadia's spine. "That's not true. I'll always need you. Besides, we needn't bother Lord Sheridan for the cost of your fare. Soon enough, I'll pay for our passage myself. You and I will sail home together, and England will be nothing more than a story we scare ourselves with before bed."

And if, late at night, she sometimes thought of kissing an arrogant wastrel with strong arms and smiling eyes and sensuous lips, well, that was her own souvenir of the journey.

A sound of warning rose in Poorvaja's throat, but Arcadia forestalled her fussing by pointing to a soft parcel wrapped in white paper. "Is that from Madame Doucet?"

The day after the betrothal ball, Arcadia had returned to the modiste's shop. When Arcadia described what she wanted to wear for her wedding celebration, the Frenchwoman's eyes had gleamed with avarice born not of greed, but of ingenuity. "Mademoiselle asks the impossible," she'd alleged, even as she began tearing books of design from a shelf. "No bride has ever done such a thing. They'll be talking about you for months." She slanted a smile at Arcadia. "*Mais,* they'll be talking about me for years." Summoning her squadron of assistants, she had dispatched several to scour fabric supply warehouses for the beaded crimson silk Arcadia now wore, sent another to the dyer, and set her best seamstress to the task of sketching out the embroidery pattern.

"Delivered this morning, while you were at church." Gently, Poorvaja unwrapped the parcel and unfolded the bundle within, a red, veil-thin sari, embroidered with peacock feathers of gold and blue and green. Round gold beads between the feathers added weight to the fabric to assist in the draping, as well as providing luster.

It might have been an overly sentimental gesture for a bridegroom who didn't intend to keep his bride, but Arcadia meant the feather design to acknowledge the motif that had brought them together—if only temporarily.

"Beautiful," Arcadia breathed, running her hand beneath the silk and marveling at the delicate transparency. "I can't believe I get to wear such a glorious thing." She lifted her arms for Poorvaja to commence wrapping.

"Not yet." Scurrying to a wardrobe, Poorvaja pulled out a small wooden chest, which she placed on the dressing table and gestured.

"What's this?" Arcadia asked, bemused. She flipped an aged brass clasp and lifted the lid. On a bed of blue silk rested a jumble of golden chains and bangles.

"From my wedding," Poorvaja said. "And now for yours."

Heart in her throat, Arcadia withdrew from the cask a bracelet of green glass and another of brass. None of it was very fine—Poorvaja had been the daughter of a younger son and the wife of a farmer—but all of it shiny and bright from fresh polishing. She cast a look of disbelief at her ayah. "You brought this from India?"

"Do not cry! You'll spoil the *kajal*. I told you, you must let me have my fun. Sit."

Dazed, she returned to her seat before the vanity mirror. Poorvaja slid numerous bracelets onto each arm and placed earrings dangling with leaf-shaped spangles at her lobes. The ayah fitted a headpiece next, two golden chains draping to either side of Arcadia's hair, with a third that nestled in her part. A medallion rested in the center of her forehead above her eyebrows, a golden filigree disc with three small pearls dangling from the bottom edge.

A knock sounded at the door. Poorvaja opened it, and Lady Delafield entered, her spare cheeks ruddy from sipping champagne punch since breakfast. "Niece, I'd like a word," she said. With a hand clutching a cup of punch, she waved Poorvaja out of the room.

"Of course, Aunt." Arcadia's adornments jangled softly as she turned her head.

"Great Jehoshaphat, what are you wearing?" Lady Delafield demanded.

"A new dress," Arcadia calmly replied, standing to show it off, "and Poorvaja's jewelry."

Her ladyship gawped. "You should be wearing Lucretia's jewelry, not the maid's."

Arcadia let the comment about Poorvaja pass. Her aunt refused to acknowledge the bond between the Indian woman and her niece. Trying to make her understand would be a waste of breath. "I wore my mother's pearls this morning."

Lady Delafield crossed the room and made as if to snatch off the headpiece. Arcadia raised a staying hand and swiftly backed away. Her aunt glimpsed Arcadia's palm and let out a low moan. "You must remove this heathen frippery at once. Lord Lothgard will accuse me of foisting a Gypsy onto his family. What will Lord Sheridan think?"

At that, the corners of Arcadia's mouth lifted. What would Lord Sheridan think, indeed. "We shall find out, won't we?"

Lady Lothgard let out another moan and sank her head against one of the bedposts. "We are ruined."

"What was it you wished to discuss, Aunt?"

Her ladyship lifted her head. "You being motherless, it is my Christian duty to inform you of the wifely duties you must soon undertake. Your husband will have certain expectations of you—"

"Thank you, Aunt, but this really isn't necessary."

"—to which you must accede with a cheerful heart. Despite the"—she gulped down some punch—"indelicate nature of the task, it is required for the creation of children, and for your husband's comfort."

His comfort? Was Arcadia to be as a favorite old chair, then? "And my comfort, as well?"

"A lady takes comfort in wisely managing her household, in easing her husband's burdens and not adding to them with imprudent expenditures or overwrought emotions."

Arcadia recalled Lady Delafield's frequent requirement of her smelling salts, but prudently said no more.

"Well," her aunt chirped, "I'm glad we had this talk so I could clarify matters for you."

She smiled. "As am I, Aunt."

Lady Delafield's "talk" was as illuminating as a gutted candle. Thankfully, Arcadia had some rudimentary inkling of the marriage act from snatches of conversation overheard in the *zenana*. Too, the response of her body to Sheri's kisses had offered a clue. The feeling of his hard thigh rubbing between her legs and the turgid ridge of his manhood hard against her abdomen had been another.

Her aunt left, and Poorvaja returned to wrap Arcadia in the splendid sari Madame Doucet had created, tucking, pleating, and draping, finally settling the last bit over Arcadia's hair and shoulders. Poorvaja stepped back, hands pressed to her heart, pride and affection beaming in her eyes.

"Will I do?" Arcadia teased.

"Come see." Poorvaja led her to a full-length mirror in the corner. A woman with sultry, mysterious eyes peered back, the hard angles of her face softened by the cloud of red silk framing her features. In deference to her English family—and the cold— Arcadia did not go barefoot as a bride in India might, but instead wore red satin shoes over silk stockings.

There was a tapping at the door. It opened a bit, then Sheri's voice. "Miss Poorvaja, I've come to take my bride down to supper. You've monopolized her since breakfast, but you must relinquish her at last."

"Come in, Sheri," Arcadia called. She turned to the door, butterflies suddenly stirring in her stomach. "I'm ready."

He entered. Stopped, she thought, to give her fluttering heart a moment to recover from the shock of his elegant male beauty. He'd changed into evening attire, a black coat and white satin knee breeches. A silver waistcoat encased his broad chest. In a double column down the center, embroidered in sapphire thread, were those—

She stepped closer. Smiled. "Peacock feathers." Her gaze lifted past the crisply perfect cravat to his parted, unsmiling lips and wide eyes.

Her own smile slipped. She should not have done this. It was too different, too much. When he told her not to change, he hadn't known that she'd spent most of her life before coming to London in saris, or that the only wedding celebrations she'd ever attended had been for Poorvaja's numerous cousins, or that Arcadia had never known to dream of her own wedding as being anything else.

His throat tightened on a swallow. "Look at you," he breathed. "Look—" His hand came to his mouth. His head tilted as his eyes roamed every inch of her. He circled her slowly, pausing to examine an earring or brush a finger over the beading on her sleeve. She felt him stop behind her. The back of her neck prickled.

"Are you angry?" she forced out. The dress she'd worn this morning was somewhere about here.

"Angry?" His hands cupped her arms. His voice purred in her ear. "Ye gods, woman, I've never been less angry in my life." A beat of silence, then a chuckle. "Peacock feathers. And I thought I was so clever. I should have known you'd take the wind from my sails, peahen."

"We will look clever together," she said, her spirits lifting once more.

He turned her around, his eyes alight with male appreciation. "You are exquisite, Lady Sheridan." He brought her hand to his lips and turned it to brush his lips over the inside of her wrist. She sighed at the caress, even as she experienced a frisson of dismay.

Lady Sheridan. Not even granted the dignity of her own name. She'd been given a courtesy title derived from another courtesy title. If he was Lord Nothing, the moon whose light was only a reflection of his father's, what did that make her? Less than nothing?

"What is this?" His finger traced the intricate reddish-brown designs on her palm.

"Mehndi," Poorvaja answered. "Do you like it?"

"It's astonishing. I've never seen anything like it. Did you do this, Miss Poorvaja?" His eyes flicked to the ayah. "Now I know what you've been doing all day. This must have taken hours."

"We did it yesterday," Arcadia said. His finger continued following the looping scrolls and flowers. Her scalp tingled.

"Yesterday?" He lifted a brow. "Your hands were decorated like this in church this morning?"

Arcadia nodded. "Under my gloves, of course. Did I commit an Anglican mortal sin? Are you angry now?"

He grinned, the crooked, boyish smile that made her knees weak. "Are you mad? This is brilliant. To think, while I was admiring my pretty, modest bride, *this* was hiding just beneath her gloves. You little minx."

He brought a finger to her chin and tilted her face, then touched his lips to hers. He brushed the tip of his nose lightly around the end of hers, then pressed another light kiss to her mouth. Arcadia's bones softened. A distant but steady thrumming began in her breasts and belly and between her legs. In her new red shoes, her toes curled.

"Supper, you said?"

Startled by Poorvaja's voice, Arcadia gasped, jerked her face away from Sheri's.

His lids drooped in a smoldering, private look that *promised*. Arcadia's toes curled tighter.

"I did, but before we go ..." He reached into his inner pocket, then paused, his eyes still trained on Arcadia's.

Married.

He withdrew his empty hand. Tried another pocket. "Ah, here we are." He pulled forth a small velvet pouch. "Just a small gift …" He winked at Arcadia, swiveled, and presented it to Poorvaja. "For you."

She accepted it with visible uncertainty. Arcadia could not recall having ever seen Poorvaja receive a gift from a man before. The ayah tipped the pouch and exclaimed as a ring tumbled onto her palm. Her fingers shook as she picked it up. An aquamarine solitaire winked in the candlelight. "I will not be your second wife, you wicked man," she blurted, but Arcadia could see how her friend struggled with emotion.

"It reminded me of the water," Sheri said cryptically, "and I thought it might do the same for you."

Blinking back tears, Poorvaja slid the ring onto her right hand. She swiped an eye with the edge of her sari.

Emotion welled inside Arcadia's chest. On the short list of things she would miss about England, the way Sheri always treated Poorvaja with such kindness and respect would be near the top.

"Thank you," she whispered, her throat tight.

Sheri nodded. "And for you, my dear …" He reached behind his back, his hand returning with a flat, rectangular box, which he extended to her on his palms.

Inside, Arcadia found a double-strand necklace of golden citrines, the oval-cut stones set end to end. Arcadia's hand flew to her throat.

"I wanted to give you something with a little sparkle, but already you far outshine my gift. You needn't wear it."

"But I want to," Arcadia blurted before she could stop herself. She couldn't accept such a gift. It was far too valuable. What had he been thinking to purchase such a thing for the wife he wouldn't keep? Still, it couldn't hurt to wear the necklace just this once.

He lowered the sari to her shoulders and fixed the jewels around her neck. They were cold against her skin and heavy enough to notice, a constant reminder of their giver. After drawing her sari back up, he offered her one arm, the other to Poorvaja, and escorted them both downstairs.

• • •

They stepped into the gallery, where the company was enjoying *apéritifs*. Sheri paused in the entryway and counted.

One ... two ...

The first gasp sounded off to his left. The second quickly followed. Soon, a chorus of soft exclamations swept the room as the heads swiveled to see the bride.

Arcadia was breathtaking. The filmy red layers of her ensemble gently caressed her curves, making of her a living flame. A soft tinkling sound accompanied her every movement. Sheri could follow at her heels for hours, just to hear the music of her passing.

She was ethereal and entirely unique and cast a spell on every man in the room. Sheri could not catch the eye of any of his friends; they were all staring at Arcadia. Even the happily married ones, like Brandon and Henry, were agog at the vision Sheri's wife presented, and for once, he didn't mind Sir Godwin's wistful expression.

Gentlemen, I know how you feel.

His modest little peahen was a fantasy come to life, erotically enticing without showing so much as an inch of her bosom. The rounded neckline of her dress revealed only a bit of clavicle, but they were the most arousing collarbones Sheri had ever seen. The hours between now and the moment he could whisk her away to privacy yawned before him, unreasonable in their number.

An expectant hush filled the gallery, as though everyone was waiting for someone else to be the first to make a move. It was Arcadia. Tucking that stubborn chin into the air, she dropped his arm and stepped forward, regal and so beautiful it made his chest hurt and graceful—and his.

His.

He wanted to whoop and pound his chest and run a lap around the perimeter of the gallery so his long-dead ancestors could marvel at the lucky bastard their line had produced.

Deborah broke from the crowd first, of course. In her quiet, kind way, she took Arcadia's hands and kissed her cheek. "How splendid you look, Lady Sheridan. Elijah?" She beckoned the marquess with a glance. Sheri's brother bowed over Arcadia's hand. "You are a vision, madam. My brother is a fortunate devil." Lothgard then clasped Sheri's hand and clapped his shoulder. "Congratulations again, Sheridan." A short distance away, the dowager met Sheri's gaze, her mouth pursed and brow raised. *Judgment withheld.*

After that, the compliments came in a rush. Claudia was in rhapsodies over Arcadia's ensemble, while Lorna was more restrained, but no less sincere, in her admiration. While women flocked around Arcadia to heap praise on her daring gown, Elsa sauntered to Sheri's side and hooked her arm through his.

He felt a spike of dread. His spine stiffened.

"Lower your hackles. I'm not going to cause trouble. Tonight." She shot him a rueful smile. When he saw that her eyes were clear, the tension between his shoulders relaxed. "She's quite the splash." Elsa nodded to Arcadia at the center of a throng. After a moment of silence, she added, "I know it's not a love match, but I do hope you'll find happiness. I think you could, with her."

There was a minor commotion from the back of the chamber. Finely attired countesses and barons hopped aside at the behest of one mightily insistent boy and the apologetic twin following in his wake.

Pushing past the last row of onlookers, Crispin pulled to a stop. His brown eyes locked on Arcadia and widened. He approached her as if in a trance. With a smile, Arcadia offered the boy her hand. He took it and continued staring, stupefied. "I wish you weren't married to Uncle Sheridan," he breathed, "I'd marry you myself." Suddenly, dimples appeared in his cheeks. "Might I give you a kiss, Aunt Arcadia?"

Cheeky scamp. "Bad form to covet another man's wife," Sheri heard himself say as he joined his wife and nephew. Hypocrisy tasted bitter on his tongue. Other men's wives comprised half or more of the population of his prior bed partners, comely widows sometimes being thin on the ground.

With a laugh, Arcadia crouched and accepted the child's embrace. Webb appeared at his brother's shoulder and offered a stiff bow of his own. "Aunt," he said, "Crispin and I happened to find ourselves in the kitchen a few minutes ago—"

"Nicking scones," Crispin clarified.

"—and noticed the appealing aroma of the supper Cook is preparing."

"The food smells good, and we want some. May we eat with you?"

"Oh, can they?" Arcadia asked Sheri, her mosaic hazel eyes filled with pleading. "I wish to be surrounded by family." His heart stuttered. It was for family that Sheri had embarked on this matrimonial enterprise. The sight of the seductress in red laughingly accepting another of Crispin's juvenile gallantries made Sheri think of things he'd never thought before. A family of his own, a wife and children who loved Sheri as much as he loved them, who would never threaten to hack him from the family tree as Lothgard had. They would never have need to, because he wouldn't want anything more from life than their happiness.

Dangerous thoughts.

The marchioness granted permission, and places for the twins were shoehorned in beside Poorvaja and the dowager.

The meal began, and Arcadia's magnificent attire was replaced in conversation by the novelty of an Indian menu. Aromatic steam lifted from platters swimming with green and yellow gravies. Tonnish ladies and gentlemen who tended to affect fashionable boredom, now exclaimed in delight as they sampled curried lamb and lemon rice. The twins dared one another to try this or that fiery dish, a challenge taken up by other intrepid diners.

Sheri particularly liked a flatbread called *naan*, tasty in its own right, but useful, too, for sopping every drop of succulent curry sauce from his plate. He leaned back in his chair, stifling a groan of repletion.

"How did you manage this?" he asked his wife across the table.

Over the rim of her wineglass, her kohl-rimmed eyes were lively. "Deborah graciously permitted Poorvaja and me to share receipts with her cook. A spice merchant near the docks had most of the seasonings we required."

After a sweet course of dense, fried dough balls dripping with a sauce of thick, sweetened milk flavored with saffron, Sheri raised a glass to his bride. The company joined him in toasting Arcadia's health, with Crispin contributing a particularly enthusiastic "Hear, hear!"

Arcadia stood, drawing the attention of all. Lashes lowered, her slim finger trailed the rim of her dessert dish while she seemed to search for words. God, she was lovely.

After a moment, she raised her eyes, meeting Sheri's gaze. A current of awareness, vital and strong, passed between them. Her cheeks colored, and she looked away before addressing the table, haltingly at first. "I don't know if it's customary for the bride to offer a toast. If not, I must plead ignorance, and I hope you'll forgive me." Sheri saw Claudia offer a smile of encouragement. Mrs. De Vere was a thorn in his side, but he was grateful for the friendship she'd so readily offered Arcadia.

Drawing a breath, Arcadia continued, her voice steadier and melodiously accented. "I wish to thank the Marchioness and Marquess of Lothgard for hosting this lovely party, and thank you all for coming. Most of you don't know me, but you know Lord Sheridan, and you know my husband is a good man." She met his eyes, the glance spearing him in the heart. "A kind man. Thank you, my lord, for all you've done for me, and for the promises you made."

Promises, such as to track down her brooch and to send her back to India. To remain legally married, but physically separated, so long as they both shall live. A single night of conjugal bliss. Tonight.

Of all the promises Sheri had made, the last was the only one he didn't regret.

"Finally," Arcadia said, "I wish to pay my respects to those who are not with us, whose company we miss." She raised her glass; all others followed. "To the memory of my father and mother, Sir Thaddeus and Lady Lucretia Parks. To the memory of Lord Sheridan's father, the late Marquess of Lothgard. And to the memory of Grace."

A cold stone dropped in his middle. His ears rang. Confused frowns passed over many faces, accompanied by murmurs of, "Who?"

"Who's Grace?" Crispin asked aloud. He demanded across the table, "Grandmama, who is Grace?"

The dowager's cheeks were white as bone. "I'm sure I have no idea," she stiffly replied.

Arcadia's wineglass wavered. "Grace, my lady. Your late daughter."

Eyes furious and brimming with hurt, Sheri's mother silently promised him a blistering set-to in the near future. Then she rounded icy hauteur on her new daughter-in-law.

Miss you, Sheri.

"You are quite mistaken, Lady Sheridan. I have no daughter."

CHAPTER TWENTY-ONE

It was going so well. That thought looped through her brain, over and over. *It was going so well.*

Until it wasn't. Until she'd unwittingly committed a grave *faux pas* so serious, Sheri had thanked his sister-in-law for a lovely evening, dashed off a joke about his eagerness for his wedding night for the benefit of the stunned audience, and all but tossed Arcadia over his shoulder in his haste to remove her from Lothgard House.

The short carriage ride was tense and silent. When Arcadia tentatively said, "Sheri ..." he raised a hand. "Grant me a few moments to reflect on that excellent repast, if you would," he said and turned his stony stare out the window, his exquisite profile taut.

A small staff met them outside the house Sheri had let, and French welcomed them home with a brief speech offering his felicitations and best wishes for a happy and fruitful marriage. "Why don't you give Lady Sheridan a tour of the place?" Sheri requested, then slipped away. Arcadia blankly looked over furnishings her husband had cozened her aunt and uncle into purchasing while French proudly led her from room to room.

She interrupted his description of an ebonized footstool. "Where did Lord Sheridan go?"

The servant blinked. "Perhaps to his chamber?"

"Please take me there."

French led the way and knocked on the indicated door, but there was no reply. Nor was Sheri in the room that served as a study and library for a small collection of books. Flummoxed, French looked at Arcadia and shrugged. "I don't know where he's got off to, madam."

She heard a thump. And a few seconds later, another.

"Where is that coming from?" Following the sound, she discovered a hidden door for the servant stairs that led up to an attic. There, she located her missing husband.

He sat on the dusty floor in his wedding finery with his back to the wall, one long leg extended, the other drawn up, his left arm propped on his knee. His coat had been tossed over the back of a rickety chair. He was rolling a cricket ball against the opposite wall and catching it when it bounced back.

Arcadia went to the wall opposite him and sank to her knees.

"You'll spoil your pretty dress," he said.

"You'll spoil yours."

The corner of his mouth raised, but it wasn't really a smile. He rolled the ball to her. The leather was warm against her palm, the dark surface roughened from use. She rolled it back.

They continued like this, back and forth, for some minutes.

"Grace was my half sister," he said, his voice hitching. "We have different mothers."

"All right." She tried to catch his eye, but he wouldn't meet her gaze. "Am I meant to be shocked?" she gently teased. "Did you forget about the *zenana*? I grew up with dozens of children fathered by one man, with ten different mothers."

His shoulders relaxed and he answered with a grin, a flash of white teeth in the dim attic. "Peahen, knowing you lived part of the time in a harem is my favorite fact of anything I've ever learned. That one's not slipping from the old memory any time soon." He waggled his brows roguishly.

Heat stirred in her belly. She ducked her face, palmed the ball, returned it.

"But things are different here. Grace was illegitimate. Her mother was the wife of one of my father's tenants. Pater took her for his mistress, put her up in a small cottage, but had her brought to our house whenever he wished to see her. My mother was mortified. That was the point, I suppose. And the woman's husband, a poor crofter, had no recourse against the mighty *Marquess of Lothgard.*" He dripped scorn on the name. "Pater couldn't acknowledge Grace, of course, so he'd send me to visit her on his behalf. Wouldn't have his precious heir's hands sullied with the task of seeing to a baseborn daughter, but it was an assignment on par with my station, he said." He addressed the ball in his hand as he continued. "By the time Grace was three or so, it became obvious that she wasn't growing normally, not walking or speaking anywhere near as well as other children her age. Pater wanted to send her away."

"But you didn't let him," Arcadia guessed, scooting across the floor and placing her hand atop the ball resting in his. "You loved your sister."

"Caring for her was a challenge. She couldn't tend to her own cleanliness, and she easily became frightened or upset and acted accordingly. I couldn't imagine her being shuffled off to some asylum or foundling home where she'd have been mistreated."

"So you cared for her."

He chuffed a laugh. "Let's not overstate things. I was a boy myself. Grace's mother did the difficult work. I just stood my ground with the old man and made sure Grace got to live at home, where she belonged."

"And you played ball with her," she reminded him, rolling the cricket ball between their hands. Sheri's fingers brushed her thumb.

"Kicked the ball, dug holes in the garden, stacked blocks … whatever she wanted. I tried to bring a little gift whenever I came—a piece of fruit or a candy. Pebbles or leaves that caught my eye. A frog from the pond, once, much to her mother's dismay." He slid an impish look her way. "Every spring, I took her to visit the new lambs, and she always rode in front of me on my pony—my horse when I was older—when I took her into the village. Spoiled her a little, truth be told, but it was so easy to make Grace happy.

And her smile …" Sheri lifted his eyes. "I would give anything to see that smile again."

And there it was, she realized, the reason he went out of his way to dance with wallflowers and flirt with spinsters. Sheri tried to make them all happy because he was looking for Grace in their smiles. The old marquess might have thought to humiliate young Sheridan by appointing the boy keeper of his illegitimate half sister, but instead had forged in his second son a compassionate, giving soul.

Arcadia brought her hand to his jaw, felt the growth of whiskers on the cheek that had been immaculately smooth for their wedding just this morning.

"I'm sorry if I shamed you or your family by speaking carelessly at dinner. That was not my intention." The Dowager Lady Lothgard's vehement reaction to Grace's name made sense now. Though in no way the child's fault, Grace was the product of an adulterous liaison the old marquess had flaunted before his wife.

Sheri's hand covered hers. He brought her palm to his mouth, pressed a kiss into it. "You did nothing wrong, Arcadia. It was a relief to hear Grace spoken of openly. And I did miss her today. You were right about that, if not the old bastard."

He stood, having to keep his head stooped in the low space, and offered a hand to help Arcadia to her feet. "I apologize for sulking on our wedding day. I wasn't abandoning you, merely putting my head to rights before plying my seductive powers upon you."

Arcadia's mouth went dry. She licked her lips. "I'd nearly forgotten." A lie.

Tut-tut-tut went his tongue. "You wound me, peahen." Hooking a finger into the collar of his coat, he swung it over his shoulder and led the way back down the stairs. At the door to his room, he paused. "Would you like to come in with me now, or do you prefer to freshen up in your own room first?"

So casually he spoke of their intimacy, as if it were of no greater import than a proposed jaunt to the marketplace. Perhaps it wasn't a significant event for him. Many women enjoyed his company, it was said. What was one more lover, even if the woman in question happened to be his wife?

"I should change out of my sari before I do it irreparable harm." She gasped. "Poorvaja! We left her at Lothgard House."

"Did we? How careless of us."

"We must return for her at once."

He shot her an incredulous look, then pushed into his room. "Darling, if you think I'm leaving home on my wedding night to fetch your ayah, you are tragically mistaken."

Arcadia peeked into the chamber. Tastefully appointed in rich greens and browns, it didn't look like a den of debauchery. After tossing the coat across a stool, Sheri untied his cravat with nimble fingers, drew the neckcloth from his collar, and discarded it on the corner of the large bed. He turned, fingers opening the buttons on his waistcoat. His brown eyes assessed her. "Still there, you little voyeur?" The elegant waistcoat was wadded into a ball and carelessly tossed to a corner.

"Your clothes are scattered everywhere."

"It gives French something to do in the morning." Kicking off a shoe, he sent it sailing to one side of the room. "His favorite pastime is waking me with a scold for the shocking way I abuse my garments." The other shoe spun beneath the bed. "And then I get to tell him they're my demmed clothes to treat however I please, and if he doesn't care for it, he's welcome to find another position." Dropping onto a stool, he tugged off his stockings and wiggled his toes. They were long and straight, the nails there as nicely groomed as those on his hands. A few hairs grew on the tops of his white feet, brown against the pale skin. His calves had an appealing shape, she thought, though she'd no basis for comparison other than the *Discobolus*. The living examples before her were firmly muscled and covered with more of that crisp brown hair, and she wondered very much what they would feel like. "Then he gives me my coffee and sets about restoring my clothes to pristine order." He lobbed one stocking to the top of a walnut wardrobe; the second found its way behind a curtain.

Smothering a laugh, Arcadia took a few steps into the room. He was being absurd, and she was glad. It distracted her from his intriguing calves.

Pivoting, he tugged his shirt free of his breeches and over his head, then sauntered slowly to her. His lids drooped and his eyes glinted, but his smile remained light, teasing. Arcadia found it very difficult to focus on his face with his bare chest *right there*. Wide shoulders were round with muscle, giving way to the hillocks of the strong arms that had carried her once and held her close not often enough. His chest was broad, the bulges flatter and firm in the places where her own was soft with breasts. Small brown nipples drew her gaze, which then slid down a trail of that tantalizing hair to his belly. Lean muscle banded his flat stomach, and his every step gave her a view of the smooth play of those muscles beneath his skin.

Her face went cold, then hot. Her palms grew moist; she hoped the *mehndi* would not run. *Discobolus* had in no way prepared Arcadia for the raw, animal beauty of this man. Shadows cast by the fire hollowed his cheekbones, drawing lines that arrowed to his sensual lips. Arcadia's mouth watered.

Shirt dangling from his hand, Sheri stopped just in front of her. Arcadia inhaled great, greedy gulps of his tea-and-leather scent. He trailed the edge of a cuff across her jaw. "The secret to a perfect cravat," he murmured, "is that the linen must have the bitter tears of a long-suffering valet ironed into it. It's a finely tuned rapport we've established, you see."

Smirking, he stepped back. Arcadia was lightheaded. He'd spun a silly tale to put her at ease, and now he was naked but for his breeches. Her lips thrummed in time with her pulse, plumping, as if to silently wave him down and request a kiss.

She touched her brow, was surprised to find the medallion there. She'd forgotten she was still wearing her sari. "Poorvaja—"

"Is having a fine time at my brother's house. It was all arranged for her to stay at Lothgard House tonight." From his dressing room, he selected a silk dressing gown, which he tugged on and loosely belted with the tie.

"Oh." Arcadia glanced down. Getting out of her intricate ensemble by herself would be a challenge, but she'd manage.

As if reading her thoughts, Sheri said, "I'll play lady's maid tonight, peahen."

"You needn't trouble yourself. I'll make do."

He smiled wolfishly. "If you think I'd be troubling myself, you're mistaken once again. Come." Slipping his hand around hers, he led her through his dressing room, at the back of which was a door.

"Open it," he encouraged.

Beyond the door was another dressing room and then a bedchamber French had neglected to include in the tour.

The room was snugly warm, thanks to a fire blazing in the fireplace. A coal scuttle on the hearth was generously heaped with fuel. Besides the fire, the room was illuminated by an oil lamp. The light revealed draperies and bedding in vibrant jewel tones, sapphire and emerald and gold like the citrines at her throat. Her feet sank into a thick rug that covered all but a few inches around the perimeter of the room. Her hand slipped across the soft pile of velvet bed curtains. Her Kashmir shawl was draped across the end of the bed heaped with pillows. Several neatly folded quilts formed a stack beside the bed. On the vanity table, she spotted her brush and comb, which Poorvaja had just used on her hours earlier at Lothgard House.

She slanted a questioning look at him. "How …?"

"Do you like the room?"

Something in the timbre of his voice, the tilt of his head, communicated that her answer mattered. It wasn't polite interest that prompted him to ask, but the earnest hope of approval that she'd sometimes glimpsed. *This is his doing,* she realized.

"It's lovely, Sheri. Perfect." She drew back the hood of her sari. "And it's warm."

His hands came to her arms. "I don't want you to be cold."

The simple sweetness of his words tugged on her heart. She lifted on her toes and brought her mouth to his.

"Thank you," she whispered, dropping back a step.

Sheri's hand cupped her jaw; his fingers jangled her earring. He brought her face back to his and sealed their mouths together. His lips parted, coaxed hers to follow. Arcadia welcomed the sweep of his tongue and met it with her own. His other hand came to her face, holding her captive for a long, slow, drugging kiss. It went on and on, giving the pleasure time to migrate from her lips down her throat to her breasts and beyond, until it went beyond pleasure to restlessness.

Arcadia brought her hand to his chest, splaying her fingers over the firm contours of flesh, his skin heating the thin layer of silk. Her other hand came to his neck, slipped to his nape. Her fingers burrowed into his russet waves. Her bangles tinkled as she explored his chest and hair.

"Mmm," he moaned, lifting his mouth only to bring it to her jaw and chin. Arcadia arched her throat, and he trailed hot, openmouthed kisses to her collarbones.

His fingers plucked at the sari. "You are stunning, Arcadia. A goddess." His tongue swirled in the hollow at the base of her throat. Her knees trembled. "You're a work of art," his whisper rumbled below her ear, his nose nudging her earring aside so he could plant kisses there, as well. "I could look at you for hours and find new details to admire. But please, for the love of God, tell me how to get this infernal thing off of you."

Her head fell back, and she laughed, her arm cradling his head. He chuckled, too, the corners of his eyes crinkling even as he continued lavishing her face and neck with kisses.

She pulled out of his grasp; his fingers lingered in the air for a moment, as if he missed touching her already.

"First, the jewelry." She held her arms out, palms turned up to display the beautiful *mendhi*. Sheri's eye caught on the swirling patterns.

"I'd rather hoped the jewelry could stay." His brow quirked over a wicked glint in his eye.

"It's borrowed. I would not wish it to be damaged."

One at a time, he drew the bracelets down her arm, carefully rocking each back and forth to work them over her hands. When one wrist was bare, he lightly trailed his fingertips down the inside of her forearm and hand, ending with a kiss in the center of her palm. Then he repeated the procedure on the other arm.

He piled the bangles on the vanity. "What next?" he asked, his voice husky.

Panting slightly, Arcadia turned her head, touched an ear.

Heeding her silent instruction, he removed the earring, then gently massaged her earlobe between his thumb and forefinger. His mouth replaced his hand as he drew the tender flesh between his lips. Again, he repeated his ministrations on the other side, treating that lobe to the same massage and kisses.

Arcadia's breath quickened. She clung to his shoulder for support as his attention to her ear and neck sent a shimmering shower of sensation pouring through her body.

"Now here." She bent her neck so he could remove the headpiece. The necklace was last to go. Almost, she didn't ask him to remove it. But it, too, was borrowed finery, she reminded herself, and so it joined the other pieces on the vanity.

She extended her arms so he could unwind the sari. Grasping the loose end of delicate material, he slowly circled her, gathering the slack into his hands as he went.

"Peacock feathers," he said, almost to himself. His fingers slipped into the space between her skirt and blouse, caressing her stomach with a touch that made Arcadia's intimate flesh throb, sudden and sharp. She shifted, pressing her thighs together to ease the heavy ache building between her legs. A tiny moan fell from her lips.

"Almost there, peahen," he murmured soothingly. Sheri folded the sari and set it on the vanity stool, then shrugged out of his dressing gown, the blue silk joining the red in a heap.

She saw the jutting outline of his erection behind the fall of his breeches. Her body twitched in anticipation, remembering how it felt to rub against him. Knowing that he was aroused by her did strange things to Arcadia's body. Her breasts grew heavier, her lips parted.

He noticed her looking. Sheri dropped a hand to his front, stroked two fingers up and down the length of his manhood. "This is my constant companion when you're near," he said, "and three-quarters of the time when you're not. I wake up in the morning hard, aching to be inside you, and go to sleep at night with only my hand and poor imagination for company."

The sight of Sheri touching himself was shocking and exciting at once, and his words caused her stomach to hollow on a shuddering breath.

"Truly?" she breathed. Her hands twitched to join his. Her skin craved the relief of his touch. "You desire me so much?"

His hand curled around his shaft on a groan. The muscles in his arm flexed as he stroked. "So much. Take off your shoes." Arcadia nearly tripped in her eagerness to comply with his command. She took off her stockings, too, the carnal hunger in his eyes making her bold.

Her hands went to the edge of her blouse at her waist. "Ah-ah." Sheri lifted a hand, padded across the rug. "I'm troubling myself with this duty, recall." She lifted her arms, and he drew the blouse over her head, the beads lightly abrading her skin. Her unrestrained breasts tumbled into view.

His breath hitched. "Sweet Christ, look at you." It was close to what he'd said before, but with an added layer of lust this time. The hands he brought to her shoulders trembled. He ran his hands down her arms as though inspecting a horse for purchase. One hand slid around her waist and came up her ribs to cup her breast. The other came to her back, drawing her close.

The feeling of her bare chest against his was extraordinary, like coming home and embarking on a voyage all at once. Slipping her arms around his neck, she pulled his mouth to her.

He released her breast, locked both arms behind her back, and, for a moment, seemed content simply to hold her like this, his hands stroking up and down her back as his tongue took possession of her mouth.

But soon, soon, that needy frustration found Arcadia again. She rubbed her chest back and forth, teasing her nipples against the soft hair on his chest.

"Yes," he rasped. She dropped an arm to his waist, then allowed her fingers to slip below. His shaft twitched against her palm; he bit back a sharp moan, and she thrilled at her power. *Look what I can do.* Intuitively, Arcadia tightened her grip, and was rewarded with a sharp buck of his hips against her.

He broke from their kiss. A sheen of perspiration on his throat glistened. "Jesus God. I'll be staining my breeches like a green boy if you don't stop."

He was trembling all over, his motions jerky as he fumbled with the tie at her waist. "You too, you too," Arcadia said, pawing the buttons of his fall free of their loops.

She shimmied out of her skirt while he shucked his breeches. For a second, she drank in the sight of him in his glory, his powerful thighs and long, thick manhood. He was as unashamed in his nakedness as *Discobolus*, but infinitely more beautiful.

Sheri's hands came to her hips, and his mouth crashed down on hers. He palmed her buttocks and kissed a path from her throat to her breast. His tongue flicked lightly over her nipple.

"*Ah!*" Arcadia cried, sensation spearing her. That wicked tongue worked circles around the sensitive peak, then he drew it into his hot mouth, while his fingers found the other nipple and teased it mercilessly.

A moan rose in her throat, primal in her own ears. Sheri lifted his head and took her mouth, his fingers plunging into her hair, freeing it from hairpins to tumble loose down her back. His hands stroked through it, over and over, while he ravished her mouth.

Arcadia wanted—*needed*—more. She wantonly rubbed herself against him, seeking relief for her aching flesh. A growl rumbled in his chest. *Thrilling.*

He lifted her by the hips. Arcadia brought her legs around him, locking her feet at the small of his back. *Yes.* This was what she wanted. To climb him and rub. Everything. Everywhere. The rubbing was bliss.

A rush of dizziness struck an instant before her back touched the bed. Sheri followed her down, covering her body with his. Her feet came flat to the counterpane, her knees bracketing his hips. Her hands roved his back; she couldn't get enough of the feel of his firm muscles moving beneath that hot, smooth skin. She raked her nails up his spine. He groaned, rolling his hips as he reared over her on his knees.

Gripping her thighs, he kissed his way down her neck and chest, his skin sliding lightly over her breasts and belly, her entire body feeling caressed all at once. His hands slid to her calves, his fingers massaging, and then his mouth was on her leg. His tongue and lips scorched a path on the inside of her knee and up her thigh on a course to her aching sex. Arcadia's heart thundered in her ears. "Oh," she gasped, uncertain whether to beg him to stop or to continue.

He decided the matter by giving her other leg the same treatment. Except this time, as he kissed his way upward, his hand came to the apex of her thighs. Sheri's fingers plucked lightly at the soft curls covering her mound, then slipped down the slit of her swollen folds. She whimpered as he parted her gently. The pad of his thumb came to the center of her pleasure and worked small circles on the throbbing nubbin.

"Sheri," she gasped, her fingers clenching into his hair. "Kiss me … please, kiss—oh!" One finger slid into her sheath as he raised his head. Greedy for his mouth, she met him with her lips open. His tongue slid right into her, and it was such welcome relief, familiar ground in this foreign realm of intimacy. He slanted his mouth, deepening the kiss further. His finger kept stroking and stroking. Pleasure darted through her abdomen. Arcadia arched her spine and threw back her head, overwhelmed by the sensations swamping her body.

"Oh, sweetheart, look at you." Sheri's voice was gravel, his pupils wide. "You're gorgeous, Arcadia. Everything about your body is perfection. Oh—" His hand rode with her as she lifted her hips, his thumb unrelenting in its ministrations. "Let me help you feel good, love."

"You do," she cried. Then, "I trust you, Sheri," because she did, and because it needed to be said.

His eyes were strained, but they softened a fraction and he smiled—pleased and cocky but a little tender, too.

Then his head dipped to her breast and covered her nipple with his mouth. He sucked hard, sending a wash of pleasure up her throat and into her face. He withdrew his finger. A needy whimper rose in her throat. He plunged inside once more, two fingers this time. He was stretching her from within. There was an edge of pain to the stretching, but mostly it was good, so good. Better than anything she'd ever felt.

He changed the tempo of his thrusting and angled his wrist higher. His thumb slipped to the base of her nub and rubbed back and forth. "Do you feel this, Arcadia?"

"Yes, yes," she sobbed, her body a writhing thing beyond her control. The pleasure was decadent—hedonistic, almost. She wanted more and more. Her body took the pleasure he served her and stored it up in ever growing heaps that were growing precariously high. Something was going to topple and fall—

"Come on, love," he rasped. "Come for me. Let me see you. Give it to me, Arcadia. Give me your pleasure."

Her face was hotter than she'd ever felt, her breath rasping in her throat. "I can't," she cried. "I can't."

"You can. Arcadia, look at me." His eyes were steady, her anchor in the storm, even as his lips blew out on huffing breaths. "Trust me, peahen."

"I do, I do—*ah!*" He rotated his wrist, twisting the fingers inside her. And she fell. Long and hard, the pleasure had its way with her, bowing her back off the bed and wrenching cries from her lips. But Sheri was there to bring her through it, whispering soothing words and kissing her mouth, her eyes, her shoulder.

She was dazed and scarcely returned to herself when he came between her legs and nudged her thighs farther apart. His shaft was thickly erect with prominent veins roping the circumference. The head was a dusky purple-red, a bead of moisture glistening at the tip.

Gripping himself, he rubbed that slickness over her nub, and she was surprised to feel another shock of pleasure. He drew his shaft down, trailing the head between her sensitized folds. His eyes were riveted on where their bodies met. "*Oooh,*" he moaned.

"You have the prettiest quim. Pink and wet and opening up for me. Just like that."

He nudged the head in where his fingers had been, then with short thrusts of his hips, fed in another inch, and then another.

The fullness was greater now, the stretching more intense. Her nails dug into his forearm. She clamped her belly and bore down against the intrusion.

"Shh, shh, shh." Sheri ran a hand down her ribs. "Breathe, sweetheart. Relax and breathe."

His words sounded so like an admonition she'd heard a thousand times while practicing yoga that she laughed.

• • •

While she was distracted, Sheri pulled back, then drove home in one long stroke. She was wet and tight and felt so good his eyes crossed.

She writhed, bucking her hips and tightening again. Her limbs were lithe, lean muscles softly delineated beneath supple skin. Her abdomen flexed. "Calm, peahen, calm," he urged, but Sheri himself was anything but. His control was wearing thin. His cock was harder than he could ever remember being. The corner of his mind that always monitored his boon companion fretted that such a raging erection might do him harm.

But he was inside her now, and everything was going to be all right. He held himself still, grinding his teeth against the animal urge to rut and pound and claim her. She liked to be kissed, and so he lowered his mouth to hers. Propping his weight on his elbows, he smoothed sun-streaked tresses from her golden face. His golden goddess.

Her tension eased. Sheri gave an experimental rock of his hips. She gasped, but pleasurably this time. And so he did it again. "Better now?"

Arcadia hummed and brought her arm around his shoulder. "Better, yes. It feels so good." Her accent was richer now, a song that reached inside his heart and grabbed his cock and filled his brain with one thought: *I make her feel good.* He was consumed with male pride. Reaching down, he hooked his hand behind her knee and drew her enticing leg to his hip.

"Put your legs 'round me."

Her soft feet slid along the outside of his legs, her firm thighs lifted around his haunches. Her notch opened further, drawing his cock deeper. His balls tightened and throbbed. He shook from head to toe. Involuntarily, his hips jerked back and forth. He moaned, grasping her hip, pulling back, and driving home.

Arcadia gave a breathy "ah!" and so he let himself loose, gave over to the primal rhythm of mating. Every stroke took him deeper, every breath drew more of her essence into his lungs. His pubic bone clapped against her mound, giving her pleasure where she needed it most with every thrust.

Sheri's climax built at the base of his spine, tightly coiling through his groin and down his thighs. His spine bowed towards her as he plunged on and on, urged by her gasps and cries. Deeper into Arcadia, deeper into madness.

She cried his name as she came, the rippling contractions of her ecstasy pulling him over the edge. "Arcadia," he groaned. He poured himself inside her, lost himself in a pleasure that went beyond pleasure, wiping his mind of any sense of self or place. There was only her, and it felt as if it had always been this way, and that it was right and good to know nothing but her. She was where he belonged.

Later—a moment or an hour, he didn't know—he held her in his arms, her head resting on his chest. Sweaty and sated, he floated on a cloud of bliss. Infinitely better than spirits, this was an intoxication to which he could become a willing slave. Eyes closed, he kissed her crown and felt her smile against him.

"So it's done, then?" Arcadia asked. "Consummated."

He squeezed his eyes tighter. He'd asked her only for this. For one night. "Yes, consummated," he confirmed. "Wedded and bedded."

She snuggled in beside him, her little hand curled over his heart, and he raged silently at a world that would continue turning and march relentlessly into the dawn, and steal his goddess from his bed.

• • •

Arcadia awoke slowly. She was cocooned in the most delicious warmth and was loathe to admit to consciousness if it meant getting out of the bed. She sighed, rolling on decadently soft pillows. Her nose bumped a male shoulder.

Sheri.

Smiling to herself, she burrowed deeper into the covers, luxuriating in the presence of her own private heat source.

"Are you awake," came his sleep-roughened voice, "or are you the most gleeful dreamer in existence?"

Reluctantly, she lifted an eyelid. "I haven't been this perfectly warm since India. It's marvelous."

He propped his head on an elbow and looked down at her. His jaw was darkened with morning whiskers, and his hair flopped over his forehead. Without thinking, she reached up and swept it back.

"So ..." he said. "We're both awake."

An unwelcome chill that had nothing to do with the air stole into her lungs. "Morning."

Their wedding night was over, the marriage consummated. Arcadia's part of their bargain was fulfilled. As soon as she found her brooch, she and Poorvaja could go home.

"It doesn't have to be." Beneath the blanket, his arm hooked over her waist. He pulled her close, tucking her back against his chest. Direct contact with the warmth. Bliss.

"What do you mean," she said drowsily, "*it doesn't have to be*? It is. Light is coming through the cracks in the curtains."

He kissed her shoulder, the softness of his mouth framed by the prickling of his whiskers. His hips rolled, stroking his hard member in the cleft between her buttocks.

"It's still tonight if we say it is." His hand came to her breast. He rolled her nipple beneath the pad of his thumb, toyed with it as it swelled and hardened. A soft cry caught in her throat. She pressed back against his cock, enjoyed the hiss of breath between his teeth. "If we don't get up, the night isn't over, you see?" he reasoned, his voice strained.

Arcadia turned her face up, meeting his mouth. Their tongues twined together, stroking and teasing. Sheri's hand came between her legs, and she parted them, inviting his touch. His finger slipped between the folds and probed gently.

"Are you too sore?"

There was some tenderness, but her spiraling desire quickly eclipsed the discomfort. "Not too much," she panted. "It isn't morning. Not yet."

Sheri turned her onto her belly. He licked and kissed his way down her back and rump. He rose onto his knees, gripped her hips, and pulled them up. Arcadia made a sound of confusion.

"Up on your knees and elbows, sweetheart."

She did as he suggested, resting her cheek on a pillow between her hands. She felt exposed and vulnerable, but then his hand was at her entrance once more, spreading her slick wetness to the taut bud at her apex. She pressed onto her palms and bore against his hand, seeking more of that delicious friction.

Suddenly his hand was gone, replaced by the round head of his member sliding up and down. He curved over her back, pulled her hair to the side, and mouthed her neck. "I love how wet you are," he said. "I love making you feel good."

Rearing up, he fitted himself to her entrance and drove forward, stretching and filling her in one long stroke.

The night's not over. It isn't morning yet.

But not even the most determined lovers could keep the sun at bay.

CHAPTER TWENTY-TWO

A week after the wedding, Sheri was quietly going insane. A beautiful woman with lean, strong limbs, perfect breasts, and a mouth he could kiss forever—if only he could simultaneously hear her bewitching voice fill his ears with the sounds of her rapture—was living under his roof but not sharing his bed. She was happy to discuss the news of the day over the morning papers, accompany him on fruitless expeditions to jewelers and pawnbrokers, and play cards after dinner. Then, like the friend she'd vowed to be, she bid him good night and retired to her room. Alone.

Night after night he lay in his bed, his eyes boring a hole in the door connecting their rooms, willing it to open. It never did. And he never stepped through it, either. They'd agreed on one night, and she'd willingly, enthusiastically, taken part. He'd even inveigled an additional session of morning sex into the arrangement. Asking for more would be ungentlemanly.

The trouble was, Arcadia made him feel quite ungentlemanly. Sleeping with her had only stoked his lust, rather than assuage it. He'd only had her twice, which left most of the school of copulation unexplored. Sheri'd never had Arcadia on top of him, riding him with abandon. He'd never had her against the wall or on a table. They'd never slipped away from a dull party to make their own entertainment in a convenient broom closet and return to the party with no one the wiser. Not once had they enjoyed the pleasures of the flesh beneath the open sky. Hell, he'd never even had her on a Tuesday.

Was he supposed to go the rest of his days without once having Arcadia on a Tuesday? It was an outrage. An affront.

Most of the time, he was perfectly content to enjoy a woman's company once or twice. Some affairs survived for a few weeks, with a notable few lingering a month or two. Arcadia was certainly the sort of girl he'd like to spend some time with. Beyond the supple body he couldn't get enough of, she was sharp and fun to cross verbal swords with. She called on Deborah and doted on his undeserving nephews. She'd even extended an olive branch to his mother, willingly shutting herself up alone in a room with the dowager for half an hour. Sheri had paced the corridor outside the drawing room door, ready to dash to Arcadia's rescue the instant he heard the *thwang* of his mother's fangs dropping in her jaws, positioned to strike.

But there had been no sounds of bloodletting from the room, only the soft murmur of feminine voices. When the door opened, his mother had patted Arcadia's hand fondly and called her "dear." The dowager never called Sheri "dear."

"Here's a note from Mrs. Dewhurst," Arcadia said while going through her morning post at the breakfast table—on a Tuesday, he gloomily noted.

"What news from that worthy lady?" he inquired placidly whilst stabbing a knife into a beef kidney.

Arcadia's eyes scanned the correspondence. "We're invited to Elmwood to spend two nights, beginning on Friday." She glanced over the paper at him. "Oh, may we? I've still not seen anything of your country besides London. It would be nice to see a little of the countryside. And I promised Claudia and Lorna a yoga demonstration, as well."

His knife clattered to the table. *Good God.* He'd done his level best to try to not think about what he'd overheard Arcadia tell Claudia. It was just more fuel for his frustrated fantasies. And now there was to be a demonstration to toss into his seething cauldron of lust? "Sounds delightful," he said.

She smiled. "Smashing! I shall write our acceptance at once."

His brows drew together. "'Smashing'? That sounds like Claudia De Vere talking. Don't let her influence you to foolhardy plans."

"Oh, the yoga demonstration was her idea."

"Of course it was."

. . .

"So"—Claudia tugged on the arm she had looped with Arcadia's—"tell, tell. Is marriage to Lord Sheridan most agreeable?"

Arcadia, Claudia, and Lorna were taking a ramble about Elmwood's park on Friday afternoon. The overcast day was cold, naturally, but Arcadia lifted her face to the air and breathed deep, grateful for the clean scents of earth and autumn leaves. A large brown-and-black dog called Bluebell loped ahead of the trio, zigzagging wildly, her snuffling nose to the ground. Occasionally she bounded off after a chipmunk or squirrel, but always returned to Lorna's side before resuming her sniffing inspection of the ground.

They paused for a moment on a rise overlooking the house. It was nothing like the grand homes Arcadia had seen in etchings in the books of Sir Thaddeus's library at home. Elmwood was a mismatched hodgepodge of architecture, each rambling addition a testament to a family history spanning centuries. It was lived in and comfortable and true, a family home, instead of a showplace. A wistful pang stirred in her breast.

"Lord Sheridan is most congenial," she answered. "He's gone out of his way to ensure my comfort." Besides the jewel box of a room he'd made for her, he had ordered that the rooms Lady Sheridan frequented be kept amply heated all the day through. Her own chamber was seemingly supplied with a bottomless scuttle of coal. Unless she went outside, Arcadia could almost forget she was in England.

Lorna looked at Arcadia askance. The slender woman wore only a single shawl over her walking dress, while Arcadia had, as usual, donned multiple layers of outerwear.

"Congenial?" Lorna repeated.

"That does seem a curious descriptor to attribute to Sheri," Claudia said. She rocked back on her heels, her gloved hands tucked behind her back. "But he is … tending to your comfort?"

"He knows I don't like the cold," Arcadia explained. "He tells the servants to keep fires burning in several rooms all day, though I'm sure it's expensive to do so."

She hadn't been as warm again as she'd been the one night she spent in his arms, but the fires were a kind consolation prize.

"Very thoughtful of him, I'm sure," Claudia persisted, "but is he *most agreeable?*"

Arcadia frowned. "Did I not answer the question?"

"Oh, look, there's Poorvaja with Daniel." Lorna pointed to where the ayah had emerged from the house in the company of her younger brother. Bluebell woofed and galloped down the hill towards them, huge ears flapping in the wind. "It was so kind of Poorvaja to agree to join us for the demonstration tomorrow."

"What I wish to know," Claudia interjected, "is whether Lord Sheridan properly attends his Husbandly Duties."

"You mean … ?"

Lorna tucked her hands into her shawl. "I'm afraid that is what she means." She turned a pointed look on Claudia. "Although it's none of your concern and you should be ashamed of yourself."

Throwing her hands wide, Claudia affected a wounded expression. "We've all heard gossip about the great Chère Zouche's prowess. Can you fault me for possessing a purely academic curiosity in the subject when I am finally given the opportunity to learn from one with firsthand experience?"

Arcadia's eyes burned. Wretched man. Awful man. She'd have been better off by far remaining a virgin to the end of her days than to have been burdened with this knowledge of what they'd had together, and what she was losing.

"Yes," she managed, her throat tight, "he is most agreeable." The things he'd made her feel that night were exquisite. Her body had blossomed at his touch, responding to every caress, every whispered word.

Claudia chuffed. "*Hmph*. Reality does not conform to the myth, I presume. Typical male posturing. *Ow!*" She rubbed her shoulder where Lorna had just swatted her. "What was that for?"

"Stop it, you ninny."

Arcadia sat down on the grass, tucking her knees up and resting her chin on them.

"Don't listen to me," Claudia said, sitting down beside her. "I'm a dreadful hoyden. Comes from growing up in a large family, I'm afraid. I almost always say the first thing that pops into my head, and it's almost always something that I should have kept behind my teeth."

"But we do wish you happy," Lorna said, coming to sit on Arcadia's other side. "Lord Sheridan is loyal and kind, in his own way. And he is terribly handsome."

"He's kind and loyal in anyone's way," Arcadia said stoutly. She knew who he was inside, the boy who had defied his father to care for his illegitimate sister. "But he doesn't want to be married," she found herself saying. "He had to marry, and so did I, and so we married each other."

Lorna picked up a leaf and twirled it by the stem. "That's not so unusual. Many marriages begin like that. But there's every hope that it will become a love match sooner or later."

"You don't understand.," Arcadia said, shaking her head. "He doesn't want a wife. He wants to be married in name only to an absent wife so he may resume his life without the burden of a spouse nearby."

"Absentee wife?" Claudia snorted. "Where does he think he's going to put you? He's got no land. Is he planning to ship you back to India?"

Arcadia sank her eyes to her knees.

"Oh," Claudia said.

"Well, don't go," Lorna said. "He can't make you go to India if you don't want to."

"But I promised." Arcadia lifted her head and swiped a stray tear from her cheek. "That was the deal we struck. I told him I wanted to fulfill my duty to my family by marrying, then go back to India like it never happened."

"But it did happen," Lorna said.

"And now you're in love," Claudia concluded, reaching an arm around Arcadia's shoulders.

She nodded miserably. "I'm afraid so."

• • •

"You're cracked," Henry observed.

"Quite possibly," Sheri admitted, "but you cannot tell me you aren't curious. You, too, Dewhurst," he shot to Brandon. "Stop scowling at me like I've tracked mud on the parlor rug."

Returning his mug of tea to the table, Brandon rubbed circles at his graying temple. "Naturally, I'm curious. From an anatomical standpoint, observing yoga postures would present an interesting study in the body's capability to—"

"Spare me your anatomical fee-faw-fum." Sheri thumped the side of his fist to the table. "I'm talking about women. *Bending* women."

A muscle in Brandon's jaw ticked. "It doesn't matter. We're not invited. The demonstration is only for the ladies."

Stretching an arm to where Brandon was seated beside him, Sheri tapped the surgeon's forehead. "Which is why I suggested we observe discreetly. And we'd best get on with it, as they are set to convene in twenty minutes." Arcadia and her friends had quit the table ahead of the men in order to prepare, affording Sheri the opportunity to pursue a harebrained scheme of his own.

"You want to spy on the ladies?" Henry sounded nonplussed. He crossed his arms across his chest, his face twisted in scorn.

Not *ladies*, just one lady. Sheri was frenzied with the desire to watch Arcadia at her yoga practice. "It's a demonstration," he pointed out. "Your wives aren't going to do anything but watch. All I'm asking is for some assistance in admiring my own spouse."

"*Pffft.*" Henry chuffed a breath, rustling the lock of straw-gold hair drooping over his brow. "And you're inviting us along to leer at her, too? You're despicable, Zouche, you know that?"

Wounded, Sheri pushed back from the table. He brushed toast crumbs from his waistcoat. "Mock all you wish. But if it was your wife planning to sail away to India, never to return—which sounds precisely like something Mrs. De Vere would cook up, you must admit—and you said to me, 'Sheri, my dearest friend—'"

"I wouldn't say that."

"'—my wife is going to leave me, and I'll never again lay eyes upon her once she's gone, but there has arisen a golden opportunity for me to feast on the sight of her, will you help me?' I would. I would do whatever was needful to assist your romantic quest."

On their way to his quizzing glass, his fingers paused to touch the silver fob. *Miss you, Sheri.* Would Arcadia miss him? Even a little? Or would Sheri once more be the only one suffering the sting of absence, as he still felt the loss of Grace?

Instead of plucking out his quizzing glass, he swiped his face, suddenly weary. "Of course I don't want you leering at Arcadia. I'm asking you to help me admire her from afar, and if the cost of your assistance is that you grab a gander at that beautiful woman, as well, then who am I to refuse? If you had the good fortune to be married to Arcadia, I would stare at her so much you'd have to call me out."

Henry rolled his eyes, but his sneer softened. "It's not a romantic quest, so much as a mildly disturbing one," he said without much heat, "but I take your meaning."

Brandon's fingertips drummed on the table. "I've never seen you like this about a woman before."

I've never been like this about a woman before. There simply was no other woman like Arcadia. She was precious and rare.

The surgeon leaned forward. "Tell her you don't want her to go. Ask her to stay." Henry murmured his agreement.

They didn't understand. How could they? Both had married for love, not in fulfillment of a cold *quid pro quo* arrangement. Arcadia had done her part. If Sheri refused to hold up his side of their bargain, not only would he be breaking his word, but he'd be asking Arcadia to sacrifice the only thing she wanted: to return to India.

"I cannot."

Brandon must have heard the desolation in his tone. He sighed. "They are meeting in what was a gun room, when that part of the house was built in the seventeenth century. The only windows are high up the wall, and there are no trees or vines to facilitate peeping." His mouth pulled to the side, his expression thoughtful. "But," he said, "there is a hidden passage that goes from the study to the gun room. Evidently, the old baron had cause to fear his tenants."

Sheri's eyes widened. "A hidden passage," he breathed. "I could crack the secret door and watch that way."

Brandon shook his head. "No good. The door in the study is still existent, but the one at the other end, opening into the gun room, was bricked over ages ago."

Sheri's temper flashed. "Then what good—"

"Ventilation," Brandon cut in. "There are narrow slits in the wall, hidden in chinks in the mortar, that provide the passageway with fresh air. Some of them are incorporated into the gun room's wall."

A grin split Sheri's face. He clapped Brandon's shoulder. "Brilliant! Let's go."

Moments later, the three friends stared into the dark corridor revealed by a hidden pocket door in the study's paneling. A cold draft blew stale air across their faces. The floor of the passage was thick with dust to the point that Sheri could not discern the color of the stone.

Dropping to the floor, he hastily pried off his boots.

"What are you about?" Henry asked. "Is this another manifestation of your madness?"

Sheri raised a brow. "Not done much sneaking about houses in the dead of night, I take it." His history of accepting invitations into the bedchambers of married women might have been morally questionable, but it had taught him the finer points of keeping secret assignations secret.

Glancing at the filthy floor of the passage, he paused to silently apologize to his stockings. *You sacrifice your lives in service of a noble cause.*

The passage was narrow and low. Almost immediately, Sheri cracked his head on the ceiling. He cursed. There was a heavy sigh behind him. "A moment."

Sheri twisted himself around and saw Brandon removing his own boots. "You can't go alone," Brandon said in answer to Sheri's look of question. "If you hit your head again, you might bleed to death inside the walls of my house. The smell would be atrocious."

"Well, I don't want to be the odd man out." Henry crossed his ankle over his knee and hopped on one foot to remove his footwear.

There was much grunting and hissed curses as the three men squeezed through a space that Crispin and Webb would find cozy. Their only light filtered through the ventilation slits. Each of those being about two inches high and half an inch wide, and spaced at intervals of four feet, the going was gloomy.

Sheri felt as if he'd run a long footrace when at last Brandon halted, peered through a ventilation slit, and gave him a nod.

Sheri brought his eye to a hole. The room that came into focus was about fifteen feet on a side. The walls and floor were gray stone, but a hodgepodge of rugs had been brought in to cover the floor.

Arcadia, Lorna, and Claudia sat on the floor, their backs to Sheri. They faced Poorvaja, who was likewise seated. The Indian woman's legs were crossed, each bare foot atop the opposite knee. He saw the bottoms of Arcadia's feet; she, too, had bent her legs in the challenging configuration.

Sheri fretted over her bare toes. There was no fire in the room, and the stone would leach whatever heat came with the sunlight slanting through the high windows. He hoped she was not too cold.

For long minutes, the women just sat. Poorvaja's eyes were closed. She spoke several times about drawing attention to the breath.

"How's the big show?" Henry whispered near Sheri's ear.

Disappointing, honestly. Sheri was pathetic, as his friend had alleged. So pathetic, in fact, that he'd worked himself into a frenzy and ruined a perfectly good pair of stockings over what amounted to a breathing lesson.

Poorvaja pushed to her feet and bid the others follow. Arcadia unfolded her legs and rose in a graceful, fluid movement. Sheri noticed that all the women had changed into loose tunics and skirts, which they'd drawn between their legs and tucked at the waist to free their legs. Poorvaja stepped one foot forward and brought her back knee to the floor. She spoke instructions, her hands tracing the lines of her own body. The other three joined in. Arcadia reached over to help Claudia find the correct posture, then turned, positioning herself in profile for the benefit of the other women—and, unwittingly, her husband.

"Mrs. De Vere and Mrs. Dewhurst are participating, too," he whispered over his shoulder.

"*What?*" He felt, rather than saw, Henry plaster himself to the neighboring spy hole.

The women reached their arms overhead and leaned backwards. Arcadia looked almost worshipful, her lovely face lifted skyward, eyes closed, the hint of a smile on her mouth. Sheri's chest hurt.

"They look like a coven," Henry hissed. "We should stop them before they summon a malevolent spirit."

They rose to standing and bowed at the waist. Arcadia's face touched her shins, as did Poorvaja's. The other two gave it a try, though they did not fold as deeply as the experienced yogis.

There was a pose in which they all stood on one foot with the sole of the other pressed to the inside of the standing leg. Lorna quickly mastered this exercise, while Claudia toppled over onto her rump. After that followed a pose that held the legs in a wide angle, the upper body bending to the side to reach the hand to the floor. There were poses that twisted the spine or stretched the joints, and others that challenged the practitioner's balance. Sheri watched, rapt, as Arcadia's bare arm and leg muscles engaged to meet the demands of each posture. This was why she was strong, he realized, why she could hold the weight of her own extended arm through an entire waltz.

Next, Poorvaja said something; in response, Arcadia spread her feet and dropped to a squatting position, her hands in prayer position at her chest and elbows pressed to her knees, while Poorvaja narrated an explanation to the others. Arcadia placed her palms on the floor and slowly tipped forward, knees pressed into her upper arms. Her feet rose off the floor; all of her weight was balanced on her hands.

Sheri felt his lungs seize. She would fall, she would be hurt—but she wasn't. Her balance was true. To Sheri's right, Brandon let out a low, quiet whistle. "Christ on a crutch," Henry muttered.

Slowly, Arcadia reversed the exercise, lowering herself back to her feet. Claudia applauded. "Oh, well done!"

Sheri felt like applauding himself. He was absurdly proud of Arcadia. How much dedication, how many years of work, did it take to master such a feat? His wife was beautiful and strong and—*just look at the smile on that face.* She grinned at her friends, accepting their praise with a silly bow, and he found himself grinning, too.

A realization jolted through his mind. *This is what she misses.* He understood then, in a new and deeper way, that Arcadia wasn't his, and she never would be. She had a life in India she loved. He couldn't keep her from it any longer.

All four women tried the next exercise. From an upright kneeling position, they reached their hands back to their heels. Arcadia bowed her spine, pushing her chest out and up. Her body followed an elegant arc from the top of her tipped head to where her knees met the rug.

Sheri's breath caught again, for a different reason. Were he in that room with her, the front of her body would be open to his perusal. He would kiss her neck and nibble those delectable collarbones while his hands took full advantage of having her breasts so flagrantly presented. Too, he could reach right between her legs—

Oh no.

He drew a shaky breath, struggling to master himself. This was neither the time nor the place for the physical stirring in his trousers. He turned his face away and looked at Brandon. That would squelch his ardor.

Brandon was looking at him.

Shit.

Back in the gun room, the women had released that pose and were making their way down to lie on their backs. That looked harmless enough. With a word from Poorvaja, both she and Arcadia raised their legs straight up into the air and kept going, lifting their backs off the floor until only the head, neck, and shoulders remained on the rug. Arcadia braced hands on her hips and propped her elbows on the ground for support.

"I can do that!" Claudia chirped. She threw her legs up, grunting and panting until, red-faced, she'd maneuvered herself into the same pose. Lorna went more slowly, finally achieving the same, albeit wobbly, result. Arcadia dropped her straight legs towards her face, her toes coming to rest on the rug above her head. Poorvaja padded over to Lorna and assisted her, and then Claudia.

"That's …" Sheri gulped on a dry throat. "That's impressive."

At Poorvaja's instruction, the ladies separated their feet, tracing an arc on the ground. Arcadia took the additional step of bending her legs and drawing her feet back towards her head, so that her rump was in the air and her knees around her ears.

He wanted to whimper.

With knowledge acquired on their wedding night, Sheri could picture her naked now, which made this so much worse. Spread before him thus, he would bend his head and lap at her swollen sex, making himself drunk on the taste and smell of her. She would squirm and beg but he would hold her still, his hands on her smooth haunches pinning her—

Henry punched Sheri's shoulder. "Enough. I don't want you perverts looking at my wife."

"I wasn't looking at your wife, idiot," Sheri corrected, "I was looking at mine." As far as he was concerned, the other women might as well not have been present. His eyes only saw Arcadia. "My wife," he whispered, the grief of impending loss already lapping at his heels.

Mine.

CHAPTER TWENTY-THREE

Lorna had allotted only one bedchamber to Sheri and Arcadia. On the first night of their stay at Elmwood, Arcadia went to bed with her heart thundering in her ears. But Sheri stayed up late with the gentlemen, and Arcadia fell asleep alone. When she awoke in the morning, Sheri was in the bed with her, but huddled on the far side of the mattress, as if he was loathe to touch her, even in his sleep.

On Saturday night, Sheri excused himself just after supper, pleading fatigue. Oddly, Mr. Dewhurst and Mr. De Vere likewise proclaimed that the trials of the day had done them in. Lorna and Claudia exchanged a knowing look, then followed their husbands to their respective chambers.

Arcadia wasn't so naïve that she didn't realize what was going on. She bid her friends good night and fought to suppress a spurt of jealousy that each of them were headed to the welcoming embrace of the men they loved.

Poorvaja had declined to sup with the group, instead taking her meal in her room. And so Arcadia found herself alone, browsing the bookshelves in the library. She wasn't an avid reader, but a tome was likely to be all the companionship she'd find this evening.

There were French novels and Greek poetry, Roman histories and German philosophies. None of these appealed to Arcadia. Of mild interest was the large collection of books pertaining to human anatomy and disease—the collection being related to Mr. Dewhurst's surgical career, she presumed.

A large atlas caught her eye at last. She pulled it from the shelf and carried it to a podium illuminated by a standing candelabrum. The leather cover made a cracking sound as she opened it to the frontispiece, a map of the world, covering two pages. Laying her hands on the vellum, she spanned the distance between England

and India in less than the width of her ten fingers. It seemed such a brief distance, but seven months of her life had been spent traveling from one to the other. She could expect roughly the same for her return—six months, if the weather was cooperative. So long. By the time she reached India, she will already have been apart from Sheri for half a year.

Would that be time enough to heal her heart?

She flipped through the pages to a map of the subcontinent. Tracing the western coast with a finger, she could almost smell the scent of rain splashing on parched earth, breaking the dry season. The sounds of the rowdy village marketplace filled her ears, and she envisioned the mounds of cardamom and turmeric powder in the spice seller's stall. Almost, she could feel the sun's rays touching her face as they broke over the horizon, and her bones echoed with the roar of tigers and the trumpeting of elephants.

In keeping Arcadia in India, Sir Thaddeus Parks had not just permitted his motherless daughter to stay in the only home she knew, he'd given her a childhood most English girls could never dream of. India had taken his wife, and so, in preservation, he'd turned his daughter over to it entirely, encouraging Arcadia to adapt and thrive. How many ladies at a Society ball could say they'd dangled their feet in a river while keeping an eye on the crocodile floating lazily nearby, or that they'd once been gifted a doll by a Mughal prince?

But then, what other lady at a Society ball could claim Lord Sheridan Zouche as her husband? In balance, which memories did she treasure more: her many long summers in the *zenana*, or a single night in the arms of the man she loved?

She was glad she'd come to England. Sheri didn't want a wife, but he would always have one. Arcadia would carry the connection in her heart forever. From half a world away, she would remember the delicious slide of his skin against hers and the rapture she'd glimpsed when he possessed and filled her.

From the corner of her eye, a flicker of movement alerted her to his presence. "I thought you'd gone to bed."

Sheri stepped into the candelabrum's circle of light. He wore his silk dressing gown and trousers. "Not so tired as I'd supposed. Where's everyone else?"

"All retired. An epidemic of fatigue has swept the house. Or something," she muttered.

He came to stand at her shoulder and studied the page. He didn't touch her, but she felt his presence like a caress on her neck anyway. "Where?"

"Here is Hyderabad State." She pointed to a region in the center of the vast land. "Our station was here"—she slid her finger—"in the northwest. The Company only controls a small area there. All around us was under Mughal command."

He leaned closer, as if trying to commit to memory the lines of ink that stood in for rivers and hills. A lock of his russet hair brushed her cheek. Surreptitiously, Arcadia turned her head ever so slightly, committing to her own memory his unique, enticing smell.

"Is that where you'll go when you return?" His voice was peculiar. Maybe he was tired, after all.

"If I return. Still no brooch," she reminded him. Then she said, half to herself, "Maybe I have to accept it's gone and leave without it. I can't have everything, can I?"

A shadow crossed his features. "It may yet turn up." A long silence passed before he spoke again. "So is that where you'll go?"

"No." She indicated an area some distance north of Sir Thaddeus's little station in the *mofussil*. "Poorvaja's uncle lives here. That's where we'll go."

"Back to the harem?" He turned his face to her, a teasing glint in his eyes. She'd not been this close to his lips in weeks. If she leaned just the smallest bit ... but the distance between them was like that on the map—small in appearance, vast in truth.

She swallowed. "The *zenana*, yes. For a short time, anyway. I'd like to find a house of my own near there. I don't want to take Poorvaja far from her family. Not again."

"Hmm." His gaze flicked back to the map. "And what will you do there, in that house of your own?"

Not too long ago, Arcadia wouldn't have had a satisfactory answer to that question. When she first arrived in England, she'd thought it would be enough to simply be in India. But her girlhood was over; there would be no more summers spent idling in the *zenana*, and no Sir Thaddeus greeting her from the shaded porch of their bungalow when she returned to the station at summer's end. She had to find her way as a woman now and make a meaningful life for herself.

"I want to help other people," she said. "Do charitable work." She bit her lip, then plunged ahead. "You inspired me."

His brows drew together in a puzzled expression; he breathed a quiet laugh. "How's that?"

"You do so much."

Sheri shook his head slowly. "I don't see how. I'm the most unproductive lump of clay God ever breathed life into."

"Sheri!" She touched his shoulder. He glanced at her hand but did not move away. "I saw you at our ball. You didn't sit down once all night. Every moment, you were busy dancing with wallflowers or tending to elderly ladies."

He did shrug her hand off then. "So my lone worth in life really *is* occupying a place in the dance formation? I'd suspected so, but outside verification is always valuable." There was a bitter edge to his sarcastic words.

"Have you any idea what it means to those women, to be noticed? And it's clear that you really do see them as people, that they matter. We ladies are very good at sniffing out feigned gallantries, you know. The smiles I saw that night were genuine."

"I hate to spoil a good run of adulation, but they were probably just laughing at me. I've had something of a presence in the scandal sheets lately."

She nudged him with an elbow. "You're their Chère. They're all half in love with you. Not just because you're ridiculously handsome, but because you're a good man."

He gave her an odd look. Arcadia turned her face, feeling heat spread up her neck. "Anyway, that's what I want to do."

"Dance attendance on old ladies at balls?"

"Help people. Spread happiness where I can. There isn't enough of it in the world. It's a good calling, I think." She closed the atlas, crossed her hands on the cover.

He tilted his head as if in thought. "Sounds demmed noble, when you put it like that." He slid the book out from under her hands, returned it to the shelf, then offered his arm. "Well then, madam, shall we to bed? I can perform the invaluable service of heating your blanket, should you require it."

She slanted a smile at him, but her heart twisted. If only he weren't teasing. If only he noticed that the person he could make happier than any other woman in the world was the one right in front of him.

• • •

An hour after their return to Town, Sheri was in his bedchamber, rifling through the case that housed his collection of cuff links and stickpins. Nudging aside monogrammed silver discs, mother-of-pearl studs, and a lone beryl come loose from its setting, he drew out the fowl he'd stashed in the box.

"Must be nice," he muttered to the jeweled bird, "to be so wanted." This brooch was the only thing holding Arcadia in England. Once she possessed it again, there would be nothing tying her to Sheri.

As he had numerous times over the last month or so, Sheri weighed Arcadia's desire of her treasure against his desire to keep her. It was a hopeless equation, for while his need for Arcadia was ever increasing, he'd seen at Elmwood that she was not meant for him. She belonged to an ancient land of mystics and spice, and he had made a promise.

Caring for Arcadia meant giving her what she wanted and needed, even if doing so broke his heart. He pocketed the peacock and entered his dressing room. Sheri rolled his shoulders and cracked his neck, as if preparing for a boxing match. He took several huffing breaths, raised his hand, and knocked.

"Come in," Arcadia called.

He opened the door connecting their rooms. He'd not stepped through it since their wedding night, and he did so now with his insides tied in knots and his mouth dry.

She sat cross-legged on the rug in front of the fireplace and smiled up at him in welcome. She wore a tunic and skirt similar to what she'd worn during the yoga lesson. Her hair was piled in a loose knot atop her head, a multitude of wayward strands providing a wispy veil over her ears and neck.

"Am—am I interrupting?"

"I was meditating, but I'm all done now." She unfolded her legs and stretched them in front of her, wiggled her bare toes before the fire. She was so lovely, it almost hurt to look at her. No, it *did* hurt to look at her—and so he didn't. He tore his eyes away and spotted the valise from their trip to Elmwood on the foot of her bed.

He nodded to the luggage. "Shall I have French see to that?"

"No need to bother French. I can unpack my own things."

He nodded. Blinked down at his shoes. Felt the weight in his pocket like stones in the pocket of a drowning man. He didn't have to do this. He could turn around and she'd never be the wiser.

"Did you need something, Sheri?" The hazel mosaics peered at him curiously.

She has a life she wants to live, you bastard—a life that, impossibly, you've influenced. Don't be a selfish clump now.

Reaching into his pocket, his fingers closed around his fate. "Does this look familiar, peahen?" He extended his hand.

Light danced over the facets of the peacock's brilliant sapphire body and winked in the blood-dark garnet eye.

With a shriek, Arcadia shot to her feet, her eyes as wide and round as the piece of jewelry. "My brooch!" Her hands trembled as she took it from him. "I can't believe it!" she exclaimed, her voice in an upper register. "How did—? Where—? Oh, Sheri, thank you." She threw her arms around his neck, and he took full advantage, pulling her close and burying his nose in her hair while his hand rubbed up and down her slender back.

"Thank you, thank you, thank you." She squeezed him tight in return, rocking back and forth.

Her reaction delighted him—could only have been better if she chose to express her gratitude with a tumble in the sheets.

As if drunk on giddiness, she staggered back a couple steps, laughing, her face flushed and eyes bright. Her chest moved up and down rapidly, drawing his notice to the points of her taut nipples pressing against the thin material of her tunic. Murmuring to herself in Hindustani, she cupped the brooch in her hand and scrutinized each part, touching its enameled head and jeweled feathers.

"It is undamaged," he assured her.

"How can this be?" she asked in wonder. "We've had no luck in our hunt. Where did you find it?" She beamed at him. "It must have been waiting for you when we returned from Elmwood this afternoon."

His delight at her elation ebbed. His stomach clenched. Rubbing the back of his neck, he tried to gather his thoughts. He had little success.

"It was at the shop we visited with Mrs. De Vere."

"The shopkeeper came across it recently, you mean? You're so clever to have left your direction." Her brow furrowed. "Did he have your direction? You weren't living in this house when we visited that shop."

"The peacock was there that day, Arcadia. When I described your brooch, the shopkeeper took me into a back room and opened a strongbox, and there it was. Evidently, he doesn't scruple to acquire quality pieces from dubious sources."

Tilting her head, her eyes flicked to the peacock, then back to him. "I don't ... I don't understand. I didn't notice—"

"You were engrossed in your conversation with Mrs. De Vere." That fact was seared into his memory, because it was the overheard tail of that particular conversation that had taught him to fantasize about Arcadia practicing yoga. "And all the business was completed in the back room. There was nothing for you to see."

"But you didn't give this to me then." She wagged the brooch at him. "You didn't say anything."

Sheri shifted his weight to the other foot. Scratched his neck. Couldn't meet her eye. "Things were going so fast. Poorvaja returned through no effort on my part. And then the brooch turned up on our second try ..." His voice faltered.

"Did you think I wouldn't marry you if you gave this to me?"

"It crossed my mind," he admitted.

One slim bare foot came towards him on a step, her expression stony. "I made a promise, and I wouldn't have broken it. This is mine, Sheri. The only material thing I care about."

"Yes, yes, your mother and father and India."

She gestured broadly with her arm. "The worry I felt, all the—" She made a sound of disgust in her throat. "All the hours we spent going to shops. Why would you do that, when you had it in your possession?"

He drove his hands into his hair, gripped the strands in a hard twist. "I wasn't ready. I intended to give it to you on our wedding day, but ..." He dropped his hands, and his shoulders drooped as a feeling of defeat settled over him. "I wasn't ready. I thought ... You were so damned beautiful, and I didn't want ... I wasn't ready ..." The words caught in his throat.

He'd wanted to keep her. He was selfish with Arcadia. Greedy. He always had been. From the moment he took her up in his arms in Hyde Park and reluctantly gave her back to her aunt, to every moment since, no amount of Arcadia was ever enough. Retaining the peacock had been his way of holding on to her just a little bit longer. But he knew now that he'd been a fool. Another day, a month, a year—it didn't matter. Nothing short of a lifetime would be long enough with this woman.

"You had no right."

"I'm sorry."

"I thought we were friends."

He flinched. *Friends.* What a terrible word. "We were. We are."

"Is this how friends treat one another in your country?" Her eyes clouded with hurt. He wanted to take her in his arms and kiss it away. She turned her back, her head bowed. "You had no right."

He lifted a hand, dropped it, useless. "Again, I apologize. You have it now."

A beat of silence. "We both have what we agreed to, then."

His jaw tightened. "Indeed. You may leave for India as soon as you like. A happy ending for all," he added bitterly.

She swiveled to face him. Her eyes were shuttered. He hated that, not knowing what she felt. "Happiness was never the object of our agreement."

"Then it's just as well we didn't ask it of one another." With a curt nod, he turned and shut the door to happiness behind him.

Chapter Twenty-Four

Arcadia climbed slowly into the coach. Her feet felt like lead. The previous night had been sleepless, and her meeting this afternoon had her head in a muddle and her heart in tatters.

Poorvaja looked up from her knitting. "You were a long time."

"You should have come in." Arcadia sank onto the squabs and leaned her head back, her eyes sliding closed. "Mrs. De Vere was distraught to hear you were sitting out here in the carriage. She fretted she'd done something at the demonstration to cause you offense."

Clack-clack-clack went the knitting needles. "I did not feel like socializing." Poorvaja's tone was testy. "What did you learn?"

She shifted her shoulders against mounting tension in her back. "Mr. De Vere's shipping company is sending a ship east. India is not the final destination, but there will be a stop for supplies in Madras. He offered us berths on the ship and wouldn't hear of accepting payment."

She kept to herself that Henry De Vere had been visibly shaken by her request and had begged Arcadia to reconsider. Only when she mentioned it was Sheri who had suggested she speak to him, and she had assured him she was quite certain of her decision, had he offered passage.

"Generous."

"He's a kind man." Arcadia would miss Claudia and Lorna, as well as their husbands. She would miss Deborah and Elijah, gregarious Crispin and somber Webb. She would even miss the Dowager Lady Lothgard. A bit.

"When does the ship sail?"

"A fortnight."

Poorvaja's needles flew faster and faster, her hands jerky, agitated. "So soon."

She shrugged. "We haven't much to pack."

Preparations for the trip would keep her busy, hopefully too busy to see much of Sheri. During the night, she had turned over and over in her mind what Sheri had said when he'd returned her peacock brooch. *I wasn't ready.* Wasn't ready for what? In the small hours of morning, it occurred to her that maybe—*maybe*—he'd meant he hadn't wanted her to leave yet, not because he feared she wouldn't follow through on their agreement, but because he simply wanted her to stay.

Hope had stirred in her chest, but it was tempered by uncertainty. And then, at breakfast, when he calmly suggested she inquire with Henry De Vere regarding her travel to India, the hope was snuffed out.

The strand of yarn tangled around Poorvaja's fingers. With a curse, she clapped the needles together and slammed her work to the seat at her side. She turned her face to the window, her eyes scanning back and forth over the busy scene on Piccadilly. "I want to walk," she said abruptly. "Let me down."

Arcadia knocked on the roof. When the carriage drew to a stop, the ayah struggled to open the door. "Poorvaja"—Arcadia touched her friend's shoulder—"are you all right?"

The Indian woman nodded stiffly. "I'd just prefer to be alone right now, Jalanili."

"Very well." Arcadia offered an uncertain smile. "I'll see you at home."

As the coach moved on, Arcadia clasped her hands tightly in her lap. Whatever had Poorvaja in such a fettle? She knew her friend could look after herself, but still, Arcadia couldn't help but fret a little.

I'll see you at home.

Arcadia's breath caught. Her heart stopped.

Home.

Her head snapped up. She glanced out the window. Knocked on the roof. Her hands shaking, she struggled to open the door and could scarcely wait for the driver to help her down.

The teeming hubbub of the street engulfed her. Merchants hawked their wares while pedestrians jostled on the walk and a gentleman driving a high phaeton shouted invective at the driver of a wagon moving too slowly for his liking.

Arcadia darted and dodged her way through the traffic, finally breaking through onto a quieter street. One lined with imposing, stately structures that cast cool shadows on the cobblestone. She scurried down the street to where a particular window bowed away from the facade of a building.

• • •

A glass of brandy floated into Sheri's field of vision. He glanced up to see Harrison Dyer standing beside his chair.

"Thanks for coming, Harry," Sheri said, accepting the proffered beverage.

"Glad to have your note this morning," Harrison replied as he took a seat beside Sheri. "You've been a busy fellow, *hmm*? Married. Sorry I couldn't make it to festivities." Harrison lifted his drink, the corners of his amber eyes crinkling. "Congratulations, old man. I wish you happy."

It was the first Sheri had seen of Harrison since the morning of the duel. His friend was leaner than he'd been several months ago, his tawny hair long and unkempt.

Tipping back his brandy, Sheri drained the glass and winced, not from the liquor's burn but from the more potent pain jabbing his heart.

"Got married, yes," he confirmed, his gaze sliding from Harry's interested expression to the mundanities passing by the bow window. A liveried footman dashed by with arms full of parcels. "And now she's leaving me."

Harrison startled. A long pause followed. "I don't know what to say."

Shrugging, Sheri shifted forward. He rolled the empty snifter between his palms. "I'm not looking for a shoulder to cry upon. I asked you here because I need you to do something for me."

"If it's in my power, you needn't even ask."

Sheri gave a weary smile. "I know." He might not have the woman he loved, but he was abundantly blessed with loyal friends. In this, he had more than most. It would have to be enough. "Arcadia, my wife"—*my wife, My Wife, MY WIFE,* shouted his brain—"is making arrangements with Henry, even as we speak, to secure passage on his ship when it sails."

Harry squinted and rubbed his temple. "Alone, I take it?"

He nodded. "I need you to watch over her for me. Keep her safe until …" *Until she's vanished over the horizon, carrying away the future you didn't know you wanted until it was too late.* "Until she's home," he finished.

Home. What a stupid word. Like *friends.* Stupid when it came to Arcadia, at any rate, he amended, shooting a look at his companion. What home would he have without her? An empty house he didn't want? Endless days with interminable hours he'd try to fill with frivolity and mindless pleasure? What was the point? Without Arcadia, he would feel just as homeless as his wife did now. Why, he might as well—

Harrison clapped his shoulder. "I'll see to her safety. You have my word."

Sheri shook his head. "No, never mind. I'll see to it myself." He deposited his glass on a table. Arcadia would be returning from her call to the De Veres' house shortly. He wanted to be there when she arrived.

Harrison's brows drew together. "See to it yourself?" he echoed. "You mean to stop her from going?"

The corner of his eye caught the flutter of a familiar paisley Kashmir shawl. Sheri turned his face, and there she was, right back on St. James's Street, where she had no business being, the difference being that this time she was his. She was his, and he wasn't giving her up.

For a moment, he studied her without reaction. Then, he lifted his quizzing glass to his eye.

Arcadia giggled and showed him a smile. God, how could he have ever thought to let her go?

Several other gentlemen were gathered in the window, and more were jostling for position, once again entertained by the spectacle of Sheri and Arcadia.

Let them look.

"No, Harry, I mean to accompany her," he informed his friend. "I'm going to India, too." Sheri slipped out of his seat and hurried to collect his things. A few minutes later he exited, nodding to the footman at the door.

"Lady Sheridan," he said, pulling on his gloves, "you are provokingly scandalous."

She hitched her shawl higher. "You told me to be as scandalous as I wished. You told me to be myself."

He slanted a wry smile. "Words I may live to regret, I see." He should get her home, he supposed, before putting his heart in her hands and hoping she didn't chuck it into the rubbish bin. He proffered his arm.

She shook her head and didn't budge. "I spoke to Mr. De Vere. He offered me passage on his ship."

Sheri's face fell at her determined tone. She didn't sound like a woman with any doubts about leaving her husband. But he had to try. He offered his arm again. "What can I do to facilitate your preparations for the voyage, Arcadia?"

She batted his arm. "Nothing, Sheri. You can't do anything. I'm not going."

He frowned. "You're not—I beg your pardon?"

"I'm not going," she repeated. She lifted her chin. "All my life, I've resented my mother for dying. I blamed her, you see. She was too much a *memsahib*, too much part of the Raj. She refused to let India touch or change her. She went right on wearing her petticoats and trying to make English flowers grow in her garden, talking always of Home. After she died, I couldn't help but think, if she hadn't put so much energy into fighting India, it could have been home, and maybe she wouldn't have died. Or at least she'd have been happy there, instead of always missing England."

Sheri's expression was guarded. "I'm afraid I don't see—"

"*I'm* my mother," Arcadia said, throwing her hands into the air. "I've spent every moment fighting England and missing India. I've tried not to let England touch me. But it has. I have friends here now, and even if my aunt and uncle haven't been all one could wish in a family, Deborah and Elijah have welcomed me into theirs. But, most importantly ..." She held out her palm.

He raised a brow. Then he took her hand, lacing his fingers through hers.

"I have you," she finished. "I love you, Sheri. This is my home, and I don't want to leave."

He brought his hand to her jaw, a wondering smile forming. "I love you, too, peahen. But you don't have to stay here. I'll come to India with you. You haven't seen a winter here yet. You may find it too cold—"

Her brows twitched over a naughty twinkle in her eye. "I was perfectly toasty when we were in bed together. Will you help me stay warm?"

His mouth lifted in a crooked smile. "I should like nothing more."

He tipped her face and lowered his head. His heart sang as their lips met. Arcadia loved him, and she was his. Sheri couldn't imagine possibly being out of countenance with the world again.

He lifted his head, his eyes scanning her face. "You really want to stay? With me?"

"Yes. But maybe you don't want me to," she said, apprehension trickling through her words.

"I love you, Arcadia," he repeated. He'd tell her a thousand times until she believed it, and then a thousand times more because the words were the song of his heart. "I love you, and I want to be with you. Now. Always. You're the most spectacular woman I've ever known. You're brave and intelligent, and you're *strong*." He gripped her hip in emphasis. "So strong. In every possible way. And I can't stop thinking about getting into bed with you. Or just getting into *you*, really, because I've no druthers as to the location, so long as I can touch you. I need you, peahen. I need you to be proud of me for dancing with wallflowers. I need you to love me for being me, in all my ridiculousness. If you got on that ship, I would follow you. To the other side of the world and beyond."

She tugged his mouth to hers; her tongue brushed his lips, and he responded with a groan, drawing her tongue into his mouth and twining it with his. His arm clamped tight about her waist, and his other hand tangled in her hair, and he held her close, so close that there wasn't any room for cold or uncertainty.

They kissed long and thoroughly, stopping only when they heard knocks on glass and the muffled hoots of their forgotten witnesses in the window. When Sheri broke away, they were both breathless. His brow creased with one nagging thought.

"What about Poorvaja?" he asked.

Arcadia rested her hand on his chest, a frown finally appearing on her face. "If you and I are staying here, I have to tell her she's going home without me."

• • •

Sheri offered a hackney, but Arcadia said she didn't mind walking home, provided he stayed close. He was more than happy to oblige. They took their time strolling, pausing to look in shop windows and listen to a street sweep sing while he worked. Sheri flipped the urchin a penny.

Contentment suffused every part of him.

That feeling lasted until they arrived home and found Sir Godwin Prickering in the drawing room.

He shot to his feet at their entrance. His hair stood on end, and he had a wild look in his eyes. His red neckcloth, Sheri noted, had been removed. It was presently located in the poet's hands, being twisted and shredded to an ignoble death.

"Lady Sheridan," he cried, "Poorvaja has told me you're leaving." He turned slightly, looking to where the ayah sat on the sofa. The Indian woman's pretty face was creased, her eyes bright with moisture. Having to tend an overwrought Sir Godwin would drive anyone to tears, Sheri mused.

"This will not do, my lady, indeed it will not." He stomped a foot. "I cannot permit this." His prodigious nose shone bright pink.

Sheri almost felt sorry for the bloke. He knew what it was to be hopelessly in love with Arcadia and want to rip one's own heart out at the prospect of being parted from her forever. Still, the sod was throwing himself at Sheri's wife in an unseemly display. He cleared his throat meaningfully and shot the man a stern look.

Arcadia looked around the blubbering poet to her friend. "Sir Godwin, I regret your distress, but I must ask you to excuse yourself. I need to speak with Poorvaja."

The older woman made a choked sound. Sir Godwin pivoted and rushed to her side, taking her hand and covering it with kisses.

"Whatever you have to say to Poorvaja you must say in front of me, Lady Sheridan. We will not be parted. I won't permit you to snatch my muse, my love, from me."

Sheri blinked. Shook his head. Was there a pebble lodged in his ear, perhaps?

Arcadia recovered first. "Your love? What … what is this? Poorvaja?"

"Oh, Jalanili." Poorvaja twisted her hand into her braid. "You are grown now, and I am still young enough to marry again and maybe—Lakshmi willing—have another child of my own. Godwin is a good man and very kind, and he has asked me to marry him. I cannot stop you from this folly of yours"—she cut a look at Sheri—"but I will not accompany you. I'm sorry, Jalanili"—her voice hitched—"but I'm staying here."

Arcadia brought a hand to her head. She looked at Sheri and laughed, a sound of disbelief and relief rolled into one. "But Poorvaja"—she sat beside her friend and took her hand—"I'm staying here, too."

"With Lord Sheridan?" the ayah asked.

"Yes." Arcadia nodded. "Are you really staying, too? We were just on our way to tell you that Sheri and I are staying—"

"Or going," Sheri interjected. "Whatever you want, Arcadia. I meant it."

She glanced at him with eyes shining with love. She laughed, and his heart radiated joy that suffused every fiber of his body. "Or going. Perhaps we'll stay here a while, then all go back to India together to visit your family, Poorvaja. Could we do that, Sheri?"

"Of course. I would very much like to see this harem of yours."

Laughing again, Arcadia turned to her ayah. "I'm so happy, Poorvaja."

The women embraced and started chattering at each other in Hindustani. Though he didn't comprehend the words, the joy mirrored in each woman's face was clear enough.

Still sniffling as he gradually composed himself, Sir Godwin wandered over to Sheri. Through his tears, he beamed fondly at the ladies.

Sheri tipped his head. "How long?" he asked. If Prickering was in any way misleading Poorvaja, Sheri would make sure he answered for it.

"From the first," the poet breathed. "I saw her in Hyde Park, and I was lost. Every opportunity to be near her, I sprang upon. It wasn't until the night of your betrothal ball, though, that I found the courage to speak. We've been meeting in secret ever since."

Sheri, too, had begun losing his heart that day in the park. All those times he'd thought Sir Godwin was mooning after Arcadia, he was really gazing at Poorvaja. Sheri supposed he'd assumed Prickering was infatuated with Arcadia because—well, who wouldn't be? She was beauty and grace and compassion. Still, he was glad the poet had had his eye on a different lady. On a day of such fine feeling, it would be regrettable to have to watch another man's heart crumble.

It was strange to feel in accord with Prickering, but love did strange things to a fellow. Sheri extended his hand. Sir Godwin gripped it. It was a nice moment of fraternal goodwill, the milk of human kindness, and all of that.

"We'll be like family," Sir Godwin declared, clapping happily. "I'll practically be your father-in-law." He nudged Sheri. "Son."

Moment over.

"Come on, peahen," he said, crossing to the sofa and sweeping his wife up into his arms. "Let's leave these lovebirds alone."

Arcadia's arms came around his neck. She pressed a kiss to the underside of his jaw and then drew his earlobe between her lips, her fingers playing in the hair at his nape. Sheri sprinted for the stairs.

"Where are you taking me?" Arcadia asked, laughing.

"To bed," he growled. "I'm feeling rather chilly."

Epilogue

A fortnight later

The embarkation of *Brizo's Woe* was a tedious affair, accomplished in several stages of final boarding and inspections before the harbormaster gave the signal. Even once the anchors were raised and the lines released from the wharf, it was some time before the wind tucked into the sails and nudged the merchant vessel towards open water.

Huddled inside her stout new coat, Arcadia lifted her hand in farewell to Mr. Harrison Dyer standing on the ship's deck. She and Sheri, Brandon, Henry, and Norman—as well as Claudia and Lorna—had all made it to the docks before dawn to see their friend off.

Arcadia recalled how her new husband had once promised to wish her *bon voyage* with a cheer and a basket of sweets, and while Sheri put on a smile for his old friend's sake, she read tension in the lines around his mouth. Besides sweets, Sheri had crammed a small trunk with every provision he thought his friend might need on his journey, from bottles of liquor to spare linens and razors, to a compass and knife, to books, playing cards, and other little entertainments.

"You fret over him more than Poorvaja ever did over me," she'd teased as she watched him pack the trunk, secretly adoring that thoughtful, nurturing side of him.

As their little group broke up and began going their separate ways, Arcadia slipped an arm around Sheri's waist. He drew her close and pressed a kiss to her forehead.

"He'll be all right, you know," she said. "If I survived that awful voyage, so will he."

"Is that a note of regret I hear?" he asked, his hand slipping from her shoulder to the small of her back as they made their way to their carriage. "Wish you were aboard?"

That small point of contact did more to dispel the morning's chill than all her layers of clothes. After mounting the carriage step, she paused and turned. The light of a new day illuminated his handsome face and the tender warmth in his eyes. Arcadia's heart fluttered inside her chest. She touched his cheek. "Not in the slightest."

They settled onto the squabs, and Sheri knocked on the roof. Then he kicked his feet up on the opposite bench and reclined, pulling Arcadia down with him.

Her eyes drifted closed, and for a few minutes she simply breathed, reveling in the feeling of his chest beneath her cheek and the love that pulsed between them, as vital and bright as the sunlight now streaming through the carriage windows.

"Will you come calling with me this afternoon?" His question rumbled against her temple, easy and natural as the gentle thunder accompanying the rain that broke the dry season.

"I'm looking forward to it," she readily accepted. Their mutual willingness now to admit their desire for the other's company was one of Arcadia's favorite things about married life. Sheri was her best friend, the person who made her laugh and challenged her to stretch her limits—and she got to spend the rest of her life with him. Lucky, lucky girl.

"Did you remember to pack the preserves in the baskets?" she inquired.

He nodded. "Lady Dane's sweet tooth will be delighted, I'm sure, although I can't speak for old Mr. Waldman."

"Who doesn't like apple jam?" She squeezed his waist. "But even if he doesn't, he'll be sure to appreciate the company. It was good of you to include a gentleman on your first round of charity visits. I know the ladies are more your forte. Soon enough, all the men will be calling you Chère, too."

He snorted, and they relaxed again into companionable silence.

She knew the instant his thoughts turned naughty, felt the hitch in his breath and the quickening of his pulse. Her own body softened in response.

"We can't go back to bed," she said, even though her fingers itched to bury themselves in his hair and her skin was hungry for the feel of his mouth. "Claudia and Lorna are coming for a yoga lesson this morning, remember?"

Sheri groaned. "Tell them to come another day, when I'm not busy having carnal relations with my wife." He slipped the top two buttons of her coat free, then cupped a possessive hand over her breast.

Chuckling, Arcadia nestled closer. "What day would that be, husband?" Since the morning they'd each finally confessed their love, not a day had passed without Sheri teaching Arcadia another way to find pleasure together—a new location, a new position, another inch of her body or his to tantalize and excite. Not a night had passed without words of love whispered in the dark before they fell asleep in each other's arms.

"Tomorrow, perhaps?" she suggested.

"No good. Tomorrow is Tuesday."

"You can't have every Tuesday—"

"The hell I can't."

"Besides," she said, "I've already lit the fire to warm the new yoga room." She paused before adding, "And you may be disheartened to hear that I checked and double-checked the walls. There are no spy holes in our house."

Sheri stiffened. "Who told? I'll drub the traitor."

Arcadia lifted her head and met her husband's unrepentant grin. "They both told, you fiend." She swatted his arm playfully. "And both their wives told me."

"Are you angry?" he asked.

She lowered her voice to a sultry drawl. "Did I seem angry this morning? Or last night? Or—"

He silenced her with a kiss that was both tender and raw, stoking her desire, promising love of every sort. Arcadia promised him right back.

And they both kept their word.

Acknowledgments

It's been said that writing is easy; you simply open a vein and bleed onto the page. Some novels demand more blood than others—this one sucked me dry and then raided the blood bank.

Jason, Sarah, Michelle, Deb, and Beth, you propped me up when my bum ankle wouldn't hold me and gave me your strength when I had none of my own. I love you.

Tara, this book wouldn't be here without you. Thank you for always being the editor I need.

Thanks to my copyeditor, Annie Cosby, for keeping me on my toes, and to Julie Sturgeon for cheering me to the finish with much needed wit and wisdom. Many thanks to the art department and everyone else at Crimson for giving my novels such exquisite care.

Channing, Nicole, Sierra, and the rest of the Pink Lotus instructors and *Kula*, thank you for teaching and inspiring me. Thank you, Amy, for keeping me sane.

And thanks to you, my dear readers. If you have ever sent me a note or taken the time to leave a review of my books, you helped bring this novel to fruition. You never know what the effect of a kind word will be. You have been my inspiration and my motivation when I needed it most. Thank you.

About the Author

Elizabeth Boyce had a lifelong dream: to be an astronaut. She has recently made peace with the fact that this dream is unlikely to come to fruition. Good thing, then, she had another dream: to be an author. This dream comes true every single day, and she couldn't be more grateful.

Ms. Boyce lives in South Carolina with her husband, children, and her personal assistant / cat.

She loves hearing from readers, so keep in touch!

Email: bluestockingball@gmail.com

Facebook: *https://www.facebook.com/AuthorElizabethBoyce/*

Twitter: @EBoyceRomance

More from This Author
Truth Within Dreams by Elizabeth Boyce

Six years later

The night was stormy, and most certainly dark. And while others might see such weather as portentous of some grave misfortune, to Miss Claudia Baxter, the rain and howling wind were as welcome as a surprise inheritance from a heretofore unheard-of uncle. The appearance of the storm had gifted Claudia an opportunity to deliver herself from a dreadful fate. Not one to ignore such a cosmic boon, she had, over the course of the last two hours, feverishly stitched together an idea.

It was a rather slapdash plan, Claudia allowed, as she padded away from the kitchen with a small bottle of pig's blood gripped in her fist. But with her wedding to Sir Saint Tuggle and his fifty years' worth of dental negligence less than a week off, what choice did she have? At this point, Claudia would have happily run away with a band of Gypsies, had any been so kind as to pass by Rudley Court. Sadly, Roma were thin on the ground in Wiltshire just now, so Claudia was left with a madcap scheme and a vial of blood.

Her bare feet made no sound as she crept through the sleeping house. She and her twin brother, Claude, had discovered—and thereafter avoided—every creaky board and groaning hinge in a childhood spent terrorizing their way through six governesses.

She made her way up to the bedchambers, keeping a keen eye out for Ferguson. The butler's highest calling in life was the preservation of Rudley Court and he'd been known to patrol the halls at least twice per night. In years past, that duty had meant defending the house against the ravages of nine Baxter children, Claudia and Claude being numbers eight and nine.

Luck was with her; Ferguson was nowhere to be seen. Claudia followed the path running down the center of the corridor rug, worn thin by decades of young Baxters and their guests. She stopped outside a guest room door and was startled by a sudden fluttering in her middle. There had been no doubts or fears until this very moment. The little bottle grew slippery in her hand. She passed it to the other and wiped her palm against her dressing gown.

If only her parents hadn't agreed to Sir Saint's proposal, then Claudia wouldn't have been driven to these desperate measures. But she had failed to make a match during her Season. She'd been just another Baxter, with unremarkable looks and an embarrassingly large family. Her two thousand pounds were nothing to brag about, and most of her gowns were handed down from her sisters. Claudia had never been the prettiest, the richest, the most fashionable. And so her Season came and went without a single proposal.

In the five years since, Claudia had resigned herself to the role of spinster aunt to her growing herd of nieces and nephews. Every family needed one, she reasoned. But then, two months ago, disaster struck in the doughy, stinky form of Sir Saint Tuggle. Sir John Baxter had accepted Sir Saint's suit without so much as a by-your-leave from his youngest daughter. Claudia had been informed of her betrothal over the fish course that night.

Sir Saint was due to arrive tomorrow afternoon and stay at Rudley Court until the wedding, and her many siblings would likewise begin trickling in over the course of the week. With the house full of people, Claudia would have no more opportunities to evade this marriage. She was out of time. Unless she took her fate into her own hands, she would become Lady Tuggle in a few days. As her intended had told her, she could look forward to producing Sir Saint's heir, followed by a lifetime of rusticating. There would be no house parties or Seasons in Town or trips abroad. Sir Saint's gout prohibited anything resembling fun from touching his life. She was too young to surrender to such a dreary existence. She couldn't do it. She wouldn't.

Steeling her resolve, Claudia turned the knob.

She slipped into the room and leaned against the beveled wood, allowing her vision to adjust to the darkness of the bedchamber. Outside, the storm still raged. A flash of lightning revealed the bed, as well as a pair of top boots carelessly discarded in the middle of the floor. Plunged once again into darkness, Claudia made her way forward, careful to avoid the boots. One noisy stumble would ruin everything.

With her free hand extended, Claudia reached the bed and felt her way to the top of the covers. A soft exhalation of breath made her heart leap. *It's only Henry*, she reminded herself.

"Only Henry" being Mr. Henry De Vere, whose family's estate, Fairbrook, adjoined the eastern side of Rudley Court. He was twenty-five, two years older than the twins, and had often been about when they were children, tossed in with the Baxters like just another puppy in the litter. Back then, Henry and the twins had been thick as thieves, roaming the countryside and playing games of Claudia's invention. Henry usually sided with her in disputes between the twins and had never let Claude exclude her from their play. Perhaps understandably, she'd developed a touch of hero worship where Henry was concerned. He was her very own champion. As she grew into adolescence, she couldn't help but dream he might come courting some day.

Claude and Henry had gone to Harrow together, and then Henry went off to Oxford. After that … well, Henry never did come courting. He'd remained a good friend, one she was always happy to see when he visited, but she had long since abandoned fantasies of her next-door neighbor returning the kind of affection she'd carried for him all these years.

Just back from London, Henry had come by earlier today to show off the new horse he'd purchased at Tattersall's. It was the first time Claude and Claudia had seen him in six months. Horse talk had led to tea in the library, which led to an invitation to stay to supper, and then the storm set in and Henry was stuck at Rudley Court for the duration—the unexpected event around which Claudia had hastily formulated her impromptu plan.

Earlier in the evening, when she'd broken the news of her betrothal, Henry's brows had drawn together. "A bit long in the tooth, isn't he?" Henry had asked. Just then, Claudia had wanted to throw her arms around his neck and weep. But the moment passed. He had kissed her cheek and wished her happiness, yet she was sure she'd seen a shadow cross his green eyes.

He would want to help her avoid this marriage, Claudia was certain, even if he didn't approve of her methods. But he would go along with her, as he'd always done.

The long, low mound of his shadow was on the opposite side of the bed. Claudia peeled back the counterpane, revealing the white bottom sheet. She worried at her lower lip while she dithered about what to do. Having seven older siblings meant she was more knowledgeable about particular matters than most young, unmarried ladies. Still, she wasn't entirely certain where to put the blood.

In the regular order of things, the fluid would be beneath her, she decided, in the region of her bottom. She tried to picture where that would be, were she lying on the bed—which she would be, in a moment. That was stage two of The Plan.

She let out a huff of annoyance. This was taking too long. "Bother," she muttered. It would be easier to place herself in the bed first. Then she'd know for sure how to set the scene.

Claudia set down the bottle of blood and untied the sash around her waist. Her dressing gown fell to the floor, leaving her in just her chemise. The decision of what to wear for the occasion of her ruin had caused a moment of consternation, but in the end she decided her usual night rail was too prim for what was meant to look like a night of wanton debauchery.

She crawled onto the bed. The mattress shifted under her weight and Henry's head tossed. Claudia froze, not even daring to breathe. As she knelt there, staring into the darkness with her bottle once again firmly in hand, Claudia realized she could use Henry as a guide.

When she was sure he still slept, Claudia pulled the counterpane back farther, revealing the side of Henry's body.

Henry's *naked* body.

Claudia gulped convulsively. She hadn't reckoned on encountering an unclothed man tonight, no matter what she meant to portray via The Plan.

It didn't matter, she told herself. Henry was asleep and Claudia would soon be—well, maybe not asleep. It would be difficult, knowing she shared the bed with a naked man. But she had to carry on. It was this, or climb into bed with Sir Saint.

Claudia unstoppered the bottle, but then guilt seized her guts, staying her hand. It wasn't just her who would be affected; Henry, too, would be subject to scrutiny. But she remembered the time a dozen years ago, when Henry had taken the blame for breaking Lady Baxter's porcelain fruit bowl, even though it was Claudia who had been pretending it was the hat portion of her regimentals during a battle reenactment in the parlor. He'd thought nothing of subjecting himself to Lady Baxter's ire to save Claudia from punishment.

But perhaps there was a better way. She hadn't explained her predicament to Henry, hadn't enlisted him in her cause. It was one thing to subject herself to her parents' disapprobation; it was another thing entirely to rope Henry into it without his permission.

Henry rolled onto his side just as lightning flashed. For an instant Claudia was blind, but the image of Henry De Vere's body was seared onto the backs of her eyelids. His torso was sculpted with broad shoulders and lean muscle, tapering to a flat stomach and narrow hips. Even relaxed in sleep, the muscles of his chest looked hard beneath a taut covering of skin. Thank heavens, his heavy thigh draped just so, concealing his most private area. Claudia was already stunned by what she'd seen; anything more intimate might cause permanent injury to her nerves. Memory provided a picture of Henry's handsome face: loose waves the color of ripe wheat falling about his ears, high cheekbones and an easy smile, hooded green eyes brimming with laughter. How on earth had she never suspected that familiar face was connected to a body straight off of Lord Elgin's Greek marbles? Probably, she realized, because she'd never given much thought to what a man's body looked like. Henry was beautiful, a word she never thought to apply to a man.

Gradually, Claudia recovered from her shock. She pulled her eyes away from Henry's recumbent form, saw the bed, and gasped. In her stupor, she'd spilled the entire contents of the bottle onto the bed, the stain stark against the white sheets, and growing larger as the fibers wicked the liquid outward from the center of the puddle.

"It's probably worse than it looks," she whispered. No, wait. That wasn't right. Drat Henry De Vere and his mind-muddling physique!

Briefly, she considered waking him. Maybe they could burn the sheets? Then what? When the sun rose, Claudia would still have an unwanted fiancé. No, she decided, better to just follow The Plan. Henry would understand; he would play along.

Claudia restoppered the bottle and shoved it under the bed, then gingerly lay down, keeping well away from the damp mess and the disturbingly alluring man across the bed.

She'd set into motion life-altering events. In the morning, she'd be a ruined woman. Sir Saint would cry off, and Claudia would be saved. Her parents would be furious, of course. Queasiness stole through her as she pictured a look of profound disappointment on her mother's face. But she couldn't allow this wedding to happen. Claudia had made her bed, and now she was lying in it.

She curled up on her side, pulled the counterpane around her ears, and willed everything from her mind but the relentless sounds of the storm.

Once a Duchess

Praise for *Once a Duchess*:

"Sparkling characters, a fast-paced plot, and beautiful descriptions of Regency England made this moving story of love lost and found once again, a book I couldn't put down. A delicious debut by an author to watch!" —Danelle Harmon, author of *The Wild One*

Once an Heiress

Praise for *Once an Heiress:*

"*Once an Heiress* combines everything readers love about historical romance with a twisting, suspenseful story that will have you on the edge of your seat ... I loved every second of *Once an Heiress*—it had the intrigue I love about historical romance combined with an excellent storyline that kept me on my toes."—The Romance Reviews

"If you like historical romances with a strong heroine that doesn't stick to society rules and a scarred hero with a wonderful hidden heart then you will like *Once an Heiress* by Elizabeth Boyce." — Harlequin Junkie

Once an Innocent

Praise for *Once an Innocent*:

"*Once an Innocent* by Elizabeth Boyce is a fantastic espionage romance that has some surprising action and gripping drama. If you are a 007 fan, you will be entertained by this novel."—The Romance Reviews

In the mood for more Crimson Romance?
Check out *Revolutionary Hearts by Pema Donyo* at
CrimsonRomance.com.

Printed in the United States
By Bookmasters